VESPER LYONS

ARTURUS REX

MARMALADE PRESS

Published by Marmalade Press
www.marmaladepress.co.uk

First published 2017

A CIP catalogue record for this book
is available from the British Library.

Printed and bound in Great Britain by Clays Ltd, St Ives plc

Typeset in Adobe Garamond Pro

ISBN 978-1-9997645-0-0

For Darcey

For a legend to be born, the greatest of lives must first come to an end.

1

A FINE TRADITION

Arthur had expected *some* whispering, but this was ridiculous. The chatter had started when he'd shuffled out of the Headmaster's study, and it had followed him as he'd trailed after the Head Boy through the winding corridors of Badon College. After the eighteenth or so hissed exclamation of '*look who it is*' he had started to consider how easy it would be to flee the building, jump back into the car he'd arrived in, and demand someone take him back to London as quickly as humanly possible. Unfortunately, there were several hundred boys, a handful of press photographers, and at least six bodyguards between him and freedom, so instead he sighed and tried to force his attention back to the tour he was being given.

Being first in line to the throne meant that Arthur had traipsed around more than his fair share of old buildings in the thirteen years he'd been alive as part of his 'duties'. He was pretty good at pretending to be interested in ancient vases and paintings of landscapes, and luckily most of the time people were only interested in hearing what his father had to say about their precious collection of antiquities anyway. Sadly, in this case, his father wasn't here, and

1

Eliot Troyes, who was taking his role of Head Boy very seriously, seemed to want to know Arthur's thoughts on everything. (The vast portrait of the founding fathers of the school? '*Impressive*'. The exquisite frescoes in the chapel? '*Remarkable*'.)

"It's such a privilege to go to school here. Badon has such an interesting history, don't you think, Sir?" Eliot asked earnestly, tilting his head in a bird-like manner.

Arthur valiantly suppressed a yawn. "Yeah, really interesting." His bank of adjectives was almost exhausted at this stage and it was becoming more difficult to feign enjoyment when all he really wanted to do was lock himself in his new bedroom and pretend this whole boarding school nonsense didn't exist.

Eliot looked pleased enough with his response though and carried on with a brief history of the school's most important moments.

The many badges on Eliot's blazer were glistening distractingly, and Arthur was certain they were regularly polished, particularly the gold shield-shaped pin proclaiming *Head Boy* in deep red lettering.

"It's even more of a privilege, being that we're so close to the university," Eliot continued. "My whole family attended university in Cambridge. I'm hoping to be accepted too."

"Well, good luck with that," Arthur replied, not really knowing what else he could say.

Eliot beamed. "Oh, thank you. Six generations of the Troyes family have studied at Catterick College. It would be a great pleasure to be the seventh."

Eliot's further chatter about his future prospects couldn't distract Arthur from the staring of those around him, and he shifted between smiling politely and keeping his gaze fixed straight ahead. He heaved a sigh of relief as Eliot blessedly announced he would take the prince to his boarding house to get settled in.

Eliot led the way towards the stone building that dominated this part of the school. He marched across the inner court, cutting through the collection of suited boys, parents, and luggage littering the grass. There was an archway in the middle of the building, that led out onto the bridge that connected the two sides of the school either side of the River Cam. Arthur had followed Eliot over the bridge earlier in the tour, but the Head Boy hadn't remarked on the building at all. Arthur realised now that Eliot had been saving this for his grand finale.

"This is Caerleon House, Your Royal Highness. It is the pride of Chapel Court," Eliot announced pompously as he stopped by a large, wooden door to the right of the archway and faced Arthur. "The House was rebuilt in Ancaster stone in the mid-nineteenth century after the original buildings were destroyed in a fire. Only the Caerleon archway here survived. Caerleon is the most sociable of all the Badon Houses. I'm sure you'll be very happy here."

Eliot gave a slightly reverent bob of his head as he waved towards the building behind him, and Arthur had to fight the urge to roll his eyes at the comment; after all, he was stuck here whether he was happy about it or not.

When it became clear that Arthur wasn't about to offer up an insightful comment about Caerleon's nineteenth-century architecture or otherwise Eliot turned and opened the door with a flourish, holding it wide so that Arthur could duck out of the early September sunshine and into the relative darkness of the entranceway.

Arthur pursed his lips. So this was it, the place he was

confined to for the next five years. He wrinkled his nose at the slightly musty smell of the corridor as Eliot gestured for him to lead the way up the narrow staircase. Arthur liked to think he had reasonable expectations when it came to life, and he hadn't expected his new school to match up to the grandeur of the palaces and stately homes he'd lived in or visited as he'd grown up. However, he would have thought that the institution responsible for educating the Kings of Britain, Northern Ireland and the Commonwealth (in her many iterations) since the thirteenth century would be a little less shabby. Fine, he'd admit that the buildings were quite impressive looking from the outside, and Badon did occupy the same stretch of the Cam as some of the University's most illustrious colleges, but Arthur was willing to bet that the staircase he was currently wending his way up hadn't seen a paintbrush in years.

Eliot didn't seem to have noticed Arthur's distaste and was still speaking when the prince tuned back in just in time to hear him say "...so you'll need to make sure you do that every time you leave college grounds."

Arthur, without even a vague clue as to what the Head Boy was talking about, nodded in response. He hoped that Hector – his primary security agent, who was also traipsing up the stairs – had been listening and would fill him in on whatever details he'd missed. Hector had been guarding Arthur since he was four, and he hadn't let him down once in all that time.

"First years have free time between four o'clock and half-past-five on Thursday afternoons," Eliot stated as he gestured for Arthur to wait on the first floor landing. "That is the only time you're permitted to leave Badon during the week, unless you have express permission from the

Headmaster." Eliot suddenly seemed to remember who he was talking to and his cheeks went as red as the blazer he was wearing. "Of course, Your Royal Highness, I mean, *Sir*, I'm sure there will be special dispensation in your case."

Arthur nodded, waving away Eliot's embarrassment. "We're allowed to go into town on Saturday afternoons though, aren't we?"

"That's right, and in the summer we're even allowed to take punts up the river to Grantchester village."

Arthur wanted to hoot with joy at the prospect of a whole afternoon of freedom - well, as much freedom as one could have when being trailed by bodyguards – but as that was exactly the kind of behaviour he'd been warned didn't befit the future King, Arthur had to arrange his features into an expression of solemn indifference. Up to this point he'd spent almost every Saturday attending events of one kind or another with his parents, and the thought of even just a few hours of choosing his own timetable *almost* made up for the fact that he'd be stuck in school for the rest of the week.

Eliot gave a short respectful nod in Arthur's direction before scuttling past him and heading for a door at the end of the corridor. "This will be your room, Your Royal Highness. The other ten Caerleon first years will be moving in over the next hour, and the older boys arrive tomorrow evening. Your Housemaster, Mr Beaulake, will meet you all in the JCR - that's the Junior Common Room - downstairs at five-thirty."

Arthur, desperate to get a glimpse of his new room, shot a blinding smile at Eliot. "Thank you for your time, Eliot," he bobbed his head, whipping the small brass key out of the Head Boy's hand. "I'll let the Headmaster know how helpful you've been. I'm sure you have lots of other important things to do though, and I think I can find my way from here."

Eliot preened slightly under the praise and didn't seem to take offence at Arthur's rather blunt brush off. Arthur ignored the way Hector frowned at him – he'd been doing that a lot recently.

"Thanks again," Arthur beamed before practically diving for the door, unlocking it and shouldering his way inside. He quickly pushed the door closed behind him and leant his forehead against it with a sigh of relief. He knew Hector would come barging through in a few seconds but Arthur just wanted to savour the brief moment of being free, and of being properly alone at last.

"That bad already?"

Arthur emitted a high-pitched squeak he'd never readily admit to as the voice came from behind him. He whirled around, immediately on the defensive, ready to call for Hector's assistance with the threat if necessary.

'The threat' turned out to be a blond-haired boy in a suit who, although a little bit shorter, looked to be about the same age as Arthur. He was giving the new arrival a suspicious once over as if *Arthur* was the one who was out of place.

"Who are you?" Arthur asked, vaguely aware that he was brandishing a pen in the other boy's direction. "What are you doing in my room?"

"*Your* room?" The suspected intruder raised an eyebrow before realisation seemed to dawn. "Oh, you're Prince Arthur."

Arthur wasn't hugely impressed by the lack of reverence in the other boy's tone. "Yes, I am. And I'll ask you again, what are you doing in my room?"

The boy only grinned at him. "I'm Merlin Montgomery." He held a hand out towards Arthur. "This is my room too. A stuffy bloke in a dinner jacket told me I wasn't supposed to call you by your first name until you told me to, but to be honest I wasn't really listening to what he said after that."

Arthur shook the boy's hand, less because he'd chosen to and more because years of ingrained propriety dictated that he must. "It's Your Royal Highness, and then 'Sir'."

Merlin laughed. "You don't really expect me to call you 'Sir' for the next five years, do you?"

Arthur's brain finally caught up with the thread of conversation. "Wait, did you say this was your room too?"

"I did." Merlin gave Arthur a look that suggested he thought the prince might be a bit odd.

"There must be some mistake," Arthur replied looking around the room for the first time. Sure enough there were two single beds, a desk each side of the large window, two chests of drawers, two wardrobes and so on. Arthur was increasingly horrified by the fact that there seemed to be two of everything, including occupants of the room. "No, I was quite clearly told that this was *my* room."

Merlin crossed his arms over his chest. "Yes, but it's also *my* room. Didn't anyone tell you that you'd be sharing with someone?"

Arthur shook his head in disbelief. He'd never had to share anything with anybody. That was just the way it was when you were the heir to the throne.

"Ah," Merlin sat down on the edge of the bed he'd clearly claimed as his own. "I can see how this might be a bit awkward for you."

"Awkward for me?" Arthur barked out a laugh. "No, I think it's going to be far more awkward for you considering it looks like you've already unpacked your… *stuff.*" Arthur wrinkled his nose at the collection of textbooks, clothes, and odds and ends that seemed be in the process of exploding from two trunks on Merlin's side of the room.

Merlin frowned and opened his mouth to say something just as Hector – perfect timing as always – strode into the room. Arthur grinned; surely the mess would be sorted out now. Merlin would leave and he could get onto reveling in the fact he had a room to himself far, *far* away from the palace.

"Ah, you must be Merlin." Hector smiled charmingly and shook Merlin's hand.

What? Arthur's mouth dropped open in surprise. *Hector knew?* Hector knew and hadn't told him?

Merlin switched straight from the irritated frown that had settled on his face at Arthur's earlier words to a blinding grin for Hector. "Are you a bodyguard? Do you have a gun?"

Hector found this far more amusing than Arthur did if his guffaw of laughter was anything to go by.

"Hector," Arthur frowned, "what's going on?"

Hector shook his head. "What do you mean, Arthur?"

"Why does *he*," he pointed to Merlin, fully aware that he was actually being quite rude now, "seem to think we're supposed to be sharing this room? And why do *you* seem to know about it?"

Hector looked momentarily horrified before slipping back into his mask of friendly professionalism. "Didn't you know about this Arthur? I assumed your parents had told you before we left this morning?"

Arthur gritted his teeth. "No," he practically growled, "they seem to have forgotten to mention that detail. How quickly can another room be found for Merlin?"

Hector shook his head slowly. "Arthur, you're already being afforded more privileges than most boys here, but there are certain conditions that even you have to meet. Your parents are keen for you to have as 'normal' an experience at school as possible, and you'll have to share a room just like everybody else."

Merlin coughed quietly. "I'll just go and find my parents. I only popped up here to dump my stuff." He shuffled towards the door and let himself out before anyone could prevent his escape.

Not that Arthur would have stopped him. "Really, Hector?"

Hector nodded gravely. "I'm sorry Arthur, I thought you knew. The school's already had to reduce the number of first year students it admitted this year so that your security team could be housed in and around the college. It would be impossible to justify giving you your own room when Badon has already made such allowances."

Arthur sighed and tried to remind himself that sulking wasn't really appropriate. He'd faced enough of these situations in life to know that tantrums never really got him anywhere. "So there's nothing I can do?"

"Not about this, my boy," Hector slipped slightly into the familiarity he'd moved away from as Arthur had grown older. "But I'm sure Merlin will be a perfectly fine roommate. Just think, you might even become good friends."

"I doubt that." Arthur shrugged. He frowned almost immediately as his brain finally latched onto the niggling thought that had been trying to make itself known over the preceding few minutes. "Hang on, is this someone's idea of a joke?"

"Pardon?"

"Is his name really *Merlin*?"

"Ah," Hector grinned slightly. "Yes to both questions, probably."

Arthur shook his head with a sigh far wearier than any thirteen-year-old had the right to produce as he sat down on the unclaimed bed. "If he turns me into a toad, you're getting sacked."

*   *   *   *   *

At least Mr Beaulake seemed like an alright kind of teacher. He wasn't a million years old like the headmaster, probably somewhere closer in age to Hector, and he'd seemed really keen to get the boys of Caerleon House involved with as many of Badon's school teams as possible. Arthur was particularly happy about that; he'd always been good at team sports, but as most of the time he hadn't been available for his prep school's matches his experience had been limited to games lessons. Most importantly though, as he went around the room to meet each boy's family, Beaulake had made a point of introducing himself to Arthur before asking how he wanted to be addressed, rather than just assuming the prince wanted formal terms used at all times.

"Arthur's fine," he'd replied and Beaulake had smiled in agreement before moving on to introduce himself to Hector who was effectively standing in for Arthur's parents. If Arthur's calculations and the clock in the JCR were correct then the King and Queen were currently somewhere over the Atlantic.

Arthur felt a familiar stab of *'something'* when he looked around to see the other first years surrounded by their parents. Some families were laughing together, whereas other parents were clinging protectively to their sons as if they weren't quite ready to let them go just yet. He spotted Merlin, shirtsleeves rolled up in complete disregard of the uniform rules, awkwardly slouching between a smartly dressed man and a woman who seemed to be wearing every colour of the rainbow somewhere about her person.

Merlin noticed Arthur looking his way and gave him a small wave that managed to look a little apologetic, but he was almost immediately drawn back into a conversation when the multicoloured woman Arthur assumed was Merlin's mother began to forcibly roll her son's sleeves back down to his wrists.

A knock on the open door to the JCR drew everyone's attention. A woman with long red hair stood in the doorway smiling warmly at the assembled crowd. One of her arms was clamped tightly around the shoulders of a teenage girl with equally fiery locks, and a small boy with a shock of dark hair was gripping the other fiercely.

"Ladies and Gentlemen," Beaulake announced, striding towards the new arrivals with a grin, "allow me to introduce Mrs Beaulake, Housemistress of Caerleon, and Chemistry teacher here at Badon."

"Hello." Mrs Beaulake smiled widely at her new charges, before pushing the teenage girl forward slightly. "This is Elaine, and the young man hiding behind my legs is Thomas."

Arthur was gratified to note that Elaine Beaulake looked even less impressed to be in the Caerleon JCR than he did. This thought was promptly followed by one of how sensible

Thomas Beaulake was as the toddler scarpered from the room as if being chased by a pack of wolves, shrieking as he did.

Mrs Beaulake nudged her daughter and the teenager gave one last forced smile to the assembled families before trotting off after her brother.

"Sorry about that," Mrs Beaulake rolled her eyes. "Tom's just reached the shouting stage."

A few mothers nodded sagely, shooting slightly pointed glances towards their teenage sons. Arthur snorted at the image, and was gratified to see Merlin's mother eyeing her own son with a slight frown.

"Mr Beaulake, the children, and I live in the family quarters at the end of the corridor so there's always someone here for you outside of school hours," Mrs Beaulake explained. "Don't worry, gentlemen, the walls of Caerleon are thick enough that you won't hear Tom shouting at all hours."

Relieved grunts filled the room and with a smile Mrs Beaulake joined her husband in order to continue the personal introductions. The rest of the JCR descended once more into general chatter, and a few boys drifted away from their parents to introduce themselves to neighbours, Merlin included.

Arthur, for once in his life, found himself completely at the edge of a social circle. Hector was chatting to the parents of a boy with a rather unfortunate mullet, and the only other person the prince 'knew' seemed to already be making friends with half the room.

"Arthur, isn't it?"

The prince startled slightly at the soft voice and turned to see Mrs Beaulake holding out a glass of orange squash. He

12

took the drink gratefully with a quiet, "Yes, Mrs Beaulake. Thank you."

"We like to call each boy by their given name in the boarding house, or if we're speaking to you as your housemaster and housemistress," Mrs Beaulake continued with a smile. "During lessons teachers are more formal. Even us."

"That's what it's like with Hector," Arthur found himself saying. "Technically he's supposed to call me 'Sir' but I've known him since I was four and it would have been weird not to keep calling me Arthur as I got older."

"That makes sense," Mrs Beaulake replied as she perched on the window seat and gestured for Arthur to join her. "Now, Arthur, I hear there was a little bit of confusion about your bedroom."

Arthur felt his cheeks heat slightly. "Just a misunderstanding."

"I'm sure you'll enjoy sharing a room." Mrs Beaulake nodded seriously. "It's nice to have someone to talk to at the end of the day."

Arthur, lacking any better response, nodded his head. He still wasn't quite sure about this 'instant friend' business, but best to let the adults think he was agreeing with them anyway.

"Your cousin's boarding house is only the other side of the bridge," Mrs Beaulake continued just as Arthur took a drink, "so I'm sure you can always pop over there if you want to see a friendly, familiar face."

He tried so hard not to choke, but the surprise of hearing Hugo, Prince of York, described as 'friendly' was enough to have Arthur spraying orange squash from his nose in a way that his father would no doubt inform him was 'completely unacceptable'.

Arthur grimaced as he wiped sugary trails of juice from his face. Mrs Beaulake was patting his back and asking if he was alright, and he knew without looking that the attention of the room was quite firmly on him. Thankfully, it seemed that Hector had established that the drink explosion was more likely down to Arthur's ability to cause havoc rather than a stealthy assassination attempt. A swoop by his security team on his first day would have been the final straw for Arthur's nerves.

"I'm fine, thank you, Mrs Beaulake," Arthur coughed slightly as he spoke. "It just went down the wrong way."

Mrs Beaulake didn't quite look like she believed him, so he hurriedly excused himself under the pretext that he should probably go and get to know Merlin a little better.

The Housemistress nodded once before smiling kindly at him again. "Go and have fun, Arthur. Don't forget to knock on our door if you ever need anything."

Merlin was chatting to two boys when Arthur reached the other side of the JCR. His roommate glanced pointedly at the prince's squash-stained shirt and rolled his eyes slightly.

"This is my roommate." Merlin nodded his head in Arthur's direction and the prince watched as the other two boys' eyes widened in slight surprise. "I'm not sure exactly what I'm supposed to introduce him as. I think it might be *Sir*."

Arthur ignored Merlin's deliberate attempt to rile him and held his hand out to the taller of the other two boys. "Arthur Pendragon." He hoped neither boy would make any connection between his and Merlin's names; Arthur had a feeling that it was going to get old rather quickly.

"Albert Dorner," the boy replied, shaking the prince's

14

hand firmly. "Most people call me Bertie though. I'm a second year, but my roommate moved schools at the end of last term, and because of the odd number of first years I'm sharing with Gareth here. Mr Beaulake asked me to arrive early so that I could get to know Gareth better, and so that the rest of you can ask any questions you have about life at Badon."

The other boy – Gareth - didn't look old enough to be anywhere near Badon. He grinned jauntily from under a mop of sandy-blond hair as he shook Arthur's hand, which only served to make him look even younger. "Hello." Then, as if he were able to read Arthur's thoughts, he added, "I'm twelve, but I got bumped up a year in school. My Dad's promised I'll have a growth spurt soon though."

Arthur thought it was probably best not to comment.

"Do you play rugby, Arthur?" Bertie asked. "Neither of these two are interested, but the Lower School selection rounds begin on Wednesday and I need to start signing people up."

Arthur perked up properly for the first time since arriving in Cambridge.

"I'm the Lower Sports Captain for Caerleon House," Bertie continued to explain. "Normally they give the job to a third year, but considering quite a few Badon teams are made up mostly of Caerleon second years Mr Beaulake nominated me for the post."

"Do you have to join a team?" Gareth looked slightly panicked.

Bertie snorted at the flash of fear. "No. Don't worry. Everyone has to choose at least one sports club to join for after school activities, but you don't have to take it too seriously if you don't want to."

"But I'm terrible at everything!" Gareth practically wailed.

"I'm sure you'll find something, Gareth," Arthur encouraged. He didn't entirely believe it himself, but part of his princely duties involved supporting others after all. "Where do I sign up for rugby then?"

Bertie held up his hand. "Here." He fished a crumpled piece of paper out of his pocket and handed it to Arthur. "The ones at the top of this list are teams holding selections this term, so have a look and see if there's anything else you'd be interested in. The clubs at the bottom are the ones that don't hold selections until after Christmas, but you'll need to sign up now if you want to have a go."

Arthur scanned the list quickly, immediately picking out four or five he'd seriously consider. Rugby was top of the list, and he'd always wanted to try out rowing.

"Clay pigeon shooting?" Merlin's voice came from somewhere over Arthur's shoulder. "Really?"

Bertie nodded again. "Some people take it quite seriously, Merlin."

"Maybe you should try that one, Gareth," Merlin grinned at the younger boy.

"You're joking!" Gareth winced. "Me with a weapon of any kind? I'd probably take someone's eye out. Actually, I'd probably take my *own* eye out."

"Better stay away from fencing then," Bertie laughed.

Arthur grimaced again. He was going to stay away from fencing too, no matter what his father said about the family's fine tradition of producing Badon fencing champions. Fencing champions like Hugo. Arthur wasn't going to let his awful cousin anywhere near him with a sword, blunt or otherwise.

"Rowing sounds good," Arthur shrugged handing the list back to Bertie. "And maybe cricket after Christmas."

"Pick two at most," Bertie grinned, "otherwise you'll have no time for a life." He turned to Merlin again. "What about you, Merlin?"

Merlin wrinkled his nose. "I don't actually like outside all that much."

Bertie's grin only widened. "Well there're plenty of indoor sports. Swimming?"

Merlin's face darkened. "Not a big fan of water either."

"Badminton?" Bertie tried. "Squash?"

Merlin shook his head. "I suppose it's too much to hope that you'd class lurking indoors as a sport?"

Arthur was alarmed to see that Bertie actually looked thoughtful for a moment.

"Well," Bertie said eventually, "we did have an Extreme Hide and Seek club last year, but Mr Beaulake banned it after it all got a bit…" he trailed off, searching for the right word. "*Extreme*, I suppose."

Arthur sighed as Merlin looked positively overjoyed. For just a minute there he'd thought that Badon College might be approaching something normal.

* * * * *

"Jim, Kofi, Alexei, Will." Arthur stated each name as he pointed in turn at the boys on the next table in the Dining Hall the following morning. Then moving his attention to another table, he added, "Marc, Sib, Ruari, Charlie. Honestly, Merlin, it's not that difficult. Were you actually listening last night when people spoke to you?"

"It's not my fault I'm terrible with names," Merlin replied before shovelling another great spoon of chocolate cereal into his mouth. "You should be honoured I can remember *your* name."

Gareth snorted. Arthur raised an eyebrow at him and the younger boy very quickly went back to contemplating his toast.

"Just wait until everyone else arrives today," Bertie said to Merlin. "Then you'll have to remember *their* names, *and* the teachers' names, *and* remember where you need to go for each lesson."

Merlin looked disgruntled and pushed his bowl away from him. "Thanks, Bertie. That makes me feel much better."

Bertie laughed loudly. "Relax. I'll give you three a proper tour of the place in a minute. Our illustrious Head Boy and his army of prefects tend to focus on the boring stuff when they give their tours."

"And you don't?" Arthur grinned.

"Course not. I'll give you a proper look at Badon. I might even tell you where the classrooms are. Funnily enough, our good old Head Boy, Troyes, doesn't seem to think that sort of information is important."

"I don't suppose you know the best way of escaping from here entirely, do you?" Merlin grimaced. "I think I've had enough already."

Bertie winked. "I know quite a lot of things, Merlin."

Merlin looked slightly cheered for the first time that morning. "Good. If I can only get out of here twice a week for the next few years I think I might go stark raving mad."

"Aren't you that already?" Arthur quipped.

Merlin narrowed his eyes as everyone else laughed, but Arthur was fairly sure there was no malice behind it.

"Are you going to eat that toast, Gareth?' Bertie asked

a few minutes later. "Or just stare at it until it starts to mould?"

"Sorry," Gareth crammed the crusts into his mouth, still looking terribly sleepy. "I'm not very good before eight in the morning."

"Come on then," Bertie stood up and grabbed his tray from the table. "You need to put your plates and things on the conveyor belt over there. Woe betide anyone who leaves a cup behind. You'll have Agnes and her kitchen team after you, and trust me when I say you really don't want that."

"Agnes seemed really nice," Gareth frowned as he followed Bertie's lead, thinking back to the kindly woman who'd found some strawberry jam for him.

"She is," Bertie replied. "And she'll give you extra biscuits and cake if she likes you. But if you cross her you'll know about it."

Arthur and Merlin exchanged a slightly worried glance before they both very dutifully placed their trays on the conveyor as instructed; Arthur because he didn't want to anger anyone, particularly not someone who seemed as friendly as Agnes, and Merlin because he was terrified at the prospect of being denied extra dessert.

"Right," Bertie announced as the other three trailed after him into the bright Sunday morning. "So our side of the river – the *better* side, obviously – has Caerleon, Winchester House, the Chapel and De Grace, which is basically the humanities building. This side starts with Kings' Court." He waved around at the perfect square of green grass surrounded on all four sides by a higgledy-piggledy selection of buildings. "That's the Dining Hall, obviously. The two red brick buildings are classrooms. The taller one, Maris, is the maths and science building; and the gym and infirmary are in there too. There's a modern bit on the back that's full of labs. The black and white Tudor buildings over there make up Kings' House; Caerleon's main rivals in everything from sport to music." He stopped walking and grinned at Arthur. "They've even got their own royal too."

Arthur grimaced. "Hugo."

"Do you not get on with your cousin, Arthur?" Gareth asked, the picture of wide-eyed innocence. "I thought it'd be nice to have someone you knew living so close."

"No," Arthur shook his head. "We don't really have much in common."

Arthur and his cousin shared a surname, and that was really where the similarities ended. Where Arthur had the dark brown hair and eyes of his mother, Hugo, and his sister Charlotte for that matter, had inherited the hazel eyes and gently-waving blond hair of the Pendragon family. Both York siblings had also been graced with the striking, angular features of their French mother, as well as her short temper and haughtiness.

"I've come across him in some inter house fencing matches," Bertie added. "He's in the year above me though, so at least there's been a limit to how many times he's had the opportunity to thrash me."

"Well Caerleon has Arthur, and his dad's the King," Merlin grinned. "Surely that trumps whatever Hugo is."

"Prince of York," Arthur wrinkled his nose.

"Exactly," Merlin nudged his roommate with his elbow, "he only gets a city. You get a whole country."

Arthur laughed at that, banishing the slight cloud that had descended over the group at the mention of Hugo. "Sticking up for me now, Merlin? You better be careful or people will start thinking we might actually get on."

"Sorry, *Sir*."

Bertie laughed again before pointing to the right-hand side of Kings' House where the architecture was even older. "That's the Headmaster's Lodge in the corner, but I'm sure you remember that from your interviews." At the other three boys' dutiful nods he added, "I suggest you make that the only time you end up in there. Not least because it's haunted."

"What?" Gareth squeaked, staring at the somewhat ramshackle building in the corner.

Arthur rolled his eyes. "He's winding you up, Gareth."

"I'm not!" Bertie held up his hands in defence. "You know how the school started, don't you?"

Arthur and Gareth nodded their ascent.

Merlin, however, shrugged. "Not really."

"Didn't read the prospectus then?' Arthur asked.

"Course not," Merlin replied with another shrug. "They let me in because I'm clever, not because I could recite the history of the place."

"Annoyingly sure of yourself, aren't you?" Arthur raised an eyebrow. Trust him to get stuck with probably the oddest roommate in the history of the school.

"Something like that," Merlin replied. "It's not my fault they decided I was brilliant and dragged me here with the promise of a free education."

"You have a scholarship?" Gareth asked in slight surprise.

"Not just *any* scholarship," Merlin adopted a ridiculously pompous tone. "The *Headmaster's* Scholarship." He rolled his eyes. "Basically, it means I'm just a lowly commoner who has to get decent marks for the next five years or I'm out on my ear. Nobody said I was going to get tested on ghost stories, but I'm sure a good haunting might liven this place up a bit. Go on then." He gestured for Bertie to recite the tale.

"Well," Bertie replied, lowering his voice to sound more dramatic, "the school was founded by Sir James Catterick, and Edward Alderley, Lord Badon, in the fifteenth century, just after they completed work on Catterick College at the University. Neither man was from Cambridge, so why they chose to settle here we can't be sure. The story goes that Catterick and Alderley were part of some secret society, and were pretty high up in the ranks."

"A secret society for what?" Gareth asked, eyes saucer-wide.

"Nobody really knows," Bertie shrugged. "They were apparently the guardians of some precious object that had to be kept safe at all costs. *And* there are some who say that Catterick and Alderley were involved with alchemists and sorcerers."

"Sorcerers?" Arthur snorted. "It sounded like quite a good story up until that part, Bertie."

"What do you mean 'involved with alchemists and sorcerers'? Merlin asked, sounding, to Arthur's surprise, genuinely interested in what Bertie was saying.

"Oh," Arthur rolled his eyes at his roommate, "don't tell me you believe in magic, Merlin. I know you're named after a wizard, but-"

"Sorcerer," Merlin cut him off.

"What?"

"Merlin in the stories wasn't a wizard," Merlin folded his arms. "He was a *sorcerer.*"

"Because there's a difference?" Arthur shrugged.

"Of course there is," Merlin replied, looking quite cross all of a sudden.

"*Anyway*," Bertie said soundly, effectively cutting off any argument that might be about to erupt, "whatever Catterick and Alderley were up to they held meetings here, in the Headmaster's Lodge, with their fellow members."

"What for?" Gareth asked.

"Nobody really knows," Bertie replied. "But for the past five hundred years there have been reports of figures in black robes outside the Lodge on very dark nights. It's the second oldest building on the river, you know."

Gareth looked horrified. "Who are the figures? Catterick and Alderley?"

"Nobody knows that either," Bertie replied. "They always wear hoods so their faces have never been seen."

A sudden gust drifted up the river bringing a chill to the air that was far too wintery for early September. Gareth shivered, and even Arthur was slightly unnerved.

"Okay, that was a bit spooky," Gareth hissed, rubbing his arms at the sudden nip.

Bertie shook his head after a long moment. "Nah, that's just England's weather for you, isn't it? It'll probably start raining in a minute and then be really sunny for the rest of the day. Come on. I'll show you how to get to the sports fields." He began walking towards Kings' House. "Oh, don't walk on the grass. Teachers and prefects only, I'm afraid, so you'll have to go around the edge at all times."

"What if we're really late for a lesson?" Gareth asked.

"Not even then. Troyes and his minions will be waiting for you to have a go." Bertie quirked his lips slightly. "I think the best bit of advice I can give you is try not to be late for lessons."

Gareth made a face that suggested that he might not be able to live up to these words of wisdom, but he remained silent as he followed the others through an archway to the left of Kings' House.

"This is Catterick Court," Bertie announced.

The back of Kings' House, the Arts building, the admin building, and the smallest boarding house, Hainault, formed the sides of the Court. Bertie explained that Hainault boys were often the sons of professors at the University and so tended to escape the confines of the College more often than others as their parents were able to take them off premises at short notice.

"And finally, this is the Back Gate," Bertie said as they reached an imposing stone archway that didn't match the architectural style of either building it was attached to, and it looked almost ridiculous between the red brick grandeur of Arts and the wooden construction of Hainault. "It's named that because it's at the back of the college, obviously, *and* because it actually leads out onto the footpath along the bit of the river known as the Backs. It's because the back of quite a few of the University colleges are along this stretch of the Cam; I don't think they were too inventive when they came up with the name."

Merlin reached forwards and slid a small wooden panel on the gate itself to the left, thus exposing a snapshot of the world beyond Badon's walls. The main road was separated from the gate by a deep grass verge and in the distance it was just possible to see how the River Cam swept back round to the left once it had passed underneath the numerous University bridges that dominated the landscape.

"Freedom," Merlin muttered as he closed the hatch with a resigned sigh.

Bertie looked at his watch. "We should really be heading back to our side," he said as he gestured for the others to follow him again. "We've got to be at Chapel for nine-thirty and you need to be in full formal and gowns because it's Sunday."

Merlin groaned. "Those gowns are ridiculous."

"You'll be grateful of that gown when it gets to November," Bertie replied as they crossed back through Kings' Court. "The Chapel's absolutely freezing at the best of times, but the winter is a special brand of torture."

Merlin looked down at his jeans sadly. "I don't see why we can't just wear normal clothes under the gowns, it's not like you'll be able to see!"

"Tradition is very important here, Mr Montgomery."

All four boys startled slightly at the new voice. They turned in comedic unison to see Mr Beaulake grinning behind them. His family was hovering behind, and Mrs Beaulake was obviously trying not to laugh at the boys' startled expressions.

"Of course, sir," Merlin replied contritely, and Arthur almost fell over in surprise such was the change from the other boy's usually rebellious behaviour.

"We enter Chapel as a united house so be ready at nine twenty," Beaulake explained. "I'm sure Bertie will make sure you're all exactly where you need to be."

"Sir." Bertie nodded.

The Beaulakes walked on, and Thomas stared up at the four older boys in a combination of interest and suspicion. Elaine barely glanced at the first years, but she did grace Bertie with a small smile and a quick 'hello.' Bertie gave a small gesture that looked like a cross between an embarrassed wave and an involuntary twitch.

"Well, well." Merlin rounded on Bertie the minute the Beaulakes crossed the bridge and disappeared through the

25

archway into Chapel Court, heading back to their home in Caerleon. "It looks like Albert has a girlfriend."

"Shut up, Merlin." Bertie nudged the other boy, but his cheeks still reddened slightly. "Elaine's just sort of my friend."

"Of course," Arthur chimed in, a slightly mocking tone to his voice. "I believe you."

Gareth opened his mouth, presumably to add a quip of his own, but Bertie got there first.

"One more word and I'll leave you to the mercy of Head Boy Troyes and his minions when we're in Chapel," Bertie replied, drawing himself up to his considerable height. "And here I was going to let you in on a little secret about how to extend your freedom. I guess I'm just going to have to hold onto that information for a little longer."

"What?" Merlin cried indignantly. "No, Bertie, you have to tell us! I was joking. A joke, you know, ha-ha isn't Merlin hilarious?"

Bertie only smirked before shaking his head sadly. "Sorry, Merlin. I just don't have anything else to tell you right now."

"Merlin!" Arthur punched his roommate's arm with perhaps more force than was necessary. "Now look what you've done."

"*Me?*" Merlin rubbed his arm. "And by the way, Arthur, *ow*. You were making fun of him too!"

Gareth piped up. "I didn't say anything, Bertie. Will you tell me?"

Arthur and Merlin were momentarily united as they glared at Gareth in outrage.

Bertie just went back to smirking. "Sorry, Gareth, you're guilty by association. Who knows? I might tell you all eventually. It depends if I'm ever feeling this generous again."

Merlin grumbled something to himself that Arthur couldn't quite catch but was sure from the tone that it was far from a friendly comment.

"Come on," Bertie said cheerfully as he headed over the bridge to the city-side of the College. "It takes forever to dress for Chapel."

* * * * *

After the initial disaster that was Merlin and Gareth's inability to tie bowties without getting into a right mess, Chapel had gone quite smoothly. Arthur had noticed there was far less whispering and pointing from the first year boys in the other houses now that they'd had a day to get used to the idea that they were attending school with the heir to the throne.

Of course there was no way Arthur's newfound sense of peace could last. The arrival of the remaining forty-six Caerleonites brought a second round of variations on 'look, that's the Crown Prince', and he couldn't even escape to his room as Mr and Mrs Beaulake had been quite firm about all first year boys remaining in the JCR so that the older students could meet them properly.

At least Bertie's friends hadn't been too bad about the whole royalty thing; Arthur was fairly certain that this was because Bertie had briefed them all in full before they'd trooped down the stairs to meet the three boys Bertie had taken under his wing. Although, one of them hadn't been able to resist making a comment about the coincidence of Arthur being stuck in a room with a boy named Merlin.

"Like the King and the Wizard then," a ridiculously tall

boy with wild red hair had guffawed as he'd shaken hands with Arthur.

"Sorcerer," Arthur found himself correcting unconsciously.

"What?" The boy had frowned in confusion.

"Ignore him, Arthur," Bertie had grinned and thumped the redhead on the back good-naturedly. "If anyone shouldn't be allowed to comment on other people's names it's him. He's stuck as Kingsley Kendal Kennedy-Kendrick for life."

Arthur had chuckled at that and Kingsley's face had turned a deep shade of beetroot.

"We just call him Kay though," Bertie added. "Seems a bit more reasonable, don't you think?"

So it wasn't until just before dinner that evening that Arthur's mood was completely ruined.

He'd been dragged into a brief meeting with his security team so Merlin and Gareth had gone on ahead to the Dining Hall with some of the second years. Hector had wanted to be very clear about arrangements for Arthur attending evening sports practices as the Badon pitches were outside of school grounds. Arthur hadn't really listened; it was always the same message anyway – '*Arthur, you mustn't go anywhere without ensuring the Protection Squad is aware of your activities*'.

The Royal Protection Squad didn't seem to be aware that Arthur wasn't supposed to be late for dinner though, and by the time they'd let him go he only had a couple of minutes to spare.

He had just skidded off the bridge and onto the gravel of Kings' Court when he had to stop short to avoid careering straight into two boys also making their way to dinner.

"Sorry," Arthur raised his hands in apology before his brain caught up with his eyes and he registered a familiar face sneering at him.

Hugo shook his head slowly at his cousin, his lip curled in obvious distaste. "So, Daddy's finally let you fly the nest, has he?"

The hulking boy next to Hugo sniggered and Arthur was immediately reminded that anyone who would choose to associate with Hugo was probably as much of a bad egg as the Prince of York himself.

"You better watch yourself, Pendragon." Hugo's dark eyes narrowed as Arthur fought to avoid taking a step backwards.

Arthur frowned. He'd never been able to pinpoint when exactly the hostility between the two of them had started. It seemed even from their earliest meetings Hugo had acted in the vilest way possible towards Arthur. Hugo's elder sister, Princess Charlotte of York, wasn't much better. Arthur had dreaded family gatherings of any kind as the adults had always suggested that the three youngest royals spend time together; all completely oblivious to the fact that the York siblings liked nothing better than upsetting their young cousin at every available opportunity. He suppressed a shudder at the memory of the cold, lonely hours he'd spent hiding from his cousins, constantly afraid that they would discover him.

On some level at least, his fear of Hugo stemmed from the fact that the York siblings had often told Arthur that he'd probably face the same fate as the King of legend; they did share a name and an ancestry after all. It didn't matter that most of the legend was complete fiction and didn't reflect the Pendragon family's true history, but it had felt like enough of a possibility to terrify a small child. Arthur had spent hours of his childhood just waiting for a sword-wielding enemy to jump out from behind a door.

But Arthur wasn't a small child anymore, and he wasn't going to let Hugo intimidate him now that they were both at Badon. "It was an accident, Hugo. Can we just forget this stupid squabble? It's childish."

Hugo barked out a harsh laugh. "A squabble? You think this is a squabble?" He looked at his friend and grinned nastily. "You see, Laurie, Arthur here likes to think he knows everything." His voice held no warmth when he addressed his cousin once more. "You don't know anything, Arthur. You're a stupid child. Nothing more."

Arthur raised his chin and turned away without another word. Hugo's taunt of *'That's right, run away as usual'* followed him into the Dining Hall. He didn't want to sit through dinner and make polite conversation; he wanted to retreat to his room and sulk for a while.

"There you are!" Merlin rolled his eyes when Arthur approached the empty seat next to his roommate at the long table. "We thought you were going to miss Grace. Bertie said if you arrive after the headmaster he usually-"

"I don't care!" Arthur snapped. "Just shut up and leave me alone." He was aware that he'd drawn significant attention from the boys around him and this only succeeded in darkening his mood further.

"Charming," Merlin huffed. "What's gotten in to you?"

Arthur felt the last fragment of his patience shatter. "What's gotten in to me is that I'm sick of being surrounded by idiots. I don't need friends here, and I'm certainly not going to be friends with the likes of a nosey, irritating *scholarship* boy like you."

Arthur regretted the words even before they'd tumbled from his mouth, and his mother's wisdom came back to him. '*Remember, Arthur, until you speak, **you** are the master of the word, but as soon as you open your mouth the word becomes the master of you.*' He'd never really understood what she'd meant until the moment Merlin's forehead knitted into a frown, the flicker of hurt unmistakable though it lasted no more than a split-second.

"Scholarship," Merlin repeated coldly. "Yes, I can see how that would cause a problem for you."

"Merlin-" Arthur tried to salvage the situation, but Merlin wouldn't allow it.

"No, no," Merlin waved his hands airily. "Save your breath. I understand completely, *Sir.*" With that he turned away from Arthur and immediately started up a horribly forced conversation with a stunned Gareth.

Arthur looked around to explain himself to anyone who would listen but Bertie, Kay and the other Caerleon boys sitting nearby were all refusing to meet Arthur's eyes.

Arthur dropped his head to his chest in resignation just as the bell rang to signify the arrival of the Headmaster. Every boy in the hall fell silent as they rose to their feet to say Grace. As Arthur recited the words mechanically he marvelled at how wrong he'd been when he'd arrived.

He wasn't looking forward to being on his own at all.

* * * * *

Arthur started awake. His heart was hammering almost painfully in his chest as he gulped in a huge mouthful of air. He rubbed a hand through his hair; pulling a face as he pushed back the damp strands that were plastered uncomfortably to his sweat-soaked forehead.

It must have been a nightmare, but he couldn't remember anything of what he'd been dreaming about. He shivered slightly as his clammy skin began to cool, his heavy duvet thrown to the floor. He was fully aware of the room around him now, but there was a crawling sense of foreboding; an awareness of a darkness he couldn't see that had settled at the base of his spine and was refusing to shift.

"Oh, stop being a baby," he chastised himself in a whisper. He looked over to the other occupant of the room to find that Merlin was still snoring and completely oblivious to Arthur's moment of panic. Not that Merlin would have been particularly sympathetic considering the way he'd stalked back to Caerleon after dinner without another word to Arthur. Merlin had already been huddled under his duvet with all the lights off when Arthur had finally made it back to their room.

Arthur sighed as he lay back down, pulling the duvet back up to his chin. Tomorrow was the first official day of Michaelmas Term and he needed to be as alert as possible if he was going to make it through the timetable Mr Beaulake had handed to him earlier.

Just as he'd closed his eyes and forced his breathing to slow down he heard a noise outside. He blinked, and for a moment he thought that he recognised the sound from his dream – it was probably what had woken him in the first place. He frowned as the noise came again; a deep, grating sound that reminded Arthur a little of nails scraping on a chalkboard.

Knowing that he'd never get to sleep if he didn't satisfy the small niggle of curiosity he clambered out from underneath his covers quietly and padded to the large window. He moved the curtain slightly and peered out into the darkness. The clouds that had descended on Cambridge around lunchtime had lingered through the rest of the day and were now obscuring any light the moon might have otherwise cast on the grounds of Badon College, leaving Arthur unable to make out anything more specific than the looming silhouettes of the buildings on the other side of the river.

The sound came again, fainter than before, almost as though Arthur was hearing it through a badly tuned radio. His head involuntarily turned to the right as the sound of dogs barking rose up from somewhere beyond the college walls. *That's odd*, he thought as he looked at the clock. Why would there be a pack of dogs out in Cambridge at half-past three in the morning?

The sound gradually faded away and Arthur shivered again. Bertie hadn't been lying when he'd said they'd really feel the cold in Caerleon, and with a final glance into the darkness Arthur hurried back into his bed, wrapping the covers tightly around his body once more.

It still took a long time for sleep to catch up with him as he stared at the ceiling and tried to convince himself that he wasn't dreading the next morning.

2

Fee-fi-fo-fum

By two o'clock on Wednesday Arthur wasn't sure things could actually get much worse. Merlin still wasn't speaking to him at all, which was more than a little bit awkward considering they were sharing a room, and Gareth hadn't said more than a hurried 'hello' to him since Sunday evening. Add to that the fact that Bertie was constantly surrounded by his second year friends, and this left Arthur with nobody else he really knew. The other first year Caerleonites seemed to have formed little groups already and Arthur had just spent half an hour listening in on Ruari O'Connell and Charlie Riordan's conversation about football as he'd sat silently on the same table as them for lunch.

He was already standing by the Back Gate when Mr Beaulake appeared clutching a clipboard and a net of rugby balls, and looking far more cheerful than when he'd been teaching History that morning.

"I'm glad to see you're here for training, Arthur," Beaulake stopped, taking a moment to send a cheerful wave towards where Hector was guarding from afar. "I've heard good things about you from your last school."

"Really, sir?" Arthur was surprised. "I wasn't really able to play for the school team. I just took part in games lessons."

"Well, let's see if we can change that this year," Beaulake grinned. "Caerleon boys tend to dominate the school teams, and I'm sure Bertie's already told you that most of the Lower School rugby first fifteen are from our house."

Arthur nodded.

"You're going up for cricket after Christmas as well?" Beaulake asked as he dropped the net on the ground before balancing his clipboard on top.

"I might join the rowing club too, even though I've never tried it before" Arthur replied. He'd had quite a lot of time to think since the weekend and had concluded that if he were doomed to have no friends at Badon he might as well join as many teams as he could.

"That's a lot of commitment for any student, Arthur," Beaulake frowned. "Not least one who I know has perhaps a little less relaxation time than others during the holidays."

"I can manage it, sir," Arthur held his chin up.

Beaulake smiled slightly at that. "Of that I have no doubt, Arthur." He looked back towards the school to see other Caerleon first years heading towards them.

"Alright, Arthur?" Charlie shouted, waving madly. "You disappeared after lunch."

"Sorry," Arthur replied with a sheepish shrug as Beaulake silently moved away. "Just didn't want to be late."

"This is going to be killer," Ruari replied with a grin. "I was talking to Sib earlier about it. His brother, Rajendra, is in second year and on the house *and* school teams. Apparently Beaulake is really difficult to impress. You have to be awesome to even get through the first round today."

Arthur's excitement gave way slightly to a pang of

nervousness. "How many rounds are there?"

Ruari shrugged. "Three or four, I think. I'll ask Sib." He looked around as they were joined by boys from all three lower years in Caerleon. "Sib!" He yelled, gesturing for a tall, laughing boy to join them. "Sib! Come over here."

Sib trotted over in the relaxed way he did everything. "What?"

"How many of these training things do we have to get through to get on to the team?" Ruari asked.

"I'm sure I told you this about ten minutes ago," Sib frowned.

Ruari shrugged. "Yeah, well my memory's not the greatest, plus Arthur wants to know."

Sib turned to Arthur. "Well, my brother said that Beaulake makes the first cut after today's session. Then everyone who is successful goes through another three or four rounds because they need to make sure first years can learn enough to be able to start playing full games for Inter house after Christmas."

"We don't find out if we've made the team for weeks?" Arthur asked in surprise.

Sib shook his head. "It's much harder to get on the Caerleon team than any of the other houses. We've won the inter house competition every year for decades, and the team's only got better since Beaulake took it on a couple of years ago."

Arthur groaned. "This is going to be impossible."

Charlie laughed and slapped Arthur on the back. "Come on, Pendragon, it won't be that bad."

"Gentlemen!" Mr Beaulake called loudly and the boys immediately ceased speaking. "We're going to head over to the pitches now. Please do not walk in groups of more than two when we're on the pavement, and try not to take up more space than you need. First years follow me; second years, you're with Mr Wade; third years, you will follow Mr Hastings. Second and thirds, you'll be starting with drills on the far pitch."

With a final nod from Beaulake they were off, filing dutifully through the Back Gate out onto the Backs. There were tourists everywhere, snapping pictures of Badon, and the surrounding University colleges. Arthur kept his head down just in case someone spotted him, pulling the collar of his rugby shirt up around his chin for extra coverage.

"Do you get to wear actual disguises?" Charlie asked as he dropped into step with Arthur. "Big sunglasses and things?"

"Sometimes," Arthur grinned. "Once, when we went to Japan, my security team made me wear three different hats on one walking tour of a city to confuse anyone out to get a photo."

Charlie snorted. "Is it really annoying?"

Arthur shrugged. "I'm used to it, I suppose. The press isn't supposed to follow me around when I'm here at school, and hopefully most people won't recognise me anyway."

"My grandmother loves you," Charlie replied, still laughing. "She can't remember my name half the time, but she knows that she thinks you're lovely. She wants you to pop in for lunch if you're ever in Ireland. She *does* make really good sandwiches."

Arthur laughed. "I'll ask my father."

They continued in companionable silence, listening instead to the heated argument Sib and Ruari were having a few paces behind.

"Elves are *way* better than dwarves!" Sib threw his hands

up dramatically as they turned into the gate at the Badon playing fields. "How could you think otherwise?"

"Because elves are lame," Ruari replied, as though this were the most obvious point in the world.

"Mr Chopra!" Beaulake called as he stopped and turned to face the arguing boys. "Why don't you go and set out these cones in a line?" He handed Sib a stack of small red cones. "You'll see there are some yellow ones already out over there. I want you to place a red one in between each yellow one, alright?"

Sib nodded and took the cones, narrowing his eyes slightly at a grinning Ruari.

"And Mr O'Connell," Beaulake added, Ruari's face dropping immediately, "you can make a list of everyone who's here." He then handed his tutee a clipboard and a pen. "Off you go."

Arthur and Charlie laughed as the two boys set about their respective tasks.

"Did you hear that Marc Dubois' family all play for the French national team?" Charlie asked Ruari, pointing as Sib's roommate walked by them. "If he doesn't make the team I'll eat a rugby ball for supper."

"The national team?" Arthur asked in awe.

"Yep," Charlie nodded sagely. "And Kofi over there is the size of a house. I'm not looking forward to practising tackling with him."

Arthur nodded his agreement. He was already feeling intimidated by the second and third years who were milling around on far side of the pitches, about to start their drills with Mr Wade and Mr Hastings.

"Right," Beaulake clapped his hands. "We're going to do some warm ups to start. They're basic versions of the drills you'll go through if you become a full member of the team. I'm glad to see most of the year group is here." He smiled at the surrounding boys.

Arthur looked around and realised that the only two first year Caerleonites missing were Merlin and Gareth.

"Mr Pendragon."

Arthur startled slightly at Beaulake's voice and looked up as a rugby ball came flying through the air towards him. He caught it securely and pulled it to his chest.

"Very good," Beaulake nodded. "Now I want you all to follow me. Mr Pendragon is going to demonstrate the first exercise."

Arthur clutched the ball tightly as they walked; following Beaulake to where Sib had neatly laid out the cones he'd been given.

"Now, Mr Pendragon," Beaulake began when they stopped walking, "I want you to keep a secure hold on the ball. You're going to weave between each cone until you reach the other end, then you're going to turn, throw the ball to the next boy in line then come and stand by me. Mr Riordan," he pointed to Charlie, "you will catch the ball and then complete the same steps when I give you the signal, alright?"

Charlie nodded. "Yes, sir."

"This drill is designed to test your speed and agility, and I'll be timing each of you." Beaulake produced a stopwatch from his pocket and laid it on the clipboard in front of him. "Are you ready, Mr Pendragon?"

"Yes, sir." Arthur took his place at the head of the line and waited for the next instruction.

"Go!" Mr Beaulake called.

Arthur took off like a shot, making sure his fingers stayed

clamped around the ball as tightly as possible. He weaved through the cones, careful to keep his line of motion as tight as possible so that he didn't take any more time than he needed to.

He reached the end of the cones and turned, the ball already at hip level. He barely gave himself time to finish turning before he nodded to Charlie and threw the ball.

Charlie neatly caught the ball with a grin and Arthur sprinted towards Beaulake as quickly as he could.

Mr Beaulake scribbled Arthur's time down on his clipboard before looking to the boy next to him. "That was incredibly quick, Arthur."

"Thank you, sir."

Arthur tried not to smile too widely as Beaulake nodded and turned to shout for Charlie to begin.

* * * * *

Arthur was tired and content as he slouched across Chapel Court and back into Caerleon, hair still damp from a well-earned shower. He was still on a high from a successful game and he grinned again when he recalled how Mr Beaulake had called Arthur's name as one of the successful first years moving onto the next stage of try outs after school on Friday.

His mind was still on the game even as he shouldered into his room and dropped his kit bag on the floor with an unceremonious clunk. It was for this reason that he'd neglected to remember Merlin would be there, still icily ignoring him from the left-hand side of the room.

It was like an invisible barrier had been constructed between each half, dividing the room into two completely separate worlds. Merlin's side was chaotic; books strewn all over the bed as he completed his prep. The lid from a tin of contraband biscuits was resting on the floor and Arthur had no idea where the rest of the tin *or* the biscuits had disappeared to. In stark contrast Arthur's side of the room looked like nobody lived there. The neat collection of stationery on the desk and the fact that the bed was made was the only clue that another boy lived there, and Arthur certainly didn't have snacks stashed anywhere. The window seat had silently been declared 'no man's land' and neither boy went near it; Hector occasionally perched there if he came to ask Arthur a question, but Merlin had taken to visiting friends in their rooms rather than inviting them in for a chat.

Arthur thought about saying something, anything really, as long as it broke the uncomfortable silence. He knew it was his fault that things were this way, but the apology still got lodged somewhere behind a dose of pride every time he opened his mouth. So ignoring the hunched figure at the far desk, he sat down at his own workspace and took his Latin prep books from where they were stored in the bottom drawer.

It was amazing, really, how quickly any final traces of his euphoria from earlier were banished at the sight of Latin vocabulary. He hadn't been paying too much attention in his lesson that morning – his mind already outside on the pitches across the river – and now he was faced with a list of unfamiliar words he had a sneaky suspicion he was supposed to learn by heart in time for tomorrow.

He scanned the first five words quickly. *Appropinquare, Effugio, Mortuus, Capere, Cognoscere.* Okay, they weren't that difficult, everything was going to be absolutely fine. He covered the words with his exercise book and tried to remember what he'd just read.

Approprin –no, that was wrong. He moved the book out of the way and looked at the words again. *Appropinquare.*

Once more Arthur covered the vocabulary list. "Appropinquare," he muttered to himself. "Effugio. Mortuus, Capere, and Cognon-something. Cognon..." he trailed off and frowned at the exercise book, momentarily hoping he'd gain x-ray vision.

"Cognoscere."

Arthur's head whipped up at the quiet voice from the other side of the room. Merlin was still hunched over his work, his pen scratching hurriedly on the paper in front of him.

"What?" Arthur asked hesitantly, not completely certain that his roommate had really spoken.

Merlin put down his pen and turned to face Arthur. "Cognoscere. That's the word you're looking for." He scratched his head, looking thoughtful. "I would've thought you of all people had been speaking Latin since birth."

Arthur frowned. "Why?"

Merlin shrugged. "I don't know. You're the prince, aren't you? It didn't seem like too mad an idea, but the way you're butchering that vocab I'd say I was way off the mark."

Arthur wasn't sure what the etiquette was in a situation like this. Merlin had just initiated a conversation after three days of silence, so was Arthur to assume that they were on speaking terms again?

A snort of laughter drew Arthur from his thoughts once more. "What?" he asked again, reduced to single syllables in his surprise.

"Your face," Merlin grinned. "You are aware you're just frowning at the carpet, aren't you?" He shuffled slightly in his chair and adopted a more serious expression. "Look, let's just forget about Sunday, alright? You were clearly in a strop about something else, and I was a bit of, well, *a git.* Sorry about that."

Was this how easy it was to apologise? If so Arthur had been a bit of a git for the past few days as well. "No, it was my fault. Hugo surprised me on the way to dinner, that's all, and he has the natural ability to bring out the worst in everyone who crosses his path."

"He sounds great," Merlin rolled his eyes.

"Hopefully I can just avoid him for the next few years," Arthur replied. He pushed his textbooks away from him just as his empty stomach growled in protest. "Eurgh, I'm starving. Is it dinner time yet?"

Merlin looked at his watch, olive branch obviously accepted. "Close enough. Shall we go over there now? We can take Gareth with us. He was caked in mud after cross country last time I saw him – I think he might need some moral support."

* * * * *

Arthur couldn't sleep again. He should have been exhausted due to the distance he'd run that afternoon, but a combination of repeating a mantra of Latin vocab in his head after Lights Out and the amount of sugar he'd consumed thanks to Merlin's hidden stash of Chelsea buns was making it impossible.

He rolled onto his side with a sigh and stared at the wall, listening to the old building settling around him. Merlin was dead to the world and had started snoring almost as soon as his head had hit the pillow, providing a fairly noisy counterpoint to the tick of the wall clock. The chapel bell chimed once and Arthur knew he was going to be falling asleep in his cereal if he stayed awake much longer. He pulled the duvet up around his face and closed his eyes, hoping to block out the sliver of moonlight that was casting an eerie glow throughout the room.

He was no closer to sleep when he heard the same scraping noise that had awakened him on his second night at Badon. He quietly pushed back the duvet and climbed out of bed, stealthily padding to the window to take a look outside.

The bright moon threw now familiar landmarks into sharp relief, and the old bridge separating the Chapel Court buildings from the rest of the school stood out proudly in the dark. Arthur squinted into the night but everything seemed as still as it should be for well after one o'clock in the morning.

"What are you doing?"

Arthur clutched his chest in fright as Merlin hissed at him, stumbling away from the window in surprise "Bloody hell, Merlin!"

"Keep your voice down," Merlin whispered in irritation. "Unless you want your security team to come barging through the door thinking I'm trying to murder you."

"They wouldn't be wrong," Arthur hissed back, his hand still pressed against his chest. "You nearly gave me a heart attack."

"Oh stop being so dramatic," Merlin sighed as he too clambered out of bed and peered out of the other side of the curtain. "What's so interesting out there that you're staring out the window in the middle of the night?"

"Nothing," Arthur replied, feeling his pulse return to something approaching normal. "I thought I heard something weird, but there's nothing out there."

Merlin made a non-committal sound before suddenly his entire body went rigid.

"Merlin?" Arthur asked, taking a hesitant step towards the other boy.

"What on earth is that?" Merlin breathed, his attention still transfixed by something outside.

Arthur frowned and resumed his previous stance. Again, he couldn't see anything particularly interesting; just trees and buildings and-

He sucked in a surprised gulp of air when his eyes finally caught hold of the same thing Merlin must be seeing. There, in the furthest corner of King's Court on the other side of the river, was a large, dark shadow.

The shadow moved and the scraping sound split the otherwise silent night once more. Both boys gulped in tandem as the shadow moved closer and closer to the bridge, the moonlight beginning to pick out a figure, perhaps human in shape, but far taller than any either boy had ever seen. Even hunched over as it was, the shadow's head was almost in line with the first-floor windows of the science building, and in its right hand it held what looked to be an enormous wooden club. The side of the weapon scratched over the ground with every step as it was dragged behind the slowly advancing silhouette.

"Arthur, you can see that too, can't you?" Merlin hissed.

"Mmm," Arthur replied just as the shadow stepped out from the gloominess of Kings' Court, the light reflecting from the river showing its features clearly for the first time. Arthur gasped in horror and dived back from the window just as Merlin did the same.

The shadow wasn't a man at all, but instead a hideous

creature with sickly grey skin. Two black holes gaped in its face in place of eyes, and its mouth had been open in a snarl that showed sharp jagged teeth glinting under the moon.

Arthur scrambled backwards on his hands and knees towards the door. "I need to get Hector."

"And what's he going to do?" Merlin hissed, his eyes round in panic as he crouched by his bed. "Wave a gun at a bloody great *giant*?"

"He could get a whole team of-" Arthur cut himself off as an inhuman snarl reached his ears. Surely that would have woken the whole school, but as Arthur remained as still as possible he couldn't hear even the smallest sound of movement from within the building. "Merlin, we need to tell *someone*."

Merlin didn't reply and Arthur was horrified to see the other boy pushing himself to his feet and edging back towards the window. Arthur would swear that he could hear the giant breathing loudly just outside.

"Merlin, what are you *doing*?" Arthur snapped, standing up himself and pressing his back to the door. "Stay away from the window."

"Something's not right," Merlin replied without turning back.

"Well of course something's not right!" Arthur waved his hands, no longer trying to keep his voice down. "There's a *monster* standing on a bridge. *In Cambridge*." Arthur opened the door. "I'm getting Hector."

He stumbled out into the hallway and hammered on the door to the room Hector and the on-duty members of the RPS were permanently stationed in. "Hector!" he yelled, using his fist to make as much as noise as possible. "James!"

46

Getting no response, Arthur decided now was not the time for politeness. "Open the door *now*!" He pushed down on the handle and his shoulder thudded painfully against the door when it didn't give way as he'd expected. Why was nobody answering? He whirled around and realised that every door on the landing remained closed. There was no way people could be sleeping through this racket.

He tried Gareth and Bertie's door and received no response. The same thing happened when he tried Sib and Marc. Arthur wasn't supposed to panic, his tutors had been telling him that since he was a baby, he was the future King for goodness sake! He was supposed to be a natural born leader under any circumstances. Yet he couldn't help thinking that he must have missed the lesson where they explained what to do when faced with an actual giant.

"Merlin!" Arthur yelled for the only other person who seemed to be aware of what was going on as he raced back towards his room. "Nobody's answering! Merlin!"

Merlin was still hovering by the window, but the curtain had been drawn back so that if the creature had paused on the bridge below it no doubt had a completely uninter-rupted view of Arthur's roommate.

"What are you doing?" Arthur yanked Merlin back harshly, frowning slightly when he realised he couldn't see the giant anymore. "Are you trying to encourage it to eat you?"

"I think I can get rid of it," was all Merlin said in reply, his eyes lingering on the window.

"What?" Arthur barked. "What do you mean you can get rid of it? With what?"

"Stay here." Merlin nodded firmly before ducking past Arthur and clattering down the corridor.

Stay here?! Merlin was completely mad if he thought Arthur was going to stay put while his idiot of a roommate went outside to take on a giant. He rolled his eyes with an exasperated grunt before turning on his heel to chase after the other boy, grabbing his brand-new hockey stick from by the door as he ran.

Arthur caught up with Merlin at Caerleon's door. "Shouldn't we see if we can raise the Beaulakes?"

"Don't you think they'd already be out there if they could?" Merlin asked with a sigh as he somehow managed to open the door, even though Arthur knew for a fact that it was locked after dark. Locked to stop boys traipsing around the college at night.

"Merlin, I really can't see how this is a good idea!" Arthur protested as Merlin marched out into Chapel Court before turning back on himself to reach the archway that would lead them to the bridge.

"It's *not* a good idea, Arthur," Merlin hissed as he pressed himself against the walls of the archway, "but it's the only one we have."

"What are you going to do?" Arthur asked. "You're wearing pyjamas, and you don't even have a weapon."

Merlin looked back over his shoulder and cast a critical eye over the hockey stick Arthur was brandishing in front of him. "And you think you'll do better with that, do you?"

Arthur opened his mouth to respond, but was cut off for the second time that night by a snarl from the giant. He jumped in surprise as he saw the creature's legs appear on the other side of the bridge once more. If anything, it looked even taller now that they were only metres from it. "Merlin," he whispered as he pointed over Merlin's shoulder. "It's there."

Merlin turned around just as the giant folded itself in half so that its grotesque face was looking straight at the boys. It inhaled noisily and Arthur really, *really* hoped it wasn't doing so in order to sniff out dinner. The two boys retreated slightly into the shadow of Caerleon's archway.

"I don't think it can see us," Merlin whispered. He was so quiet Arthur barely heard him. "Don't move again."

Neither boy breathed for a long moment, terrified to make even the slightest movement if it would alert the giant to their location. Just as Arthur was sure he was going to have to take a breath if he didn't want to pass out the creature straightened up and walked back towards the buildings of King's Court.

"Arthur, I need you to listen to me." Merlin turned and he had that rather serious expression from his earlier apology back on his face again. "Go back upstairs and try to get hold of Hector again."

"Merlin, for the ninetieth time, *what are you going to do?*" Arthur hissed, blocking Merlin's way as the other boy tried to set foot on the bridge.

Merlin sighed in exasperation. "We don't have time for this conversation, Arthur."

"*Merlin!*"

"Oh for-" Merlin scrubbed a hand through his hair. "Look, I don't even know if my plan's going to work. It all tends to be a bit temperamental."

"What tends to be a bit temperamental?"

Merlin didn't answer, just dodged past Arthur again and hurried over the bridge making enough noise to wake the dead. The giant turned immediately and sloped back towards them, still dragging his wooden club.

Arthur was torn between staying in the shadows to

possibly delay his inevitable death for a little while longer, and storming after Merlin with only a hockey stick to protect himself.

He'd just about decided on the hockey stick plan of action when Merlin threw his hands up above his head and yelled something that sounded suspiciously like gibberish at the giant.

The giant stopped in its tracks, and tilted its head in such a way that Arthur was reminded immediately of an inquisitive puppy. An inquisitive puppy that just so happened to be twenty feet tall and the most grotesque thing Arthur had ever seen.

For a few seconds there was complete stillness.

Then the giant burst forward with a menacing roar, shocking Arthur out of his stupor enough to see that Merlin wasn't even attempting to move out of the way.

"Merlin!" Arthur yelled, rushing forwards to where the other boy was still standing with his hands outstretched above his head as the creature bore down on him.

Merlin was shouting again. It was a word that Arthur didn't recognise, repeated over and over again, and he was sure it wasn't in any language he'd ever come across; there seemed to be far too many consonants strung together to make any kind of sense. Each utterance was slightly more desperate than the last as Arthur's feet pounded over the bridge.

"Merlin, move!" Arthur barked, latching his hand around the other boy's arm and pulling him out of the way just as the giant brought his club down with a brutal roar.

Both boys tumbled to the floor just as the weapon hit the ground with enough force to send gravel flying in every direction, the tiny stones pelting Arthur and Merlin as they scrambled to get out of the way.

"What were you doing?" Arthur pulled Merlin to his feet and half-dragged him back over the bridge towards the relative safety of Caerleon's archway. "Trying to get bludgeoned to death?"

"Yes, that's exactly what I was trying to do." Merlin was breathing hard as he leaned against the wall. "I told you my plan might not work."

The giant was now resting the club on its shoulder, clearly prepared for another attack should it be given the opportunity.

"How did it get in?" Merlin asked, frowning in concern.

"Yes, because that's what we should be worried about," Arthur huffed sarcastically, "Badon's lax security. Never mind that nobody else seems to have noticed there's a giant attacking the school or, oh I don't know, *the fact that a giant's attacking the school!*"

Arthur's raised voice caught the creature's attention, alerting it to their hiding place, and it began to move towards the boys once more.

"Oh, well done," Merlin snapped as the giant placed one enormous foot on the bridge in front of him and reached a calloused hand towards the archway.

Arthur and Merlin shrank back further into the shadows as the giant's fingers grazed the woodwork of the bridge just short of where it met the stone wall of Caerleon House.

"At least it can't reach us here," Merlin sighed in relief. "And there's no way it'll be able to get across the bridge; it wouldn't hold its weight."

Merlin's moment of triumphant logic was short lived as the giant took another step forwards. The bridge creaked dangerously under the strain, but instead of retreating

51

entirely the giant moved to the left and stepped straight off the bank and into the river, oblivious to the cold water rushing around its legs as it waded slowly towards its prey.

"I think it can reach us now!" Arthur hissed. "We need to get out of here."

"Let me try it again, Arthur," Merlin replied. "I know I can do this, but you need to leave."

"Merlin!" Arthur fought the urge to drag the shorter boy away by the scruff of the neck. "Shouting at it only makes it angrier. Did you miss the part where it tried to club your thick skull?"

Merlin ignored him in favour of holding his hands out towards the advancing giant once more and repeating that same guttural word from earlier.

"How is chanting rubbish at it helping?" Arthur could no longer keep the note of panic out of his voice. He needed to get out of there, but he couldn't just leave Merlin to the mercy of the creature. He held the hockey stick tightly in both hands and pointed the toe-end towards the steadily advancing giant. He hoped he wasn't going to regret this.

"What are you doing?" Merlin looked appalled when Arthur stepped forward so that they were shoulder to shoulder.

"Being your backup," Arthur replied as steadily as he could. "What kind of roommate would I be if I let that thing eat you?"

Merlin shook his head, but didn't argue any further. He began his chanting again and Arthur noticed that the pronunciation of the word changed slightly every few times Merlin repeated it, almost as if he wasn't entirely sure of what he was saying.

The creature didn't seem too worried about the two

boys under the arch, walking steadily as it raised its hand towards them, each finger pockmarked and studded with blackened warts.

Arthur swallowed loudly as Merlin's chanting increased in volume. "Merlin," he said quietly, hockey stick shaking slightly in his hand. "Merlin, I really don't think this is working."

Merlin ignored him, and so did the creature.

"Merlin." Arthur repeated, his voice rising to match Merlin's shouts. "Merlin!"

The creature was scant metres from them now and Arthur's courage could take no more. He grabbed Merlin's arm and hauled him away from the edge of the bridge again. Unfortunately, Merlin put up less resistance than Arthur had anticipated and the force of the prince's heave sent Arthur stumbling backwards slightly until he tripped over his own feet and landed with a bone-shaking thud on the grassy bank.

Merlin inexplicably remained upright, his eyes widening in horror as the creature reached the City-side of the river. He ducked just as the creature's fingers reached out to him, dropping onto his knees and scrabbling out of the way in the nick of time.

"If we die, Merlin," Arthur hissed as they both tried to scramble to their feet again, "I'm going to kill you."

"That doesn't make sense," Merlin retorted.

The giant roared, perhaps in response to the boys' ill-timed sniping and leaned down towards them, suddenly moving with a sense of urgency it hadn't demonstrated in its passage across the gaping stretch of river. Even though it didn't have eyes it seemed to be able to locate them with precision accuracy.

"Arthur, look out!" Merlin bellowed.

Arthur looked up to see the wooden club descending towards him just as Merlin shouted a different, but still wholly unfamiliar word. He couldn't think fast enough to move his legs, but he refused to close his eyes even as he was struck with a sense of certainty that he was about to die.

But the expected blow didn't come.

Arthur blinked, then blinked again. No, he decided, he wasn't seeing things, and he was fairly sure he was still alive; the creature was still looming over him, its expression twisted into indignant rage, but it was completely still as though suspended outside of time.

Arthur had to blink again to make sure he wasn't imagining the blue shimmer that seemed to be surrounding him, acting like a barrier between him and the giant. He turned his head to look for Merlin and caught the look of pure surprise on the other boy's face as his hands remained raised above his head.

"Are you okay?" Merlin asked, a note of sheer panic in his voice.

Arthur's brain suddenly whirred into action and his eyes widened in surprise as he processed the thought he'd just had. *Merlin somehow made the creature stop.* "Merlin," he whispered in amazement, "is there anything you want to tell me?"

Merlin, whose eyes were as wide as Arthur's own, gulped. "Um…surprise?" He grinned feebly, the corners of his lips barely quirking upwards before he switched back to looking stunned and terrified at the same time.

The blue haze flickered and Merlin looked panicked. "Arthur," he said hurriedly, "I can't keep this up for much longer. Can you get out of the way? *Please?*"

Arthur didn't need telling twice this time. He stumbled away from the creature, and a split-second later the blue tinge to the air disappeared with an audible pop.

The wooden club came crashing down in its inevitable arc and the crater left in the grass was visible even in the slowly deepening night. Arthur shivered at the thought that he'd had been standing there only moments earlier.

The creature paused, and Arthur imagined that if its face had held human features it would have been frowning in confusion at the fact that its target seemed to have impossibly disappeared.

As it twisted its head around the black holes in the creature's face created such a terrifying image that Arthur found himself twitching in horror once more. What *was* this thing? And why was it here?

Just as Arthur was about to silently suggest to Merlin that they scarper while they still had the chance the sound of distant barking sliced through the night, punctuated by howls. It was the same unsettling chorus that Arthur had heard on Sunday night and he didn't miss the connection between the sound and the creature's appearance.

The giant jolted backwards, almost stumbling as its legs thrashed in the river. It twitched and jerked as though being pulled in two opposing directions by invisible lengths of rope as the barking dogs seemed to grow closer. Arthur felt his attention drawn back through the archway and over Badon's walls, towards the just visible chimneys of Queens' College on the adjacent street.

With a final snarl the creature curled in on itself and the boys could only watch in astonishment as it slowly faded into something unsubstantial before finally disappearing entirely.

A single, mournful howl drifted over the College walls before abrupt silence fell for the first time since Arthur had climbed out of bed.

Almost immediately a light flickered on in the Headmaster's Lodge, followed by a few others in Kings' House.

"I think we better get back inside," Merlin whispered hurriedly as he turned his head to see lights snapping on in the windows of Caerleon above them. "Quickly, before Beaulake finds us outside. Or worse, your security team does instead. Everyone seems to have woken up."

Arthur nodded silently, not sure he could actually say anything to his roommate even if he had the mental capacity to form words, which in that moment he most certainly did not. He picked up his previously discarded hockey stick and followed Merlin under the archway and back towards Caerleon's front door.

Lights were blazing in the windows Arthur knew belonged to the Beaulakes and so it was with a sense of renewed urgency that he bolted up the stairs as soon as Merlin opened the door, his roommate keeping pace behind him.

The pair of them had just reached their bedroom when the door next to them opened and Hector's confused face appeared.

"Arthur?" The bodyguard frowned. "What are you doing out of bed? Why are you hiding a hockey stick behind your back?"

The prince opened his mouth to mumble something in response, but was saved when the door to Bertie and Gareth's room flew open too.

"Did you hear something weird as well?" Bertie asked, looking between Merlin and Arthur.

"Yeah," Merlin butted in when it became clear that Arthur wasn't regaining the ability to speak just yet. "We just came out into the corridor to see if anyone else had heard it as well."

Doors to the other bedrooms on the corridor opened almost immediately after that, and a variety of different faces popped out into the corridor.

"What's going on?" Marc asked, rubbing his eyes sleepily. "It sounded like every dog in Cambridge was outside in the Court."

Seconds later Mr Beaulake appeared at the top of the stairs. He looked slightly ridiculous dressed in a pair of striped red pyjamas, but Arthur was sure he'd never seen such a serious expression on the housemaster's face.

"Is everyone alright?" Beaulake asked, his eyes pausing on each boy's face long enough to ensure their safety. He looked at Arthur with particular concern and the boy shuffled slightly in embarrassment.

"It sounded like a pack of dogs," Hector stated, frowning at the housemaster in puzzlement. "They must have escaped from somewhere in the city."

Mr Beaulake ran a hand through his hair and Arthur would have dared to say that the teacher looked nervous. "Yes, that must be the case. I'll make a quick call to the police to make sure there's nothing untoward going on."

Arthur tried not to pale. If only everyone else knew what had just happened outside.

"Boys, there's no need to worry yourselves," Mr Beaulake nodded, his expression clearing eventually. "Please return to bed and try to get some sleep. It's far too late to be

57

wandering the corridors and it's a school day tomorrow."

Bedroom doors immediately started closing in response and Arthur was sure to quickly herd Merlin in and close the door behind them before Hector could remember that he hadn't received an answer about the hockey stick.

Merlin was sitting in the middle of his bed with his knees drawn up to his chest when Arthur finally looked at him. "Well," he sighed tiredly, "that was fun."

3

PRACTICAL MAGIC

Arthur had been waiting, very patiently in his opinion, for nearly five minutes when Merlin finally found enough words to string together into a sentence that didn't cut itself off after a syllable or two.

"Are you going to tell Hector? Or your father? Or the newspapers?" He asked, blanching just enough for his already pale skin to take on a translucent, almost ethereal glow in the moonlit bedroom.

Arthur's face crinkled into a frown. "What?" He'd been expecting an explanation for the way Merlin had seemed to stop the creature in his tracks, not the increasing look of fear on his roommate's face. "Why would I do that?"

Merlin shrugged, but it was anything but casual. "I don't know. What does a person normally do when he finds out he's sharing a room with a wizard?"

"You're a wizard?" Arthur's frown deepened, testing the words as he spoke them. "Not a sorcerer?"

Merlin snorted slightly. "So you *were* listening the other day. Yeah, okay, you're sharing a room with a *sorcerer*."

"What's the difference?"

Merlin looked surprised, and Arthur wondered whether

it was because the other boy really had been expecting to be marched straight to Hector and his armed comrades; which was ridiculous, not least because Hector probably wouldn't believe a word of it anyway, but more importantly because Arthur – who was usually a fairly decent judge of character – hadn't even considered that Merlin could be dangerous.

"Well..." Merlin replied eventually. "Both wizards and sorcerers are born with magical abilities. Generally speaking, a wizard needs spells, but a sorcerer can also wield magic without the need for an incantation if necessary. They can harness the power of earth, air, fire and water." He frowned again. "Apparently."

"But you were shouting at the creature," Arthur replied with a glance towards the window, "weren't you?"

"Yes," Merlin nodded. "What I said about my grasp of magic being unpredictable is true. There's a lot of it, and it's difficult to control. I've been trying to find spells to use so that I have a better idea of what might happen when I..." he trailed off and waved a hand. "Rather than just, you know, hoping for the best."

For a moment, Arthur wondered whether he was in some kind of shock, considering the ease with which he was accepting Merlin's explanation. An hour earlier - *half* an hour even - he hadn't believed that magic was anything more than a clever party trick, or indeed that a creature like the one he had just seen with his own eyes could exist outside of the pages of the most fantastical of stories. But here he was, perched on the edge of his bed having a conversation with a sorcerer who had just saved his life.

"The problem is," Merlin continued, scraping his hand through his wild hair for the millionth time since the conversation had started, "there aren't exactly books of spells lying around in libraries. And the number of weirdoes on the internet who think they're sorcerers is horrifying, so searching there for stuff isn't too useful either. The few spells I know are from some ratty little paperback I found in a bargain bin at a tourist shop in Glastonbury. Most of the pages are missing, but considering what just happened I'd say it was ten pence well spent."

"So there *are* other sorcerers then?" Arthur asked.

Merlin shrugged. "To be honest, I don't know. I've never come across one before, and I'd started to think I might be the only one. But now I'm not so sure."

"What about your parents?"

Merlin laughed loudly before clamping a hand over his mouth and lowering his voice to a whisper again. "My parents are about as magical as lampposts. My mum's always been a bit obsessed with the weird and wonderful, which you probably already guessed considering she named her only child *Merlin*, but that's where their connection to magic ends. Odd stuff's always happened around me, but Mum and Dad don't know what I can do."

"Who else *does* know?" Arthur asked, struggling slightly with the concept that Merlin could have kept such a big secret from the rest of the world for such a long time. Then again, Arthur thought, Merlin didn't have people following him around twenty-fours a day the way the prince did.

"Ah," Merlin quirked his lips again, "you get the honour of being the first person who really knows about this."

Arthur gaped. "None of your friends from home know?"

Merlin shrugged. "I'm pretty good at keeping secrets, Arthur. Good job really, don't you think?"

Arthur said nothing and just continued to impersonate

a goldfish.

"You know," Merlin added with a frown, "you're taking this surprisingly well."

"Would you prefer me to freak out?" Arthur asked with a tilt of his head. "I could start shouting and have Hector wave his gun around a bit if you'd like."

Merlin's eyes widened.

"I'm kidding, Merlin." Arthur backtracked at the horror-struck expression. "Bloody hell. I'm not going to tell anyone, alright?"

Merlin clearly didn't believe him. "Really? Why not?"

Arthur rolled his eyes. "Anyone would think you actually *wanted* me to tell everyone you're a sorcerer. But that's what friends do, isn't it? Keep secrets."

"We're friends?" Merlin looked pleased.

Arthur shrugged as nonchalantly as possible for a boy who'd just used the dreaded, and rarely-uttered, 'f' word to describe someone who'd just spent three days regarding him in frosty silence, and who had also happened to stop time earlier that evening.

"And you won't tell your dad?" Merlin gulped out, looking a little on edge again. "I think he'd probably chuck me in a dungeon in London or something."

"Don't be ridiculous," Arthur replied. "We don't really use the dungeons anymore. It'd be a bit awkward with all the tourists around if my father kept locking people up in the gift shop. It would definitely hurt ticket sales."

Merlin looked like the weight of the world had suddenly been lifted from his shoulders. "Well that's very good to know. Although, I wouldn't mind if you locked up whoever is responsible for that creature."

"So you don't think it's just, I don't know," Arthur

62

shrugged, "wandered in here by mistake?"

"I doubt it," Merlin looked pensive. "After all, it didn't seem like the brightest crayon in the box, did it? I can't imagine it figured out how to get into the college by itself. Plus, there's the way it just disappeared."

"Could a sorcerer have created it?"

"I suppose so; there are lots of stories of giants and monsters in history, and there must be some truth to them somewhere. And magic must be behind the way nobody else seemed to even stir when that thing was roaring its head off outside."

Arthur shivered at the thought. "Someone could really be that powerful?"

"I'm sure of it," Merlin nodded. "I once blew out every single window on my parents' street when I tried to move a pen from my desk to where I was doing homework on my bed."

Arthur gaped again. "How the hell did you explain that?"

Merlin shrugged, and Arthur started to think it was his default setting. "I didn't have to explain anything. Everyone freaked out until the local police announced that the RAF had been testing planes in the area and it must have been a sonic boom that caused all the damage." He wrinkled his nose. "Not sure I would have had enough pocket money to cover the repairs if they'd known it was my fault." He turned very serious again. "But that was without even really trying, Arthur, and back when I really didn't understand anything about magic. If a sorcerer has complete control over magic I dread to think what might be possible."

That wasn't reassuring. Arthur folded his arms and scooted backwards so that he could lean against the wall.

"How come we heard the monster when nobody else did?"

"I don't know," Merlin answered honestly. "Either something about this room, possibly something to do with me, protected us from the spell, or…" he trailed off looking slightly ill again.

"Or what?" Arthur asked, his stomach dropping in anticipation of the bad news he just knew Merlin was about to reveal. "Merlin?"

"*Or* we were supposed to hear it." Merlin shuddered. "It wouldn't be completely nuts to think that it was here for you, would it? You *are* the prince."

"But why send a giant?" Arthur waved his hands. "Why use magic at all? People have threatened royalty before, and I don't ever remember fantastical creatures being involved."

"Well your namesake was a famed giant killer after all," Merlin replied. "Maybe the sorcerer thought it would be a fitting end for you."

"I'm not named after King Arthur," Arthur snapped. He'd corrected so many people on this point he'd lost all patience with it. "My mother lived with her grandfather when she was a little girl and she named me after him."

Merlin frowned. "What about Hugo? Wasn't there a big hoo-hah about his middle name being Mordred. Isn't he the one in the legends who k-"

"Yes," Arthur replied quickly. "Mordred from the legends is based on a real person too, but he wasn't responsible for King Arthur's death. That's all just a story."

"Are you sure about that?" Merlin asked, arching an eyebrow in suspicion. "Because your cousin's a bit of a…" Merlin trailed off with a cough. "And he's worryingly good with a sword."

Arthur shook his head firmly. "Hugo is named for a

relative on his mother's side of the family, but despite how horrible he is, I'm fairly confident he wouldn't actually stretch to murder. Plus, somebody would have noticed if he'd started magicking creatures up out of the ground. Trust me when I say that even though he's shown his true colours on more than one occasion, he's not behind this. He can't be."

"So what are we going to do about this?" Merlin asked after the silence stretched for a long moment. "Should we tell Beaulake? Or Hector?"

Arthur bit his lip in thought. He'd always been told that he should alert an adult in a position of responsibility if he was ever worried about anything, and he'd promised his mother a million times before he'd left for school that he'd be careful. But what was he supposed to do now? There's no way Beaulake would believe them, and why should he when it all sounded so ridiculous? As for Hector, well that was a difficult one; on one hand the bodyguard might not believe him and just think Arthur was being difficult, but there was also the possibility that Hector *would* believe him and either ban Arthur from ever being out of his sight again, or worse, suggest Arthur leave Badon forever and face being educated alone within the walls of the palace in London.

"Well?" Merlin asked after a long moment.

"I think we should keep it to ourselves for now," Arthur replied. "We don't know that the creature's going to come back. For all we know, tonight could be the last we see of it."

Merlin's face suggested he didn't believe a word of that, but as Arthur didn't believe it himself he didn't take too much offence.

"But in the meantime," Arthur added, "I think we should try and see what you can do with your magic, just in case."

Merlin was startled enough that Arthur thought he might actually fall off the bed. "You want to help me learn about magic?"

"Well it wouldn't do for you to blow up Badon by accident, would it?" Arthur shrugged. Then he grinned as he added, "and it would be a shame if you didn't get to have some fun with it too."

"What do you mean?" Merlin asked warily.

"Just think of the pranks, Merlin," Arthur's grin widened.

Merlin snorted, but still looked slightly horrified. "And here everyone else was worrying that *I* was going to be a bad influence on *you*."

Arthur's responding laugh turned into a yawn almost immediately. "Well in that case I'll have a responsible moment and say we should probably at least try and get some sleep."

Merlin nodded silently before crawling under his covers just as Arthur did the same on the opposite side of the room. "Night, Arthur."

"Goodnight," Arthur replied as he turned to face the wall. "And thanks, Merlin, you know, for saving my life out there."

"No problem," Merlin replied quietly. "I couldn't just let my roommate get killed now, could I? That's probably an expellable offence."

Arthur grinned into the darkness and it wasn't long before Merlin's familiar snoring filled the room. Arthur listened very carefully to the sounds of the College and it was only when he was very, *very* sure that the giant was gone for good that he allowed himself to close his eyes and slip into a dreamless sleep.

* * * * *

Rather disappointingly, the Latin test during first period turned out to be the highlight of the morning. Arthur remembered everything he'd drilled into his memory the night before and scratched each word onto the paper at the same speed as Merlin a few desks away, but by the time he reached Chemistry, the final lesson before lunch, he was starting to wilt.

"Are you alright, Arthur?" Gareth asked as the prince's head drooped dangerously for the second time in under a minute.

Arthur turned to his lab partner and blinked a few times to clear the haze. "Sorry, Gareth. I didn't get much sleep last night."

"I'm not surprised," Gareth replied, pouring an unknown substance into a beaker. "Those dogs were really loud, weren't they?"

Arthur nodded. He'd almost forgotten about the pack of dogs considering he was still rather focused on the fact that a giant had almost clubbed him to death yards from the boarding house. He realised Gareth was expecting a verbal response and had to shake his head before he added, "Merlin snores like a beast too."

Gareth grinned. "Thankfully I sleep like the dead." He frowned at the beaker in consternation. "That should really have turned purple by now."

Arthur looked around the room, horribly aware that he had absolutely no idea what the purpose of this experiment was. Indeed, it appeared that everyone else was in possession of a beaker of purple liquid. Even Merlin, who didn't have a partner for this experiment thanks to the odd number of boys in the year group and looked about as awake as Arthur felt, was slumped next to the product of a successful experiment.

Mrs Beaulake was wandering between the benches, stopping to speak with each boy and talk through their results with them. She was almost finished with Ruari and Charlie by the looks of things, which meant that Arthur and Gareth were the final pair to be observed.

"Maybe I did something wrong." Gareth wrinkled his nose at the instruction sheet in front of him, squinting through the compulsory safety goggles.

"Maybe we should just add some more of this." Arthur picked up the conical flask Gareth had been pouring from and tipped it to allow a steady flow of clear liquid to drizzle into the beaker below.

"Arthur, no!" Gareth practically shrieked. "Not that one!"

Mrs Beaulake, alongside every other boy in the room, had turned at Gareth's yell and Arthur now had an avid audience as the liquid in the beaker cycled towards a cloudy pink colour before settling as a deep, angry red.

"Boys!" Mrs Beaulake shouted, her voice far more commanding than Arthur had ever heard it before. "Move away from the bench now."

Gareth hopped off his stool and hurried past Arthur to where Mrs Beaulake was pointing next to her. Arthur, stumbling slightly as his legs felt like jelly, wobbled away slowly. He'd just reached Mrs Beaulake's side when a terrible hissing sound reached his ears. Arthur turned, horrified to see the red liquid bubbling and fizzing over the top of the beaker and covering the entire workbench in a noxious foam. His eyes widened as the various bits of discarded stationery that dared to be in the way of the cherry–coloured wave were being destroyed.

From next to Arthur, Gareth squeaked when his fountain pen seemed to sizzle and then almost immediately begin to dissolve. Arthur pulled off his goggles and opened his mouth to say something, but he ended up channelling all remaining energy into glaring at Merlin when he realised his friend was smirking tiredly at him from the other side of the room.

"What happened?" Mrs Beaulake rounded on Gareth and Arthur, not a trace of their kind Housemistress in her voice or expression.

"It was my fault, Ma'am," Arthur replied as Gareth shrank back. "I wasn't paying enough attention and I picked up the wrong flask. Gareth had nothing to do with it."

Mrs Beaulake's stern expression only softened slightly. "Thank you for being honest, but I'd like you to stay behind at the end of the lesson, Mr Pendragon." She looked to Gareth. "Mr Allard, we'll try this experiment next time so that you can receive a proper mark for your work."

Gareth nodded as he shot Arthur a grateful look.

Their teacher turned to the rest of the class. "Right, boys. Instructions for prep are on the board; please make sure you write everything down carefully. This week Mr Kaverin will be in charge of collecting your work from you before breakfast and dropping it off in my pigeonhole at the staffroom before eight o'clock."

Alexei looked slightly fearful until Mrs Beaulake smiled kindly at him. "Don't worry. Everyone takes turns to collect work for me so that I don't end up with an entire year group of boys dropping work off in the morning."

Arthur shuffled his feet in embarrassment when he realised that his error had led to both his and Gareth's prep planners being destroyed.

"Just use some paper for now," Mrs Beaulake instructed the two boys as the rest of the class followed her instructions. "Although, Mr Pendragon you will be making a visit to the first-year office later today to replace both planners, and perhaps also retrieve a new pen for Mr Allard."

Arthur nodded, ducking his head as he could tell his cheeks were probably the same colour as the disastrous experiment.

"I'm really sorry, Gareth," Arthur swallowed heavily as their teacher walked away. "I'll replace everything."

"It's alright," Gareth replied. "I'm sure I'll do far worse than that at some point."

Arthur still felt terrible when Gareth just grinned at him and went in search of some paper. The other boys had already begun packing their bags when the bell rang to signal the end of that morning's lessons and the start of lunch.

"You can copy up from me later."

Arthur's head jerked up in surprise as Merlin's voice came from next to him. Merlin didn't look in the least bit sympathetic, in fact he was still grinning at his friend.

"Oh come on, Arthur." Merlin rolled his eyes at Arthur's slumped shoulders. "Mrs Beaulake's the nicest teacher here. Just go and see her. I'll wait outside for you with Gareth." Merlin shrugged his satchel over his head. "Just don't take all day. Jim said he saw Agnes baking apple pie this morning when he went out with the cross-country lot, and if it's all gone by the time we get there that's the end of our friendship." He gave one final grin before zipping out of the classroom with a gesture for Gareth to follow him.

"I'm very sorry, Mrs Beaulake," Arthur bobbed his head meekly when the classroom had cleared of the other boys.

Mrs Beaulake pulled two tall stools out from under a lab bench. "Come and sit down, Arthur."

Arthur pulled his satchel onto his shoulder and did as he was told, but he kept his eyes fixed firmly on his feet even as he clambered onto his seat.

"How are you settling in?" Mrs Beaulake asked when Arthur finally looked up at her. She no longer looked stern, and in fact was smiling faintly at Arthur's awkward behaviour. "Normally we give all our boys a couple of weeks to get used to being here before we start interrogating you about your welfare." Her smile grew slightly at that. "But you seem to be somewhere else entirely today, Arthur, and there's nothing in any of the reports from your previous school and tutors to suggest that you're one who's likely to daydream in lessons."

Arthur worried his lip. "I'm sorry, Mrs Beaulake. I didn't sleep well last night, that's all."

Mrs Beaulake nodded. "But at least it looks like you've patched things up with your roommate."

Arthur dropped his eyes again. "How did you know there was a problem?"

Mrs Beaulake smiled. "It's impossible to keep secrets at Badon. One boy overhears a single comment and five minutes later it seems that the whole school knows."

"Oh," Arthur could taste the slight tang of copper as he worried his lip with his teeth. So it was impossible to keep secrets at Badon? That didn't bode well for Arthur, or

Merlin for that matter. "Yes," he added when Mrs Beaulake continued to look at him questioningly. "It was just a bit of a misunderstanding, that's all. My fault."

"You aren't responsible for everything, Arthur," Mrs Beaulake frowned.

"No," Arthur shook his head, "I know, but that really *was* my fault. I was angry about something else and I took it out on Merlin. But it's okay, we're friends."

His Housemistress looked positively delighted at that statement, "That's great," she beamed. "It's very important to have people around you when you're somewhere like Badon for the first time. It's important to have people you can really trust and rely on when the time comes."

Arthur tilted his head at the slightly cryptic comment, but Mrs Beaulake wasn't forthcoming with any further explanation.

"Try and sleep well tonight," Mrs Beaulake said eventually. "This half term is always busy and you don't want to tire yourself out so much that you can't enjoy the holidays. If you replace those two prep books by the end of the lunch break, and promise not to doze during experiments again we'll call this the end of the matter, alright?"

Arthur nodded in relief. "Thank you, Ma'am."

"Now, get yourself to lunch, Arthur," Mrs Beaulake smiled, nodding towards the door. "Merlin looks like he can't wait another second for that pie."

Arthur grinned, sliding off his stool as he caught sight of his friend practically bouncing up and down in the corridor. "Yes, Mrs Beaulake."

"Arthur?"

Arthur paused as he reached the door, turning to see his housemistress giving him another inscrutable look.

"Just remember," Mrs Beaulake said seriously, "that you can always talk to me if you need to. Or Mr Beaulake, of course. No matter how small or silly you think something is, alright?"

Arthur nodded as he pushed open the door. "Of course."

Gareth and Merlin were waiting on the other side as promised. The younger of the two still looked slightly shell-shocked from the Chemistry incident.

"Did you get into trouble?" Gareth asked worriedly as they headed for the exit.

Arthur shook his head as they strolled into the sunlight. "Nah. Mrs Beaulake was really nice about it."

"Told you, didn't I?" Merlin pushed the other two boys towards the Dining Hall. "Now come on, I'm starving."

Arthur allowed himself to be propelled forward, but he was only half-listening to Merlin and Gareth's chatter as they queued up for lunch. He couldn't shake the feeling that Mrs Beaulake knew something that she wasn't sharing with her student, perhaps something about what had really happened the night before.

No, Arthur told himself firmly as grabbed a tray, that would be impossible.

Wouldn't it?

* * * * *

Arthur and Merlin's brilliant plan to find somewhere to work on magic outside of school was scuppered completely in the first week. Thursday's after school trip into the city centre turned into a guided tour by the prefects instead of the free time the first years had imagined. Arthur had almost groaned aloud when he realised that Eliot Troyes himself was in charge of Arthur's group, but he'd gritted his teeth and endured two hours of monotonous lectures on the history of the University and the surrounding city.

Then, Arthur's Saturday afternoon was commandeered by Mr Beaulake and another rugby trial, which left Merlin wandering the streets of Cambridge with Gareth, getting hopelessly lost and reappearing back in College almost an hour late, laden down with boxes of biscuits and cakes.

So, it wasn't until well over a week after their meeting with the giant that Arthur and Merlin finally found themselves able to escape into the city on a chilly Saturday afternoon. Admittedly, Hector and a group of guards were hovering somewhere behind them at a covert distance as they left Badon and headed for the cinema, but Arthur had managed to negotiate with Hector for some more freedom. If Arthur and Merlin swore to behave Hector would allow them to watch the film in peace while the guards remained in the foyer.

Arthur was wearing scruffy clothes and had a woolly hat pulled down over his ears in an attempt to keep attention away from him. He tugged the hat down further towards his eyes as he slipped out of the cinema's fire exit with Merlin twenty minutes into the film during a well-timed action sequence.

"Finally!" Arthur grinned as they hurried around the side of the building, flattening themselves as close to the walls as possible. "That film was terrible."

"We've got just under two hours," Merlin replied as they darted across the car park. "It's the longest film they were showing without resorting to a romantic comedy."

Arthur stuck his tongue out. "Eurgh."

"Exactly."

As they reached the main road a man jostled past as he

darted onto the pavement in a hurry. Arthur took a second to revel in the fact that as the man looked back in apology quickly he received nothing more than a 'sorry, mate' before the stranger continued on his way.

"Arthur!" Merlin hissed, waving his friend over to the pedestrian crossing. "Hurry up, we've got a little bit of a walk."

Arthur hurried after his friend, dodging pedestrians and cyclists alike as they left the cinema car park, and therefore Hector and the RPS, behind them. They didn't speak as they walked, both still concerned that they'd be caught and their plan would go immediately to waste.

After a few minutes, Merlin turned left through a gate. Arthur followed blindly and said nothing when Merlin produced two Badon College IDs from his pocket and handed them to a woman in a ticket booth. She glanced quickly at the boys, more interested in their ID cards than their faces before wishing them a nice visit.

Arthur frowned as he followed Merlin into a large, green space dotted with bursts of brightly coloured flowers and the odd group of people.

"*This* is your brilliant plan?" Arthur arched a sceptical eyebrow as he turned in a slow circle taking in the large gardens he was standing in. "The Botanic Gardens? I thought you said you didn't like outside all that much."

"Close enough to the cinema that we can get back quickly," Merlin replied as he started marching towards a secluded area, "free entry, and because we're Badon students we don't need an adult with us. Plus, there are plenty of places to stay out of sight. Can't exactly start levitating objects in front of the general public, can I? If I wanted that we could have stayed in school."

Arthur frowned, but followed his friend anyway. It was with a sense of guilt that they'd escaped from Badon without telling Gareth where they were going, but it was partially because of their younger friend that they'd had to resort to such drastic measures anyway. With second year friends monopolising Bertie's time Gareth had taken to spending almost every free minute with Merlin and Arthur. Even though Arthur could completely understand why Merlin didn't want Gareth to know about the magic it didn't stop the slight creep of shame up his spine at the thought of leaving him behind.

"What?" Merlin asked as Arthur caught up with him and settled himself at the foot of an enormous tree. "You're frowning again. I thought you were looking forward to an afternoon without Hector."

"I am," Arthur replied, pulling off the hat to shake his hair out, "but I feel bad about Gareth."

Merlin sighed and dropped on to the grass opposite his friend. "Yeah, I know. So do I, but he'll be alright. Bertie will be around, and Marc's been on at him for ages to show him where that fudge shop is."

Arthur nodded even if it still didn't sit quite right with him. "Alright then, Houdini, show me what you can do."

"Houdini was a *magician*, Arthur." Merlin made a face of deep dissatisfaction.

"Magician. Wizard. Sorcerer. Whatever." Arthur grinned and was fully expecting the punch to his arm when it came.

Merlin rolled his eyes and retrieved a twig from underneath the tree and placed it on the grass in front of him. "Okay, we'll start small." He held his right hand out in front of him in the general direction of the twig. For a long moment nothing happened, but just as Arthur was about to make a snide remark the twig rose from the grass and hovered under the force of Merlin's glare.

Arthur had been expecting it really, but that still didn't stop a strange combination of thrill and fear sparking under his skin. This display was nowhere near the scale of magic Merlin had demonstrated on the night they'd faced the giant, and yet Arthur found he couldn't tear his eyes away from where the twig hovered impossibly before him. "That's cool."

Merlin grinned and snapped his fingers back towards his palm, the twig falling back to the ground as he did so. "That's nice and simple. It's the bigger stuff that causes a problem, which is why I've resorted to trying spells."

Arthur nodded. "What spell did you use to stop the creature?"

Merlin fished a scrappy looking book out of his back pocket. "This is the book I was telling you about."

Arthur eagerly took the book from his friend's hand. How many people got to hold a real-life book of spells? His face fell almost immediately as he read the cover and looked up at his friend. "A pocket dictionary of Old Irish?" He made a face. "I thought you said it was a magic book."

"It is!" Merlin snapped defensively before retrieving the book from Arthur. "Spells are nothing more than normal words with the strength of magic behind them."

Arthur's eyebrows knitted together as he puzzled this through. "So, you could say, I don't know, *boat* and make a boat appear?"

"Not really," Merlin shook his head. "You have to be quite specific about the words you use, so if I wanted to make a boat appear I'd have to use the correct words for 'boat' and for 'appear', otherwise nothing would happen.

Even then, it doesn't seem to work like that most of the time."

"This sounds depressingly like a lesson," Arthur stuck his tongue out in distaste.

Merlin laughed. "At least you're hearing about this now. Imagine what it was like when I first started trying things out."

"But why Old Irish?" Arthur pointed to the book. "Is Ireland more magical than other places?"

Merlin gave another of his shrugs. "I don't know. Maybe. I tried Latin first, because I thought it would be the obvious choice, but I didn't achieve anything more than learning more vocab than any person could ever need. Old English was a disaster. I came out in a rash when I tried Middle English." Merlin shuddered. "And I'm not even going to talk about what happened when I experimented with Old Norse."

Arthur looked disgusted on his friend's behalf. "Well at least you found something that works."

"Sort of." Merlin replied, flicking through the browning pages of the book and pointed to a word. "*That's* what I used when you almost got clobbered. I thought it would be a useful one to learn when I was younger. I was quite small for quite a long time."

Arthur squinted, immediately hearing his mother telling him to put on his reading glasses, and nearly went cross-eyed as he struggled to read the tiny script;

turthugud – protection or sanctuary.

"The problem is…I don't really know how to pronounce things properly." Merlin admitted. "There's quite a lot of trial and error involved."

Arthur remembered the way Merlin had shouted slight variations of his chosen words at the giant. "So, unless your pronunciation is perfect it doesn't work?"

Merlin nodded meekly.

"Which means that if you hadn't found the right pronunciation I would have ended up as a splatter on the riverbank?" Arthur shivered.

"Possibly." Merlin flinched. "Although the magic tends to come in to its own if I'm angry or scared or something. Hopefully it would have put that shield up in front of you anyway. The first thing I tried on the giant was using the word for 'banish', but that didn't seem to have much effect. Either I said it wrong, or the giant was just too big to repel like that. I think I need to try it out on smaller objects first, because at least then I'll know that it's not my pronunciation causing the problem."

Arthur nodded as he clapped his hands together and pushed up onto his knees. "Right. Try it on me."

"What?" Merlin's eyes bugged. "No way! Weren't you listening when I said I don't have proper control over it?"

Arthur rolled his eyes at Merlin's aghast expression. "Oh, come on. You said the giant might have been too big for it to work on, and while it's all well and good that you can move a twig I doubt we're going to be attacked by a hedge anytime soon. You need to practise."

"Arthur, no!" Merlin shook his head firmly. "Do you have a death wish? I could just as soon kill you by accident."

Arthur sighed in defeat, knowing he wasn't going to get anywhere. Merlin was annoying stubborn when he wanted to be. "Alright, fine." He looked around, a small smile twitching at the corner of his mouth as his gaze landed on a rockery garden. "But I've got an idea."

Merlin followed his friend's line of sight and he gulped loudly. "Arthur, this plan wouldn't involve throwing rocks at my head, would it?"

"It's up to you to stop them," Arthur replied, still grinning as he clambered to his feet and ambled towards the waiting rocks. "You're the sorcerer after all."

"I take it back," Merlin grumbled as Arthur selected a particularly nasty looking rock. "I think I'd rather try this out on you."

*   *   *   *   *

It took nearly two weeks for Merlin's bruises to fade completely, and Arthur spent most of the fortnight covering up the desire to laugh with incredibly serious expressions; this tactic was employed mainly because he was slightly concerned that Merlin's stalwart refusal to use magic against his friend might be waning, if the particularly dark looks the prince kept receiving were anything to go by.

Explaining Merlin's purpling face to everyone at Badon had been a lesson in creativity, particularly to Hector who'd been more than a little surprised to see Merlin wander into the cinema's foyer at the end of the film looking like he'd just gone a couple of rounds in a boxing match.

"He tripped over his own feet," Arthur had replied airily when Hector had rounded on them. "He was paying far too much attention to the popcorn he was carrying."

Merlin's glaring, which contained an already fairly impressive level of rage, had actually darkened considerably, but he'd gone along sullenly with Arthur's story.

Gareth and Bertie were treated to an altered version of the truth too. Merlin swore blind that Arthur had been teaching him the basics of rugby tackling and that the prince had become decidedly too aggressive because he was, in Merlin's words, 'a competitive idiot with no bloody restraint'. Much to Arthur's chagrin Bertie had seemed fairly satisfied by Merlin's account of his potential future teammate, and Gareth had accepted the explanation only once he had stopped sulking about being left behind.

The Beaulakes had been much harder to convince. Mrs Beaulake had shrieked in horror when she'd seen Merlin's face before heading off to the kitchen with Tom who had started wailing at the clearly terrifying sight of Merlin's rapidly swelling eye. Mr Beaulake ended up hearing a strange cross between the cinema trip story and the tale of Arthur's competitive tackling and looked neither convinced nor like he wanted to question the boys further by the time they had finished their halting rendition of the afternoon's activities.

However, it all became far less amusing to Arthur when he reached the final trial for the Caerleon rugby team selection and ended the activities bruised to within an inch of his life from tackling second and third years who were less like boys and more like brick walls.

"Good work, Pendragon!" Rajendra Chopra, a particularly tall second year, said as he clapped Arthur on the back.

"Thanks," Arthur heaved out as he rested his hands on his hips and took a deep breath, but Rajendra had already disappeared, heading across the pitch to where his younger brother, Sib, was still trying to get his breath back.

"You're really bloody fast!" Bertie grinned as he came over and stood next to Arthur, looking more like he'd just been for a casual stroll into town than racing around

Badon's pitch for an hour.

"Excellent work, Arthur!" Mr Beaulake beamed and Arthur wanted to collapse on the pitch in relief. Mr Beaulake wasn't terribly easy to impress, and he *had* to impress if he wanted a chance to play for Caerleon and then later for the school.

"No more, right?" Arthur asked, finally standing up straight and looking to Bertie as Mr Beaulake had a quiet word with his fellow coach, Mr Wade.

"That's it," Bertie replied. "Beaulake will either put us out of misery now or let us stew overnight."

Arthur made a noise of disapproval. "Overnight?"

"Right, boys!" Beaulake called loudly, drawing everyone's attention immediately. "Gather round over here, please."

Arthur dutifully trudged after Bertie to take his place in the semi-circle of twenty boys who'd made it this far.

"The standard this year has been exceptionally high, and once again Caerleon has the highest turn out of boys for trials." Mr Beaulake continued when everyone finally stopped shuffling. "You haven't made it easy for us, but we we've decided on the squad that will represent Caerleon in lower school tournaments after Christmas. This is not to say that our decisions today are final – you will have to live up to the high standards we set you and you will be moved between the first team and the reserves accordingly. Boys in the reserve pool should be prepared to act as substitutes for the first team where necessary, so you will still be required to attend all practices."

Arthur sighed. He knew it would come to this but he also knew he'd be more than a little disappointed if he didn't make the first team. He balled his hands into fists at his sides and wished to any greater power listening that he'd be selected.

"Mr Wade will read out the names of the boys who have made the first team," Mr Beaulake explained. "When you hear your name please collect your kit bag and come to stand over here next to Mr Wade as you'll be heading back to school with him immediately."

"Alright," Mr Wade cleared his throat as he looked around at the hopeful faces. "We'll start with the third years."

Arthur nearly shouted in frustration. Why were they doing it this way round? First years should go first, shouldn't they?

"Morahan, Levy, Lewis and Drurie."

The four triumphant third years grinned to each other before nodding their thanks to the coaches and retrieving their kit bags from the side-lines.

"Second years," Mr Wade cast his eyes back to the clip-board he was holding. "Millions of you lot again." He laughed. "Okay, Dorner."

Bertie nudged Arthur in the ribs with a grin before heading for his bag. Arthur grinned back, but he was feeling less hopeful as the seconds passed.

"Chevalier, Kennedy-Kendrick – let's stick with just *Kay* again shall we -, De Vere, Chopra, Firth and Troyes." Mr Wade looked up. "That's *all* of you then."

Arthur's heart sank as he watched every second year that had tried out for the team cheer loudly and make their way to stand with their official teammates. He'd been counting as Wade read out the names. There were only four places left, and six first year boys remained.

"First years." Mr Wade paused to fix each boy with a steady gaze. "You've all been very impressive, and you've had a lot to learn in a very short period of time, but we can only give four of you places on the first team."

Arthur bowed his head and waited.

"Chopra."

Sib laughed loudly as his older brother led a wave of whooping from the other side of Mr Wade.

"Yes, thank you, Rajendra," Mr Beaulake shook his head, but he was grinning too.

"O'Connell and Riordan."

Ruari and Charlie bumped fists; the two of them always seemed to come in a pair so it wasn't much of a surprise that they'd been picked together. Arthur would admit to the fact he was a little bit jealous of how well Ruari and Charlie worked together on the pitch, as though each could tell what the other would be thinking in five seconds' time and anticipate that move.

One place left. Arthur looked around to see Kofi and Marc both smiling nervously at him. He didn't know how this would go. He knew he was quick, but Kofi had taken to tackling like a duck to water, and Marc came from a family that had already produced four players for the French national team.

"Pendragon."

Arthur jumped in surprise at the call of his own name. "What?"

Mr Wade frowned slightly. "Pendragon. Go on, grab your bag and head over to your teammates."

Arthur shook himself before he dazedly picked up his bag, returned the huge grins Kofi and Marc were shooting him and headed over to the waiting crowd of boys, all of whom were quick to thump him on the back in congratulations.

"Well done, Pendragon!" Bertie laughed. "Knew we could do with you on the team."

Arthur couldn't do anything but grin back in surprise.

* * * * *

"Alright, you've proved your point, Merlin," Arthur waved his hands in exasperation. "Can you stop hovering this above my head now?"

Merlin's infuriating smirk grew wider, but he didn't look up from the work he was completing at his desk. "You're the one who said I wouldn't be able to finish this maths prep *and* use magic at the same time. I'm just enjoying proving you wrong." He wriggled the fingers of his left hand slightly and the glass of water suspended a few feet above Arthur wobbled precariously.

Arthur had tried moving from his desk to the bed, then to floor, anywhere to get away from Merlin's threat, but the glass of water had followed him around the room until he'd given up and headed back to where he'd started. "Merlin, if you get my laptop wet I'll kill you."

Merlin made a non-committal sound, but made no attempt to stop what he was doing.

He'd rather not admit it right in that moment, but Arthur was certain that Merlin's control over his magic was improving every day. There were still some burn marks in the carpet and some interesting dents in the walls of the bedroom they'd need to sort out before room inspection in the morning, but it had been days since Merlin had set anything on fire or blown something up. He'd also proven earlier that afternoon that his verbal spell casting had improved when he'd managed to trip up Hugo's horrible friend Laurie on the other side of Kings' Court with nothing more than a quick whisper. It only would have been more perfect if it had been Hugo instead, but then again Arthur was thrilled that he'd barely seen his cousin in the six weeks he'd been in Cambridge.

They were quietly confident that Merlin might be able to do something more useful if they came up against the giant again. But as the days passed the creature had made no sign of reappearing, and the initial flurry of local newspaper articles covering the mysterious pack of dogs roaming the city had died down fairly quickly. Nothing odd had happened at Badon in weeks, but even now that they'd reached the eve of the half-term holiday Arthur wasn't ready to forget the 'incident' just yet. A giant didn't just wander into the courtyard of a school, try to eat two students and then disappear into thin air.

It was as Arthur was thinking (again) about what a bizarre time he'd been having at Badon that the door opened without warning. He whirled in his desk chair to see Gareth and Bertie framed in the doorway, both holding bright green water pistols, manic grins on their faces.

Merlin, to his credit, did manage to shift the glass slightly far enough to the left so that when it inevitably tumbled towards the carpet it didn't crack his roommate over the head. Although the liquid did slosh everywhere, soaking Arthur, his laptop and the Chemistry homework he'd just finished. Miraculously the glass stayed intact and rolled harmlessly under Arthur's bed.

"Merlin!" Arthur spluttered as cold water dribbled down his face.

"What...?" Bertie asked, looking between the other occupants of the room. "What just happened?"

Gareth had gone as white as a sheet and opened his

mouth as if to release an almighty shriek of surprise. Arthur, with reflexes to rival an Olympian, managed to vault over his satchel, pull the two visitors into the room, slam the door and clamp his hand over Gareth's mouth all in one fluid movement.

Arthur glared at Merlin, who was ignoring him in favour of staring at Bertie in horror. Bertie, for his part, was staring back with an equal look of fear. Both water pistols clattered to the floor in unison.

"Gareth," Arthur said as calmly as possible, "don't freak out, okay? If you shout, Hector will come running in and bad things will happen." *Bad things will happen* didn't really begin to cover what would probably happen if people found out about Merlin's magic, but Arthur didn't want to go into any more detail than was necessary. "Just…don't shout."

Gareth nodded weakly and Arthur pulled his hand back. Gareth remained silent, but he still wasn't blinking, and looked ready to flee in panic at any moment. Arthur carefully took a few steps away so as not to spook the younger boy further.

"Was that glass of water floating in the air?" Bertie asked slowly, looking immensely discomfited. "Because that's not possible."

"Well?" Arthur looked over at Merlin, taking a second to push his damp fringe away from his forehead. "Do you want to tell them, or should I?"

Merlin twitched but remained silent.

"Okay," Arthur sighed. "I'll tell them then. The thing is, Mer-"

"No. Let me." Merlin held up his hand. "I…um. *I'm a sorcerer.*" He stood up abruptly and Bertie flinched,

87

stumbling backwards until his back hit the door. Merlin's words had been completely garbled, but the word 'sorcerer' still stood out loud and clear.

Arthur frowned at his teammate's reaction. "He's not dangerous, Bertie."

"You're a *sorcerer*?" Gareth squeaked, all remaining blood draining from his face. "But you can't be. Magic doesn't exist."

Arthur sat down heavily on the end of his bed. "Merlin, if you're done having a nervous breakdown over there, can you dig out a box of those Chelsea buns you've got hidden somewhere? I think we're going to need the sugar."

Bertie and Gareth looked at each other warily and Arthur could see the unspoken question of *'should we run?'* on their faces. They were good friends and deserved the truth, but they also needed to know that Merlin wasn't to be feared, and that this secret was one to fiercely protect.

Merlin was rifling under his bed with a faintly terrified expression, so Arthur assumed his instruction had been acknowledged. He looked up at his two neighbours who were still wide-eyed and silent. "Well," he said with a forced smile, "I think you should both sit down. This might take a while."

4

Sweet Revenge

For the first few days of the half-term holiday Arthur had wanted nothing more than to get back to Cambridge as soon as possible. His parents were once again on a trip to goodness-knows-where to meet goodness-knows-who, and he was bored wandering around the palace in London on his own. He'd asked as politely as possible to be allowed to go to the house in Cornwall - at least there he could easily go outside and roam around the grounds without the need for Hector to create complicated security plans detailing his every move down to the second - but his father had refused for no good reason that Arthur could see.

By Tuesday he was convinced that the reason he couldn't sleep properly was because his room was far too quiet, lacking in Merlin's impressive snores and the sound of the river slowly moving past his window. He hadn't heard a peep from his roommate since he'd left, which wasn't altogether surprising since Merlin never knew where his phone was five seconds after it went into his pocket or his bag when they were out in Cambridge.

Thankfully he'd had a few messages from Gareth and Bertie who had, after some quite spectacular hyperventilating on Gareth's part and a trip to the JCR for a cup of tea, seemed to accept that Merlin was telling the truth about magic. Bertie had text him about upcoming rugby training, whereas Gareth, completely unexpectedly, seemed to be taking the threat of a creature very seriously and was sending Arthur daily updates of his online research into dark magic.

Arthur had also received two identical messages from Ruari and Charlie seconds apart, and was starting to suspect that they were doing this to wind him up in retaliation for Arthur informing them that they were 'basically just one person' at breakfast on Friday.

But the Wednesday of the holiday brought Arthur some news that had him wanting to stay in London for the rest of the year. He didn't really need to go back to Badon after all, did he? Being tutored at the palace would probably be fine, and Merlin and co. could deal with any problems without him, couldn't they?

"Arthur," his father had said brusquely over the phone, "I expect you to continue to maintain close ties with both of your cousins whilst you are all in Cambridge."

"*All* in Cambridge?" Arthur had asked, dropping onto his bed in surprise. He had the sudden feeling that he hadn't been listening to a very important conversation at some point in the past.

His father had sighed, obviously of the same opinion. "Yes, Arthur. Charlotte started her studies at the University a few weeks ago. She's at Catterick College, which isn't too far from Badon."

Arthur couldn't have stopped the shiver if he'd tried "Great."

There had been silence on the other end of the line,

and Arthur had thought his father might finally be about to address the fact that his only son didn't really see eye to eye with the York siblings. "Arthur, you are the heir to the throne," the King had replied eventually, "and it is your responsibility, alongside your cousins, to promote a positive image of this entire family."

Arthur had wanted to tell his father that Hugo and Charlotte weren't exactly good role models for anyone, but he held his tongue as he knew it would get him nowhere.

"Catterick College is holding a feast on Saturday evening, and you and Hugo will both be attending with Charlotte as the special guests of the President of Catterick, and his wife."

Arthur had nearly choked. "I'm not supposed to be back in Cambridge until Sunday evening."

"Hector will be taking you back on Saturday morning instead." His father's tone suggested he would take no arguments from Arthur. "You will meet Hugo and both of you will be taken to Catterick for seven o'clock. I'm sure I don't need to remind you of the importance of impeccable behaviour when attending public events. The Pendragon family has always had strong links with Catterick College, Arthur, and as you yourself will one day be applying to study there I suggest that you take the chance to show why you should be given such an opportunity when the time comes."

It wouldn't do to inform his father that he had no intention of going to Catterick College to study politics like *everybody else* in his family had done for over a hundred years. His mother was aware of this, but always said they'd 'talk about it later'. 'Later' had yet to arrive.

"Yes, father," Arthur had replied eventually, and that had

been the end of that.

Now it was six-thirty on Saturday evening and Arthur was sitting alone at his desk. Nobody else had returned to Caerleon earlier than expected, and the few Kings' boys he'd seen were fourth years and therefore had completely ignored Arthur over lunch.

He was only seconds away from faking a stomach ache, or even a coma if necessary. He was so focused on how much he was going to hate the next few hours that he completely missed the sound of the bedroom door opening.

"Bloody hell, you look like a penguin!"

Arthur's head shot up so fast he almost jarred his neck. "Merlin! What are you doing here?"

Merlin closed the door, dropped his rucksack in the middle of the floor and took a seat on his bed. "Mum's terrible with dates. She booked my train ticket to come back today instead of tomorrow. When I realised what she'd done it was too late, and far too expensive, to change it, so here I am. But none of that explains why *you're* here, and why you look like you're about to leap through the window in panic."

Arthur tugged distractedly on the cuffs of his dress shirt, not able to muster up even the tiniest bit of amusement at Merlin's story. "I've got to go to dinner with both of my cousins tonight."

"*Both* of your cousins?" Merlin looked confused.

"Hugo, obviously," Arthur replied with a look of distaste, "and his sister, Charlotte. Apparently, she's just started studying at Catterick College. I hadn't realised it was this year."

"Sorry, wait." Merlin shook his head slowly, still looking baffled. "Your family go out for dinner dressed like that?

92

You lot are ridiculous."

"Merlin, focus," Arthur snapped. "That's really not the problem here. The problem is I have to spend the next few hours making polite conversation with two people who hate my guts."

"It can't be that bad, surely?" Merlin frowned. "I know Hugo's a…" he trailed off. "Well, he's a word I can't use in polite company, but there'll be loads of other people there, right? Maybe you'll find someone else to chat to."

"You think university students will want to *chat* to a thirteen-year-old?" Arthur raised an eyebrow.

Merlin rolled his eyes. "You seem to be forgetting who you are."

Arthur was about to hit back with a snarky retort when Hector knocked on the door and poked his head around a second later.

"Arthur, are y-Oh, hello, Merlin! I wasn't expecting you!" Hector grinned. "Get the day wrong, did you?"

"Not me," Merlin looked affronted. "It was my mum. Some new dig site near Glastonbury got her all excited and she ended up booking the wrong train for me. To be honest it's a miracle she didn't send me to Glasgow by mistake. She just keeps talking about the dig, and about how someone really dull is making some really dull discoveries about some really dull ancient battle site or something. It's made her worse than usual."

"Your mum didn't say 'really dull', did she?" Arthur asked as he stood and pulled his dinner jacket on.

Merlin sighed. "No, but the enthusiasm she has for digging holes in the ground with a bunch of weirdoes makes me feel a bit ill, to be honest."

"It explains a lot," Arthur grinned, feeling much better

now that he could mock his friend.

"Arthur," Hector said warningly, but he was clearly trying not to laugh at Merlin too. "The car will be at the Back Gate in a few minutes."

"That's early," Arthur frowned. "I thought we didn't have to be there until seven."

Hector cleared his throat. "It's a matter of security, Arthur."

Arthur's frown deepened. A matter of security? That usually meant that something was going on and everyone would be making it their business to completely avoid letting on to Arthur what that 'something' was. The last time he'd heard those words he'd been nine and Hector had just pulled him out of a school trip due to kidnap threats.

"That sounds ominous," Merlin said looking between Hector and Arthur.

"Nothing to worry about, Merlin," Hector forced a smile. "Just the usual."

Merlin looked about as convinced as Arthur did, but he didn't question Hector any further; he just shrugged and got to his feet, dusting imaginary crumbs from his jeans. "I'll wander down with you. A few of the international students in Winchester and Kings didn't go home for the holiday so Agnes is still here making food. Mrs Beaulake wants me to sit with the family so that I don't feel left out."

"Don't try to impress Elaine, Merlin," Arthur snorted as he followed Merlin and Hector out into the corridor. "Bertie will have your head."

"Elaine?" Merlin looked horrified. "You're joking, right? I know Bertie thinks she's the best thing since sliced bread, but she terrifies me. Don't you remember what she said to Jim when he winked at her?"

Arthur laughed as they descended the stairs. Jim Fletcher, fellow first year and resident Romeo (or so he thought) had made the error of trying to impress Elaine Beaulake. She had been distinctly *unimpressed* and cornered him in the Caerleon entrance corridor before delivering a very inventive threat that would have had her mother blushing in horror if she'd overheard.

Hector, with a quick wave to Merlin, strode on ahead as they stepped outside, hurrying over the bridge and across Kings' Court to look out for the car.

Merlin inhaled deeply as they crossed the bridge. "That smells like lasagne! Oh good, finally, *actual* food. My Dad suggested we go out for dinner on the first night I was back and my mum just nudged him in the ribs and said '*No, Tim. We've still got those lentils Sandra brought back from Peru, and I'm sure Merlin would love lentil stew. Wouldn't you, love?*"

Arthur laughed again at Merlin's impression of his mother. "And you didn't love the lentil stew?"

"I might have done if it tasted anything like lentil stew," Merlin replied, "but it was a fairly unrecognisable taste *and* texture. Poor dad has to put up with it every day though so I guess I'm lucky."

"You've brought the little wizard for protection, have you?"

Arthur's grin froze in place at the new voice. He looked up to see Hugo standing in front of them, a black robe swishing around him in the breeze.

"Hugo." Arthur nodded his head and averted his eyes.

"Oh, hello!" Merlin grinned cheerfully up at the older boy. "You look like a complete tit."

Arthur wasn't sure if he was more surprised than Hugo

at Merlin's insult, and there was a bizarre moment where the cousins seemed to agree on something for the first time in their lives – *Merlin* was actually the complete tit, and he was probably about to die.

"What did you just say?" Hugo hissed, towering considerably over Merlin.

"Oh, I think you heard me," Merlin replied steadily. "I know the uniform for this place is ridiculous, but I don't remember seeing super flappy bat cape on the list. Was it on a special letter only received by poncey gits?"

"*This* is a robe of Catterick College," Hugo replied coldly. "It's a mark of the University's heritage."

"Yeah," Merlin shrugged unimpressed, "but why do *you* have one?"

"I'm wearing one as a sign of respect, considering the feast we're attending tonight is in honour of Catterick College's five-hundredth year."

"A feast?" Merlin laughed loudly. "This gets more ridiculous as it goes on. Well, you both enjoy your *feast*. I'm sure there'll be lots of roast swan, or whatever. You guys can eat swans, can't you? Because Arthur's dad owns them all, or something? Although that's just weird in my opinion; the owning, *and* the eating, I mean."

Arthur wasn't sure whether he wanted to laugh or just stare at his friend in disbelief.

Hugo smiled without a trace of humour. "You think you're hilarious, don't you?"

"Sometimes."

"You have no idea who you're messing with." Hugo spat, taking a step closer to Merlin who didn't back away.

"Did you *really* just say that?" Merlin arched an eyebrow, before turning to look at Arthur. "I didn't know there was a comic book villain in your family. Arthur, you're completely normal compared to this one."

Arthur wasn't particularly surprised when Hugo's fist shot out from under the ballooning black material to land squarely on Merlin's jaw. Merlin, for all his bluster, was still only a thirteen-year old boy and he reeled backwards from the force.

"Hugo!" Arthur may not have been surprised, but he was still appalled as his cousin advanced towards where Merlin was crouching on the gravel, a hand pressed to his face.

Merlin mumbled something.

"Are you trying to say something?" Hugo sneered.

"Okay, *ow!*" Merlin looked up and suddenly smirked at his attacker underneath a grimace. "But that was a bit of a mistake."

"What's going on here?"

All three boys turned as Mr Beaulake stormed over the bridge, barking out his question.

"Nothing, sir," Hugo replied calmly. "Just a misunderstanding."

"A misunderstanding?" Beaulake asked, helping Merlin to his feet. "Because from my study it looked like you just assaulted one of my tutees."

"I was provoked, *sir*," Hugo answered, and his use of Beaulake's title was anything but respectful.

"The Headmaster's office, Mr York." Beaulake glared at Hugo. "*Now.*"

Hugo only smirked slightly. "I'm afraid I can't do that, Mr Beaulake, sir. I'm attending an event at the request of the King. Arthur is attending too."

The sound of the Back Gate opening had Arthur turning

to see Hector gesturing for him to hurry.

"Our cars are here, Mr Beaulake," Hugo added. "I'm sure my parents will be happy to talk through any concerns you have about my conduct when they return from their current state visit." With that, he turned and walked away, his robe billowing out behind him once more.

"Are you alright?" Arthur asked Merlin in alarm once Hugo had retreated.

Merlin grinned, but then winced almost immediately. "Oh, I'm fine," he replied. "Hugo's come out the worst, trust me." He wiggled the fingers of his left hand very subtly and Arthur's eyes widened at the implication.

"Merlin, you and I are going to have a very serious chat over supper," Mr Beaulake said before he turned his attention to Arthur. "Arthur, I think you should go to this event as planned, but I want to see you and Merlin in my study straight after breakfast."

Arthur nodded solemnly. "Of course, sir."

Mr Beaulake patted Arthur once on the shoulder. "You're not in trouble, Arthur, but I'd like to understand what's going on; we don't like bad blood between students here at Badon."

Arthur nodded again. "Yes, sir. Excuse me, sir. I'll see you later, Merlin."

Merlin waved, looking slightly less perky now that the adrenaline was wearing off.

"Come on, Merlin," Arthur heard Mr Beaulake say as he walked away. "A quick trip to the matron before dinner."

Hector stopped Arthur at the Back Gate with a frown. "Arthur, what just happened?"

"Nothing." Arthur shook his head. "But I'd appreciate it if I don't have to sit next to Hugo this evening."

Hector looked ready to ask another question, but changed his mind at the last second. "Don't worry about that, my boy. I'll make sure his Royal Highness is miles away."

"Thanks, Hector." Arthur smiled grimly before bracing himself to get into the idling car. All he could do now was grit his teeth and wait to see what Merlin had in store for the Prince of York.

* * * * *

Dinner was roughly as bad as Arthur had been expecting. On the plus side, Hector, true to his word, had made a few quiet comments to the President of Catterick College upon arrival and Arthur had found himself sitting at the other end of the long top table from the York siblings. The food had also been brilliant, although he knew Merlin would be disappointed to hear that there hadn't been a swan in sight.

However, even though he'd managed to escape the clutches of Hugo and Charlotte, Arthur had instead found himself surrounded by various elderly professors who spoke *at* him, rather than *to* him. He was certain that they probably *were* researching very interesting things, but he didn't have a clue what they were talking about most of the time, and he'd just nodded in what he thought might have been the correct places. On top of that he was sitting next to the President's wife, Lady Burton, who was wearing such an alarming shade of pink it was proving to be quite the distraction.

Most disappointingly though was the fact that Hugo had appeared unaffected by Merlin's mutterings. He and Charlotte had been holding court over their end of the table all night; the guests around them listening intently and throwing their heads back in appreciative laughter at regular intervals.

Arthur only realised that he'd been staring into space when the view in front of his eyes changed. He blinked rapidly to clear his head as he saw Charlotte excusing herself from her seat and sashaying towards him.

"Arthur, darling," Charlotte beamed at him as she stopped behind his chair. "Weren't you going to come and say hello?"

Arthur's years of practised politeness kicked in. He stood immediately and allowed himself to be wrapped in a hug. He held his breath for fear of suffocating in a cloud of his cousin's perfume. He wasn't an expert but he could have sworn that Charlotte was swaddled in the scent of dying flowers.

"Sorry," he said as politely as possible when he pulled away. "I was just talking to Professor Elody here." He pointed at man hunched over his half-eaten dessert, and frowned when he thought he heard the professor snoring.

"It looks like he was very interested in what you had to say," Charlotte smirked. "Now, who do you think I can move so that I can sit down and have a proper chat with you?"

A proper chat? Arthur was willing to bet everything he owned that Charlotte had never said 'a proper chat' to anyone in her life, least of all Arthur,

"Oh, she looks dull," Charlotte whispered conspiratorially, before stepping past her cousin and tapping the Master's wife on the shoulder.

Lady Burton's eyes widened as she turned, scrambling to her feet so quickly the chair skidded on the tiled floor behind her. "Your Royal Highness." She briefly looked

Charlotte in the eye with a weak smile, then averted her eyes to the floor, before finally settling on a midpoint somewhere near the princess's shoulder.

"I was wondering if you wouldn't mind switching places with me for a while?" Charlotte smiled sweetly. "I haven't seen my cousin in such a long time, and it would be a shame to miss the opportunity to speak to him now."

Lady Burton didn't answer; instead she bobbed her head vigorously, snatched up her bag (also horrifyingly pink) without another word and hurried away.

"There," said Charlotte as she gracefully took the vacated seat, "that's much better."

Arthur, who realised that he was still standing in surprise, silently returned to his chair and waited for Charlotte to make her intentions clear. She had always actively avoided her younger cousin, and when they *had* been forced to spend time together she had never been anything other than cold.

"Hugo tells me your friend wasn't very nice to him earlier," the princess said after a visibly nervous waiter had brought her a new glass of champagne.

"Did Hugo also tell you that he punched my friend, who's a first year?" Arthur asked before he could stop himself.

"He did," Charlotte said, shaking her head as she placed the glass carefully on the table. "It's a horrible business. Hugo should know better."

Arthur nearly fell off his chair. "He should?"

"Of course he should," Charlotte replied in surprise. "He's two years older than you, and he's *supposed* to behave like a member of the royal family at all times. I want you to know that I've discussed his behaviour with him and he won't be attacking any of your friends in the future."

Arthur was fairly certain that his jaw had dropped to the floor and scuttled away under the dinner table in shock.

"Don't look so surprised, Arthur." Charlotte laughed, a high-pitched tinkling sound that skittered around the room. "I know we haven't always been close, but I'd dearly love for that to change now that we're all in Cambridge."

"Um…" was all Arthur could manage after a long moment of silence.

"Oh, Arthur!" Charlotte laughed again. "Surely you can't hold the past against me! I was a child. We all were. It was just harmless teasing; it didn't mean anything,"

Arthur would disagree. Harmless teasing didn't usually include locking a ten-year-old child in a wardrobe for an entire day, and pushing your young cousin into a lake in the middle of winter wasn't normally considered hilarious.

"I'm sorry, Arthur," Charlotte frowned. "I know we were horrible, but it was only because we were silly little children who didn't know any better."

When Arthur was eight or nine his nanny had passed on her words of wisdom with grave seriousness; *Now Arthur,* she'd said, *when you apologise you should never try to excuse your behaviour afterwards. Never say 'sorry' and then 'but'.*

Charlotte, however, did look genuinely sorry for the first time in her life. She looked like Arthur's forgiveness was the most important thing in the world to her at that moment, and even though it felt wrong to do so Arthur nodded his head slightly.

"Brilliant," Charlotte beamed, a hand dramatically resting above her heart, drawing attention to the blood-red ruby she had worn around her neck for as long as Arthur could remember. "Now tell me about your first half-term.

Do you really have a friend named *Merlin?*"

Arthur nodded. "His mum really likes magic and other weird stuff. I guess somebody thought it was funny to put us together when they were deciding on room allocations."

Charlotte grinned. "So he's not actually a wizard then?"

"No," Arthur shook his head. "That would be ridiculous. And there's no such thing as magic anyway. No way."

Charlotte frowned slightly, and Arthur had to admit that maybe his denial had been a little too vehement to be considered normal. Luckily all further conversation was halted by a shriek from the other end of the table.

In a burst of fuchsia, Lady Burton sprang up from her seat as though she'd been burned. Her face had paled so much that, added to the colour of her clothes, Arthur couldn't help thinking she looked just like a marshmallow. She was pointing at something in fright.

"What's going on?" Arthur craned his neck, his interest increasing as other guests rose from their seats near the head of the table.

"What's happening?" Hugo demanded, his voice cutting over the commotion. "Why are you pointing at me?"

Arthur's frown morphed immediately into shock as his cousin's face suddenly came into view; Hugo's skin was green! Not a subtle, sickly shade, but instead a rich, deep green that reminded Arthur of a freshly cut Christmas tree. A slow trickle of realisation began to filter into his awareness; *Merlin.*

Charlotte's eyes flew open in surprise and she hurried towards her brother with a shriek. "Hugo! Why are you green?"

"What?" Hugo yelled back in confused annoyance. "*Green?!*"

Arthur watched as the Prince of York held up his hands, which were now the same colour as his face. Hugo's expression contorted into horror as gasps and shouts of surprise echoed around the college's Old Hall at breakneck speed.

"What's happening?" Hugo wailed again, and Arthur was only slightly disappointed in himself at the sheer level of joy his cousin's anguish was bringing him. He decided in that moment that he was definitely going to have to get Merlin the best Christmas present ever.

The prince's amusement, however, was halted immediately when he noticed Charlotte turn away from her brother and look around the room in question. Her frown was deep and her eyes calculating, looking as though she knew exactly what she was looking for.

Charlotte's eyes paused on Arthur and he made sure to look back with his best impression of dignified horror. The princess's eyes narrowed slightly, but a split-second later her gaze moved on and Arthur felt the brief clutch of inexplicable fear release its grip on his heart.

"Arthur!" Hector clamped a hand on Arthur's shoulder and hauled the prince to his feet. "Come on!"

Arthur stumbled slightly as Hector propelled him towards the door, barging through the guests who by now were all standing up to get a good look at Hugo's predicament. Arthur was pretty sure that if he tried to resist this forward motion Hector would just pick him up and carry him out of the Old Hall so he kept his eyes fixed straight ahead to where a team of RPS agents in dinner jackets had gathered by the door.

"The car's ready, sir." A suited man nodded at Hector as the grand old door was opened.

Arthur was marched towards the exit at speed, and he

nearly tripped over when he didn't quite manage to completely dodge one of the suits of armour that adorned both sides of Catterick College's oldest passageway.

Hector was barking instructions, not at his young charge, but into the highly sensitive microphone Arthur knew was hidden under his guard's collar. Arthur didn't understand what Hector was saying as it seemed to be a code involving the repetition of words like 'owl' and 'barrel'. What an owl in a barrel had to do with anything, Arthur had no clue.

The pitch-black four-wheel-drive was parked right up against the main gate so that Arthur barely had to step onto the cobbles of the side street before he was in the backseat of the car. Hector climbed in hurriedly after him and slammed the door before tugging the seatbelt from Arthur's hands and locking it with a secure *snap*.

"Go!" Hector barked and the car sped away from Catterick College, wheels spinning on the damp tarmac.

"What's happening?" Arthur asked as he watched the centre of Cambridge flit by his window, a convoy of other cars suddenly surrounding the one he was travelling in. "Is this because of what happened to Hugo?"

Hector ignored him in favour of rapidly tapping on his mobile and holding it to his ear. "Proceeding as initially intended unless informed otherwise," he snapped rapidly. "Has His Majesty been informed? Good." With that he hung up just as the car hurtled past the back of Queens' College.

Arthur didn't think the car was going to stop outside Badon, but it braked at the last second, sending both backseat passengers scooting forwards slightly only to be restrained at the mercy of their seatbelts.

"Okay, that wasn't pleasant," Arthur muttered as he

unlatched his seatbelt with a huff of breath when Hector clambered out of the car. His complaints probably would have continued if the door hadn't immediately been pulled open so that Hector could reach in and yank Arthur out of the car and through the Back Gate.

Arthur found himself hemmed in on all sides by men in suits and once again he had to just keep striding forward for fear of being trampled. He was tall for his age, but he still couldn't see past the towering height of each RPS agent as they marched him over the bridge and through Caerleon's arch.

"Clear." Another man in a suit announced as the door to the boarding house opened in front of them. "Wizard is inside. Should I remove him?"

Arthur's eyes nearly popped out of his head. *Wizard?* Had they found out about Merlin? What had the idiot done to get himself noticed? Surely nobody knew what had really happened to Hugo? And most worryingly of all, was *remove* code for assassinate or something equally awful?

"No." Hector's reply cut through Arthur's thoughts. "He's not a threat." He turned to the rest of the team. "Ensure the exterior of the boarding house remains secure this evening. Only those with full clearance should be permitted entry."

Arthur found himself pushed through the main door, Hector shutting it behind both of them a second later. "Merlin's not a wizard," he blurted out at the bottom of the stairs.

Hector chuckled. "I'm fully aware of that, Arthur. It's just the code name the security team use, for obvious reasons."

The prince once more found himself frozen in surprise. So they *didn't* know about Merlin's magic. He sagged in relief against the wood panelling of the staircase.

"Are you alright, Arthur?" Hector asked in concern. "Do you feel ill at all?"

Arthur nodded hurriedly. "Sorry, I just wasn't expecting to be hauled out of dinner like that."

Hector nodded, and gestured for Arthur to lead the way upstairs. "You know how it works, Arthur. If there's any credible threat to your safety we have to remove you as soon as possible."

"Hugo turning green is classed as a 'credible threat'?" Arthur asked in disbelief.

"When it's highly likely that your cousin has been poisoned then yes, Arthur, it's certainly a credible threat," Hector replied.

"Poisoned?" Arthur almost laughed. "Is *that* what you think happened to him?"

Hector paused as they reached the top of the stairs. "What else would I think happened?" He narrowed his eyes. "Is there something you're not telling me, Arthur?"

Arthur tried not to gulp, but Hector could be rather intimidating when he wanted to be; a useful trait for a royal bodyguard, but not necessarily a side to the man that Arthur wanted to see regularly. "No, of course not," he replied, hoping he had imagined the slight squeak in his voice. "What would I not be telling you?"

Hector tilted his head slightly, but his gaze didn't waver. "I know you don't like your cousin, Arthur, but I thought you might be a bit more concerned than you are."

Arthur tried to adopt an expression of complete innocence, with just a hint of worry for Hugo's welfare. Unfortunately, he felt like he ended up making a face that screamed '*guilty!*' instead. Thankfully the bedroom door at the end of the corridor opened and Merlin appeared, half hidden under a mess of bruising and dishevelled hair.

"There you are!" Merlin announced, letting the door swing wide so he could lean against the frame. "What's going on? I got told by a big bloke in a suit to 'stay here unless I wanted to regret it.'" He waved his arm towards the room behind him. "Clearly I chose a life without regret."

Arthur turned away from Hector and strode towards his friend. "Everything's probably fine," Arthur said as he got closer, "but Hugo turned green."

"Green?" Merlin asked in mock surprise, a grin desperately trying to escape. "What do you mean, *green*?"

Arthur shot Merlin a look he hoped communicated a desire for his friend to shut up while Hector was around, then he turned around to face his bodyguard. "Will you let me know as soon as you hear what's happening with Hugo?"

Hector was still frowning at him. "Of course," he said eventually. "Goodnight Arthur."

"Goodnight." Arthur replied hurriedly before herding Merlin through the door and closing it quickly behind them.

They managed to last a whole four seconds before dissolving into laughter.

* * * * *

"We thought there was something wrong with the television when they showed the picture on the news!" Gareth nearly choked on his toast he was laughing so much as he spoke. "Mum kept hitting the side of it with her hand and Dad just swore at the remote control. Your cousin was *so* green!"

Arthur had barely stopped grinning since Saturday

night, and even the prospect of lessons starting again in under an hour couldn't dampen his good mood. Hugo was fine; Hector had announced on Sunday morning that the Prince of York had been tested for every poison known to man and the best his doctors could come up with was that he'd had an allergic reaction to the wine at dinner - Wine he shouldn't have been drinking considering he was far too young. To add to Arthur's joy, it looked like Hugo was going to have to miss at least the first week of term to recover from his 'ordeal'.

The press had had a field day with the whole situation and Monday morning's papers, which had been delivered to the JCR before breakfast, for the second day in a row each had a photo of Hugo's bright green skin under headlines such as '**A little green around the gills!**' and Arthur's personal favourite, '**Too much fun for His Royal Greenness?**' Some of the second years had been in the middle of pinning the front pages to the JCR notice board with glee when Arthur and Merlin had wandered past.

"Did you really do that to him, Merlin?" Bertie asked quietly, looking around to make sure he wasn't overheard. He'd arrived with Gareth and hadn't taken his usual place at the next table with his fellow second years.

Merlin nodded silently. He was still uneasy about the fact his secret was much less of a secret than it had been when he'd first arrived at Badon. Arthur knew that Bertie and Gareth weren't going to tell anyone about the magic, but he could understand why Merlin looked like he was just waiting for someone to turn on him.

"I mean, it was *brilliant*," Bertie added with a grin. "Really brilliant."

Merlin relaxed immediately and his white-knuckled

grip on his glass of orange juice relaxed slightly. "Well he did make my face go purple." He pointed at his obviously bruised jaw. "It seemed only fair for him to share my pain."

Gareth was now looking at Merlin as though he'd discovered his new idol. "I wish I could do magic."

"What did Beaulake say?" Bertie asked, dropping his voice again.

Arthur shrugged. "Not much really. He wasn't happy that Hugo had punched Merlin, obviously, and Hugo's been banned from crossing the Caerleon bridge unless it's for lessons or Chapel just in case. I'm supposed to stay out of his way; not that I'd actually spend time with him unless I was forced to!"

"I'm not allowed to talk to His Royal Awfulness at all." Merlin rolled his eyes before a wicked grin spread across his lips. "Doesn't mean I can't have some fun from afar."

Gareth looked thrilled even as Arthur shook his head at his roommate.

"Well, come on then, Gareth," Merlin said when he finally paused for breath between his usual shovelfuls of cereal. "Arthur said you'd been looking into *stuff* over half term."

Gareth nodded with more enthusiasm in his expression than Arthur had ever seen on anyone, and certainly not on perpetually worried Gareth. "I have!"

"And?" Arthur asked after a few seconds of expectant silence.

"Oh!" Gareth rolled his eyes at himself. "Sorry! Yes, well I thought the best thing to do was to see what I could find out about magic on the internet."

"Bunch of weirdoes," Merlin mumbled into his juice.

Gareth nodded. "Yeah. I didn't get very far for the first

few days. It took ages to read through all the forums I came across. There's a surprising number of people who think they're wizards like Merlin."

"Sorcerer!" Merlin corrected, looking offended again. "How many times? Sorcerers and wizards are *not* the same thing!"

"I know!" Gareth defended himself. "*I* know, but they don't. They really like Merlin though."

"Clearly they haven't met him," Arthur snickered.

"Oh, thanks, Arthur," Merlin rolled his eyes again. "Anyway," he frowned at Gareth, "they don't know me so how can they like me?"

"Not you." Gareth shook his head. "They really like proper old Merlin, with the beard and the pointy hat from the King Arthur legends. They think he's the most powerful wizard or *sorcerer*, ever to live and that one day he'll come back, just like King Arthur will."

Arthur and Merlin exchanged a glance at Gareth's suddenly uncomfortable expression.

"No way," Merlin said as he realised exactly what Gareth was thinking.

"Not a chance," Arthur added. "I'm named after my grandfather and Merlin's mum's a bit mad. No offence, Merlin."

"None taken," Merlin nodded at his friend. "It's just a coincidence. You don't really expect us to believe that this idiot next to me is *the* King Arthur. No offence, Arthur."

"Hey!" Arthur snapped. "Well it's far more likely that I'm *the* King Arthur than you're some great powerful sorcerer. Obviously."

"Oh really?" Merlin looked genuinely offended. "And why's that?"

"Whoa! Hold it!" Bertie held up his hands. "God, you two are awful sometimes. Stop bickering and listen to Gareth."

Arthur and Merlin adopted suitably chastised expressions.

"Anyway," Gareth said when Bertie gestured for him to continue, "whether you believe it or not, you have to admit it's a bit of a coincidence, Arthur. Particularly with Hugo's middle name being Mordred. Oh, and I found out that Princess Charlotte's full name is Charlotte Louise Morgainne. Morgainne's a bit like Morgan, isn't it? Morgan le Fay was the witch from the legends."

"Their mother liked the names!" Arthur protested. "Don't be ridiculous. People can't just come back from the dead like that. Anyway, the stories aren't true. There wasn't an actual person called Merlin; he was just invented to make the stories a bit more interesting."

"No disrespect, Arthur," Bertie interjected, "but, to be fair, none of us, Merlin excepted, knew there was such a thing as real magic until recently. What if the stories have a bit more truth to them than you thought?"

"That's ridiculous," Arthur said after a long moment of stunned silence. "You can't all really believe that?"

"I don't," Merlin replied. "Although maybe you're right to avoid going up against Hugo with a sword, Arthur."

Arthur tried to ignore the fact that this had been his entire reasoning for not joining the fencing team even though his father had wanted him to. "I'm not King Arthur and Merlin's not the greatest sorcerer ever, alright?"

Gareth looked totally unconvinced. "Okay. Ignore all of that then, but I did find some interesting things out about the giant you saw, and I have an idea about why none of

112

the rest of us heard anything."

"Bertie!"

Gareth whirled in surprise as Kay and Leo appeared behind him just as he was about to explain.

"Yeah?" Bertie looked up at his friends.

"Beaulake wants to see all second years before first period," Leo explained. "Come on."

"Yeah, hang on a second," Bertie replied. "Let me get rid of my tray and I'll meet you outside."

Leo gave a brief wave to the others as Kay added, "Glad to see Hugo got his comeuppance for what he did to you, Merlin. Don't worry, we're all more than ready to taunt him the minute he dares show his face back at Badon."

"Thanks!" Merlin grinned. It had been a surprise to see how readily every boy in Caerleon, even those in their final year, had been to show Merlin support since they'd all started arriving back from holiday the night before.

"I'll tell you the rest later," Gareth said quietly as Leo and Kay left. "Do you want me to bring everything to your room after prep tonight, Arthur?"

"Wait until after dinner," Arthur replied. "We've got rugby tonight, and Ms Bell is bound to give us hours of Latin prep."

"I'll see you at training, Arthur," Bertie said as he stood up with his tray. "See you later."

"Bye, Bertie," Gareth added.

Merlin waved, his mouth full of cereal again even though Arthur could have sworn that the bowl had been empty a moment ago. He frowned at his roommate who just chewed noisily in response.

* * * * *

113

Arthur hadn't been wrong about the amount of Latin prep they'd receive. Dinner was long over and he was still translating the final paragraph of text when Gareth and Bertie knocked on the door.

Merlin, who had finished his work at his usual supersonic speed, was the one to yell 'Come in' and wave his arms around in a manner that Arthur assumed meant 'take a seat anywhere you like', but could just as easily have been decoded as a gesture of irritation.

"Give me five minutes," Arthur replied, not taking his eyes off the page in front of him. He adjusted his reading glasses on his nose and squinted at the block of text that was starting to bring on a headache. "I've got two sentences left."

"Oh for pity's sake," Merlin sighed from where he was perched on his bed. "The sentences are basically 'The girls led the cattle as far up the mountain as possible before the sun began to set. As night fell the air filled with the sounds of strange creatures.' Just write something like that down and put it away. I can practically feel your annoyance from over here."

Arthur momentarily considered arguing; after all he was a firm believer in completing work independently. Then again, Merlin had produced yet another box of assorted biscuits from somewhere, and Gareth was clutching a stack of paper and looking fit to burst. He scribbled down two final sentences and closed his textbook with a satisfied thud.

Gareth waited until everyone had chosen a biscuit from the quite impressive selection before beginning to recount what he'd discovered. "Well," he began, brandishing a custard cream, "the first useful thing I found out was that giants feature quite a bit in the Arthur stories."

"Told you," Merlin folded his arms and stared pointedly at Arthur. "Giant killer!"

Arthur shook his head and turned his attention back to Gareth. "And?"

"*And* that the giants generally spent their time eating people." Gareth gulped.

"Eating people?" Bertie looked mildly ill and put his half-eaten biscuit down on Merlin's desk.

Gareth nodded. "Now, according to everything I read, a giant wouldn't have any magical ability. So, the way you described its disappearance doesn't make any sense when you just look at the giant on its own."

"What exactly are you getting at, Gareth?" Arthur asked.

Gareth took a deep breath. "To create a giant like that – a creature that hasn't been seen in a few hundred years – you'd need to be a really powerful sorcerer. Someone who's learned magic from books, or even a wizard, probably wouldn't have the natural power to be able to bring something of that size into existence. Even the most powerful of sorcerers would need to be close by to maintain the giant's existence."

"So the sorcerer was here at Badon?" Merlin asked, wide eyed. "But we didn't see anyone else!"

Arthur shook his head. "Merlin's right. There was nobody else out there."

Gareth shrugged. "It's the only explanation. The sorcerer wouldn't need to actually be at Badon, but they'd need to be fairly close to the grounds. Dark magic requires more skill and power than any other kind of magic. If I'm right, that giant wasn't just created by the sorcerer, it was raised from the dead."

"Necromancy?" Merlin asked, looking as stricken as Gareth.

Gareth nodded. "I think so."

"Necro-what now?" Bertie asked, although he looked rather like he didn't really want an answer.

"Necromancy," Merlin croaked. "It's where a sorcerer can raise a spirit, or even bring a body back to life, sort of."

"Sort of?" Arthur shivered.

"No sorcerer, or anybody else for that matter, has the power to really bring someone, or *something*, back from the grave," Merlin replied. "A body can be reanimated, but its actions would be entirely controlled by the necromancer. It's a bit like having a really, really twisted version of a puppet."

Arthur let out the breath he'd been holding in anticipation of Merlin's answer. "What if it comes back? How do you stop something that's already dead?"

"Well the simplest way would be to stop the sorcerer at the source," Gareth shrugged. "If the sorcerer's concentration was broken they wouldn't be able to maintain the magic required to keep the giant animated. I think."

"Sorry," Arthur said slowly, "did you say the simplest way to defeat the giant if it returns is to basically *distract* a really powerful sorcerer who clearly has reason for setting a giant loose in the grounds of a school?"

Gareth shrugged again. "I didn't say you'd *like* the simplest way."

"What's the more complicated way?" Bertie asked. He still hadn't picked up his biscuit again.

"Well," Gareth sighed, "just because the giant's technically already dead, it doesn't mean it can't be killed again."

"How do you kill a giant?" Arthur asked.

"Traditionally with a sword," Gareth replied.

"Well we haven't got one of those Gareth," Merlin replied. "We've got sports equipment, your violin, and my magic.

And before anyone suggests it, yes I *have* tried to change objects into other things before and the best I managed was to get a pencil to turn into a shoe."

"Were you *trying* to turn it into a shoe?" Arthur asked with a frown.

"I was aiming for an ice-lolly," Merlin replied. "So, unless you want a hockey stick irreparably transformed into a deckchair, or something equally useless, I suggest we don't try to make a sword."

"Okay," Bertie waved his hand, "look, I know this is all a bit mad, but maybe we should just tell someone. Hector? Mr Beaulake, maybe?"

"You think they'd believe us?" Merlin scoffed. "Can you imagine just casually saying *Oh, hey Hector, did you know there's a lunatic sorcerer on the loose? And to make it worse, the sorcerer has a pet giant?*"

"Um…" Gareth said quietly.

Arthur's stomach dropped. "What does 'um' mean, Gareth?"

"I haven't actually told you everything yet," Gareth said slowly.

"What else could there possibly be?" Merlin asked, arching an eyebrow.

"The sorcerer who created the giant was also strong enough to maintain a spell that kept everyone in the college asleep or protected from the sounds outside." Gareth pointed at Merlin and Arthur. "Everyone except you two, that is."

Arthur nodded. "We think maybe Merlin's magic somehow protected us from whatever spell was cast."

"I don't think so," Gareth replied. "Look, you're *really* not going to like what I'm going to say."

"Is this about the Legends again?" Arthur asked in exasperation.

Gareth scrunched up his face. "I'm not sure about Merlin. Maybe magic is the reason he wasn't affected by the spell. But Arthur, I really think *you* were supposed to hear that giant and go looking for it."

"You seem very sure about this, Gareth," Arthur replied.

"It's because of the barking," Gareth nodded.

"The barking?" Merlin asked. "The pack of wild dogs, you mean?"

"I found this in a translation of the Legend." Gareth retrieved a sheet of paper from the pile resting on his knee. "*And as he sat so, Arthur thought he heard a noise of hounds, to the sum of thirty,*" he read. "*And with that the King saw coming towards him the strangest beast that ever he saw or heard of. So this beast went to the well and drank, and the noise was in the beast's belly like unto the questing of thirty couple hounds.*" He looked up at the confused faces of his friends. "It's not a pack of dogs, guys, it's the Questing Beast."

Arthur shook his head. He didn't know what a Questing Beast was, but it didn't sound good, and more importantly, he refused to believe that somebody was raising creatures from Arthurian Legend. "It can't be."

A roar of laughter floated up from the JCR and all four boys jumped in surprise.

"I think I've had enough for tonight," Bertie mumbled as he stood up. He glanced to the right as he did so. His forehead creased into a frown. "What the..." He trailed off and leaned forwards to peer through the slight gap in the curtains. He jerked back almost immediately.

"What?" Arthur jumped to his feet and moved towards the window, but Bertie grabbed his arm to stop him.

"Wait." Bertie hissed. "Gareth, Merlin, turn all the lights off. Quickly."

Both boys did as instructed and the room was plunged into darkness immediately.

"Arthur, look out there and tell me what you see," Bertie whispered.

Arthur couldn't see Bertie's face in the dark, but the older boy sounded even more apprehensive than he had done throughout Gareth's explanations. He approached the window, just as he had done the night he'd encountered the giant, and carefully inched the curtain to the left.

"You've got to be joking," Arthur whispered as he looked over to Kings' Court. It was difficult to see with clouds obscuring any moonlight there would otherwise have been.

"Is it the giant?" Gareth squeaked.

"What?" Merlin elbowed Arthur out of the way to take a look himself. "Seriously?" he added after a few seconds. "Bertie, I thought you were *joking*."

"So did I," Bertie gulped.

"What is it?" Gareth asked, although made no attempt to move towards the window.

"Remember when Bertie told us that ghost story about the hooded figures near the Headmaster's Lodge?" Arthur asked into the black room.

"Yes," Gareth replied, the uneasiness clear in his voice.

Arthur watched at least ten figures clad in black robes moving towards the Headmaster's Lodge. They were hugging the shadows, remaining in single file as they appeared to glide along the unlit side of Kings' Court. "Well, it looks like it wasn't just a ghost story."

5

The Brotherhood

"They still haven't come back out," Arthur whispered, stationed at the window as he had been since they'd first seen the robed figures. The fifth year prefects had knocked for lights out at nine-thirty so Bertie, and an equally uneasy Gareth, had left with the promise that they'd be the first to know if anything of note happened.

Merlin sighed from where he was lying on his bed, still in his after-school clothes. "I still think we should be out there. We're not going to learn much staying up here and spying on them like nosey old women, are we?"

"How are we supposed to get outside?" Arthur asked. "Hector's been hovering more than usual since he mentioned that 'matter of security' before the Catterick dinner."

"Oh, yeah," Merlin frowned. "Do you have any idea what he meant?"

Arthur shook his head. "No, but it does mean that it's going to be a lot harder to sneak away from him for a while." His eyes suddenly lit up in wonder. "Merlin?"

"I don't like that face, Arthur," Merlin replied warily, "and I know I'm going to regret asking but, *what*?"

"You're a sorcerer!"

"You're just getting that now?" Merlin arched an eyebrow.

Arthur rolled his eyes. "You can make us invisible!"

For a long moment Merlin said nothing, but then he burst out laughing as though Arthur had told the funniest joke known to man. He quickly covered his face with his pillow to muffle the sound. "You're kidding, right?"

Arthur was distinctly *not* kidding, and he stared pointedly at his roommate until the peals of laughter quieted slightly.

"Arthur," Merlin said when he'd composed himself enough to speak, "you do remember who you're talking to, don't you? I'm sure a sorcerer could make us invisible, and one day I might even be that sorcerer. But knowing our luck I'd end up making us invisible for the rest of our lives; you wouldn't be a very good King if nobody could see you!"

"Good point." Arthur was loathed to admit that Merlin was right, but when he thought about it he didn't really fancy explaining his sudden invisibility to his father. "Any other ideas?"

"Well, that depends," Merlin replied as Arthur pulled on a jumper. "Are there any of your guards outside?"

"There shouldn't be," Arthur shook his head. "Hector's team monitors Caerleon from this floor, and if we can get past them we should be alright. Neither school gate is constantly monitored, but there are two nearby security teams who will turn up if there's even a hint of trouble."

"That's an awful lot of security guards, Arthur." Merlin glanced over in surprise.

"Well I'm a very important person, Merlin." Arthur stuck his tongue out with a grin.

"Not at all big-headed, are you?" Merlin rolled his eyes.

"I could try a shielding spell. It won't make us invisible, but it means someone would have to look *directly* at us for them to know we were there. The spell would stop us from being noticed if anybody glanced out of a window."

"You can do that?" Arthur asked in slight awe.

"I said I'd *try*, Arthur," Merlin replied. "I've never really used this spell before. To get past your guards next door we're going to need more than that. I can charm the room so that they can't hear anything on the other side of their door." He bit his lip. "It wouldn't be anywhere near as powerful as the spell the sorcerer used to block out the giant, but I've done it a couple of times at home when I've needed to practise spells and didn't want mum to come running at the sounds of explosions."

"Do it." Arthur said without hesitation. "Should we get Bertie and Gareth on the way?"

Merlin nodded. "The more the merrier, I say. Plus, Bertie's kind of scary when he wants to be."

Arthur grinned as Merlin reached up to his bookshelf to grab the ratty text that would hopefully help them on their way.

"I don't need this for the silencing spell," Merlin said as he shoved the book into the back pocket of his jeans, "but it might be useful to have with us, just in case…"

Arthur looked at his friend when he trailed off. What they were about to do wasn't really anything less than incredibly foolish, probably terribly dangerous, and, of course, absolutely necessary.

He dutifully remained silent and watched in fascination as Merlin held out a hand towards the wall they shared with Arthur's security team. After a few seconds of concentration, Merlin muttered a string of words. Arthur tried to pick out the individual syllables, but he only heard something that sounded like 'fun id toast' which he guessed probably wasn't Merlin had said.

"That's it," Merlin announced. "We should do the same to the Beaulakes' door, just in case."

Arthur nodded. "Are you sure it definitely worked?"

Merlin shrugged. "Only one way to find out." He grinned, pulled open the bedroom door and then knocked on the security team's door loudly enough that anyone inside would clearly hear.

Arthur held his breath. A few seconds passed but the door remained closed. "Brilliant," Arthur hissed quietly, giving his friend two thumbs up. He then padded softly to Bertie and Gareth's room and knocked very quietly so as not to disturb the other boys on the landing.

Bertie's face appeared in increments as the door inched open. Arthur held his finger to his lips and gestured for Bertie to follow him and Merlin down the corridor. Bertie nodded, then pointed his finger back into the room and mouthed 'Gareth's staying here.'

Arthur couldn't really blame the younger boy; not many people would willingly go trailing around in the dark when there was at least one sorcerer on the loose, as well as a giant, a mythical beast, and, by the looks of things, some ghosts in robes. Actually, when Arthur thought about it he couldn't quite work out why *he* was so keen to go outside.

The three boys made their way silently towards the stairs, before taking each step down with infinite care, and making sure to avoid the creaky board near the bottom.

Merlin whispered the same words as before, this time his hand pointing towards the Beaulakes' apartment, before turning his attention to unlocking Caerleon's door with a flick of his hand.

"Did he say something about toast?" Bertie hissed as they made their way outside.

Arthur just shook his head silently, and tried not to laugh at the ridiculous situation. "Merlin, the shield?"

Merlin held up his hand towards Bertie. "Relax. I promise I won't maim you, kill you, or otherwise damage you irreparably. It's just a shielding spell."

Bertie flinched slightly, but nodded his assent after only a second of hesitation.

"Sciath," Merlin whispered, then tilted his head appraisingly. "I think that's worked." He then repeated the same word in Arthur's direction, before finally turning his magic on himself.

"We should still try and stay in the shadows," Arthur murmured as they hurried across the bridge. He led the way to the Dining Hall, pressing close to the brickwork as the other two did the same behind him.

"What exactly is the plan, Merlin?" Bertie asked.

"Plan?" Merlin asked in mock surprise. "I don't have one. Arthur?"

"You didn't really expect a plan, did you?" Arthur responded with a grin as they moved stealthily towards the Headmaster's Lodge. There was the unmistakable flicker of candlelight in the lower windows. Whatever was going on surely couldn't be happening without the awareness of the headmaster himself.

"So, what? One of us is just going to wander up to the Lodge and take a peek through the window?" Bertie asked in exasperation as they crouched by the untamed rose bushes covering the front wall of the Dining Hall, before crawling behind an evergreen hedge.

"What an excellent idea, Bertie," Merlin replied. "What do you reckon, Arthur?"

"Thanks for volunteering, Bertie," Arthur added. "We'll keep a lookout from here." He wondered for a moment if he should really be taking this whole thing more seriously.

"What?" Bertie spluttered.

"Oh, go on," Merlin mumbled through a mouthful of leaves. "Nobody will see you."

"Why don't *you* go then?" Bertie grumbled back.

"Because I'm a weed," Merlin replied, "and you're quite intimidating, which would be helpful if there *is* a ghost lurking around.

"You think a ghost can be intimidated?" Bertie asked sceptically.

"We don't actually know that they're ghosts," Merlin grumbled. "That's why you need to go and have a look."

"Guys!" Arthur hissed. "I'll go, alright?"

"No," Bertie replied, stepping out from the safety of the foliage. "I'm going. Merlin, if they see me, I'll kill you. If a ghost comes after me, I'll kill you. Are we clear?"

"Crystal," Merlin replied. "If anything happens to you, I'm a dead man."

"Good lad," Bertie whispered. "Right, I'll be back in a minute."

Bertie darted forwards, stooped low to stay out of sight as much as possible. His feet barely made a sound, even as he navigated the gravel that had spilled out from the borders and littered the path around Kings' Court.

"This is a terrible idea," Merlin whispered as he peered out, trying to avoid being poked in the eye by a thorn-covered branch.

Arthur faced him. "This was *your* idea."

Merlin shrugged. "Yes, but it's still a terrible one."

Arthur shook his head in disbelief as he turned back to check on Bertie's progress, craning his neck and elbowing Merlin when his roommate stepped on his foot.

"I can't see," Merlin complained.

"He's almost there," Arthur hissed.

Bertie was only a few feet from the window. The candlelight reflecting on the panes made it almost impossible for Arthur to see anything through the glass from a distance, and he hoped that Bertie would fare better. As he squinted into the shadows Arthur was suddenly utterly convinced that although this might seem to be the worst idea in the history of the world, it was important for him to find out who, or what, the figures were if he was to understand what was really going on.

"What's happening?" Merlin whispered behind him.

Arthur shook his head to clear it and focused once more on Bertie's progress. "He's at the window."

Merlin, now having reached the threshold of his limited patience, rearranged his limbs so that he could wriggle out from behind the rose bush and take a better look for himself.

Bertie wasn't moving. He was crouched beneath the large window and Arthur was about to whisper to him when suddenly all the lights in the Headmaster's Lodge were extinguished at once.

"What just happened?" Merlin asked quietly, one foot frozen in mid-air as he stilled immediately. It would have been comical if not for the large, wooden door to the Lodge creaking open slowly only metres away from their hiding place.

Arthur reached out and grabbed the back of Merlin's

jumper, pulling him back into the shelter of the rose bushes. Merlin's back hit the wall of the Dining Hall, and the quiet *'oomph'* that escaped his lips in surprise sounded, to Arthur at least, loud enough to wake the dead.

Merlin pressed his hands over his mouth, his eyes wide in shock as Arthur tugged on his sleeve in a soundless instruction to crouch down. Merlin inclined his head slightly in the direction of the Lodge and the silent question was clear; *Where's Bertie?*

Arthur, careful to take shallow breaths instead of the gulps of surprise his lungs seemed to be begging for, shifted slowly to peer out through the bushes. He frowned when he realised that he couldn't see Bertie anywhere. He ducked his head, eyes darting around Kings' Court for any clue to his friend's whereabouts.

"Arthur," Merlin breathed, his hand appearing in Arthur's peripheral vision, finger pointed towards the Lodge.

Arthur followed the direction of Merlin's gesture and had to fight the urge to run as four black-clad figures emerged from the Lodge in silence. The hooded robes still obscured their faces, but Arthur was sure that they weren't ghosts as he watched white clouds of breath condense in the cold night air. Ghosts didn't breathe, did they?

The group moved in the direction of the Caerleon bridge, passing only inches from the two boys who were barely breathing for fear of being discovered. They could only hope that they wouldn't be noticed, and that Merlin's charm would be enough to keep them out of sight.

The first two figures drifted past Arthur and he could feel Merlin backing away even further next to him. It was only now that they were here that it occurred to Arthur that the hooded figures might be the ones responsible for the giant. They might be sorcerers, and if that were the case, there was no way the boys could defend themselves if discovered. Merlin might be a sorcerer, but Arthur doubted he'd be able to take on a group with a proven ability at necromancy.

The figure at the back paused. Slowly it turned its head towards Arthur and Merlin's hiding place as if it knew it was being observed.

Arthur held his breath completely and was slightly concerned that Merlin's heart had stopped because he'd gone so rigidly still beside him. He could only hope once more that Bertie had managed to conceal himself safely elsewhere around the Court.

The figure did not move as another joined it, standing just to the right.

"What is it, Lyonesse?"

Arthur couldn't help flinching slightly at the deep, *familiar* voice. He clenched his fists, fighting the urge to close his eyes and will himself to disappear as his stomach twisted in horror. He turned his head slightly towards Merlin and he saw his thoughts mirrored on Merlin's face; it was the headmaster's voice they had just heard.

"I'm not sure," the first figure – Lyonesse – replied, sounding much younger than the headmaster. "I thought I heard something."

The figure who'd spoken first turned down his hood and Arthur's suspicions were confirmed. Even in the shadows, the dark calculating eyes and oversized nose of Cecil Catterick were recognisable. "There is enchantment in the air."

Merlin somehow managed to tense up further at the headmaster's words. It hadn't occurred to either boy that anyone else would sense Merlin's spells, and now here they were surely about to be discovered.

"The necromancer?" Lyonesse hissed, removing his own hood to reveal a face Arthur thankfully didn't recognise. Scars crisscrossed the man's cheeks in silver threads, standing out in stark contrast against his dark hair. "The creature has been summoned?"

"No." Catterick replied, moving one hand slowly in front of him. "But this too is old magic, perhaps even more ancient than the necromancer we are hunting. There is great power here, although the enchantment itself is weak."

"Can you find the source?"

"No," Catterick replied again. "Weak as it may be, this magic is still drawn from the Earth itself, Brother; An old conjurer like I couldn't hope to unravel the threads of magic here. I've had a sense of this sorcerer before. The night we first suspected that the beast had been resurrected."

"And you're sure it's not the boy?" Lyonesse snapped urgently. "This Merlin Montgomery?"

Arthur was certain Merlin stopped breathing entirely.

"I've told you before, Lyonesse," Catterick sighed. "I could barely detect the magic surrounding him when he arrived here. I doubt he's even aware of his potential abilities. He is *not* our Great Sorcerer. His name, and indeed his slight connection to magic, are nothing more than coincidence."

"And the prince?" Lyonesse cut the headmaster off, a sneer evident in his tone. "Is he also nothing more than a coincidence? Arthur Pendragon, born under the exact stars that were prophecised, is at Badon, and the creature that has stalked our Brothers throughout history has returned. Yet you all still believe it to be *coincidence*."

"Lyonesse," Catterick barked, "I know it's disappointing, but even after all the signs we've received over the past decade, it's likely neither boy is who we've waited for. Arthur is a pleasant young man, but I cannot sense anything of the warrior about him."

Arthur wasn't sure whether he should be offended or relieved at Catterick's judgement.

"However," Catterick continued, "we must still ensure the safety of Arthur Pendragon for the sake of future generations, else our Brothers' work, their sacrifices, will be for naught. The Brotherhood must ensure that the Pendragon line is preserved."

"Is this magic a threat?" Lyonesse seemed to be growing even more impatient, looking around him as though he might be able to pinpoint the sorcerer.

Catterick tilted his head and seemed to ponder on the question. "That remains to be seen," he replied eventually. "*This* power could rebuild the world in an instant, but could destroy all in the blink of an eye."

Arthur's mouth dropped open and out of the corner of his eye he could see that Merlin's jaw had also slackened in surprise. They couldn't possibly be talking about Merlin's concealment charm, could they? Not when Catterick had just explained that he doubted Merlin had magic at all.

"Then surely it must be neutralised," the younger man replied forcibly. "If the great sorcerer truly has not returned then this magic has no place being here. It must be one of *them*. One of *his*."

Merlin risked a questioning glance towards Arthur, but Arthur could only reply with a baffled shake of his head. He had no idea what the two men were talking about now.

"If this sorcerer proves to be a threat then we will

intervene as we have always done," Catterick replied steadily, reaching out to briefly grasp the other man's shoulder in a fatherly gesture. "But you must not forget all that has been foretold, Brother. If the signs *have* been correct, and our time is indeed upon us, then this is magic to be embraced, because without it nothing shall come to pass as it should. Although the Great Sorcerer may not be the boy we expected him to be, that doesn't mean that he has not returned to us in some form. The reports of the giant within our very walls disturb me greatly, but I n-"

"And if it is not our time?"

"Then we protect the legacy as our birth rights dictate, and as our many Brothers have done before us," Catterick inclined his head reverently. "We wait for our king, as our duty commands us."

The sound of small pebbles sprinkling onto the path from a height startled everyone. Arthur and Merlin shrank back even as Catterick and Lyonesse turned abruptly away from the rose bush towards the source of the noise.

"See!' Lyonesse muttered, throwing up his hood immediately. "There is someone here."

"It was nothing more than a bird," Catterick replied. "Or that awful cat the boys at Hainault have adopted."

It was clear to Arthur, even though he could no longer see his face, that Lyonesse was still ready to pounce if any threat was identified.

"Come, Brother," Catterick said quietly. "It is time for all of us to retire. The months ahead will be difficult and we must rest if we are to be fully prepared for the challenges we will face."

Lyonesse remained silent for a long moment, but eventually bowed to Catterick briefly before turning once more and disappearing from Arthur's view.

Catterick made no move to leave, instead he turned his focus back to the other side of the Court. He was obviously more interested in the sound than he'd suggested to Lyonesse, but he remained still as more figures filed out from the Lodge, each bowing respectfully to him as they passed.

When the last figure had departed Catterick turned back towards the Lodge and slowly made his way back inside, the old bolts sliding shut noisily when he closed the door behind him.

Merlin gasped, slipping down the wall until he was sitting in the soil at the base of the roses. "Arthur, what just happened?"

Arthur shook his head mutely. Even if he wasn't wary of making a sound he didn't think he'd be able to find the right words to express his reeling thoughts. "Come on," was all he managed eventually, helping to haul Merlin onto legs that were arguably as unsteady as his own. "We have to find Bertie."

The two boys crept out from their hiding place, jerking in surprise when they saw a figure hurrying across the grass.

"Bertie!" Merlin whispered in relief.

"Are you both okay?" Bertie asked, his voice barely audible as he gestured for the other two to follow him on the grass towards the bridge. "I tried to distract them with the pebbles. I thought for sure they were going to find you!"

Arthur swallowed heavily. "We're okay, but we need to get back inside. I don't know where they all went, but I don't want to run into any of them."

Bertie nodded silently, picking up his pace as they stepped off the forbidden lawn and onto the gravel in front of the bridge. There were still no lights on in the back of the boarding house and thankfully this held true for the front as they scarpered across the bridge and hurried through the archway.

"Arthur, they know about me," Merlin whispered, his fear causing him to speak even though he knew he should be silent.

"No, they don't," Arthur replied. "Not really. Catterick doesn't think you know about your abilities, otherwise he would have known it was you there tonight."

Merlin shook his head, feeling ill, as he flicked his hand towards the door and the locks silently obeyed his request. He twisted the handle gently and pushed the door open wide enough for the three of them to dart into the sanctuary of Caerleon.

They paused at the bottom of the stairs, all three boys taking a moment to revel in the fact they'd somehow managed to escape unseen.

The Caerleon door suddenly opened once more and they froze completely, unable to do anything but blink in surprise as a hooded figure glided into the entranceway and shut the door firmly behind themselves.

Arthur screwed up his face and hoped that Merlin's charm would hold for just a little bit longer. If the figure didn't know to look for them he or she shouldn't be able to see the teenagers.

The figure moved slowly down the corridor, passing only inches from Merlin, who curled into himself for fear of being discovered, but thankfully did not stop. The figure did pause, however, just in front of the door to the Beaulakes' apartment and it was with a sick sense of certainty that Arthur watched the figure draw back his hood to reveal their housemaster.

Merlin clamped a hand over his mouth for the second time that night, just about holding onto a squeak of surprise as Mr Beaulake shrugged off his robe, took a key out of his pocket and disappeared quickly into his family's home.

Bertie looked like he'd been punched in the stomach when Arthur finally got his limbs to obey him and turned towards his friends. Merlin looked distinctly ill, and Arthur knew his expression would closely resemble that of the other two.

A door opened and closed softly somewhere in the house, and the boys raced up the stairs as quietly as possible. They didn't speak as they reached the landing, and Bertie disappeared into his room without another word and only a short nod to the others.

Arthur and Merlin traipsed into their room, both remaining silent as they sat down on their beds and faced each other with matching expressions of alarm.

"Um…" Merlin mumbled eventually.

Arthur could only shrug helplessly in response.

* * * * *

The weeks following that night were strained with a tension that only seemed to tighten as the days raced towards Christmas. Even as the bustling streets of Cambridge began to twinkle in celebration, a shadow seemed to have settled over Badon College tainting the end of Arthur's first term with a bitter hint of foreboding.

"Bad luck, Pendragon." Sib clapped him on the back as they slouched off the sopping rugby pitch, covered from head to toe in an unpleasant combination of rain, mud and grass strains. "It just wasn't your day today."

Arthur ran a hand across his bloody lip, wincing as he pulled once more at the tender skin and felt it split again under his palm. The final rugby session had been an absolute disaster as far as Arthur was concerned. He'd missed passes, botched tackles, and an unfortunate skid on the wet pitch had resulted in a split lip and an achy shoulder.

"Mr Pendragon!" Beaulake called, just as Arthur was about to disappear through the gates with his teammates.

"Yes, sir?" Arthur asked, keeping his face as neutral as possible. He'd avoided interacting with his housemaster any more than was completely necessary after discovering Beaulake was part of this so called 'Brotherhood'.

"What happened out there today?" Beaulake was frowning at him as he gestured for Arthur to wait as he locked the gates to the pitch.

Arthur shrugged. "I'm not sure, sir. My mind was elsewhere."

Beaulake stared hard at him for a long moment before nodding. "Are you going to have a proper opportunity to rest over Christmas, Arthur?" he asked as they followed the others back towards Badon, Hector remaining a respectful distance away.

"Of course, sir," Arthur replied. It was true enough. He had one more evening of freedom here before he'd be whisked off to Cornwall the following morning for the traditional family Christmas; ten long days of formal dinners, dull speeches and plenty of time for Arthur to lock himself in his room and pretend he didn't mind.

"The next couple of terms might be quite challenging," Beaulake added, and Arthur was once more reminded of the conversation he'd overheard between Catterick and Lyonesse. *The months ahead will be difficult and we must rest if we are to be fully prepared for the challenges we will face.*

Arthur just nodded, unable to meet his housemaster's eyes as they crossed the road.

"Arthur…" Beaulake trailed off, looking unsure of himself for a moment. "Has everything been as you expected here at Badon?"

Arthur tilted his head. "Yes, sir." Which would be true if he'd expected to discover that magic existed, his friend was a sorcerer, and a shadowy group of people in robes skulked around Badon at night whispering about enchantments and legacies.

"No more problems with your cousin?"

Arthur shook his head again, and *that* really was the truth. Hugo had returned after a few days at home, and had been conspicuously elusive ever since. In fact, Arthur could count on one hand the number of times he'd seen his cousin around school apart from in the Dining Hall or during Chapel.

"And you've made friends?" Beaulake seemed to be looking for an answer to a question he hadn't really asked. "And you get on well with Merlin?"

"Yes, sir." Arthur replied as they stepped through the gate into Badon. "Merlin's a good friend."

"And he's settled completely too, has he?" Beaulake asked. "No problems?"

A great big neon warning sign starting flashing in Arthur's mind. Beaulake, as part of the Brotherhood, must *know* about magic, might even be capable of magic himself like the headmaster seemed to be. The question now, however, was *did he know about Merlin's magic?* Which quite neatly, and terrifyingly, led on to the question of what they would do if they *did* know.

136

"None, sir," Arthur replied as they crossed the bridge behind the other Caerleonites. "Apart from the fact he's addicted to biscuits and doesn't know how to keep his side of the room tidy."

Beaulake laughed, but it seemed much more strained than the cheerful grins he'd given freely to everyone at the beginning of the year. "Well, I'm glad to hear that, Arthur. It's very important to have friends you can trust."

Arthur did a slight double take. Mrs Beaulake had said almost the exact same thing to him on his first night at Badon all those months ago now. What exactly were the Beaulakes getting at?

"Well, make sure you enjoy your last night here," Beaulake smiled as they reached Caerleon. "Are you going into town?"

Arthur nodded and he couldn't quite keep hold of his grin even though it pulled at his lip once more. "Yes, sir."

"Make sure you pop into Matron before you go so that she can check on that lip," Beaulake nodded sagely. "I'm sure I can trust you all to remember to be back here by eight o'clock?"

"Yes, sir," Arthur nodded as dutifully as he could before clattering up the stairs as quickly as possible. He practically burst through the bedroom door, startling Merlin enough that his friend dropped the duffle bag he'd been carrying across the room in surprise.

"Bloody hell, Arthur!" Merlin clutched his chest dramatically. "Are you trying to give me a heart attack?"

"I think Beaulake knows about your magic." Arthur said hurriedly.

"What?" Merlin paled immediately. "What? How? What?"

"He just asked me if everything had been as I expected it to be here at Badon," Arthur explained, very aware of the fact he was dripping mud on the carpet. "He wanted to know if there were any problems with you. He told me it was good that I had friends I could trust."

Merlin frowned. "That doesn't mean he knows about my magic."

"Maybe," Arthur replied, "but I got the feeling that he *thinks* he knows. Remember what the headmaster said about the Brotherhood having their 'suspicions'. Even if Catterick didn't pick up on your magic when he met you, maybe the coincidence of your name, and you and me being here together is enough for him. Maybe you should avoid doing any magic for a while."

"Arthur I haven't cast a single spell since Catterick said he could sense that concealment charm," Merlin replied. His frown deepened into annoyance as more mud dripped off Arthur's shoes. "Seriously, could you at least stand on a towel?"

"Merlin, focus!" Arthur barked, but grabbed the towel from the end of his bed and dropped it on the floor to collect the muddy droplets running down his rugby kit.

"I'm not planning on using magic any time soon," Merlin held up his hands. "Alright? Beaulake won't find out."

Arthur could only hope this wasn't a case of 'famous last words'.

*　*　*　*　*

"I wish we were allowed out like this all the time!" Gareth announced from somewhere beneath the enormously fluffy hat and scarf combination he was bundled up in. He was gripping a takeaway hot chocolate in one hand and a plastic bag stuffed to the brim with fudge in the other. Sib had to keep pulling him back onto the pavement when he got distracted by various window displays.

"Don't even think about it!" Merlin shouted without even turning around.

Arthur gawped, the arm holding the snowball he'd just been about to let fly into the back of his friend's head dropping to his side instantly. "How did you know I was going to do anything?"

"He's got eyes in the back of his head!" Kay brayed loudly.

"Nope!" Merlin grinned cheekily. "Arthur's just really predictable."

Arthur felt he was then well within his rights to re-aim the snowball and send it hurtling right into Merlin's surprised face. He led the raucous laughter that followed, Merlin muttering about revenge as he dusted off his coat.

"Busy Christmas ahead, Arthur?" Leo asked as they filed around the corner onto Watling Street.

Arthur shook his head. "Not too bad. You?"

Leo shrugged. "Back home tomorrow, then off to Switzerland with Mum, Dad and my sister on Friday. Then we'll go to my Gran's for New Year; she's a complete disaster in the kitchen. Her Christmas cake is feared for miles around!"

Arthur grinned. He liked all of the Caerleon second years, but Leo especially could be relied upon to lighten any situation, even though he was incredibly serious when it came to schoolwork and rugby. "That sounds fun."

"'Fun' isn't quite the word I'd use," Leo replied.

Arthur wanted to disagree; it all sounded far more

interesting than the schedule his father had emailed through to Hector just before they'd escaped for the evening. According to the numerous typed pages, Arthur was expected to be in the car and ready to leave at eight the next morning, and then he was booked solidly into engagements until he returned to Badon a few days into January. Merlin had taken one look at Arthur's timetable ("You have a *printout* for Christmas?") and immediately declared that the Pendragons clearly had no idea what Christmas was supposed to be like.

"Do you at least have mince pies?" Merlin had asked in horror after he'd tried to pronounce the names of Arthur's seventeen Swedish relatives who were attending dinner on Christmas Eve.

"Of course we have mince pies," Arthur had rolled his eyes. "We have a pastry chef."

"You know," Merlin had wrinkled his nose in distaste, "there are times when I forget just how weird your life is."

"*My* life is weird?" Arthur had exclaimed.

"Yeah." Merlin had shrugged in his usual manner. "I'm a sorcerer and my mum's nuts, but you have a pastry chef, and seem to be related to everyone in Sweden. Don't you just want a boring old normal Christmas?"

Arthur had taken a leaf out of Merlin's book and shrugged back. Merlin was annoyingly right, as he often was; Arthur *did* want a boring old normal Christmas, but he'd never had one, and he was never likely to either.

"It's our final night here!" Gareth waved his arms towards the towers of Badon's entrance and for a second he looked a bit taller than usual. Maybe his father had been right about that growth spurt after all.

"Only for a couple of weeks, Gareth," Eric replied with

140

a laugh. "Don't get too excited."

All four housemasters were waiting on the other side of the gate, ticking boys off as they returned from their evening in the city.

"Ah, good," Beaulake grinned as Arthur and his friends trooped in. "Dorner, Chopra the elder, Kay, Montgomery, Allard, Chopra the younger, Troyes, Chevalier and Pendragon." He crossed Arthur's name out with a flourish. "Ten minutes to spare, well done. I'll see you all for breakfast."

A chorus of variations on "Goodnight, Mr Beaulake' was returned as the boys trooped across Chapel Court and into Caerleon House, pulling off various layers and woolly items as they shook the light sprinkling of snow from their clothes.

"It's a shame old Catterick banned snowball fights," Rajendra said despondently as he looked out of the entranceway's small window. "I bet we'd have time for a good one in the morning."

"Yeah, well we can blame the Kings' lot for that," Bertie shook his head. "Hugo included."

"What?" Arthur frowned. "Why?"

"Last year there was a snowball fight between Caerleon and Kings'," Kay said, dropping into storyteller mode as everyone hung up their coats to dry. "We were lowly first years then - no offence to you four obviously - so we weren't invited. Let's just say Caerleon was winning by miles when His Royal Highness over there, and his idiot friends, decided to take matters into their own hands and start an actual fight."

"That sounds about right for Hugo," Merlin grumbled. Arthur knew he was still annoyed about the fact he hadn't had much opportunity to exact any further revenge on the Prince of York since he'd returned to school.

"I've never seen Catterick so mad," Kay continued.

"And Mr Beaulake wasn't far behind," Leo added. "If Hugo was anyone else he would have been sent away for Christmas and never allowed back."

Arthur swallowed heavily. He knew the others were his friends, but he still felt tarnished by the same brush whenever his cousin did something awful.

"The perks of being royal," Arthur tried to joke, but the words tasted like sawdust.

"Well, our royal's far superior!" Bertie announced, nudging Arthur with a grin. "And we'll show them who's better next term when the inter house matches start!"

Arthur tried to grin back as Kay led a chant of 'Caerleon! Caerleon!' as they trooped up the stairs, but he couldn't quell the now familiar feeling of unease that had settled in his stomach weeks ago. Something was wrong; but he just didn't know what.

* * * * *

Arthur was dreaming again. It was nothing more than a mishmash of reds and blues, gold and black, and featureless faces fading in and out of his vision. There was a crackling in the air and he thought that if he could reach out and touch it, it would make the hair on his arms and the back of his neck stand to attention immediately. There were voices, but what they were saying he couldn't tell; low, gravelly tones fighting for dominance with a high-pitched scream.

"Arthur," a voice said, and Arthur squinted into his dreamscape wondering why it sounded familiar suddenly.

Fog began to roll in at the sides of his vision, scooping

up the faceless figures and twirling them into oblivion before they disappeared completely.

"Arthur."

That voice was definitely familiar and he looked around for the source.

"Oh, for crying out loud, Arthur!"

Arthur's eyes snapped open to see Merlin standing by his bed, hands folded across his chest in a familiar expression of impatience.

"What?" Arthur grumbled, rubbing at his face and glancing towards the clock. His mouth opened in surprised. "It's quarter past two in the morning, Merlin!"

"Yes, I know that, thank you," Merlin replied, "but I thought you might want to know that you've got post."

"Post?" Arthur frowned, pushing himself up into a sitting position. "What do you mean, *post*?"

"Post!" Merlin announced again holding out an envelope to Arthur. "That just came under the door. It's addressed to you, and considering it's weird to get post in the middle of the night I thought it might be important."

Arthur reached to switch on the bedside lamp, but Merlin stopped him.

"Wait," Merlin said, "if you put the light on people might see and then you'll have teachers trooping over here demanding to know why we're awake."

"Well I can't read in the dark, Merlin," Arthur replied. "And we don't get our phones back until morning so it's not like we can use them as torches. Oh, and you're *not* using magic, remember? So it's the lamp or nothing."

Merlin looked annoyed, but also as though he completely agreed with the logic. He was the one to switch on the lamp, with a hissed, "Make it quick."

Arthur ripped open the envelope and pulled out the small piece of folded paper. He frowned as he read the words, and then read them again to make sure.

"Er," said Merlin peering at the paper from above. "It's upside down from here, but I'm fairly sure that says you've just been summoned to a snowball fight on the rugby pitches in fifteen minutes."

Arthur scratched behind his ear in confusion. "It does say that, doesn't it?"

"Well that's weird," Merlin replied, blinking as if that would help him make sense of the situation. "Someone's idea of a joke?"

"Maybe," Arthur replied. "Maybe not."

Merlin's eyes widened. "What if it's the sorcerer actually challenging you to a duel!"

"Why would a sorcerer challenge me to a duel, Merlin?" Arthur asked, putting the letter down next to him.

"Maybe it's just trying to lure you out of Badon," Merlin replied with a shiver. "Then the giant's going to eat you, or that Questing Beast thing will do it instead."

"Could be," Arthur replied, eerily calm.

"You're not thinking of going, are you?" Merlin hissed.

A very soft knock at the door startled them. Arthur padded over to the door and opened it a crack to find an agitated looking Bertie on the other side.

Bertie opened his mouth to speak and Arthur held up a finger to silence him. Then he turned to Merlin, titling his head towards the RPS's room and wiggling his fingers in a silent instruction. Maybe now wasn't the best time for Merlin to be holding his magic back after all.

Merlin, with only slight hesitation, held up his hand and mumbled the charm that sounded like it had something to do with toast again. When he nodded, Arthur beckoned Bertie into the room and closed the door behind them, knowing that Hector and co. wouldn't be able to hear a thing.

"What's going on?" Arthur asked quickly.

"Someone put an envelope under our door," Bertie replied. "It said something about a snowball fight on the rugby pitches. Caerleon versus Kings'. I haven't heard anything about it and wanted to know if you'd got one too."

Arthur held up his envelope. "I did."

"There's something weird about this, Arthur," Bertie replied. "If anyone was planning this they would have made sure we knew about it earlier. The bottom of the note says that the doors and gates will all be unlocked. Nobody has the keys to be able to do that other than the caretakers, the housemasters, and the headmaster himself."

Merlin frowned. "Bertie, at the beginning of term you said you knew how to get out of school without people knowing, so someone else *must* have a key. You, maybe?"

Bertie seemed to go pink. "Elaine sometimes unlocks the door for me if I really need to get out of school."

Merlin twitched. "Now isn't the time, but can one of you remind me to mock Bertie mercilessly about this when we know what's going on. I'm not letting this opportunity pass."

Bertie ignored him, which was probably the sensible thing to do. "Gareth thinks it might be the sorcerer. Somehow they've found out that we know about magic too and we're being lured out of school."

"That's what I said!" Merlin hissed. "Look, I think it's finally my turn to be the sensible one again and say we really need to tell someone about this."

"Who?" Arthur asked. "If we tell Hector he'll probably send a team down there. If it *is* the sorcerer then they'll be completely defenceless. I can't do that to Hector, Merlin, and don't you dare say 'that's his job'!"

Merlin looked suitably chastised. "What about Beaulake then? He and his hooded friends might actually know how to get rid of the sorcerer!"

"And how do we explain how we know about magic?" Arthur asked, crossing his arms. "Hmm? Do you *really* want them to find out about you? Remember what Catterick said about the magic he could sense? What he said about *your* magic, Merlin. He said the Brotherhood would intervene if it needed to. If they see you as a threat you don't know what they'll do to you…what they'll do to any of us."

A creak on the staircase called time on their conversation. Arthur, frowning again, hurried to the door and opened it, but he couldn't see anyone on the far side of the landing.

"Er, guys?" Merlin said hesitantly a few seconds later from where he was looking out of the window. "Gareth's just run over the bridge."

Arthur and Bertie looked at each other in horror.

"We have to go after him!" Arthur said, pulling on shoes and a jumper over his pyjamas.

"We need to tell someone," Merlin repeated even as Bertie left the room, presumably to prepare for going outside.

"Merlin," Arthur said seriously, "if you think it's the right thing to do then you go and tell someone. I'm leaving right now with Bertie, and I'm sure we'll be fine, but Merlin, I'd be an awful lot happier if we had you there as well."

Merlin looked at him for a long moment. "Oh, fine," he huffed eventually, digging around for his shoes in the dark. "But if you get us killed, we're not friends anymore. And my Mum will probably become an anarchist. Just so you know."

If it hadn't been so apparent that they might genuinely be in real danger, Arthur would have laughed at that. Instead he waited silently for Bertie to return, and then the three of them made their way noiselessly down the stairs, Merlin whispering the concealment charm once more, just in case they should encounter anyone else.

"This is definitely the stupidest idea yet," Merlin announced when they made their way through the unlocked Back Gate. "Where the hell has Gareth got to? I thought he said he was terrible at running?"

"I thought he said he was terrified of monsters," Arthur added as they ran across the blessedly empty road. The snow was still coming down, peppering their clothes with enough flakes that Arthur knew they'd be soaked to the skin within minutes.

"He kept saying he felt guilty for not coming down to the Headmaster's Lodge with us," Bertie replied with a sigh. "He thought he'd let his friends down by hiding in his room."

"That's' ridiculous," Arthur replied as they reached the tall iron gate that separated the rugby pitches from the pavement.

"Try telling Gareth that," Bertie replied, in a tone of voice that suggested he *had* tried telling Gareth that. More than once.

Just like at Badon, the gate to the pitches swung open with just a push from Arthur. The pitch, which had been so damp earlier that day, wasn't covered in anywhere near enough snow for a snowball fight. Arthur guessed the grass had been too wet for the snow to settle as even now there was nothing more than a light dusting in stark contrast to the inch or so that had covered the pavements across the Backs.

Gareth was standing at the far edge of the first pitch and the boys immediately took off across the grass towards him.

"Gareth!" Bertie hissed as they ran. "Gareth!"

Gareth turned to face them, a look of surprise and embarrassment crossing his features. He was clutching a piece of paper in one hand and he stuffed it into his pocket quickly.

"What's that?" Arthur asked, pointing to the concealed note.

"Nothing." Gareth shook his head. "It doesn't matter. The sorcerer's not here anyway."

"Nobody's here," Merlin added as he turned in a slow circle to survey the pitches. "Nobody at all."

Arthur frowned again. It didn't make any sense; why would someone, or some*thing*, lure them away from Badon for no reason?

A snarl ripped through the night air, immediately derailing Arthur's thought process as he whipped around looking for the source of the noise. "*Nobody at all*, Merlin?" He snapped when the familiar shape of the giant rose up at the perimeter of the pitch, silver ribbons of light whirling around it as it raised the wooden club above its head and roared again. It seemed much larger than before, as though it had been stretched to twice its original height, and it now dwarfed the tall screening trees that ran the whole way around the pitch.

"Surely that's woken someone," Bertie said as the four boys moved closer together. "Surely."

Gareth squeaked, in a way that Arthur presumed demonstrated fear, but then the younger boy started running *towards* the giant.

Merlin, who despite his lack of athletic ability actually had decent reflexes, made a grab for the running boy but his fingers only closed around air as Gareth darted to the left in a move that wouldn't have been out of place in a rugby match.

"Gareth!" Arthur yelled, racing after him, Bertie on his heels. "Gareth, what are you doing?!"

Gareth just kept running. But Arthur hadn't made it onto the Caerleon team for nothing, and with a silent apology to his friend Arthur increased his pace for a few strides before lunging for Gareth and sending them both toppling to the ground with a bone-shaking thud.

Gareth cried out in surprise, and Arthur groaned when he rolled onto his back and jarred his already aching shoulder again. Sib had been right, today really hadn't been Arthur's day.

"Up!" Bertie barked as he hauled Gareth to his feet, before reaching down to help Arthur to stand.

Merlin reached them then. "I hate running," he grumbled.

"Well, I suggest you start liking it," Arthur said, keeping his eyes fixed on the advancing giant as the boys began to back away. "It can't see us, but it knows we're here."

"Please tell me you have a plan, Arthur," Merlin muttered out of the corner of his mouth. "Banishing rocks is one thing, but you know it didn't work with the giant last time."

"Did you bring the book?" Arthur asked quietly. The giant had paused and was looking around and inhaling deeply, searching for any hint of prey.

"Ah…" Merlin replied sheepishly.

"You didn't bring the book?!" Arthur shouted, immediately alerting the giant to their presence.

"Why do you *always* shout when there's a giant around?" Merlin shot back.

"Everybody shut up and run!" Bertie ordered, leading the way back towards the gate.

Arthur didn't argue. He waited for Merlin and Gareth to pass him and then took up his place at the back of the group. He chanced a look over his shoulder and was horrified to see the wooden club arcing through the air towards them. "Look out!"

The others all turned awkwardly at Arthur's shout, and Merlin, with a yelp of surprise, tripped over his own feet and stumbled so violently that Bertie had to grab his arm to keep him upright.

The club was getting closer, whistling through the air as it reached its peak and began swooping towards the boys. Merlin held up a hand and started muttering the same word he'd been practising at the Botanic Gardens, but the club showed no sign of changing its trajectory or slowing down even a fraction. Impact was imminent and the boys were perfect targets.

"Get out of the way!" Arthur dived to the left, hoping that the others would heed his instruction and make it to safety in time. He winced as the club hit the ground with enough force to make the pitch shake beneath him, and the booming sound ricocheted around the sports ground in a repeating loop.

Arthur scrabbled to his feet, his eyes wide as he took in the crater the club had punched into the ground. For a split-second he allowed himself to wonder what the teachers would think when they discovered it, but then he was looking around frantically for his friends. "Is everyone okay?"

Bertie was the first to emerge. He was white as a sheet and had his mouth open in horror as he crawled to his feet only scant inches from the club. "That was close."

"Merlin?" Arthur called. "Gareth? Bertie, can you see them?" He looked to Bertie, but the older boy shook his head. Arthur's heart sank at the sight; surely his friends had jumped out of the way in time, they *must* have escaped somehow. They *must* have.

"Arthur! Look!"

Arthur's head snapped up and he followed the direction of Bertie's arm. He was immediately hit by a welcome wave of relief as he caught sight of Merlin and Gareth's silhouettes in the distance. This relief was short lived, however, when he realised that his friends were once more heading towards the giant rather than away from it.

"What are they doing?" Bertie exclaimed as Gareth stopped and started waving his arms around.

"I have no idea," Arthur replied as he sprinted alongside his teammate. As they got closer they could hear snatches of Gareth yelling at the giant, which was now advancing towards him at a quicker pace than before.

The giant roared, raising its arms above its head before bringing them down with force onto the pitch. The ground around the boys trembled in response and Arthur had to rebalance himself with a quick change of direction.

"Give me that!" Merlin shouted to Gareth just as Arthur

and Bertie reached them.

Arthur watched as Merlin grabbed Gareth's closed fist and tried to retrieve the piece of paper being grasped there.

"Gareth! You're not a sorcerer, it won't work without magic!" Merlin cried, trying to pry the other boy's fingers apart.

Gareth yelled incomprehensibly at the giant but refused to give up the hold he had on the paper. "I can do this! I can do this!"

The giant was bearing down on them, only strides from where they were.

"Gareth!" Merlin yelled, grabbing his arm roughly. "Give me the spell!"

"Gareth!" Bertie barked, just as Arthur shouted, "Merlin!"

Merlin looked up. The giant was nearly upon them; its grasping fingers reaching out to snatch whichever boy it could reach first.

"Do something!" Arthur implored.

Merlin threw his arms above his head, but had only managed to utter the first breath of a syllable when the giant's hand swiped at him. Merlin was tossed up into the air like a ragdoll, his arms flailing wildly as he was thrown across the pitch to land in a crumpled, unmoving heap by the gate.

Arthur and Bertie were frozen in shock as Gareth yelled Merlin's name in panic. Their fallen friend wasn't moving even as the giant strode towards him.

"Stay here!" Arthur said firmly to Bertie and Gareth. "Wait until I've distracted that thing, then get to Merlin as quickly as you can."

"Arthur, it's too dangerous!" Bertie shook his head.

"We've got no way of stopping it if it comes after you."

"Just do it!" Arthur snapped. Bertie was right, but doing nothing wasn't going to help Merlin. He turned and sprinted behind the giant, his legs burning with the effort as the sodden ground seemed to get slicker with every stride.

"Oi!" Arthur shouted as he closed the gap between them. "Turn around! Hey! Over here! HEY!"

Arthur was firmly aware that shrieking at a murderous giant seemed like a fairly terrible thing to do, but he still almost grinned in triumph when the creature stopped and turned its sightless face in Arthur's direction.

"Come on!" Arthur yelled as loud as he could manage. "Come and get me!"

The giant snarled just once in warning before it began lumbering towards the shouting boy. Arthur twisted and began running again, shouting encouragement to the giant as he led it away from Merlin, straight past a gobsmacked Bertie and Gareth, and onto the far pitch, changing direction every few strides to ensure he wasn't caught. An idea had taken seed in his mind and he turned abruptly to find himself right in the middle of the pitch.

"Is that the best you can do?" Arthur shouted over his shoulder as he ran in a straight line towards the goalposts. He heard the giant speed up behind him and could feel a rush of air every time it planted a foot on the pitch, gaining on him with every step.

Arthur closed his eyes for a brief second and hoped with every fibre of his being that his half-formed plan would be enough. A hand swooped down next to him and he leapt forwards, throwing himself over the mottled grey fingers in a desperate lunge.

His lungs emptied on impact with the ground and he

barely had time to register what had happened before the giant's other hand reached down to him. Arthur rolled out of the way before scrambling to his feet, skidding slightly on the snow-covered grass.

The giant roared in dissatisfaction as Arthur darted forwards. He was only steps from the goalposts and the sight gave him the energy for a final burst of speed as he ran under the crossbar, just about managing to stop an inch from the line of trees that separated Badon's pitches from the University-owned ones on the other side.

Arthur turned just in time to see the giant run straight into the goalpost. He watched in fascination as the creature's legs hit the crossbar and it flailed forwards. Its arms reached out to grasp at nothing as it tumbled over the bar and landed, face down on the grass, one arm flattening a clump of trees.

"Yes!" Arthur shouted in triumph as the creature remained motionless on the ground, but the smile dropped off his face when he looked into the distance and could just about make out two figures standing by the gate. Two, not three.

Arthur wasted no more time on the giant and began sprinting towards his friends. He swiped at his face, cringing when he realised that his lip had begun bleeding once more. With every step, he told himself that Merlin would be up and about being completely insufferable by the time Arthur reached him.

When he was only metres from his friends, a light blinked in Arthur's peripheral vision. It was the same weak silver as the wispy threads that had heralded the giant's appearance. He turned his head immediately to locate the source and his eyes widened in surprise when he saw a hooded figure standing at the edge of the pitch. He couldn't see the figure's eyes, but Arthur instinctively knew he was being watched.

He was about to call out to the figure when a terrifying roar rose up behind him. Arthur whirled on instinct, his heart racing as he discovered that the giant was no longer face down on the ground, but instead striding towards him and far, far closer than it should be.

There was nothing Arthur could do to halt the sweep of the giant's hand as it reached to close its fingers tightly around him. He couldn't even make a sound of distress as he felt his ribs protesting against the crushing weight around his chest.

Arthur kicked his legs desperately, but even as his foot connected with the giant's palm he knew it was useless. How could a teenage boy possibly take on the wrath of a giant and expect to win? But Arthur refused to give in and held on tightly to every thread of instinct that told him to keep fighting.

He was concentrating so hard on his predicament that Arthur was more than a little surprised when the giant released him suddenly and he dropped onto the pitch with a dull thump. He barely had time to thank his lucky stars that the giant hadn't been holding him particularly far off the ground before he was rendered useless in astonishment.

Merlin was standing – Bertie propping him up slightly on the left – arms raised towards the giant, a look of intense concentration on his face. Gareth was backing away towards the gate.

The air was filled with the same static Arthur had sensed in his dream and he couldn't help but remember what old Catterick had said about Merlin's magic being the kind that could bring destruction in the blink of an eye. It wasn't difficult to believe that when the look on his friend's face was unsettlingly blank, with not even a hint of the bumbling schoolboy he usually was.

Merlin brought his hands together in a clasp and Arthur watched in fascinated horror as the giant copied the motion. The angered roars that followed suggested that the action was against its will. The giant struggled against binds Arthur couldn't see and the most he could do was turn to stare at his friend in ever growing wonder.

Just as Arthur thought the situation had reached maximum weirdness Merlin finally spoke, in a low voice devoid of warmth.

"Scrios mé tú."

Arthur had no way to translate the words Merlin had said, but he shivered as he *felt* the meaning behind the words. *I destroy you.*

Lightning arced through the sky over Cambridge, streaking through the snow clouds and tinting them a deep blue. With a cry, Arthur scrabbled backwards on his hands as the giant began to dissolve into ash before his eyes.

The silence that followed was almost louder than the crack of thunder that had accompanied the giant's final breath.

Arthur pushed himself to his feet, wrapping an arm around his aching ribs as he stared at his three friends. "What just happened?" He staggered towards Merlin. "Are you alright?"

Merlin nodded weakly, looking as astounded as Arthur felt.

Gareth was wringing his hands, his back pressed against the gate when Arthur looked over at him. "I found a spell," he babbled. "I found a spell that I thought would work. I thought I could stop it. I thought I could stop it."

Arthur opened his mouth to respond when a slight movement on the other side of the gate caught his eye. He looked, expecting the hooded figure who had inexplicably disappeared from the side lines, but instead Elaine Beaulake was staring back at him with a look of sheer horror frozen on her face.

"Elaine?" Arthur gasped.

"Elaine?" Bertie frowned before he whirled around quickly. His jaw dropped as he saw the same sight as Arthur.

Elaine remained motionless for a long moment and Arthur's mind floundered desperately for something to say; something that would somehow explain to Elaine what she had just witnessed.

Elaine, however, had no intention of staying for the explanation. She darted away from the gate and was lost to the shadows of the Backs before anyone could call her back.

"Oh great," Merlin breathed, slithering out of Bertie's grasp and sitting down hard on the grass. "She's going to tell her father, isn't she?"

Arthur couldn't bring himself to reply. He just sank slowly onto the grass next to his friend and hoped that they hadn't just ruined everything.

6

CATTERICK & ALDERLEY

Describing Arthur's Christmas holiday as tense would be the world's greatest understatement. From the second he'd set foot in the Pendragon's Cornish residence he'd been expecting a summons to his father's office where he would inevitably have to explain what had happened on the rugby pitches the night before term ended.

But the days passed and Arthur heard nothing from Badon; no letters or phone calls announcing that he'd been expelled for breaking a million school rules and harbouring a sorcerer. Even if Elaine hadn't told her parents, surely the hooded figure on the pitch would have reported back to the Brotherhood, and therefore the headmaster. Arthur tried not to dwell on the thought that even though he'd heard Catterick say that the Brotherhood was bound to protect the Pendragon line, the hooded figure may well have been the headmaster himself.

Arthur and his friends hadn't managed to catch up with Elaine on the way back to Caerleon because they'd had to work together to prop Merlin up for long enough to return him safely to his bed, where he'd promptly passed out until well after Arthur had been required to leave the next morning.

Bertie had called Arthur just once, only a few hours after he'd left Cambridge, and told him that he hadn't spoken to Elaine before leaving either as she'd been conspicuously absent from the final breakfast.

Arthur had sent a handful of texts to Merlin but hadn't received anything back. The only reason Arthur wasn't worrying about whether Merlin was alive and well was that he'd phoned him once, a few days into the holiday, and Mrs Montgomery had answered.

"Merlin can't talk right now, I'm afraid," she'd said. "He's stirring the jam and if he stops it'll burn."

"Oh, right," Arthur had replied, not daring to ask if the stirring could possibly be interrupted for just a few seconds. "Would you mind asking him to call me, please?"

"Of course, dear." Mrs Montgomery had responded in a distracted voice. "Who did you say was calling again?"

"Arthur."

"And you're Merlin's friend from school?"

"That's right." Arthur was reminded of Merlin's inability to recall names. "Would you tell him it's important?"

"I'll tell him. Merry Christmas, Andrew!" She'd then cheerfully rung off and Arthur had been left holding the phone with the distinct impression that Merlin wasn't going to receive that message at all.

The silence that had followed had confirmed his suspicions.

As for Gareth; he seemed to have retreated into a cave of shame. He'd barely spoken on the way back to Badon after the giant had been destroyed other than to apologise for thinking that he would have been able to stop the giant himself, that he'd just wanted to help.

Arthur wasn't stupid; he knew that there was no way they'd be able to get away from what happened in Cambridge, not with Elaine as a witness and the Brotherhood skulking around. So it was with a sense of dread therefore that Arthur answered the knock on his bedroom door on Christmas Eve just as he was knotting his tie.

"Mother?" Arthur frowned in surprise as he opened the door to reveal the woman on the other side.

The Queen smiled at her only child, nudging Arthur gently until he moved out of the way. She floated into the room and the familiar scent of flowers surrounded her in an invisible cloud. She was already dressed for the formal dinner with their Swedish family, and her dress shimmered with the deep reds, blacks and golds of the Pendragon ceremonial colours.

"We haven't had a chance to catch up, have we?" she asked softly as she took a seat on the edge of Arthur's bed and gestured for her son to join her.

Arthur shook his head as he sat down. "You've been busy."

"Tell me about school, Arthur," his mother prompted. "Hector's been keeping us informed, and your teachers seem very pleased with you." She smiled at him. "You always have been a hard worker."

Arthur ducked his head at the praise. "It's been interesting." He chose his words carefully. "I like it there. I have some good friends."

"Good," the Queen replied, and the note of relief in her voice was clear. "Your father hoped that you would enjoy your time at Badon as much as he did when he was your age; although perhaps not get into quite as much trouble as he and his friends did."

Arthur felt he shouldn't point out that his father's occasional acts of schoolboy rebellion paled in comparison to the events of Arthur's first term, so he simply smiled as best he could in response. "Of course, Mother."

"Your father and I will try to come to one of your rugby matches next term," the Queen promised. "We're so proud of you for making the team."

Arthur wouldn't get his hopes up. His parents had made him many promises throughout his life that they hadn't been able to keep; not through choice, but because duty demanded that they be elsewhere. "I'd like that. If you can."

"Now," his mother whispered conspiratorially as she leaned forward slightly, "your father's family has just arrived and Henrik has already started sampling the mulled wine."

Arthur snorted. His father's cousin, Henrik, tended to drink too much wine and then become very argumentative over the smallest of matters. Last Christmas, a gentle discussion about which game they should play after dinner erupted into all-out war when Henrik's choice of Battleship was vetoed in favour of Trivial Pursuit. Subsequent visitors to the parlour had found pieces of the game for weeks afterwards following Henrik upending the board in a fit of rage and scattering the plastic wedges and cards everywhere.

"Come and help me keep the peace?" his mother asked standing up and holding out her arm for her son.

Arthur took her hand with a grin. "I'll try, but if Henrik starts shouting I'm going to pretend I have a headache and go straight to bed."

"Clever boy." The Queen laughed as they left the room behind and descended the vast, winding staircase. "I really *am* glad that you've settled so well at school, Arthur. I was so worried that you'd find it too much of a change."

An almost overwhelming sense of guilt washed over Arthur as they approached the drawing room. He hadn't spent much time with his mother in the past few years, but they'd always been close when he'd been younger, and somehow not telling her the truth about Badon felt like a betrayal.

"Mother?" he asked hesitantly as they reached the drawing room door. "If you knew something, but thought that nobody would believe you if you told them because it all seemed so impossible, should you try and tell someone anyway?"

The Queen blinked a few times. "That sounds rather complicated, Arthur." She frowned. "Is there something you need to talk to me about?"

"No." Arthur shook his head quickly. "It's just a hypothetical question, that's all."

His mother's frown deepened. "I think you should always be honest with the people you trust the most," she replied eventually. "Particularly you, Arthur."

"Even if it means giving up someone else's secret?" Arthur asked carefully.

"Keeping secrets often leads to trouble, Arthur," his mother replied with a sigh. "Has something happened at school?"

"No," Arthur repeated, forcing a tight smile onto his face. "Honestly, it's nothing. I was just curious."

His mother seemed ready to ask another question, but then Henrik's raised voice came from inside the drawing room and ended the conversation prematurely. The Queen lifted her chin into as regal a pose as possible and nodded to her son. "Duty calls."

Arthur sighed as he followed his mother into the fray.

* * * * *

Arthur frowned as he looked at his watch again. It was heading towards six o'clock, as it had been the last few times he'd checked. There was still there was no sign of Merlin, even though it was long past when all boys were due to be back in school after the holiday.

That really should have been the first sign that something was wrong.

The second sign came when Hector opened the bedroom door without warning and asked Arthur to follow him to the Headmaster's Lodge. He'd only been back at Badon for a few hours and had spent most of that time alone in his room, waiting for his friends; he certainly hadn't done anything that would draw the headmaster's attention.

Arthur gulped, hesitantly unfolded himself from where he'd be lying on his bed and followed Hector out of the room and down the stairs, tugging on his suit jacket as he went. As they passed the boys of Caerleon on their way out of the boarding house and across the bridge Arthur couldn't quite bring himself to return the grins and friendly waves he received.

This is it, he thought as they crossed Kings' Court. *This is the end of my time at Badon. Catterick knows what happened before Christmas.*

"What's this about?" Arthur asked as Hector pulled the chain that would ring the Lodge's doorbell.

"I don't know," Hector replied. "One of the older boys was sent to pass on the message to me, and here we are."

The door creaked open and Arthur half-expected a robed member of the Brotherhood to be waiting on the other side, but in reality it was just the headmaster's housekeeper;

a stern-faced woman whose hair was drawn so severely back from her face it pulled her skin taut and widened her eyes into a permanent expression of surprise.

"Good evening." The housekeeper nodded her head at Hector. Arthur had no idea what her name was – he'd never been told – and she continued to ignore him as he followed Hector into the building.

Arthur had only been in the Lodge once and then he'd been nervous enough about his interview that he hadn't really paid attention to his surroundings. As he followed Hector and the housekeeper up the narrow staircase to the first floor he found his eyes drawn to the paintings on the wall. There were portraits of every headmaster since the school's foundation; each man a Catterick by blood, except for the very first, staring down at Arthur as he passed below.

He wondered, as the housekeeper led them along the landing to the headmaster's study, just how many of the beady eyes above him had once been concealed underneath the robes of the Brotherhood.

"The headmaster would like to see His Royal Highness alone," the housekeeper announced in a clipped tone. The disrespect skirting the edge of his formal title reminded Arthur of Merlin, but without any of the open friendliness that would usually follow any mockery.

Hector narrowed his eyes at the woman, but eventually gave a short, sharp nod. "Very well." He turned to Arthur. "I'll be downstairs."

Arthur resisted the urge to gulp loudly as the house-keeper rapped on the wooden door.

A muffled voice floated back almost instantly. "Enter."

Arthur, with a gentle shove from Hector, pushed open the door and entered the expansive study. Just as last time he was in there, his eyes were drawn to the enormous wall-hanging to the left of the fireplace. The hanging was a hand-drawn map of part of central Cambridge with the outlines of each prominent building and street standing out in a mix of red and gold ink that didn't seem to have aged in tandem with the canvas it covered.

"Mr Pendragon." A deep voice demanded Arthur's attention and he turned towards the tall figure by the window and sucked in a breath of surprise.

"You're not the headmaster!" Arthur groped behind him for the door handle.

The man he'd heard called Lyonesse stood before him. The crisscrossing scars that ran in a web across the right side of his face looked even more menacing now that he was bathed in light rather than shrouded in shadow. Dark hair fell over his eyes, but not enough to hide the steely gaze pinning Arthur to the spot.

"Indeed I am not. I am known as Lyonesse. You can leave if you like, Mr Pendragon," he said calmly. "Or you can sit down and listen to what I have to say. I won't stop you if you choose to walk away from here without the knowledge I could give you. However, you should know that this opportunity exists only in this moment, and I will not take steps to contact you again."

Arthur hesitated, assessing the situation. Would Lyonesse really try to harm him with Hector just downstairs?

"Well?" Lyonesse asked, his eyes appearing almost black as he moved away from the dimmed lamp on the window ledge.

"What do you know?" Arthur kept his voice steady and waited to be instructed further.

"Do take a seat." The ghost of a smile seemed to cross

165

Lyonesse's face, but it was gone as quickly as it had appeared.

Arthur did as he was told, shuffling to the high-backed wooden chair that faced the headmaster's desk. His father's voice filled his head, reminding him that it wasn't appropriate to show anxiety, and certainly not to fidget in the presence of others.

Lyonesse turned back to the view outside. "The history of a place is very important."

Arthur wasn't sure if he was supposed to answer or not. Eventually he chose silence and waited for Lyonesse to speak again.

"These walls have been built and rebuilt by the Catterick family," Lyonesse eventually continued. "Every stone, beam and door handle was chosen to create a haven of learning." He finally turned to face Arthur properly; fixing him with an unwavering stare. "For over five-hundred years Badon has provided education for future kings, and indeed any boy who has demonstrated particular promise."

"Yes, sir." Arthur dropped back into a default tone of respect as he lost his battle against fidgeting. He shifted slightly and ended up kicking himself in the back of the leg. He only just held onto a grimace.

"For every generation of Catterick that has watched over Badon there has been a son of the Pendragon line entrusted to their care." Lyonesse seemed suddenly weary as he sank into his chair on the opposite side of the desk.

Arthur already knew this as his father had told him at least a million times about how every boy in the family had passed through Badon 'on their way to greatness'.

"And for every Catterick, and every Pendragon, there has indeed also been an Alderley." Lyonesse's eyes seemed to darken at the utterance of the name.

Arthur frowned. *Alderley. Alderley.* Alderley had founded the school, Arthur was sure of it.

"You recognise the name." Lyonesse looked pleased about that. "Edward Alderley was a staunch supporter of James Catterick and his plan to found a college at the University. He was the first headmaster of Badon, and the only member of the Alderley family ever to hold the position."

"Why was he the only one?" Arthur tilted his head, remembering the story Bertie had told. "Alderley was Lord Badon, wasn't he? So the school was named after him?"

"Very good." Lyonesse twisted a dial on the oil lamp on the desk. The flame sputtered slightly before burning brighter than before as he studied his hands. "Edward Alderley was indeed Lord Badon, and he gave his name to the very institution we are in now. He was a just and honourable man who served his King and country until death."

Laughter and boisterous chatter drifted through the thin window and Arthur was very aware that he was going to be late for dinner.

"Edward Alderley's son, Richard, received the title of Lord Badon upon his father's untimely death. For years, he had been considered by many as the natural replacement for the position of headmaster." Lyonesse looked directly at Arthur again. "Unlike his father, Richard Alderley was a cruel, twisted soul who was interested in nothing more than power and wealth. He was a master of deceit and there are those who swear he was well-versed in the ways of dark magic."

Arthur's eyes bugged before he could control his expression. "Magic?" He almost choked on the word. "Magic isn't real."

Lyonesse stared at Arthur in silence for a long moment, and the prince was certain that his every twitch and breath was being scrutinised. Had Lyonesse realised that he was being watched by both Arthur and Merlin on the night of the Brotherhood's meeting? Did he suspect that Arthur knew about Merlin's magic?

"Quite," Lyonesse replied just as Arthur thought they were lapsing into an eternal silence. "But magic or no, Richard Alderley was barred from becoming Badon's headmaster once he turned to murder, and thus the dubious honour passed to the Catterick family instead; a mantle they accepted even in the midst of their grief."

For the third or fourth time since he'd entered the room, Arthur wondered why he was being told this.

"There were those who remained loyal to Richard Alderley, even after he was arrested for treason, stripped of his title and sentenced to death by the King." Lyonesse's voice seemed to chill the air and Arthur could have sworn every candle dimmed in response. He shivered and hoped that this cryptic meeting was almost over.

"On the night before his execution, Richard Alderley disappeared from the Tower of London," Lyonesse added. "To this day, nobody knows how he managed it, but it seemed as though he simply spirited himself away from right under the noses of the King's guard."

Arthur shook his head. "That can't be true."

"And why not?" Lyonesse raised his eyebrows.

"Because no prisoner accused of treason ever escaped from the Tower of London," Arthur replied steadily. "My father definitely would have told me that story."

Lyonesse's face twisted into a mocking smile. "The events

surrounding Alderley's escape were scrubbed from history. It wouldn't do for a traitor to the King to disappear and never be heard from again, would it?"

Arthur supposed not, but he was still convinced that Lyonesse had simply been taken in by a good story.

"I'm sure you're wondering why I'm telling you all of this." Lyonesse clasped his hands and pressed them under his chin. "Alderley and his supporters believed that there was something inherently rotten about the monarchy at the time. They saw the sovereign as an oppressor and vowed to end the reign of the Pendragon dynasty."

"I still don't understand."

"I'm telling you this because over five-hundred years have passed since Alderley escaped from the Tower, and every monarch this nation has seen has been from the Pendragon line. I believe that you should know that Alderley's supporters have never really faded away completely and that their mission, no doubt, remains the same."

Arthur finally stopped fidgeting and froze completely. He opened and closed his mouth a few times, waiting for his brain to catch up and be able to form a sentence. "Someone is trying to kill my father?"

Lyonesse shook his head. "No, I don't believe that is the case. I think that there are those who have tried to make it seem as such, to provide a distraction from their true cause. I believe you are aware of recent security concerns?"

Arthur nodded dumbly. His head was spinning; Lyonesse's words weren't making anything clearer for him.

"Threats have been made against your father for as long as he has been King, as you already know, but I believe that the real target is someone else entirely," Lyonesse added. "You."

Arthur's blood ran cold. It was one thing to suspect you were a target, but it was something else entirely to have it confirmed to you by someone else.

"I believe that you should know, even though there are many who would have my head for telling you this." Lyonesse barely blinked as his eyes bored into Arthur. "You must prepare yourself for a battle, Arthur Pendragon. You must be careful with who you trust, for it takes only one wrong decision to bring down an empire."

"I don't understand." There was that thing about *trust* again. Was everyone at this school aware of something that Arthur was yet to be privy to?

"I'm not a fool." Lyonesse was almost snarling now. "Despite what my Brothers may think. I *know* you are aware of your friend's true nature, as is he. I *know* you were out in the Court that night, and that he was with you. I might not be able to sense magic as old Catterick can, but I *am* a soldier and I know when I'm being watched.

"Just as I know that it was you and your friend who fought the giant, even if my Brothers are far keener to believe that it was neither of you. Even if they are far keener to believe that someone other than a thirteen-year-old *boy* could possess real, true Magic, and far keener to believe that we do not have to rest the hopes of centuries on a pair of children. If your friend can hide his true nature from even Cecil Catterick he is far more dangerous than you can possibly imagine. I will not allow my Brothers to discount him, and If I discover that he is a danger to anything we have worked so hard to protect I can assure you that I will not hesitate to destroy him."

Lyonesse's eyes blazed angrily as he struck the desk with his fist and Arthur resisted the urge to sprint from the room.

"What is the Brotherhood?" Arthur asked after it seemed Lyonesse had finished speaking. There was no point in pretending he didn't know what Lyonesse was talking about, but he wanted to lead the conversation away from the subject of Merlin. If Arthur had only this one chance to ask questions he was going to take it.

Lyonesse made no move to brush the question off. "The Brotherhood was formed many years before Catterick and Alderley first came to Cambridge. The Brothers were chosen from the oldest families in the kingdom - as they still are today – to protect the most important of truths."

"What truth?" Arthur asked, leaning forward before he was even aware he was moving.

Lyonesse shook his head gravely. "I cannot tell you that."

"Why not?" Arthur stood up, planting his hands on the desk in front of him. "If it's important, you need to tell me."

Lyonesse rose from the chair slowly, looming over the teenager as he spoke. "I do not *need* to tell you anything. You know more about what is going on only because I have *chosen* to tell you."

Arthur, chastened and perhaps a little afraid, sank back into his seat.

A minute passed before Lyonesse spoke again. "The Brotherhood firmly believes that Fate had already written the full story of the world long before the first man breathed air. They believe that there is nothing that can be done to change the events foretold by those who came before them. Richard Alderley was always sure that the future was not set in stone, and that although his father had aligned himself with the Brotherhood, Richard believed that he had the

171

power to change everything."

"And did he?" Arthur asked, not sure he really wanted the answer.

Lyonesse gave a short nod. "The prophecies told of a traitor who would be sent to the Tower and beheaded for his treason. According to the Brotherhood, Richard Alderley should have died that day; his escape went against everything they believed in. Since that day they have done everything in their power to ensure that Fate's path is never strayed from again. They watch, and only intervene when they absolutely must."

"But why?" Arthur ran a hand through his hair in frustration. "Why are they trying so hard to follow a stupid prophecy?"

"Because," Lyonesse once more fixed Arthur with a dark glare, "that *stupid prophecy* has foretold almost every important event in this country's history. Success, defeat, battles, plagues; *all* of them were warned of in the prophecy. It is the Brotherhood's sole responsibility to ensure that events come to pass as promised; for if they do not, then the world will be lost to darkness."

Those words seemed familiar to Arthur in a way he couldn't explain. The sounds outside had lessened, but Arthur couldn't tell whether that was because he was now the only boy at Badon not seated in the Dining Hall, or whether his mind had chosen to block out anything that wasn't Lyonesse's words.

"I have risked more than just my life by telling you this, Pendragon." Lyonesse raised his chin. "I will stand alongside my Brothers in everything but this. They believe you will be safe here because the prophecy predicts that you will be a great king one day. But I wouldn't wish to believe wholeheartedly in the words of a prophecy that has already been disrupted, would you? I have told you what you need to know, and more besides. It is up to you to make the right choices; as only then will you begin to understand your place in the world."

Arthur could only nod dumbly in response. There was a threat beneath Lyonesse's words, and Arthur knew this was the end of their 'meeting'.

"Be watchful of those around you," Lyonesse added. "Do not trust so easily, but equally do not shun those who wish to help you. Nobody is to know what has passed here tonight. These words are for you, and you alone, and you will promise me your silence. If I discover that you have broken this vow, then the consequences for us all will be unimaginable."

The bell on the top of Kings' House pealed its usual chime before declaring it six o'clock.

"You'll be late for dinner," Lyonesse said as he made to cover his head with the hood of his robe. "Tell nobody of this meeting, Arthur Pendragon. Nobody."

Arthur was fully aware that he didn't really have a choice. Who knew what Lyonesse would do if Arthur called out for Hector, or if Arthur told his father. As Lyonesse turned his back on him again Arthur took that as his cue to leave and made towards the door.

He paused at the last minute; he had one final question he couldn't refrain from asking. "Why didn't you help us with the giant? It was *you* I saw on the rugby pitch, wasn't it?"

Lyonesse's head whipped around, a look of pure surprise on his face. "It was not. We were unaware of the giant's attack until the following morning."

"Then who was it?" Arthur asked. "Someone in a hood, just like the Brotherhood, standing on the side of the pitch, just watching."

Lyonesse seemed to pale further. "I believe, Arthur Pendragon, that you may be in even more danger than I thought. *They* must be g-" Lyonesse cut himself off abruptly. He stared at Arthur for a few more seconds in silence before waving his hand in a dismissal.

Arthur didn't wait for anything else and hightailed it out of the room as fast as he could.

"Woah, woah, slow down!" Hector called after him as Arthur clattered down the stairs and straight past his bodyguard without stopping. "Arthur?"

Arthur didn't stop until he was outside. He glanced up at the headmaster's window and wasn't surprised to see Lyonesse's silhouette behind the glass.

"Arthur!" Hector grasped the prince's sleeve. "What's happened?"

Arthur forced a smile onto his face, never more aware of being watched as he was in that moment. "Nothing. I'm just starving, that's all."

Hector frowned, narrowing his eyes at Arthur. "What did the headmaster want?"

"Nothing." Arthur replied quickly. "He just wanted to make sure that I'd had a nice Christmas."

"Really?" Hector folded his arms, and if it was anyone else Arthur might have called him out for being impertinent.

"Honestly, Hector," Arthur rolled his eyes, feigning a lightness he didn't feel, "you're so suspicious about everything."

"Hmm," was all Hector said in reply.

"Now can we *please* go to the Dining Hall?" Arthur wondered if it would be a step too far to drag Hector after him. He was acutely aware that the headmaster could appear at any moment and demand to know why Arthur was loitering outside the Lodge.

Hector studied him for a long moment. "After you."

Arthur just about refrained from breathing a sigh of relief as he led the way to the Dining Hall. There were no stragglers around, and Arthur just hoped that the headmaster was somewhere else on the school grounds and wouldn't look like he'd magically transported himself from the Lodge without Hector seeing.

Thankfully the headmaster was nowhere to be seen when Arthur opened the door and ducked inside, and by some miracle everyone was still milling around and hadn't taken their places in preparation for saying Grace.

"I'll be over there by the staff tables," Hector said quietly before moving away towards the teachers grouped on the far side of the Dining Hall.

Arthur looked around for his friends. It was always more difficult to find people you knew when everyone was dressed for formal dinner, particularly when many boys were still standing in crowds around tables as they caught up with friends after the holiday. Eventually he spotted Bertie's towering height when the older boy stood up and moved from one side of a table to the other.

Just as Arthur was about to step into the fray he was jostled by someone attempting to push past him; someone who wasn't dressed for formal dinner; someone who looked like a rather soggy version of Arthur's roommate.

"There you are!" Arthur grabbed Merlin's sleeve, forcing him to turn back. Arthur grinned. "Did your mum book the wrong train again?"

Merlin, however, wasn't grinning back. Instead he was pale-faced and had clearly been caught out in the icy downpour of earlier that evening if his hair and clothes were anything to go by. But it was Merlin's expression that caught Arthur's attention. Merlin looked haunted.

Arthur's own face fell immediately. "Bloody hell, Merlin. What happened?"

Merlin just shook his head.

Arthur was about to ask him again when the door opened and Mr Beaulake appeared. He looked almost as horrified as Merlin.

''Arthur," the housemaster greeted him before focusing his attention on the other boy. "Merlin, are you sure you wouldn't rather wait in Caerleon? I'll bring some food over for you. I can give Arthur permission to miss dinner and wait with you."

Merlin shook his head again. "I'd rather just have dinner with everyone else, sir."

Beaulake frowned.

"*Please*, sir." Merlin pleaded quickly. He didn't wait for a response before pushing his way into the crowd of boys, presumably to find his friends.

"Sir, what's happened?" Arthur asked, staring after his friend in concern.

"Merlin's had a bit of…" Beaulake trailed off. "An *ordeal*, I suppose."

"Is he alright?"

"You'll probably be better at answering that than me. Do try and speak to him, Arthur." Beaulake replied. He seemed like he was about to walk away, but then he narrowed his eyes and studied Arthur carefully. "Are *you* alright, Arthur?

You look a bit shocked."

Arthur shook his head. It wouldn't really do to give the game away to Beaulake, would it? "Sorry, sir. Just worried about Merlin, that's all."

Beaulake nodded slowly and the door opened behind him, heralding the arrival of the headmaster.

"Quick, you'd better find a seat," Beaulake patted Arthur on the shoulder once, before hurrying away to join the teachers.

"All rise for the headmaster!" Arthur heard Mr Wade boom from the front of the Dining Hall. He couldn't help but think it was a bit of a pointless request considering most boys were already on their feet as he made his way in the general direction of where he'd spotted his friends

Arthur dodged some particularly rowdy Kings' fifth years, just missing an elbow to the face. It was so much harder to navigate the Dining Hall when it was laid out with the long banquet tables reserved for formal dinners and other special occasions.

"Silence!" Mr Wade added, and it was a credit to the respect the teachers commanded at Badon that the Dining Hall fell silent almost immediately.

Arthur caught movement out of the corner of his eye and turned to see Charlie waving at him and motioning towards an empty space at his table. Arthur darted to the right and hurried into place between Charlie and Merlin just as the headmaster began his walk towards the top table. With a quick glance around him it was clear that Gareth was still enacting his self-imposed isolation and was sitting at the other end of the table with a group of boys from Winchester.

"Cutting it a bit fine, aren't you, Arthur?" Charlie

whispered out of the corner of his mouth as the headmaster passed. "Although," he added with a nudge, "at least you're wearing formals. Merlin's in jeans!"

Arthur turned slightly towards his roommate. The look on Merlin's face was one that suggested he wasn't paying a blind bit of notice to the world around him, and Arthur wanted to ask again what on earth had happened to force the usually talkative boy into complete silence.

"Merlin?" Arthur hissed as quietly as possible.

Merlin didn't reply, and any further attempt of questioning on Arthur's part was halted as the headmaster welcomed the boys back, just as he'd done at the first formal dinner in September. There was no mention of damage to the rugby pitch, and Arthur noticed that Elaine Beaulake kept her gaze firmly on her plate throughout Catterick's address.

When they were eventually permitted to sit down Charlie immediately launched into a monologue about the upcoming inter house rugby match against Hainault, and didn't seem to mind that Arthur barely blinked in response.

It was only when Charlie prodded his arm a few minutes later that Arthur realised he'd spaced out entirely.

"Well?' his teammate asked, the picture of excited earnestness. "Do you think we'll win?"

Arthur swallowed heavily, and he wasn't thinking about sport when he replied. "I really hope so, Charlie. I really, *really* hope so."

* * * * *

Merlin's mum *had* mixed up the trains again. When attempting to book the ticket that would have sent her son back to Cambridge first thing on Sunday morning, Mrs Montgomery had become distracted by an owl in the garden and selected an afternoon train instead. Merlin had subsequently had to take two replacement bus services; the first was due to seemingly never-ending engineering work near Peterborough, but the second had been for far more sinister, but currently undisclosed, reasons involving the police. That was all Arthur had managed to learn by the time they'd left the Dining Hall, and Merlin had lapsed back into silence as soon as they'd ventured back to Caerleon in the crisp night air. Even if Merlin hadn't been as white as a sheet for the hour they were at dinner, Arthur would have known something was terribly wrong by the fact Merlin didn't so much as pick at a roast potato, and then he also turned down dessert.

When Merlin eventually spoke, it was hours and hours after dinner had ended and both boys should have been soundly asleep. "Arthur?"

"Yeah?" Arthur replied, only flinching slightly in surprise.

As he lay in the dark, waiting, Arthur knew with absolute certainty that it wasn't going to be a pleasant conversation.

"I overheard the policeman explaining what had happened," Merlin whispered, his voice cracking at the edges. "He was telling the driver about it when they were making us leave the station and get on the coach. He said they think it was a wild animal attack; that it was just an unfortunate case of someone in the wrong place at the wrong time."

Arthur listened silently. Not really understanding the story, but knowing that he should allow Merlin to get there at his own pace.

"They didn't know his name," Merlin continued. "Just that he'd been walking through the fields near the train line - probably heading home from the pub or something

– when he was attacked."

Silence fell again and there wasn't an ounce of comfort to be found in it. Arthur was beginning to put together the pieces of the puzzle he was being handed, and together with Lyonesse's proclamation of impending doom earlier that evening, he had a rather bad feeling about all of this.

Merlin's breath hitched slightly. "As far as I know, there aren't any lions roaming the fields of Cambridge, but that's what they're saying must have done it. A lion! And before that there were reports of dogs barking." Merlin lapsed into silence again for a long moment. "Arthur you know what this means, don't you?"

Arthur *did* know, or at least he thought he did. "Gareth said the Questing Beast was part-lion, didn't he?"

Merlin's silence was enough of an answer.

Arthur felt sick. In all his moments of bravado, when he was sure that they'd be able to stop the beast - or even the necromancer - themselves he'd never really considered that other people would be hurt. He wondered if Merlin was thinking the same thing.

"I don't understand, Arthur," Merlin said quietly. "Why is someone creating all these creatures? Why now? Is it because of *you*?" He swallowed audibly. "Or is it my fault, because of the magic?"

Arthur pushed himself up into a sitting position, drawing his blanket up from the bottom of the bed and wrapping it around his shoulders. He'd made his decision to tell Merlin the minute Lyonesse had let him leave the headmaster's study. Arthur believed in keeping promises, but not when it would keep his best friend in the dark, and possibly endanger everyone around them even more. "Merlin, something else happened tonight, before you got back."

Merlin copied Arthur's actions on the other side of the room and became a matching hulking silhouette. "What do you mean?"

Arthur recounted the story of his meeting with Lyonesse, grateful for Merlin's unusual silence for the first time that evening. It was a complicated enough story and Arthur wanted to be sure he didn't forget to mention anything that might be important.

"Bloody hell," Merlin breathed. "This place gets weirder with every minute. So Lyonesse is a member of the Brotherhood, but he doesn't believe in this prophecy he talked about?"

"That's about it," Arthur replied. "How could there possibly be a prophecy that's accurately predicted the events of the future? That's not possible, surely."

"Arthur," Merlin said, and there was a slight hint of humour there now, "*none* of this is possible, so I think that's rather beside the point. If you can believe in magic, and giants, and secret societies, why not in the idea of a prophecy?"

Arthur thought for a long moment. "I suppose I don't like the idea that certain things are supposed to just happen."

"But Lyonesse said things can be changed," Merlin added. "Maybe this prophecy is just one version of how the world could be."

"I suppose that makes sense," Arthur replied. "But he also said that I'm a target for these people. Wouldn't my father know about them if they really existed? Wouldn't Hector?"

"What reason does Lyonesse have to lie to you?" Merlin

asked steadily.

"None I can think of," Arthur replied. "But what reason does he have for telling me anything of what he did? Why did he risk himself by coming here tonight and meeting me in the Headmaster's Lodge no less?"

"Because he believes he's doing the right thing?"

"Maybe." Arthur shrugged. "And he mentioned '*them*' again, whoever they are."

"Do you think he knew? About the Questing Beast, I mean."

Merlin was quiet for a few seconds. "Do you think Lyonesse knew? About what happened with the Questing Beast, I mean. When I got off the coach at the train station in Cambridge, Beaulake was in the car park. He said he was there waiting for me, but I don't think he was. There's no way my mum would have remembered to call and tell school I was on the wrong train, and my Dad's away for work. I'm sure he looked surprised to see me, but he covered it up well enough, and it's only now that I think about it that it seemed a bit odd. If Beaulake knew, then surely the rest of the Brotherhood did too."

"Probably. Was Mr Beaulake investigating what happened to the man who died?" Arthur asked, his stomach rolling slightly at his words.

"It wouldn't be completely unbelievable, would it?"

"I guess not," Arthur sighed. "Merlin, if it *is* the Questing Beast and it's here for me, then why has it killed someone else?"

"I don't know. Maybe you're too well protected here and this is just a warning."

"Do you really believe that I'm protected here?" Arthur asked.

182

"Well, you've got the Brotherhood looking out for you by the sound of things," Merlin replied.

"They haven't been a brilliant help so far, have they?" Arthur asked, a slight sting to his words. "Remember what Catterick said – they would only intervene if they needed to. *And* it looks like Lyonesse isn't the only one who's gone rogue; remember, we don't know who it was that night on the rugby pitch."

"Well you've still got me," Merlin replied eventually, his voice steady again. "I can work on some magic. See if I can use that spell I used against the giant again."

"What was that anyway?" Arthur asked, remembering the sheer power he'd felt as the giant had disintegrated before his eyes. "Where on earth did Gareth find it? Has he tracked down a spell book or something? Do spell books even exist?"

"What?" Merlin sounded confused. "Gareth didn't find the spell."

"Yes, he did," Arthur countered. "He had it on that piece of paper he tried to keep from you.'

"Gareth's spell wouldn't have worked. It was a brilliant idea – he wanted to shrink the giant – but the words were wrong."

"Then where did you get that spell?" Arthur asked. He hadn't forgotten the weird moment when he'd understood what Merlin's words had meant. "You completely destroyed the giant."

"I know what I did," Merlin replied, and his voice shook slightly. "But I don't know how I did it. I had never uttered those words before in my life. They came from nowhere, Arthur."

Arthur didn't know what to say to that, and the silence

that followed eventually lulled them both to sleep.

* * * * *

The next morning the Dining Hall was awash with the news that a wild animal was stalking the streets of Cambridge and had already selected its first victim. Rumours that Merlin had actually seen the body (*and* the lion) were fuelled by the Caerleon's protective huddle that formed around the boy in question over breakfast.

"Ignore it," Arthur muttered to Merlin as a couple of Kings' boys made growling noises as they wandered past. People were clearly looking for a reaction after Merlin had made quite the spectacle by sitting through formal dinner in casual clothes the night before.

"Buzz off!" Sib threw a banana at the boys. "Stupid Kings' idiots. I swear any boy immediately turns rotten when he becomes one of them."

"They're probably already like that," Arthur replied as his cousin strode into the Dining Hall, looking as supercilious as usual. "Kings' just makes it worse."

"I wish you could just zap them with a spell like that old wizard, Merlin," Sib said, trying to cheer the other boy up.

Arthur almost snorted at that, but remained silent as Merlin retreated further into his cereal, which was a worryingly sugarless affair that looked completely out of place in front of him. Obviously, the discussion last night hadn't made Merlin feel too much better about magic, or the general safety of everyone at Badon.

"Alright?"

Arthur looked up to see Leo Chevalier hovering by their table, holding a plate of toast. He nodded and gestured his head towards Merlin.

"I'm fine," Merlin said, not looking up from his spoon.

"Nasty business though, isn't it?" Leo frowned as he sat down next to Sib. "Apparently Mr Beaulake knew the guy who was attacked last night."

"What?" Arthur, Merlin and Sib all asked at the same time.

"Mmm." Leo chewed his toast thoughtfully. "They went to school together. Here, obviously."

"The man who died went to Badon?" Merlin asked.

Leo frowned. "Yes," he said slowly. "I just said that. Merlin, are you sure you're alright? I mean, you did have a bit of a shock yesterday."

Merlin just gave Leo a silent thumbs-up and Arthur shook his head in silent warning to leave it be.

"Anyway," Leo said with a final glance at Merlin, "don't quote me on this. This is just what Gareth's told Bertie."

"Gareth?" Arthur looked around. The younger boy hadn't spoken to him at all since they'd arrived back, and hadn't been spotted yet this morning.

"Yeah." Leo replied. "What's up with him, anyway? Bertie spent ages trying to coax a sentence out of him when he bumped into him in the JCR earlier."

Arthur shrugged. "I don't know." He *did* know, but he couldn't exactly explain it to Leo.

"Well, apparently Gareth actually reads the newspapers delivered to Caerleon," Leo explained, "and that's how he found out. But according to Ben – you know, Kay's roommate – someone in the city's gone missing now, and the police think it might be the same thing."

Merlin's spoon clattered into his bowl noisily just as Arthur's jaw dropped.

"Ben's managed to hide a spare phone somewhere in

his and Kay's room." Leo explained, assuming the shock on the other boys' faces was nothing more than general surprise. "He looked online this morning and there are a couple of journalists who've found out that a student at the university went for a bike ride yesterday down near the train tracks, as bad luck would have it, and he hasn't returned."

"That's horrible!" Sib said, pushing his plate away from him. "I hope they catch the creature soon. Whatever it is."

Arthur, his appetite now completely evaporated, dropped his head into his hands and hoped that this was just coincidence. He hoped that someone had just got the story wrong, and that the missing student was actually happily enjoying breakfast at home.

Coincidence, Arthur pleaded silently. *Just once let it be nothing more than coincidence.*

7

THE BEAST STRIKES

It wasn't coincidence. It only took a quick glance at the local newspapers early on Wednesday morning to confirm as much.

The disappearance of a final-year student from Catterick College has sparked a police search across the city and the surrounding villages. Twenty-year-old Rupert Daunton, originally of Aberdeenshire, was last seen by his friends leaving his room as he headed out on a cycle ride through the villages south of the city. This was a typical activity for the keen sportsman, who rowed for his college and was a member of the Varsity rugby squad last year.

Daunton's disappearance follows the death of Cambridge local Lawrence Hildon, forty-two, who was killed in a suspected wild animal attack on Sunday afternoon.

Both Daunton and Hildon are alumni of the prestigious Cambridge boarding school, Badon College, with Daunton being the recipient of the Headmaster's Scholarship during his time there. The Headmaster's Scholarship is a prestigious full-scholarship granted to boys of exceptional academic ability and promise. Badon College recently gained nationwide attention as His Royal Highness, Prince Arthur began his secondary studies there in September.

Detectives are not linking the two investigations at this stage, but have advised that this may be a possible course of action in the future.

Sources close to the investigation reveal that a team of experts called in from London Zoo believe that Hildon's injuries were consistent with those expected to be sustained in a lion attack. Police are advising the public to remain vigilant, but have stressed that there is no need for widespread panic regarding the potentially violent creature on the loose.

"You mustn't worry yourself about that."

Arthur dropped the newspaper in surprise. He looked up to see Mrs Beaulake looking down on where he was slouched in the old, green-leather armchair in the JCR.

"Sorry." She smiled slightly as she clutched a mug between her hands. "I didn't mean to startle you."

Arthur shrugged with a smile of his own. "That's alright."

"You're up very early, Arthur." Mrs Beaulake perched on the arm of the sofa by the fireplace.

"Physics test this morning," Arthur explained as he gestured to the neat pile of books on the coffee table. "I'm just reading over my notes again."

"A wise idea." Mrs Beaulake nodded. "Did you have a nice holiday though? You should have seen Tom's face when he saw you on the news with your family on Christmas Day. I thought his little head was going pop in surprise."

Arthur laughed. "Well I'm glad someone found it

interesting. It was just the usual really; lots of hands to shake and food to eat. Did you have a good Christmas, Mrs Beaulake?"

"Yes, thank you," she smiled. "Tom was a bundle of excitement about Father Christmas. Elaine had lots of schoolwork to do so spent most of the time in her room. Although, she somehow managed to make it to the kitchen whenever the oven timer beeped and fresh mince pies appeared."

At least that seemed to confirm that Elaine hadn't said anything to her parents about what she'd seen at the rugby pitch.

"Oh, good morning Mrs Beaulake."

Arthur was surprised to hear Gareth's voice. He craned his neck around the side of the armchair to see the other boy hovering in the doorway and clutching his own Physics books.

"Gareth!" Mrs Beaulake beamed. "I was just having a nice chat with Arthur. Come in."

Gareth looked ready to bolt at the thought of being in the same room as Arthur, but Mrs Beaulake was still smiling encouragingly at him, and there was nowhere else for him to go, unless he decided to scarper back to his room.

"It seems everyone's up early," Mrs Beaulake said as Gareth sat down as far away as possible from Arthur.

"Physics test," Gareth mumbled.

"Well in that case, I should leave you boys to it." Mrs Beaulake was shooting the two of them a mothering look, and Arthur could tell that she knew something was wrong. "I'll see you both in Chemistry this afternoon."

"Bye, Mrs Beaulake," Arthur replied, and Gareth waved silently as their teacher left them alone.

Arthur really hated awkward silences, and yet he let this one go on for a good long while. Eventually, he couldn't take it anymore. "Good holiday, Gareth?"

Gareth looked up from his textbook in surprise. "Er, it was alright, thanks."

"Good." Arthur nodded encouragingly, and thought that perhaps Gareth would then take the lead.

Gareth dropped his eyes back to his work. Ah, perhaps not then.

"Worried about the test?" Arthur asked.

"Not really," Gareth replied. He sighed. "Arthur, why are you talking to me?"

Arthur scrunched up his face in confusion. "Why *wouldn't* I be talking to you?"

Gareth closed his book loudly. "Oh, I don't know, maybe because I nearly got us all killed."

"But you didn't, Gareth." Arthur shook his head. "You tried something and it didn't work. At least you had a plan."

"I just wanted to help," Gareth sighed again. "You and Bertie are both so good at sports, as well as being clever, and Merlin's a sorcerer, and he knows *everything*. I didn't want you all to realise that I'm a bit useless in comparison."

Arthur seriously considered throwing a cushion at his friend. "Gareth, that's the most ridiculous thing I've ever heard."

When Gareth's face fell even further Arthur realised that maybe he hadn't been quite as tactful as he could have been.

"Gareth," Arthur added carefully, "did you know that Merlin thought the spell you found was brilliant?"

"He didn't say that," Gareth mumbled. "You don't have to try and make me feel better."

Arthur decided that completely tactless might actually

be a better option after all. "Gareth, you idiot!"

Gareth's eyes widened, dumbstruck at Arthur's raised voice. "What?"

"Listen to me," Arthur shook his head. "I'm not friends with Bertie because he's good at rugby, and I'm not friends with Merlin because he knows everything – that's actually a kind of annoying thing about him. I'm friends with them because I like them, and the same goes for you. And yes, Merlin *did* think that spell was a stroke of genius, you can even ask him if you like."

Gareth wasn't going to ask him, Arthur knew that, but if the slight reddening to the tips of Gareth's ears was anything to go by, Gareth had taken the compliment as intended and might be beginning to understand.

"You'll have to start sitting with us again in the Dining Hall, you know," Arthur added eventually, "unless you want to keep sitting with Winchesters, that is."

"No," Gareth shook his head firmly. "All they ever do is talk about how they want to be bankers when they leave school."

Arthur snorted. "Sounds exciting." He grinned at Gareth before reaching for his exercise books. "Now, I think I should really read over this before breakfast."

"Do you want some help?" Gareth asked quietly a few seconds later.

"Yeah," Arthur replied, seeing the question for the olive branch it was. "Yeah, Gareth, thanks."

* * * * *

Two weeks passed with no sightings of Rupert Daunton. It looked like the police were close to giving up, but Arthur found that he could only be thankful that nobody else seemed to have gone missing in suspicious circumstances. There'd been no reports about the creature, and not a whisper of magic had been sighted at Badon (except for Merlin's stealthy efforts to improve a few small spells).

However, the threat of the creature was great enough that, aside from fifth years, the boys at Badon hadn't been allowed off school grounds outside of lesson times, and the younger boys were suffering from varying degrees of cabin fever in response.

Arthur had explained what had happened with Lyonesse to Gareth and Bertie, once more deciding that it was far more important that his friends had knowledge that could protect them, than to keep his promise to a man he didn't know, and couldn't really trust. They'd listened intently to Arthur's account of the meeting, and Gareth had immediately announced his intention to try and track down any truth to the story about Richard Alderley and his escape from the Tower.

He had barely sat down at his desk following rugby practice when the bedroom door flew open and Merlin stalked into the room, flinging his sports bag into the corner. A rather unhappy looking badminton racquet followed a split-second later.

Arthur didn't even have time to ask what on earth was going on before Merlin was standing in front of him, arms crossed and glaring.

"You need to teach me how to fence," Merlin demanded.

"What?" Arthur frowned, pulling off his reading glasses and dropping them onto his open prep books.

"You need to teach me how to fence," Merlin repeated slowly, enunciating each word as though Arthur wouldn't understand otherwise.

Enunciation or not, Arthur still didn't have a clue what Merlin was on about. "What do you mean I need to teach you how to fence?"

"*Someone*," Merlin spat, "thought it would be hilarious to tell Mr Beaulake that I haven't been going to sports sessions every week."

Arthur frowned. "Well, you *haven't* been going to sports sessions every week. You've told every games teacher that you're trying a different sport 'this week' and then slope off to the library to hide."

Merlin threw his arms up. "That isn't the point, *Arthur*! I hate sport and I had a nice little system in place, and now, having had Beaulake lecture me for half an hour and threaten to tell the headmaster, I have to join a club permanently, and they'll be checking up on me to make sure I attend."

"Ah," Arthur replied. He knew his roommate hated sport more than most other things in life, and Merlin had been so proud that he'd worked out how to avoid taking part in activities of any kind. "But why fencing?"

"Because," Merlin's glower darkened, "it was your git of a *cousin* who dobbed me into Beaulake."

"Are you sure?" Arthur frowned again. "It could have been anyone."

"Yeah, it could have been," Merlin flopped back onto his bed, "but it was Hugo who came into the library with Mr Beaulake to find me. And it was Hugo who told Beaulake – while I was *standing there*, by the way – that he had only told Mr Beaulake because he didn't want me to get into trouble with the headmaster. Oh, and that he was just trying to make amends for his behaviour last term. I nearly clobbered him with my badminton racquet, but had to

193

settle for whacking the gravel outside with it instead. *Make amends!* What a load of-"

"Merlin!" Arthur exclaimed, holding up a hand before his friend launched into an epic rant that would probably descend into nothing but cursing fairly quickly.

Merlin sat up and silently glared back at his friend.

"Hugo's a champion fencer," Arthur sighed. "Honestly, it's the only positive thing I can say about him. You wouldn't stand a chance against him."

Merlin folded his arms again. "Oh yes I would. Because I have something he doesn't." He waved his hand. "Magic. There's no way he can beat me if I use magic. Total public humiliation. It'd be perfect!"

Despite the sheer glee now radiating from Merlin's face, Arthur needed to be diplomatic about this. "Merlin, I know Hugo's a git, and trust me I'd love to see anyone beat him, but don't you think we have more important things to worry about?" He gestured to the photocopies he'd taken of the newspapers covering Rupert Daunton's disappearance. "We can't exactly save the world if Hugo skewers you in a fencing match, can we?"

Merlin grumbled, "He can't skewer me. You told me before that you wouldn't be able to do much damage in a proper fencing match."

"This is *Hugo* we're talking about," Arthur raised one eyebrow. "I don't think he'd fight fair against you, even with the whole school watching."

Merlin's expression changed to one of judgement. "'Wait, did you say, 'save the world'?"

Arthur shrugged. "I was aiming for dramatic to prove my point. Alright, maybe not save the world, but at least focus on the fact there's at least one mythical beast stalking the residents of Cambridge. Plus, can't you just pretend to like some form of non-contact sport?"

"For the next four and a half years?" Merlin curled his lip in distaste.

"Well, you did choose to come here," Arthur replied.

"No, I didn't!" Merlin exclaimed. "I'm here because someone my mum knows convinced her it would be best for me to go away to boarding school. I could just as easily have ended up at Eton, or Harrow, or somewhere else completely ridiculous."

"Why didn't you pick one of the other places then?" Arthur asked, slightly snippily considering he hadn't been given a choice at all.

"Because, as luck would have it, my parents had to read rejection letters from four other schools before I was accepted here," Merlin huffed. "*Then*, after I'd accepted my offer here and agreed on the scholarship - within about three minutes of the letter arriving, *and* with my mum practically signing my name for me, mind - all of the other schools suddenly wrote to my parents to say that they'd made a mistake with their admin, and that I actually *had* been given offers from them." Merlin stopped, a look of confusion creasing his face. "Actually, that's really weird now that I think about it."

Arthur's eyes widened in realisation at the same time as Merlin's. "Oh!"

Merlin jumped to his feet, clearly incensed. "It was *them*, wasn't it? The Brotherhood? They made sure I had to come here! *It's their fault I have to go to stupid games lessons!*"

"Now who's missing the point?" Arthur asked in exasperation. "Merlin, it had to be the Brotherhood. And if you're supposed to be here, then maybe that really means we *are* supposed to go after the Questing Beast."

"Arthur, I'm not sure you should start believing in that prophecy stuff now." Merlin shook his head. "You were the one who didn't like the idea of having your choices made for you, after all."

Arthur chewed his lip. Merlin was right; he really *didn't* like thinking that he had no real free will. "Maybe you could just try and be the bigger person here?"

"Alright," Merlin sighed after a long silence. "I'll stick with badminton. *For now.*"

Arthur grinned. "You need a new racquet."

Merlin waved his hand in the vague direction of the discarded sports equipment and Arthur watched - in the same stunned awe as he usually did at moments like this - as the racquet head righted itself, each string pulling taut and reforming as necessary. In seconds it looked as good as new.

"That's a good one," Arthur remarked with a nod.

"Yep!" Merlin lay back on his bed.

"You'll have to remember that for when you *do* clobber Hugo on the head with a badminton racquet."

Merlin snorted with laughter and Arthur joined in a moment later.

The fragile peace they seemed to have reached only lasted a few seconds before it was shattered by a knock on the door.

"Come in!" Arthur called, assuming it would be Gareth or Bertie knocking before heading down to dinner.

It was neither.

"Everything alright in here?" Hector asked, looking round the room. His eyes landed on Merlin's sports bag, which was still half-resting against the wall and upside-down. "Shouting followed by silence isn't normally a good thing in my line of work."

Merlin started laughing again at that.

Arthur just rolled his eyes. "No, we're fine. Merlin just had a bit of a tantrum."

"Oi!"

"Sorted now!" Arthur grinned at Hector.

Hector shook his head and Arthur once more thanked his lucky stars for ending up with the most patient man in the Britain as his primary bodyguard.

"Can I have a word, Arthur?" Hector asked.

"Do I need to leave the room?" Merlin asked before Arthur could reply.

"Why?" Hector frowned at him.

"I don't know." Merlin shrugged. "Are you going to have a conversation about state secrets, or something else I'm not allowed to overhear?" Merlin's smile grew, "Ooh! Are you going to communicate in code?"

"Yes, Merlin," Hector replied, completely deadpan. "Code."

Merlin's humour morphed immediately into surprise. "Really?"

"*No*, not really." Hector shook his head. "It's about the trip tomorrow."

Knowing that this could potentially continue for hours, Arthur piped up. "What is it Hector? They're not cancelling the trip, are they?"

He wouldn't actually mind all that much if Badon *had* decided to cancel the excursion. He was terrible at Art, and a trip to the Fitzwilliam Museum to draw various artefacts didn't exactly fill him with joy. Then again, getting out of school for the first time in over two weeks did sound quite nice, so perhaps he could bear it just this once.

Hector shook his head. "No. But you'll be accompanied as though it were an official engagement."

"No!" Arthur shook his head vehemently. "No way! *Hector!*"

"Sorry, Arthur." Hector did look apologetic. "Orders from His Majesty, I'm afraid."

"Well, I'm not going then!" Arthur folded his arms and stared defiantly at Hector.

"What?" Merlin asked, looking between them. "I don't understand. What's the problem?"

"Due to various complications, Arthur's security needs have changed." Hector explained. It was clear he was choosing his words so as not to give too much away, even though he probably suspected that Arthur had told Merlin about the threats the King had apparently received recently.

"It means I can't go anywhere beyond a 'secure' location, like here, without at least six security agents tailing me at all times," Arthur huffed. "It means I have to arrive in an official car and can't just walk up the road with the rest of you. It means that they'll have to shut the whole museum down to visitors before we get there so that they can do a security sweep. You know, just in case there's a ninja assassin hiding in a Grecian urn or something!"

Merlin wrinkled his nose. "A ninja assassin probably couldn't hide in a Gre-"

"Merlin!" Arthur snapped. "What is it with you and missing the point?" He turned to Hector to plead, "Hector, come on, can't you do something? If I take an entourage on a school trip I'm never going to hear the end of it."

"Sorry, Arthur." Hector held up his hands. "I'm just the messenger, and I'm afraid my hands are tied. Your car will head off once the other boys have left."

Arthur growled in frustration. *Great.* Now even the slight freedom of the trip had eluded him. How long until they just started locking him in his room?

Well if they did that, Arthur thought bitterly as Hector nodded once more and left the room, *at least he could probably persuade Merlin to magically pick the lock.*

* * * * *

Merlin and Gareth were standing just inside the entrance to the Fitzwilliam Museum when Arthur strode through the door flanked by a group of men in black suits.

"Hello, Your Royal Highness," Merlin smirked. "Did you have a pleasant journey, Sir?"

Arthur was sorely tempted to gift his friend with a rude hand gesture; but as it would only end up in the tabloids and with his father threatening to disinherit him he refrained. Just about.

"Here you go!" Merlin cheerfully handed over Arthur's sketchpad and pencils. "Miss Parker asked for volunteers to wait and give these to you. We offered to do it."

Arthur rolled his eyes.

Hector swooped over and took the sketchpad before Arthur could clasp his fingers over it.

"Seriously?" Arthur hissed. "It's paper."

"Protocol, Arthur." Hector whispered back. "*Sir.*"

"Oh, fine." Arthur snapped quietly. He was aware that various staff members were craning their necks to see him so he smiled as pleasantly as possible while Hector flipped through the pages of his sketchbook looking for any sheets intending to murder the heir to the throne with a deadly paper cut or something.

"Here you are, Sir." Hector sounded pleasant enough as

he handed the book over to Arthur, but the prince could see the hint of warning in the bodyguard's eyes. He didn't have to worry, Arthur wasn't planning to make any more of a scene than he already had.

"I assume I can still walk around with my friends." Arthur nodded his head towards where Merlin and Gareth were getting impatient near the main staircase.

"Of course," Hector replied tightly. "We'll be with you at all times."

Arthur plainly heard the *Don't even think about trying to wander off* implied in the ensuing silence. He nodded once and moved towards his friends.

"Finally!" Merlin rolled his eyes. "Come on. Miss Parker said she wasn't giving us extra time just because you're late."

"Which is a bit mean," Gareth grumbled as they climbed the stairs and headed through a door of Merlin's choosing. "It'll take me ages to draw something decent."

"Gareth you'd draw something brilliant in about five seconds," Merlin laughed as they found themselves in a room full of portraits. "I'm sure Miss Parker expects nothing better than stickmen from me, and Arthur's even worse than that. Next to the rubbish we'll end up with one of your doodles will look like a Botticelli."

"Botticelli?" Arthur arched an eyebrow.

"What?" Merlin shrugged. "I can't draw, but I have actually seen art before, Arthur."

"Can we just draw something quickly and go to the gift shop or something?" Arthur grumbled as he caught sight of yet more of his security team in the distance.

"I think it's nice that so many people want to make sure you stay alive," Gareth said as they continued to follow Merlin through various doorways and corridors.

Arthur had the distinct impression they were going in circles. "Thanks, Gareth, but being followed everywhere gets old very quickly."

"Let's go through here!" Merlin announced, holding a pencil above his head in a way that reminded Arthur of a tour guide.

"We've been through here already," Gareth said as he looked around in bewilderment.

"I know" Merlin replied, striding forwards as though he had great purpose, completely ignoring the questioning stares of their fellow Caerleonites who looked up from their work as the three of them wandered by again.

"Are we going to stop anywhere, Merlin?" Arthur asked, hearing at least one security agent break protocol and grumble quietly behind him.

"Eventually," Merlin replied with a maddening grin, "but I thought we'd take your men in black for a bit of exercise first."

Arthur tried to cover his mouth when he guffawed loudly, but he still attracted the attention of Miss Parker, who hurried over with her long blonde hair swishing behind her.

"Gentlemen." She narrowed her eyes at the three of them. "Please remember where you are. We're very lucky to have such a wonderful institution to visit, so please find an object, or artwork, and begin the task I've set you."

Arthur smiled sheepishly at her and shuffled towards a collection of small paintings in the corner. Gareth appeared at his shoulder a second later.

"Mr Montgomery," Miss Parker hissed as Merlin attempted to follow his friends, "I rather think that corner of the gallery is crowded enough. Why don't you come with me and we can find something else for you to work on? Somewhere where you won't be causing a distraction to your classmates."

Arthur covered his mouth again to smother another laugh as he heard the shuffling sounds of Merlin's footsteps counterpointing with the clack of Miss Parker's heels as they left the room. Gareth was doing an impressive job of keeping a straight face at his side. Merlin had been convinced that Miss Parker was out to get him since their first Art lesson in September.

"Shall we go find something a bit more interesting than paintings of flowers?" Gareth asked as the footsteps faded away. "There's some really old weaponry by the gift shop. There are swords and shields, and stuff like that. My parents brought me here in the summer, and mum had to shout at Dad for trying to put his arm around a suit of armour for a photo."

Arthur laughed again. "Brilliant idea. Let's go."

It didn't take long for Gareth to lead the way to the dimly lit section by the gift shop that did indeed hold a display of weaponry. Arthur was interested to see that most of the items on show were far older than the ones his father kept in a couple of the palaces.

"They dug most of this stuff up from the villages around the city," Gareth explained as he sat cross-legged on the floor to start work on his sketch. "They don't really know who it belonged to because Cambridge didn't really exist as a city for a really long time and so didn't keep records. But they dated it all, and lots of it is from the fifth and sixth centuries."

Arthur nodded towards the full suit of armour in the corner. "Is that the one your dad wanted a picture with?"

Gareth looked up and grinned. "Yeah. I thought my mum was going to kill him. She started shrieking about priceless artefacts, and was so loud the security guards had to come and ask her to calm down. She didn't take too kindly to that."

Arthur grinned, trying (and failing) to imagine his parents ever causing such a scene. "Well, I'll draw a picture of it and we can send it to your Dad as a joke."

Gareth grinned back, already sketching an outline of the shield he was studying. "But we shouldn't say who sent it. Just let it arrive mysteriously in the post."

"I'd better get started then."

Arthur walked over to the armour, squinting as he looked closely at every dent and scratch in the metalwork. The gauntlets of the suit were clasped one on top of the other, resting on a shoddy-looking sword. To the right of the display there was a small silver plaque.

- ***Suit of Armour & sword (Visigoth)*** *c.500AD*.
  Excavated during drainage of the River Cam 1986

The armour, and the sword for that matter, didn't gleam like the suits at the palace in London, and weren't covered in intricate detailing like the collections in Cornwall. This was much older - far more primitive in a way - and Arthur was fascinated. How could he not be? He'd grown up with the King Arthur stories of swords and battles, just like everybody else, and the Arthur Pendragon of his family's history was a great warrior, even if he hadn't been quite as adventurous as the character from the stories.

When he was very small he'd once asked his father if Excalibur had been a real sword. The King had laughed at his young son, ruffled his hair and told him that the *real* King Arthur wasn't the same man as the one in the book Arthur kept by his bed.

Arthur, being an inquisitive little soul, had wandered around the palace for days afterwards inspecting the weapons at close range and looking for one that might be the great sword of the Legends. He'd grown bored when he discovered that none of the ceremonial swords at the palace were lodged in stone, and that had been the end of his childish wish to find the mythical blade.

And now here he was at almost fourteen, and as drawn to the shabby looking object before him as he had been by any of the shining, perfectly-formed swords tucked away in his childhood memories.

His right hand was reaching for the pommel, just below the clasped gauntlets, before he was consciously aware that he'd moved. The tips of his fingers grazed the cold metal, and he frowned as the blade looked far more flawless than it had a moment ago. It seemed to catch the light from somewhere, even though the spotlights above were angled away from the display.

"Get your hands off that!" A sharp voice bellowed from behind him.

Arthur turned just in time to see a short, balding man rushing towards him, and he pulled his hand back as though he'd been burned.

"Sir! Stop!" Hector bellowed.

The man continued to barge towards Arthur, eyes narrowed in a ferocious glare.

Hector grabbed Arthur by both arms and hauled him out of the way at the same time a couple of the other RPS agents tackled the man to the floor.

Arthur had no time to protest before he was being pulled through a door and into the outside world. He just about caught a glimpse of the members of his security team split between talking rapidly into concealed microphones or barking at the balding man being held securely by a particularly burly agent.

He was bundled into the awaiting car, just as had happened the night of the Catterick dinner, and had barely caught his breath before he was sped away up the street.

It was only when he shook his head to clear it that he realised that Gareth was sitting in the back of the car next to him, blinking owlishly across at him in confusion; he'd obviously been scooped up by Hector or another security agent in the fray.

"Woah!" Gareth breathed, clutching his sketchbook to his chest. "What just happened?"

"I think," Arthur sighed as he ran a hand through his hair, "that I just caused that scene I was trying to avoid. Sorry, Gareth."

Gareth just grinned in reply. "Merlin and Bertie are going to be so jealous they missed this!"

Arthur was fairly certain he was right.

* * * * *

"Aww, did the nasty man at the museum give you a fright?"

Arthur's head snapped up in surprise to see Hugo, the ever-present Laurie, and a tall, dark-haired boy Arthur vaguely recognised from around Badon, smirking at him.

Arthur glared back for a moment before shaking his head and returning his attention to the sport notice board outside the gym. The boys in Caerleon had teased him mercilessly over the two days following the events at the museum, but there had been nothing malicious about their jokes. Hugo's every action, however, always held at least a spark of malevolence and Arthur wasn't thrilled to have found himself alone with his cousin.

"I knew you were a coward," Hugo sneered, "but calling in the big boys to protect you from a little old gift shop worker? That's ridiculous even for you, *Pendragon*." Hugo spat as though the name tasted foul on his tongue, even though he was a much a Pendragon as Arthur was.

Arthur told his cousin to go away, using a rather colourful phrase he'd always considered to be one of Merlin's most imaginative creations.

A split-second later, Arthur's cheek connected painfully with the notice board as Hugo pushed him forwards and twisted his right arm behind his back. Arthur wasn't scrawny, but his cousin had two years of height and bulk on him, making it impossible to wriggle out of the hold he was in. He sucked in his breath, refusing to make any other show of discomfort. He cursed the fact that Mr Beaulake had left the gym the second rugby drills had finished; he could really do with an intervention from his Housemaster.

"Hugo," Arthur said as levelly as he could," let go of me."

"Why would I do that?" Hugo hissed in his ear. "You still haven't learned, have you? Just because Daddy's the King you think everyone will just do as you want. Well you're wrong."

"What have I done to you?" Arthur replied, wincing as Hugo jarred his arm. "What is it that I did that made you hate me so much?"

Hugo didn't answer and Arthur stumbled slightly as he was suddenly released. He looked up to see Bertie, Leo, and Eric Troyes glowering at the older boys.

"Back off, Hugo." Bertie growled.

"Oh, I'm terrified, Dorner," Hugo's lips twisted into a parody of a smile. "You're too much of a little saint to try anything."

"Saint Bertie!" Laurie brayed.

Bertie was *not* amused. "Hilarious." He narrowed his eyes and Arthur was gratified to see Laurie shrink back slightly.

"Alright there, Arthur?" Leo asked, although he kept his eyes fixed firmly on Hugo's other friend.

"Fine, thanks," Arthur replied as he stretched his arm out. That was a bit of an exaggeration considering he could feel his cheekbone throbbing in time to his heartbeat, but he wouldn't give Hugo the satisfaction of knowing he'd hurt him.

"Come on," Eric said to Arthur, nudging him in the direction of the Caerleon bridge.

"Oh, and the Head Boy's little brother comes to the rescue," Hugo spat. "I bet your parents were *thrilled* when you didn't get into Winchester. Is little Eric not quite as bright as his brother?"

"Shut up, Hugo," Eric replied. "My brother might be a stuck-up git who plays by the rules, but I won't think twice about thumping you if necessary."

"Terrified," Hugo drawled, pretending to yawn.

Arthur held his chin up to shoot a final dark look at his cousin. Unfortunately, Hugo seemed completely unaffected by Arthur's show of defiance, and his smirk just grew wider.

"Go and cry to Hector!" Hugo called after them as they walked away.

"Ignore him," Leo muttered. "Your cousin's a total git, Arthur."

Arthur nodded as he gingerly pressed the tips of his fingers to his face. He hissed as he touched the tender spot under his eyes. "Thanks, guys. You didn't have to do that."

"Don't be stupid. Course we did." Bertie shrugged as they all trooped under Caerleon's arch. "You know, if it wouldn't end in me getting expelled I'd throw him in the Cam without a second thought."

Arthur grinned slightly at the thought.

All four boys jumped slightly as the door to the boarding house opened and Elaine Beaulake appeared, arms crossed over her chest. Her body language suggested she was barely keeping a lid on irritation, and Arthur hoped she'd just let them pass without incident.

"Bertie." She greeted coolly, ignoring the others. "Can I have a word, please?"

Normally such a request would probably have ended in catcalling from the other boys, and jokes made at Bertie's expense for days afterwards. However, as Elaine looked ready to destroy anyone who didn't do her bidding Bertie nodded meekly, and not a word was uttered by anyone.

"You too." Elaine's eyes flashed dangerously as she looked over at Arthur.

Arthur was too surprised to do anything but nod.

"Good." Elaine tilted her head back slightly. "The JCR's free." She turned on her heel and disappeared inside.

"Um..." Bertie gestured towards his friends.

"Okay" Eric replied slowly, "we'll see you at dinner." He ducked into the boarding house and headed for the stairs.

Leo nodded as he followed Eric inside, muttering, 'That was weird."

"She didn't look happy," Arthur whispered as he and Bertie made their way to the JCR.

Bertie shook his head. "I guess this was going to happen eventually."

The two boys pushed open the door to the JCR and were surprised to see Merlin and Gareth sitting on the sofa looking slightly bewildered. Clearly Elaine had summoned them and she looked rather pleased with herself as she leaned against the fireplace.

"Sit." Elaine pointed to the sofa. "There."

Merlin and Gareth shuffled up until there was enough room to just about squash all four boys onto the sofa.

Arthur wriggled slightly trying to find a space for his shoulders between Bertie and Merlin. He sent poor old Gareth a sympathetic look as the youngest boy curled into the arm of the sofa he was wedged against.

"What happened to you?" Merlin asked, gesturing towards Arthur's eye.

Before he could answer, Elaine decided to waste no more time in getting to the point. "I want to know what I saw on the rugby pitch." She turned the full force of her glare on Merlin. "And no more smart comments from you, whatever the hell you are."

Merlin made a face. He looked livid enough to start hurling charms at the teenage girl if she wasn't careful, and Arthur thought it was probably time to intervene.

"It was a giant." Arthur said. "I know it sounds ridiculous, but you saw it yourself."

Elaine's eyes widened minutely. "It really *was* a giant?"

"No," Merlin muttered sarcastically, "it was just a really tall friend of ours."

"Oi!" Elaine put her hands on her hips. "What did I tell

you about smart comments?"

"Who died and put you in charge?" Merlin snapped. "I think you technically need to kill Arthur and a few others before you get your hands on a crown."

"Merlin!" Arthur hissed in warning.

"What?" Merlin turned on his friend.

"Shut up," Arthur replied, shaking his head.

"Magic's real!" Bertie piped up, stepping into his familiar role of peacemaker. He held his hands up in placation as Elaine focused on him instead. "Someone is using dark magic to bring these awful creatures into the world." He paused to take a deep breath. "The giant that you saw was only the beginning of it. There's something else on the loose. It's something that's responsible for what happened to that man near the train line."

Elaine blinked silently. Eventually she nodded her acceptance, although she did look somewhat discomfited.

"*And*," Bertie continued, "we think it's all happening because of Arthur."

"Yeah," Merlin mumbled, "let's just tell her everything. *Brilliant* idea,"

"And Merlin's a sorcerer!" Gareth piped up. "And there's this group tha-

"Gareth!" Merlin was bordering on incensed again as he twisted awkwardly to glower at Gareth.

"You just said let's tell her everything." Gareth frowned. "Bertie hadn't sa-"

"It was *sarcasm*, Gareth!"

"I have a right to know what I saw," Elaine said snippily, glaring at Merlin again. "So, you'd better tell me what's going on. I don't have to keep your stupid secret from my parents, you know. Not when you could be dangerous. For all I know, you're the one who magicked-up the giant in the first place. I mean, what's stopping *you* from using this so-called dark magic?"

Merlin threw up his hands, and by some miracle he managed to get to his feet without too much trouble.

The same couldn't be said for the other three, who lolled awkwardly at the sudden space they found themselves in, completely unbalanced by Merlin's departure. Arthur rolled slightly into the middle of the sofa and it took a second for him to sit up straight and reclaim his dignity.

"Look," Merlin levelled a glare first at his friends then at Elaine, "I didn't agree to telling anyone else about the giant, or about magic in general, but, fair enough, you don't need my permission for that, even if I think we're in enough trouble as it is, without involving someone else." He narrowed his eyes at the boys. "But none of you get to decide who else knows about *me*, about magic. If it were up to me none of you would know." He stared pointedly at Arthur. "Not even you."

"Merlin-" Arthur started.

"No." Merlin shook his head before turning back to Elaine. "As for you, yeah, you saw something on the rugby pitch, and I can understand that you'd want an explanation for what that was. But you don't have a *right* to demand that explanation, and you definitely don't have a right to accuse me of something like that." He shrugged at his friends. "You lot can do what you want, but I'm leaving."

Merlin left without another word.

"I think I'd better go talk to him." Arthur nodded slightly at Elaine. "Sorry, Elaine, but you shouldn't have said that. Merlin would never use magic to hurt people."

Merlin was leaning against the wall in the corridor

outside of the JCR.

"That was a bit dramatic." Arthur tried for light-hearted, but Merlin glared at him.

"This is why I don't want people to know, Arthur," he replied. "Elaine seeing what happened is one thing, but her suggesting that *I'm* the one responsible for those...things!" He lost the thread of his argument and ran a hand through his hair in frustration. "Arthur, you even said it yourself when you spoke to Lyonesse - the Brotherhood doesn't trust me, they don't think *you* should trust me. What do you think happens to me if they decide I'm dangerous? What happens if Elaine Beaulake makes a fuss and her father finds out that we're all aware of what's going on?"

"Merlin," Arthur said carefully gauging his friend's reaction, "we all know it isn't you who summoned the dragon, *or* the Questing Beast,"

"You do." Merlin nodded. "But she doesn't. There's something off about her, Arthur. I don't know what it is, but there's *something*. I can feel it."

"What do you mean?" Arthur frowned.

"I don't know." Merlin shrugged again with a sigh. "I'd never noticed anything about her before, but then again she'd never actually spoken to me before today."

"Do you think she's magic too? Another sorcerer, or something?" Arthur dropped his voice to a whisper. "Do you think she's lying about not knowing anything?"

Merlin shook his head. "No, I don't think it's that. It's-"

The door to the JCR opened and Elaine appeared. She looked uncharacteristically sheepish as she glanced at Merlin. "Sorry,' she said, "I got a bit carried away. I didn't mean it."

Merlin remained silent.

212

Elaine persevered. "Bertie explained a bit more. I really didn't mean it. I'm not very good at not knowing everything."

"Fine." Merlin replied eventually, and Arthur supposed that was almost a miracle under the circumstances.

"I'm not going to tell my parents," Elaine said bluntly, "unless I think my family's in danger."

"We think everyone's safe, as long as they're inside Badon," Arthur replied when it was clear that Merlin's selective mutism was going to continue. "We think I'm the target." Arthur wrinkled his nose at how self-conscious a ridiculous phrase such as that made him feel.

"I could help." Elaine nodded seriously. "Really, I could-"

The door to the Beaulakes' home at the end of the corridor swung open, the handle clanging loudly off the wood-panelling as it connected with considerable force. Mr Beaulake strode through the door, buttoning up a black, woollen coat as he marched towards the group of teenagers.

"Elaine!" Beaulake barked in a tone that was uncharacteristic of the housemaster. "You need to go inside and look after your brother. Your mother and I have to go out for a while."

"What's going on?" Elaine frowned.

"Elaine!" Beaulake snarled, staring hard at his daughter until she nodded.

"Okay." She shot the boys a look of confusion, but turned and hurried through the door as her father had instructed.

"You two," Beaulake pointed between Merlin and Arthur, "should go to your room and stay there."

"What? Why?" Arthur asked before he could stop

himself. "But it's dinner t-"

"Go!" Beaulake's voice was hardened by an edge of steel neither boy had heard before; not even after Hugo had attacked Merlin had he sounded so severe.

"What's going on?" Gareth poked his head out of the JCR, Bertie close behind as Merlin and Arthur practically ran past them.

"Upstairs!" Beaulake snapped from behind them, and the two boys heard the footfalls of their friends behind them as they ascended the stairs.

"Arthur!" Hector practically grabbed the prince by the scruff of his neck as they reached the landing. "What happened to your face?"

"What's going on?" Arthur asked as he was pushed towards his room; his friends behind him.

"Stay in there!" Hector ordered, glaring at each boy as they shuffled past him and into the room.

The door closed behind Hector, and Arthur just about heard his bodyguard bark "Secure!" before footsteps barrelled away from the room down the corridor.

Merlin immediately made for the window, practically pressing his nose to the glass, before Arthur elbowed him out of the way to have a look.

Mr Beaulake was striding across Kings' Court as other teachers filtered out of buildings to converge around Caerleon's housemaster. The lights in the Dining Hall were blazing, casting eerie shadows of the teachers across the Court, rather than acting as the usual, welcoming sign that dinner was almost ready.

"What's going on?" Bertie asked, using his height to lean over the other two boys at the window. "Is that Mrs Beaulake?"

Sure enough, Mrs Beaulake was sprinting across the bridge. Her scarf was billowing out behind her as she pulled on a pair of gloves, and the fabric was tangling with her hair as she swiftly covered the distance to reach her husband.

"Guys!" Gareth called from behind them. "Guys! I can't see!"

Mr Beaulake turned and looked up towards the boarding house. His face darkened immediately and he waved irately at the boys in a clear warning for them to get away from the window.

The three boys darted backwards. Merlin tripped over a hovering Gareth with a yelp of surprise as he did so.

"Gareth!" Merlin grumbled into the carpet in annoyance.

"Sorry!" Gareth squeaked, helping his friend up. "What did I miss?"

Bertie chanced a glance through the window again only to find that both Beaulakes were now looking up at him. He retreated immediately and sat on the edge of Arthur's desk. "Okay, there's definitely something really weird going on. I've never seen Mr Beaulake look that angry before."

"Do you think it's got something to do with the Questing Beast?" Arthur looked warily at his friends. "I wish they'd let us keep our laptops after prep, or at least our phones. We could check the news, see if anything's happened."

"But why would the Beaulakes be involved?" Gareth asked.

"It must be something to do with Badon," Merlin said. He was inching towards the window again. "What if something's happened to one of the students? Hey! They've all disappeared."

The other boys were at the window in a split-second. True enough Kings' Court was deserted; even the lights in the Dining Hall had been switched off, plunging the other side of the school into shadowy darkness.

A knock on the door came a split-second later. All four boys jumped slightly at the unexpected noise.

Arthur made his way warily across the room and inched the door open; it could never hurt to be too careful, after all. The tension left his shoulders when he saw one of the Caerleon prefects, standing there.

"Hi, Arthur," the prefect said. He looked past the prince to assess who else was in the room. "Guys. All boys are to remain inside their rooms until you hear otherwise."

"Gabe, what's going on?" Bertie asked from the other side of the room.

Gabe shrugged. "Honestly, I have no idea. Whatever it is, it must be bad. Mr Beaulake's never shouted at the prefects before, but he pretty much threatened us with expulsion if we don't make sure everyone stays in their rooms until he gets back. It's probably okay for you all to be in here together though."

"What about dinner?" Merlin mumbled and Arthur couldn't help but roll his eyes at his friend.

"No idea about that either, I'm afraid," Gabe replied with an apologetic shrug. "They won't let us starve, I'm fairly sure of that, but it might be a while until we're allowed over to the Dining Hall."

"Is it just Caerleon locked in?" Gareth piped up.

Gabe shook his head. "No, the whole school's effectively in lockdown."

Arthur ran a hand through his hair. "And you really have no idea why?"

"Sorry." Gabe repeated. "Look, if I hear anything I'll come and let you know, alright?"

"Alright." Arthur agreed. "Thanks, Gabe." He shut the door as the fifth year left them alone again.

"Well," Merlin flopped back onto his bed, "I guess we're waiting for something to happen. *Again.* I'm bloody starving as well."

"Haven't you got any biscuits left?" Arthur asked as he sat on the edge of his own bed next to Gareth.

"Just a few custard creams. They're for real emergencies only." Merlin grumbled. "I have to do a supply run in town, if we're ever allowed back into Cambridge." He sat bolt upright. "What if they don't let us out of here anytime soon? What am I supposed to do then?"

"Yeah," Arthur shook his head, "because that's what you should be concerned about - a biscuit drought!"

Merlin grumpily muttered something about resorting to chewing his own arm off in response. Arthur just settled himself back against the wall for yet another evening of waiting.

* * * * *

"Gentlemen."

The Dining Hall fell silent immediately as the headmaster's sombre tone cut through the nervous chatter. Nobody had felt much like eating when they'd been summoned there twenty minutes earlier after being locked in their rooms for almost three hours, but the headmaster had insisted that the boys eat dinner before any explanation would be given.

Arthur pushed his half-eaten bowl of crumble away from him and turned to face the teachers' table. The noisy shift of chairs and bodies as those boys with their backs to the headmaster moved so that they could see him started up, but was over within a few seconds, which was, no doubt, a record for Badon.

Cecil Catterick gave a solemn nod. "Thank you all for behaving so impeccably this evening, and I would like to extend particular thanks to the house prefects for carrying out their duties immediately, and without complaint."

Arthur flinched slightly when his ankle was kicked. His head snapped around to face Merlin, who was clearly the culprit, sitting next to him. "Ow," Arthur hissed.

"Beaulake's not here," Merlin replied quietly, not even a hint of apology to his tone.

Arthur looked back to the teachers. Merlin was right. Mrs Beaulake was at the table in her usual place, almost expressionless as she stared into the middle distance, but Caerleon's housemaster was conspicuously absent.

"It is with much regret that I have to inform you of some events that have taken place this evening," Catterick continued. "I must ask you all to remain calm and rational in the hours that follow."

Arthur swallowed loudly, his mind already racing through the possibilities.

"As you are all aware, an ex-student of Badon College disappeared from the University a couple of weeks ago." Catterick paused to rove his gaze over the collection of boys before him. "I am sorry to report that Rupert Daunton has been found under similar circumstances to the reported wild animal attack at the end of the Christmas holidays."

A flurry of whispering started up and Arthur took the opportunity to turn to Merlin again. "That doesn't really explain why they've locked us in."

Merlin shook his head. "I've not got a brilliant feeling about what's coming next, Arthur."

"I'm sure you have many questions," Catterick added as the chattering died away once more, "and they will be answered, no doubt, in the coming days through the news reports that will inevitably follow. However, Rupert's death is not the main reason that such unusual measures were put into action this evening."

"Here we go," Merlin whispered, and Arthur wanted to kick him back a little bit, just to relieve a some of the tension creeping up between his shoulders.

"During the fifth years' allotted hours for visiting the city centre this afternoon, a group of students had planned to meet at the cinema," Catterick explained.

Arthur glanced around the tables, and he frowned when he realised that the fifth years from Caerleon and Winchester didn't seem to be anywhere in sight. A few of the younger boys seemed to be absent as well.

"One member of the Winchester fifth year group did not arrive as expected."

Surprised gasps rippled through the Dining Hall, loudest from the tables where the remaining Winchester boys had congregated. A picture was beginning to form in Arthur's mind, and it was becoming more unpleasant by the second.

"To avoid rumour and gossip, and to ensure the continued safety of all of you, it falls to me to report that our Head Boy, Eliot Troyes, has not been seen since this afternoon."

Arthur barely had time to process what the headmaster had said before the Dining Hall erupted into chaos.

8

THE ARCH OF CAERLEON CASTLE

"Arthur, I'm sorry, but it's not up to me. Your father wants you back in London."

"But that's not fair!" Arthur just about managed to control the urge to throw his pillow at Hector in frustration.

Hector had been repeating variations on that apology since he'd pulled Arthur out of the Dining Hall and back to Caerleon at the end of the headmaster's announcement. Apparently, the Royal Protection Squad, MI5, *and* MI6, were apparently deeply irritated that they'd only been informed of Eliot's disappearance a few minutes before the boys had been told.

"Give me my phone then," Arthur demanded, holding out his palm. "I'll talk to him."

"Arthur, His Majesty wants you back in London this evening," Hector replied with a sigh. "He believes that it's too dangerous here. I'm sure you'll be able to come back once-"

"Do you believe that?" Arthur asked, not retracting his arm. "Do you think it's too dangerous to stay here?"

Hector hesitated long enough that Arthur knew that

220

he wasn't in agreement with the King. "Arthur, it doesn't matter what I think."

"I don't want to leave, Hector." Arthur shook his head vehemently. "I like it here. I have *friends* here. So please, *please*, Hector, can you give me my phone?"

Hector looked back in silence for a long moment, and Arthur was about ready to give up and collapse back onto his bed in frustration when his bodyguard finally sighed loudly and reached into his jacket.

"Thank you," Arthur breathed as Hector held out the phone.

"A word of advice," Hector said as Arthur's fingers closed over the handset, "don't approach this as an argument, Arthur. Your father won't respond well if you start shouting at him. Be reasonable, my boy.".

"I will," Arthur replied quietly as Hector turned to leave. "Thank you, Hector."

"You've got fifteen minutes, Arthur, but then we're leaving as planned, unless I hear otherwise."

Arthur didn't waste any time. His fingers flew across the keypad, bringing up his father's number as the door clicked closed. Despite the sense of urgency he felt, his finger hovered over the number for a few seconds rather than making the contact that would connect the call.

Steeling himself for the inevitable battle ahead, he took a deep breath and allowed his phone to dial.

Ring-ring.

"Come on, come on, come on." Arthur tapped his foot impatiently against the carpet as he sat down at his desk.

Ring-ring.

Arthur ran through his argument in his head. He'd have one chance to petition his father, and he couldn't afford to stumble over his words.

Ring-ring.

No answer.

Arthur hung up in frustration and swiped a hand over his face. He stared at his phone for a few seconds before returning to his list of contacts and selecting his mother's number instead.

The phone had barely finished its first ring when Arthur heard the tell-tale click of the call being answered.

"Hello?"

His mother sounded cautious. Arthur wasn't surprised; after all, he never really called his parents from his phone. He usually waited until they contacted him through Hector.

"Mother." Arthur smiled slightly, feeling almost overwhelmingly pleased to hear her voice. "It's me."

"Oh, Arthur," his mother replied, the worry evident in her voice, "your father told me what's happened. I'll be glad to have you back home."

"But I don't…" Arthur trailed off for a moment. "I don't want to come home. Not tonight."

His mother was quiet for a long moment. "Arthur, your father has already made up his mind. There was that terrible business of that young man from the university, and now that poor boy from your school is missing. I can't say I was surprised when he told me you were coming home. We can't have you somewhere where there's a wild animal roaming the streets. You're the heir to the throne, Arthur."

As if he could forget that.

"Please, Mother." Arthur was only slightly surprised to feel a horrible prickling sensation at the back of his eyes.

"Please don't make me come back."

If Arthur left Badon he knew what would happen. The Questing Beast would strike again, and Arthur wouldn't be there to stop Merlin from doing something stupid. He also wouldn't be there to stop Bertie and Gareth from running after Merlin to help with whatever that 'something stupid' was. Arthur couldn't live with that. It was his fault that monster was in Cambridge in the first place, and there was no way he was abandoning his friends.

His mother still hadn't replied. Arthur remembered Hector's advice, knowing that his mother wouldn't appreciate a tantrum either, so he gathered his thoughts before appealing to her again.

"I'm safe here. I have Hector, and twelve members of the Protection Squad in the city. Whatever this animal is, it isn't in the school, and it can't possibly care that I'm the heir to the throne, can it? I'm not in any more danger than anyone else living in Cambridge. In fact, I'm probably the safest person in the city."

Arthur never really enjoyed lying, and particularly not to his mother. He hated the fact that there was already so much he couldn't tell her about his time at Badon, but telling the Queen that her only son was being hunted by a mystical creature would be a sure fire way of ensuring Arthur was locked in a room for the rest of his life. He also wasn't going to point out that nobody was actually certain yet that Eliot had been spirited away by a creature; mystical or otherwise.

"Please, Mother," Arthur repeated.

The Queen sighed loudly. "I'll speak to your father, darling. I can't promise you won't still be back in London this evening though. You know what he's like when he gets an idea into his head. Just give me a few minutes."

Arthur almost grinned. "Thank you."

"I love you, Arthur. Be safe."

"I love you too."

With that his mother was gone and Arthur was left to wait and see if the King's mind could be changed. If anyone could make the King see reason it was his wife, and Arthur knew that if this didn't work he'd be in the back of an armoured car and on his way to London without any hope of further discussion.

He was saved from waiting in tense silence by a commotion in the corridor outside the bedroom a minute later.

"Do I look like a bloody lion?" That was Merlin. Nobody else could sound that petulant in the face of, what Arthur assumed anyway, was an armed member of the Royal Protection Squad.

Arthur sniggered slightly and waited for his friend to appear, which he did a few seconds later.

"There you are!" Merlin closed the door behind him and sat on the edge of his bed. "Gareth was convinced you'd already be on your way back to London by now."

Arthur's mood immediately soured again. "Yes, well, I might be doing just that in a few minutes."

"Really?" Merlin asked, managing to sound incredibly disappointed in Arthur with just one word. "You're leaving?"

"It's not up to me." Arthur replied with a huff.

"But what about Eliot?" Merlin asked, chucking a pillow at his friend as though it didn't matter one jot that he was the future king. Arthur supposed it *didn't* matter at all really, did it?

"I don't actually *want* to leave, you know," Arthur

replied, throwing the pillow back and missing Merlin by a mile. "It's up to my father. If he says I've got to go back to London, then I've got to go back to London."

Merlin frowned. "Hmm."

"What's that supposed to mean?" Arthur turned to face his friend properly.

Arthur didn't find out what 'hmm' meant as a knock at the door heralded Hector's reappearance.

"Well?" Arthur asked, unable to avoid leaping to his feet in anticipation. "Did you speak to him? What did he say?"

Hector smiled slightly. "We'll make a diplomat out of you yet, Arthur."

"I can stay?"

"You can stay." Hector nodded before holding a hand up at Arthur's grin. "But, your father has some very strict conditions that we will be enforcing from this moment on. Alright?"

Arthur could tell from the look on Hector's face that he wasn't going to like what came next.

"You may not leave Badon at all until half-term, unless it is to attend a function at the request of your parents." Hector gave a sympathetic wince before continuing. "That means no trips into the city, and..."

"And what?" Arthur asked, stomach already sinking, as Hector trailed off.

"It means that you're off the rugby team until further notice."

"What?!" Arthur squawked. "Why? The pitches are school property."

"I'm sorry, Arthur, but your father wants you within the walls of Badon at all times."

"But-"

"Arthur." It was Merlin's turn to cut him off. "Arthur, I think you should just agree to it. It means you get to stay here, right?"

Arthur really wanted to argue, but the look on Merlin's face suggested that he might actually thump him in full view of Hector if Arthur didn't just shut up and agree. It wasn't fair, of that Arthur was certain, but he was also certain that he and his friends were the only people in a position to at least try and help Eliot right now.

"Fine," Arthur replied eventually.

"Fine?" Hector asked carefully and Arthur realised that Hector had expected a lot more in the way of rebellion than he'd received.

"Fine," Arthur repeated. "I haven't got a choice really, have I?"

Hector narrowed his eyes and Arthur momentarily wondered if he should have put up more of a fight just to get Hector to stop looking at him as if he were trying to figure out what Arthur wasn't telling him.

"Okay," Hector replied eventually, still appearing to be wholly unconvinced of the sincerity of Arthur's agreement. "I'm sure your father will want to speak to you later."

Arthur nodded. "Thanks, Hector."

Hector graced Arthur with a final inscrutable look before nodding shortly and leaving the room.

"So, you're *not* leaving?"

"Apparently not," Arthur replied. "But, forget that. What happened after I left the Dining Hall? Have you seen Eric?"

Merlin shook his head. "Mrs Beaulake said he was in the Headmaster's Lodge waiting for his parents. She sent me up here, by the way, to make sure you didn't want any more food? They brought biscuits and tea out after the announcement about Eliot. Everyone's stuck in the Dining Hall until Eric's gone. I suppose they don't want everyone looking out of their windows at him."

Arthur nodded. He couldn't even begin to imagine how Eric must be feeling knowing that his brother was out there somewhere, possibly in grave danger.

"Did Catterick say anything else about Eliot?" Arthur asked eventually.

"A little. Hang on one second." Merlin crouched down to pull the familiar biscuit tin out from under his bed and offered it to Arthur. "Go on, have a custard cream. I think this probably constitutes an acceptable use of the emergency stash."

Arthur only hesitated for a moment, before realising that it was going to be another long evening, and that, really, a custard cream felt quite necessary.

"Apparently, the lot from here and Winchester who were supposed to meet Eliot in town are with the police," Merlin explained. "It sounds like he was supposed to meet them after he'd run some sort of last-minute errand in town, and then he just didn't turn up at the cinema. Mrs Beaulake said they were hoping he'd just gone somewhere else and lost of track of time. She also said I didn't need to worry about the 'lion'."

"Do you think she knows?" Arthur asked. "About Mr Beaulake, I mean, being part of the Brotherhood. Or about the Questing Beast?"

Merlin shrugged. "I don't know. Surely she'd notice a great big hooded robe hanging in their wardrobe?"

Arthur was quiet for another long moment as he

considered something that had occurred to him when Catterick had been breaking the news. "Rupert Daunton was a student here. He had the same scholarship as you."

"Yeah." Merlin nodded. "I know."

"And we already know that the man they found by the train tracks - Lawrence Hildon - he was a student here with Beaulake, right?"

"Yeah," Merlin repeated slowly. "Where are you going with this?"

"To get that scholarship you have to be quite clever," Arthur continued, "don't you?"

"No, not *quite* clever. You have to be *very* clever, Arthur," Merlin replied, with just a little bit of smugness.

Arthur rolled his eyes. "Okay, you have to be *very* clever. The kind of clever that might be appreciated by a secret society. So, what if Rupert Daunton was part of the Brotherhood? What if he wasn't just out for a bike ride. What if he'd gone looking for the Beast?"

Merlin considered the idea for a moment. "And, what? You think Lawrence Hildon being at school with Beaulake means he could be a member of the Brotherhood too?"

"Well, it wouldn't be a completely ridiculous idea, would it? The Brotherhood isn't just made up of teachers from here. There's Lyonesse, remember."

"It's a nice theory, Arthur," Merlin said eventually, "but what about Eliot? You can't possibly think he's a member of the Brotherhood too."

"No, I suppose not." Arthur sighed.

"Although," Merlin added as a frown settled deeper onto his forehead, "you might be right about there being a link between them and Eliot."

"What do you mean?" Arthur asked.

"Everyone in that Dining Hall immediately thought about the 'lion' when they heard that Eliot had gone missing, didn't they?"

"Well, yeah, because Catterick had just announced that Rupert Daunton had been found dead." Arthur shrugged.

"Right, but someone would have noticed if a bloody great mythical creature had swooped down in the centre of Cambridge, wouldn't they?" Merlin continued. "We know he went into town to do something before he was supposed to meet his friends. How likely is it that he was somewhere completely alone?"

Arthur thought about how busy Cambridge always seemed to be. Tourists, students and residents were out and about at all hours of the day, so unless Eliot had strayed very far from the centre it was unlikely he'd ever have been too far from another person.

"What if the Questing Beast has nothing to do with Eliot's disappearance?" Merlin added, looking like he had everything figured out all of a sudden.

"So, what?" Arthur asked, trying to follow Merlin's train of thought. "You think Mrs Beaulake is right? That he's just going to turn up soon, apologising for not being back before dinner?"

"Of course not! Come on, Arthur, keep up." Merlin shook his head in exasperation. "People would notice a giant creature, but they wouldn't necessarily take any notice of a person they passed in the street, would they? Someone who looks ordinary enough, but could actually have the power to bring giants into the world."

It clicked and Arthur's eyes widened. "You think Eliot's been taken by the sorcerer rather than the Beast?"

Merlin nodded.

"But why?" Arthur asked. "Why take Eliot of all people?"

Merlin deflated slightly. "I have no idea."

"Neither do I."

* * * * *

By the following lunchtime, the rumours surrounding Eliot's disappearance had reached fever-pitch in the Dining Hall. The morning's lessons had continued in as normal a fashion as possible, but all boys had been banned from leaving the school grounds unless they were with a parent or guardian. Arthur didn't have the heart to be cheered by the fact that it was no longer just him who'd been confined to within Badon's walls, not under such awful circumstances.

During final period Arthur had seen two men in suits walking across Kings' Court when he'd been asked by Mrs Beaulake to get the box of safety goggles from the supply room. At first, he'd assumed they were a couple of MI5 agents or something, but Arthur had a lifetime of observing the men who protected him, and as he watched the pair striding away from the Headmaster's Lodge he could tell from the way they carried themselves that they weren't employed by his father or the Secret Intelligence Services.

"You can tell that from the way they walk?" Gareth had asked when his lab-partner had retaken his seat and shared what he'd just seen.

Arthur nodded. "Just watch Hector next time you see him. Even when he's being 'relaxed' he looks ready to pounce. The two men I just saw weren't like that; they were a bit too..." he trailed off searching for the right word. "Slouchy, I suppose."

"Who do you think they were?" Gareth asked quietly as

Mrs Beaulake began to circulate the room, checking the setup of each pair's experiment and pausing to ask questions.

Arthur shrugged. "I'm guessing policemen. Maybe they've got some news about Eliot."

"Do you think they have any idea about..." Gareth trailed off as he carefully added some water to a beaker. "You know what I mean."

Arthur shook his head and glanced over to where Mrs Beaulake was finishing her conversation with Ruari and Charlie. "Not here, Gareth."

Gareth looked like he wanted to say something else, but Arthur shot him a warning look as their teacher approached their bench.

"Everything okay over here, boys?"

Arthur looked up at his Housemistress and frowned. Up close he could see that she looked different to how she usually appeared. Sadder, somehow.

"Yes, Mrs Beaulake," Arthur and Gareth answered in tandem.

Arthur glanced down to the worksheet they'd been handed at the beginning of the lesson; he'd been so focused on the events of the evening before that he hadn't really listened to a word Mrs Beaulake had said in her explanation of the experiment. He hoped that she wasn't going to ask him any direct questions about what they were doing.

Mrs Beaulake opened her mouth as if to say something, but seemed to think better of it. Eventually she nodded before moving away to the next bench

Gareth frowned. "That was a bit weird, wasn't it?"

Before Arthur could reply there was a knock at the lab door. A boy Arthur thought might be a Hainault third year appeared a moment later.

"I'm sorry to disturb your lesson, Mrs Beaulake," the boy said with a slight bob of his head.

"How can I help you, Ross?" Mrs Beaulake asked.

"I'm to bring Arthur Pendragon to the Headmaster's Lodge, Mrs Beaulake," Ross explained.

Arthur's head snapped up in surprise.

Ross glanced at Arthur briefly, and immediately misinterpreted Arthur's expression. "Oh sorry, I mean, His Royal Highness. I think that's correct?"

Arthur fought the urge to face-plant the lab bench in embarrassment.

Mrs Beaulake frowned. "Right now, Ross?"

"Yes, Mrs Beaulake," Ross confirmed.

Arthur must have looked suitably terrified as Ross added, "The headmaster said that it's nothing to worry about. Sorry, I was supposed to say that first."

"Alright," Mrs Beaulake said eventually as she looked at Arthur. "You may go, Arthur. Please make sure you copy up this evening."

"You can have my notes, Arthur," Gareth said quietly as Arthur packed his books into his bag.

"Thanks, Gareth."

Arthur gave Mrs Beaulake a small smile before heading across the lab to the door. He caught Merlin's eye on the way past his bench.

"I have no idea," Arthur whispered to his friend as he walked by, interpreting the silent question. He followed Ross into the corridor and closed the door behind him.

"Any idea what this is about?" Arthur asked as he followed the older boy.

"Sorry," Ross shook his head. "Oh, I mean sorry, Your

232

R-"

Arthur cut him off with a quick shake of his head. "Just 'Arthur' is fine, thanks."

"Right, Arthur, okay," Ross replied with a short nod. "Sorry, I was on the way back from a clarinet lesson when the headmaster passed me in Kings' Court. He just said to come and get you and to tell you that you weren't to worry about it."

Arthur didn't look convinced about the last part of that statement.

"I'm sure it's nothing," Ross replied with a supportive smile. "The headmaster likes to catch up with first years during the first couple of terms."

Arthur couldn't help but think this was a strange time for a headmaster to schedule a chat with a first year, what with the Head Boy being missing, but he nodded as he followed Ross across Kings' Court and to the Headmaster's Lodge. The older boy pulled the chain and the bell rang inside.

The door was opened a moment later by the stern-faced housekeeper Arthur had encountered before. She narrowed her eyes as if daring the prince to bring up the circum-stances surrounding their last meeting. She had to have known that she'd been leading Arthur to Lyonesse. Arthur had to remind himself that couldn't be happening again; not when Ross had spoken to the headmaster himself only a few minutes earlier.

"The headmaster asked me to get Arthur for him," Ross explained.

The housekeeper turned her beady eyes on the other boy. "Well, His Royal Highness best come in immediately then. Shouldn't you be in a lesson, Mr Clipstone?"

Ross gulped slightly, bobbed his head and scarpered with only a quick sympathetic glance towards Arthur.

The housekeeper said nothing, but ushered Arthur into the hallway with an irritated wave of her hand. As the door closed heavily behind him, Arthur briefly wondered if he should have requested Hector's presence.

"Go on. Up the stairs," the housekeeper said curtly as she pointed in the direction of the Headmaster's study.

Arthur did as he was told. This time he ignored the painted stares of the Catterick portraits as he steeled himself for whatever awaited on the other side of the door.

The housekeeper swept passed him when they reached the first-floor landing, knocking on the study door.

Arthur had to hurry to catch up with her, only reaching the door as it was opened in front of him. He almost sighed in relief when he caught sight of the man standing in the room; it was the Headmaster himself this time.

"His Royal Highness is here to see you, Headmaster," the housekeeper announced, and Arthur was surprised to hear the respect in her tone.

"Thank you, Mrs Tilbury," Catterick said with a quick smile. "Mr Pendragon and I can take it from here."

Mrs Tilbury gave Arthur one final inscrutable look before nodding at Catterick and closing the door behind her.

Catterick was standing in front of the large hand drawn map of Cambridge. The twists and turns of the city centre were represented in a faded red ink, with the colleges of the University outlined in gold. Badon, too, was marked prominently.

"This map is almost as old as the school," Catterick explained as he caught Arthur looking at the wall. "The colleges and streets have been added as the city has grown, but much of this was drawn by James Catterick when he presided over the first students here. I still find it rather impressive. Don't you?"

"Yes, sir," Arthur nodded politely, still on edge for not knowing why he had been summoned.

"Have a seat, Arthur," Catterick said as he sat behind his desk and gestured to a chair on the opposite side. "I hope Mr Clipstone informed you that there was nothing to worry about."

Arthur sat, nodding mutely before he remembered himself. "Yes, sir. He did remember."

"I like to see all of our first years for a quick chat," Catterick explained. "Just to make sure that every boy is settled here now that the first term is over. I have heard from your teachers, and they believe that you've settled into life at Badon remarkably quickly."

"Yes, sir." Arthur was hoping that this was going to be over quickly. There was something about this room that made him feel off-kilter, but it wasn't anything he could put his finger on if he'd been asked.

"It's a terrible business about Eliot." Catterick shook his head sadly.

Arthur nodded. "I hope they find him soon, sir."

"We all do, Arthur," Catterick said. "We all do."

Catterick was silent for a long moment before leaning forward slightly in his chair. "Arthur, how much do you know about Merlin Montgomery?"

Arthur's eyes bugged. Was this Catterick asking if Arthur knew about magic?

"Pardon, sir?" he choked eventually.

The headmaster sat back slowly, a look of deep

concentration etched on his face. "Your roommate, Merlin Montgomery, what do you know of him?"

"I don't understand, sir." Arthur shook his head.

"I assume you are aware of his scholarship status?" Catterick asked.

"I am." Arthur replied, locking his hands together on his lap.

"Then you are aware that Mr Montgomery must live up to certain academic and behavioural standards in order to remain here." It was a statement, not a question.

Arthur could only nod. "Has something happened with Merlin, sir?"

"Your cousin," the headmaster continued as he glanced down at the open notebook in front of him, "has made an official complaint about Merlin's conduct towards him, and indeed towards the rules and values of Badon College."

"What?" Arthur spluttered. "*Why?*"

"The exact particulars of Hugo's complaint have yet to be determined," Catterick replied, clasping his hands together on top of the book. "Although, he was quite keen to let me know that Mr Montgomery failed to attend a single sport's club last term."

"But that's all sorted," Arthur explained quickly. "Merlin's joined badminton."

"Yes," Catterick replied. "Mr Beaulake had already made me aware of Merlin's renewed interest in sport *before* Hugo made his objections known to me. However, I am concerned that there is bad blood between your cousin and your roommate."

"He's my friend, sir," Arthur corrected. "Merlin, I mean. Not Hugo."

Catterick nodded slightly. "Then I would be delighted

236

to hear your thoughts on the matter. We don't encourage animosity between our students, and we certainly will not allow it to fester for any length of time."

"My thoughts?" Arthur scrunched up his face in confusion. "Why, sir?"

"It strikes me that you are the person here who knows them best," Catterick replied. "Feuds rarely end in anything but catastrophe, Arthur, and it is my role to ensure that Badon boys continue to uphold the values of courage, honour and brotherhood."

Arthur knew the headmaster had seen him flinch when he'd said 'brotherhood', but Catterick passed no comment. Instead he waited in silence for Arthur to answer his earlier question.

"I don't think Merlin and Hugo will ever get on," Arthur replied eventually. "But, then again, I don't think I'll ever get on with Hugo either, sir."

Catterick looked both unsurprised and faintly amused by Arthur's response. "I see."

Arthur didn't know what else to say. He tried not to fidget as the Headmaster continued to study him.

"Your family has always been a part of this place," Catterick said as he stood suddenly and gestured towards the school outside. "The keystone at the top of the archway to Caerleon House was salvaged from the ancient Pendragon home of Caerleon Castle. As was the foundation stone for this very building."

"I didn't know that," Arthur answered, turning to look through the window at Caerleon bridge before he could stop himself. "Um, sir."

Catterick nodded sagely. "The Pendragon line is in the very fabric of Badon's walls, Arthur."

This was the strangest 'meeting' Arthur had ever been a part of - his brush with Lyonessee not included. Catterick seemed to be jumping from topic to topic, and Arthur wasn't sure what this was all leading towards.

"It is very important that you come to understand that, Arthur," Catterick continued, seemingly oblivious to Arthur's confusion. "So very, very, important."

Arthur didn't understand, not even a little, but he didn't feel like he could tell the headmaster that. He waited for the Catterick to expand further, but the silence stretched on for longer than Arthur expected. The only sound in the study was the faint ticking of a clock, and Arthur glanced around

"It is also very important to choose your friends wisely, Arthur," Catterick added as he turned away from Arthur, his focus entirely on a painting of a young woman hanging above the fireplace. "We must all have allies that we can trust. When the time comes and we face challenges that seem impossible to overcome, we must be sure of who our friends are."

* * * * *

Arthur had been trying, and failing, to fall asleep properly for hours, only managing to doze lightly a couple of times. His meeting with Catterick had unnerved him; and he was still regretting telling Merlin what Hugo had done. Arthur was all for honesty with his friends, but if he'd just kept quiet about this then Merlin wouldn't have marched off to sign up for fencing, dragging Arthur with him. He hadn't even managed to tell Merlin properly about the links to Caerleon Castle because his friend had been so incensed about Hugo.

"I really don't think this is a good idea." Arthur had muttered to Merlin as they'd crossed the bridge and headed for the noticeboard outside the gym after dinner.

"Doesn't matter," Merlin had replied "Your cousin needs taking down a peg or two, and if you're not going to do it, then I am. How hard can it be, anyway?"

"Hugo's been fencing since he was five, and he hasn't lost a match in years. Not to mention, Miss Tristram was in the Olympics a few years ago. She's not going to mess about when she's teaching, Merlin, and she's definitely not going to let you anywhere near Hugo. No offense, but he'd totally destroy you."

"Oh come on, Arthur." Merlin had rolled his eyes.

"What happened to being the bigger person?"

Merlin had looked deadly serious for the first time that evening. "That went out the window when your cousin tried to get me expelled."

"Can you stop referring to him as my cousin, please?" Arthur had sighed.

"But he *is* your cousin."

"Yes, but you're making me feel guilty by association. Come on, just stick with badminton."

Merlin had rolled his eyes again as they reached the noticeboard, but he'd still scribbled his name at the bottom of the list of boys interested in trying out fencing next term.

And now here Arthur was, wide awake in the middle of the night, wondering how exactly this could possibly end well.

"Arthur, are you awake?" Merlin whispered.

"No."

Merlin snorted. "Well, in that case wake up, because I think there's something going on outside."

Arthur turned his head slightly and was surprised to see that Merlin was out of his bed and peering through a crack in the curtains.

"What do you mean?" Arthur climbed out of bed as quietly as possible and tiptoed to the window.

"It looks like our friends are back," Merlin explained as he stepped away from the curtain to allow Arthur to have a look.

Arthur carefully parted the curtains and squinted into the darkness. He could just about make out the shapes of hooded figures standing together near the Headmaster's Lodge. There were far fewer than had congregated on the night he, Merlin and Bertie had gone to investigate; just three or four, but it was impossible to tell exactly with the way they hugged the shadows.

"What are they doing?" Arthur whispered. "They look like they're just waiting."

"No idea." Merlin shrugged. "I thought I heard someone cough about ten minutes ago, which, considering it's the middle of the night is weird, so I looked out the window. They haven't moved since I spotted them."

"Hang on, someone's just come through the arch. They're on the bridge."

"Who?" Merlin jostled Arthur's shoulder. "Move. I can't see."

"Shhh," Arthur murmured. "You look out that side, and I'll look out this one. Alright?"

Merlin did as he was told, pressing his face against the wall and closing one eye as he tried to look out without moving the edge of the curtain more than he had to. They both knew how much trouble they'd be in if they were caught.

The lone figure crossed the bridge slowly, the now-familiar hooded robe billowing out behind them as they reached the other side. Most of the lights around Kings' Court had been extinguished and it was impossible to tell who the arrival was, but the slight jerk to their steps was obvious enough; whoever was underneath the hood appeared to be limping

"Maybe it's Beaulake back from wherever he's been for the past couple of days," Merlin suggested, fidgeting slightly as he tried to get a clearer view.

"Could be."

"Next year they're definitely going to give us a room on the opposite side of the building," Merlin mumbled into the curtain fabric. "Seriously, how can they be so sure they're not going to be seen by anyone? Why not meet somewhere else?"

The figure suddenly stopped dead in the middle of the Court.

"Arthur, don't move!" Merlin hissed quickly as the figure turned suddenly raising its head as if to stare directly at the two concealed boys.

"They can't see us," Arthur breathed. "There's no way they can see us. Right?"

"I don't think so," Merlin whispered back. "At least, I hope not."

The hooded figure below them didn't move and Arthur didn't dare draw breath for fear of being discovered.

Long moments passed before the figure finally turned away and joined the others by the Lodge.

"This place is going to be the death of me," Merlin hissed. "Why couldn't I have just gone to the bloody local comprehensive like everybody else?"

A weak glow emerged in the corner of Kings' Court as the door to the Lodge opened briefly to admit the awaiting the members of Brotherhood. The light wasn't enough to help Arthur identify the hooded figures, however he did manage to see that the door had been opened not by Catterick, but by a woman he'd encountered before.

"That's Mrs Tilbury," Arthur said.

"Who?" Merlin asked in confusion.

"Catterick's housekeeper," Arthur replied, as they watched the woman raise a hood to cover her head just before she closed the door

"She's part of the Brotherhood too?" Merlin breathed. "How many of them are there?"

"No idea. Lyonesse just said that they came from the oldest families in 'the kingdom'," Arthur replied. "He wasn't actually very helpful."

"We need to find out more about them." Merlin shook his head. "For all we know, every single teacher here could be one of them."

Arthur frowned. "You're not suggesting we go out there now, are you?"

Merlin looked at his friend in exasperation. "Of course not. One session of hiding in those rose bushes was enough for a lifetime, thank you very much. Not to mention I don't fancy meeting your friend Lyonesse in person."

"He's not my friend," Arthur grumbled. "Go on then, what's your grand plan?"

Merlin grinned when his friend looked over at him. "Gareth."

"Gareth?" Arthur scrunched up his nose. "You want to send *Gareth* out there?"

Merlin rolled his eyes for the umpteenth time that

evening. "No, Arthur, I'm not suggesting we send Gareth out there. I'm suggesting that Gareth is far, far better at researching things than either of us."

Arthur nodded slowly, understanding. "If there's any information about the Brotherhood, then Gareth will be able to find it."

"Think about it; I tried for ages to find out about magic, and the best I could come up with was an Old Irish dictionary," Merlin explained, "and then Gareth learned more about all of it in a few days than I did in a few years. When it comes to research, Gareth's our man."

Arthur had to agree with that. "Well in that case I'm going back to bed. If I fall asleep in Latin tomorrow Ms Bell will murder me."

"Well, you *do* murder her favourite language on a regular basis."

"Haha," Arthur muttered dryly. "Hilarious, aren't you?" He shook his head and padded back towards his bed. Maybe he'd finally be able to fall asleep now.

"Er...Arthur?"

"What now?" Arthur asked with a sigh as he reached for his pillow.

"Who's that?" Merlin was peering through the curtains again.

"Who's what?"

Merlin waved his arms towards Arthur. "Quick, come here, and look."

Arthur did. He carefully peeked through the gap in the curtains and was surprised to see someone else creeping stealthily over the bridge. There was no robe this time and Arthur's eyes widened when the figure turned their head enough for their features to be visible.

"Merlin, that's Elaine!"

"No, it's not," Merlin replied. "It can't be."

"That is definitely Elaine Beaulake." Arthur was sure of it, even in the darkness.

"I need to get a better look." Merlin began to pull the curtains wider apart.

"What are you doing?" Arthur hissed in horror as he grabbed at the material. "You can't just open the curtains! What if someone sees you?"

"They won't!" Merlin yanked the curtains back again.

"Merlin!"

"Shhh!"

"Merlin, seriously, stop!"

Merlin suddenly let go of the curtains as if he'd been burned. "Uh-oh."

"*Uh-oh?*"

Merlin tilted his head slightly in the direction of outside. Arthur warily glanced out the window to see Elaine Beaulake standing on the other side of the Caerleon bridge staring up at the two boys.

"Uh oh," Arthur agreed.

"What do we do?" Merlin asked before his face paled. "Arthur, what if she's one of *them*?"

Elaine certainly didn't look like a member of the Brotherhood. For a start, she was wearing a coat, not a robe, and, secondly, she looked horrified that she'd been spotted. Arthur said as much.

"Yeah, well, I still don't trust her," Merlin replied as Elaine as she remained rooted to the spot on the bridge. "What's she doing out there?"

Arthur opened his mouth to reply, but before he could utter a word Elaine's eyes had widened and she'd sprinted off the edge of the bridge and dropped to her knees, pressing her back against the Dining Hall's red bricks as she crouched in the shadows.

"What's she doing now?" Merlin asked, squinting into the darkness.

"Get back," Arthur hissed to Merlin as another robed figure materialised on the bridge beneath them.

Both boys flattened themselves to the wall either side of the window.

"How many times is this going to happen?" Merlin mumbled, trying to peer out to see what was happening below. "I'd love a good night's sleep at some point."

By the time Arthur chanced another look outside the figure had disappeared, but he could still just about make out Elaine still concealed in her hiding place.

"Merlin, she's hiding from them," Arthur said as he stepped away from the window and reached down to retrieve his trainers from next to the bed. "If she's one of them she wouldn't be hiding, would she?"

Merlin pointed at Arthur's shoes. "What are you doing?"

"She needs our help," Arthur replied. "We can't just leave her out there to get caught, can we? We don't know what they'll do if they find out she's there."

"It was *her* decision to go out there, Arthur," Merlin replied. "I'm sure she can get herself back to Caerleon. You can't go out there."

Arthur silently stared at his friend for a long moment. "Is this because you still think there's something weird about her?"

"Yes." Merlin nodded immediately. "Because there's *definitely* something weird about her. Plus, I'm pretty sure *at least* one of her parents is part of that Brotherhood."

"Merlin, we can't let her get caught," Arthur replied firmly, standing up to grab his coat. "Imagine what will happen if she does talk to them. What if she tells them that we know about the giant? About the Questing Beast? What if she tells them about *you*?"

Merlin paled. "Oh."

"Exactly. So, you can either stay here, or you can come with me," Arthur said as he moved towards the door, "but I'm going out to help her."

Merlin stuffed his feet into his shoes. "No. Just wait here for a second. I have a better idea."

"What better idea?" Arthur asked, frowning as Merlin shrugged on his own coat. "What are you going to do?"

"Something that will probably get me expelled," Merlin replied with a sigh. "Just wait here, okay? I'll be right back. Be ready to pretend you're surprised."

Without any more explanation Merlin opened the bedroom door carefully and tiptoed out into the corridor.

After a couple of seconds, Arthur crept across the carpet and peeked out around the doorframe. Merlin had made it to the other end of the corridor and now looked to be whispering at the wall in front of him.

Arthur's eyes widened as he realised what Merlin was trying to do a split-second before the fire alarm started wailing loudly throughout Caerleon house.

Merlin bolted back up the corridor to the bedroom, barging passed Arthur, closing the door behind him and diving onto his bed just as doors started opening on the corridor and panicked voices of their friends reached them. Arthur didn't need to pretend to be surprised.

The bedroom door burst open almost immediately and Hector appeared, already reaching to grab hold of Arthur's arm.

"Arthur, outside now!" Hector ordered. "You too, Merlin."

Merlin, who was pretending to be half-asleep as he pulled on his coat gave Arthur the slightest grin before he followed his roommate and accompanying bodyguard down the stairs.

As they reached the outer door, Arthur lost sight of his friend as the prefects joined the hoard of boys leaving the building, jostling each other slightly as they tried to calm the younger boys into silence.

Arthur approached the bridge, Hector close behind him, and saw that Elaine had managed to reach the group of Caerleon boys forming on Kings' Court. She wasn't stopping there though, instead she was striding quickly towards Caerleon with a panicked look on her face.

Elaine caught Arthur's eye before she drew level with him. "Thomas," was all she said as she tried to get past him.

Hector stopped her by holding his arm up. "Miss Beaulake, I'm afraid you can't go back inside."

Elaine looked ready to argue, but Arthur knew there wasn't a chance she'd get around Hector. Not when the bodyguard thought that the building could actually be on fire.

"Elaine!" Merlin called loudly from behind them.

Arthur turned to see his roommate hurrying towards them, clutching a tearful Thomas to his chest as best he could even as the toddler tried to escape from the unfamiliar arms clamped around him.

Elaine scooped Thomas into her arms and held him close. She looked stricken as she glanced quickly at Arthur and Merlin, opening her mouth as if to say something.

She seemed to change her mind and instead turned away abruptly before she hurried over to where the rest of Caerleon House had gathered in Kings' Court, speaking quietly to Thomas as she did so.

"You're welcome," Merlin muttered irritably with a small shake of his head as he and Arthur went to join their friends, trailed by Hector, who was frowning slightly at Elaine. Arthur could only hope Hector wouldn't ask why Elaine would have left her brother behind.

Gabe was in prefect mode again, waving his arms to get the boys' attention. "Right, everyone, year group alphabetical order, please. Quickly and silently. We need to take the register."

As Arthur slipped into line he noticed Mrs Beaulake hurrying across the court from the Headmaster's Lodge to speak to her children. Even though he'd been suspicious that she had been at the meeting with the others, Arthur's stomach still flipped at the confirmation that his housemistress was part of The Brotherhood.

"Merlin, loo-" Arthur cut himself off, looking around in surprise when he realised that Merlin was no longer standing nearby. There were only two spaces between them in the alphabet so his roommate should have been right there.

"Mr Montgomery!"

Arthur's head snapped up at Mrs Beaulake's angry shout. He caught sight of Merlin frozen in place near Gareth at the very beginning of the line. The hushed muttering of the other boys fell silent immediately.

"Does your surname begin with 'A', Merlin?" Mrs Beaulake continued in a clipped tone.

"Um...no, Mrs Beaulake," Merlin answered quietly

after recovering himself.

"Exactly, so you currently have no business being anywhere near Mr Allard." Mrs Beaulake replied.

"Sorry, Mrs B-" Gareth started.

Mrs Beaulake held up her hand for silence, and Arthur cringed in sympathy for Gareth. "Come over here, Mr Montgomery. *Now.*"

Merlin, head down, shuffled towards the housemistress. Even from a distance Arthur could tell his friend's cheeks were burning.

A slight movement in the corner of his eye caught Arthur's attention and he instinctively glanced up towards the Headmaster's Lodge. He wasn't completely certain as the building was shrouded in inky darkness, but Arthur thought he could make out two figures looking down to where the Caerleon boys were gathered.

Looking quickly around Kings' Court Arthur realised that although Mrs Beaulake had appeared, as had the housemasters of Winchester and Hainault, Mr Beaulake was still nowhere to be seen, nor any other teaching staff. Who was up there watching them? Had they seen Elaine?

Arthur shivered, not just because he hadn't thought to grab a jumper in his haste to get out of Caerleon with everyone else.

"Arthur?" Ruari hissed quietly from his place next to him. "I think Gareth wants you."

Sure enough, a quick glance confirmed that Gareth was waving at Arthur as subtly as he could from further up the court.

Even though Mrs Beaulake's attention still seemed to be firmly on Merlin, Arthur was very careful about signalling back to Gareth. It wouldn't do for them all to get into trouble tonight.

What? he tried to ask using only a twitch of his eyebrows.

Gareth silently mouthed something back to him.

Arthur frowned. *What?*

Gareth tried again, obviously trying to enunciate even in his silence. He held up three fingers quickly.

"Okay, three words. Way. Frown...*what?*" Arthur scrunched his nose trying to decipher the message. "That doesn't make any sense."

"Watch out, Arthur," Ruari warned out of the corner of his mouth as Mr Holland from Kings' looked over at them briefly.

Arthur shook his head and frowned as Gareth repeated his actions, widening his eyes meaningfully after each word.

"They," Arthur whispered slowly, trying to copy Gareth's movements. "Found..."

Arthur sucked in a breath of surprise as he realised what the final word Gareth was mouthing to him was. "*Eliot.*"

"What?" Ruari asked, loud enough for quite a few boys to look at him in surprise. "*They've found Eliot?*"

The whispering started immediately, building to surprised exclamations as the news carried through the line of Caerleon boys.

Arthur caught Merlin's shocked expression just as the wail of fire engines approaching Badon cut through the din. Merlin looked as unsettled by the news as Arthur felt.

Gareth had said Eliot had been found.

But he hadn't said *alive*.

9

Arturus Rex

Arthur's sense of unease didn't disappear overnight, and a fitful sleep had left him feeling a bit sick. He'd barely nibbled a slice of toast at breakfast to settle his stomach, but now, as the whole school headed for an impromptu morning assembly, his insides were twisting into knots.

"Eliot's fine, Arthur," Bertie said as they trooped out of Caerleon with Gareth and Merlin close behind. "You heard what Eric said."

That wasn't strictly accurate. He'd heard *Bertie's version* of what Eric had apparently said about his brother that morning. Eric wasn't even back at Badon yet, so the news was second-hand at best. Just like Gareth's mime the night before.

Before the news that Eliot had been found had made it to Arthur, Gareth had been told by Bertie, who'd been told by Leo on the way over the bridge during the evacuation. Arthur wasn't sure if Eric himself had text Leo's secret phone, or if the news had travelled through a few more second years first.

"He had an accident," Gareth added as he noticed Arthur's concern. "He really is okay."

"I still don't like it," Merlin said shaking his head. "It's too much of a coincidence."

Arthur was slightly cheered that he wasn't the only one still concerned that Eliot's disappearance, however temporary, *had* to be related to everything else that had happened.

Bertie only shrugged in response as they crossed the bridge into Kings' Court and headed for the Dining Hall for the second time that morning.

They rounded the corner of the building and joined the scrum of boys trying to fit through the single door to the hall. Arthur, feet shuffling slowly forward, watched as the headmaster emerged from the Lodge, smiling as he gestured for the woman accompanying him to walk ahead.

"I wonder who that is," Gareth said. "Do you think she's a policewoman or something? Here about Eliot?"

Arthur shook his head, certain that he'd seen her before. "No, I don't think so. I'm sure I know her from somewhere."

A vague memory was still niggling at Arthur's mind when Merlin shoved him through the doorway. "Oi! What was that for?"

"Mrs Beaulake's coming," Merlin hissed trying to squeeze himself past his friends and into the crowded hall. "I don't want her to see me."

Arthur frowned. "Why not?"

"Because I don't think I'm forgiven for breaking out of line last night. She was threatening me with a visit to Catterick's office and you know I don't want to go anywhere n-"

"Ah, Merlin, there you are."

Merlin tensed immediately at Mrs Beaulake's voice behind them.

"So much for escaping," He whispered to Arthur with a grimace before pasting on a thoroughly false smile and turning to face their Housemistress. "Good morning, Mrs Beaulake."

Mrs Beaulake smiled at Merlin, but there was a slightly frosty edge to her voice as she fell into step beside him. "Merlin, you will be sitting next to me this morning. I'm still not sure you can be trusted not to distract your friends. The headmaster would also like to see you briefly after assembly"

For one moment Arthur thought Merlin was going to argue, but in the end, he just sighed and nodded, looking utterly miserable as he followed Mrs Beaulake. Arthur knew that although Merlin was worried about Mrs Beaulake's probable connection to the Brotherhood, he was genuinely petrified of what might happen to him if Catterick ever learned that Merlin was the one who possessed the powerful magic the Brotherhood seemed to be so in awe of.

"It's my fault Merlin's in trouble," Gareth whispered as the remaining Caerleonites took their seats and waited for assembly to begin. "I was the one who called him over to tell him about Eliot. I should go and speak to Mrs Beaulake."

"I bet she wouldn't be half as cross if she knew Merlin was the one who'd gone back for Thomas," Arthur replied, sulking slightly on behalf of his best friend.

Any further conversation was halted by the appearance of the headmaster at the front of the hall. The teachers and students rose as one as Catterick approached the podium. The woman Arthur had spotted outside had followed close behind and was standing only a few steps away from the headmaster.

"Good morning, ladies and gentlemen," Catterick

began, nodding slightly as the congregation took this as the cue to sit down.

"I'm very relieved to be able to give you the news that Eliot Troyes has been found safe."

This news wasn't exactly a surprise as the story had spread like wildfire during breakfast that morning.

"As I'm sure many of you are already aware…" Catterick paused as he waited for silence to resettle itself over the Dining Hall. He cleared his throat and started again. "As I'm sure many of you are already aware, Mr Troyes was found close to the river in Grantchester last night. Due to the injuries he sustained when he fell from his bike he was unable to search for help, and without his mobile phone in his possession he could not reach the emergency services. I am happy to report that he is now under the care of medical professionals, and is being treated for his injuries, as well as for the effects of spending over twenty-four hours outside at this time of year. It is truly a joy to be able to share this good news with you all this morning, and we must all now look forward to welcoming Eliot back to Badon shortly."

From the other side of the Dining Hall Merlin shot Arthur an incredulous look.

Arthur agreed with the sentiment. It certainly was remarkable. Until he saw Eliot with his own eyes there wasn't a chance he would believe that the Head Boy was alright, and that somehow this wasn't linked to the sorcerer.

Catterick shuffled slightly, looking uncharacteristically nervous as he continued after a slight pause. "However, I am sorry to say that city-privileges will continue to be revoked for the time being. This is for all year groups, including our fifth years."

Even the combined glares of the full teaching staff

couldn't stop the surprised grumbles that rippled through the hall.

"Due to the continued threat of the wild animal, the University has a strict curfew in place for its students, and therefore we have been advised to ensure that all Badon pupils remain on the school premises for the foreseeable future," Catterick added. "This is to continue to assure the safety of you all."

The headmaster turned slightly to nod the to the woman he had entered the hall with before continuing. "However, Lady Burton from Catterick College has joined us this morning to explain how we are going to be working closely with the University to ensure that you all have some time outside of school to pursue other interests."

Emma Burton, Arthur finally realised as the woman replaced the headmaster at the podium, was the lady he had sat next to for most of the dinner at Catterick College before Hugo had turned so spectacularly green. He probably would have recognised her immediately if she'd been wearing a truly horrendous shade of pink again.

"Good morning, gentlemen," Lady Burton began, smiling at her audience. "It's lovely to be back in Badon, although I wish it were under happier circumstances. This school and Catterick College have always shared a close relationship, and with your headmaster's permission this relationship will continue by allowing you to visit Catterick College under supervision to make use of our indoor sport, music, and arts facilities until such time the curfew is lifted. Your first visit will be this coming weekend and will be for every boy at Badon."

Excited chattering replaced the silence immediately.

Arthur sighed. He knew that none of this made a

difference to his father's edict that Arthur remain within Badon at all times, so he allowed his mind to wander away from the Dining Hall for the remainder of assembly and his thoughts once more drifted miserably towards the rugby team he was no longer a real part of.

It took Gareth nudging him painfully in the ribs some time later to realise that assembly was over and that the rows of chairs were already emptying of boys around him.

"Oh, that looks bad," Bertie said, wincing slightly as they left the hall and headed back to their rooms to change out of their formals before lessons started.

Arthur followed the direction of Bertie's nod to see Merlin being led towards the Headmaster's Lodge by Mrs Beaulake. Merlin's head was bowed towards his chest and he was shuffling his feet even more than usual.

"Actually, it looks worse than 'bad'," Gareth added, pointing towards Kings' House. "Arthur, your cousin's looking a bit too pleased with himself right now."

Gareth was right. Hugo was standing with a few of his cronies, grinning and laughing as Merlin trudged across Kings' Court.

"Leave it, Arthur" Bertie warned as he watched his younger friend curl his fists. "You don't know what's going on. You know Hugo will find some way of blaming Merlin for it if you start a fight, and we really don't want to make this any worse for him. Mrs Beaulake already seems far angrier with him than I would have expected."

Arthur grumbled slightly but dropped his hands to his sides. He knew Bertie was right. Arthur had managed to avoid Hugo for weeks now, and, even though he was sure his father would call it cowardly, he would rather keep his distance unless absolutely necessary.

As the boys rounded the corner into Caerleon, Arthur's shoulder was jostled violently by someone marching in the opposite direction. Before he could yell at the other boy to watch where he was going an envelope was shoved into his hand with a hissed *I owe you one.*

It was only as the figure hurried across the bridge, head bowed beneath the hood of a black coat, that Arthur realised that it hadn't been another boy at all, it had been Elaine Beaulake.

"Um, what just happened?" Gareth asked as Arthur looked down at the white, misshapen envelope he was now clutching.

"Was that Elaine?" Bertie's confusion mirrored the other boys', as he stared after the retreating figure as it ducked through the passageway at Kings' heading for the Back Gate.

"Shouldn't she be at school already?" Gareth asked, ever the rationalist. He then pointed at the letter. "What's that?"

"No idea," Arthur whispered. "But I don't think we should open it out here."

Bertie nodded in agreement. "Good idea. The prefects will be along to make sure we're all off to lessons in ten minutes."

"Lunchtime then?" Arthur asked as they trooped up the stairs to the first year corridor.

"Rugby," Bertie replied with an apologetic wince.

"Prep in your room, Arthur?" Gareth offered.

Arthur nodded. "Come straight after lessons."

"Will do," Bertie replied as he opened the door to his and Gareth's room. "And Arthur?"

Arthur paused, his hand on his bedroom door. "Yeah?"

"Make sure Merlin's really alright, won't you?" Bertie

asked. "I've been in trouble with the teachers here before, but I've never seen Mrs Beaulake get cross with anyone before. She's usually the first to defend any of us, not march us straight to Catterick's study."

* * * * *

Arthur didn't see Merlin again until lunchtime. His wayward roommate hadn't made an appearance in Chemistry, nor had Mrs Beaulake. Merlin also apparently hadn't turned up to Geography with Gareth, he'd been missing from his usual spot near the JCR's biscuit tin at break time, and Arthur once more had an empty desk next to him during Latin. Even Hector had commented on the fact that Arthur seemed to be without his shadow.

By the time he headed back to his room at the beginning of lunchtime to dump his books on his desk Arthur was starting to think that Merlin had been spirited away. This was *not* a comforting thought when Arthur considered that this might be something the Brotherhood was actually capable of.

So, he was more than a little surprised when a few seconds after he arrived, the door to the bedroom opened and Merlin appeared.

"Where have you been?" Irritation coloured Arthur's words as the worry that had been steadily increasing all morning evaporated instantly. "What happened?"

"Not much," Merlin replied with a shrug, unceremoniously dropping the formal robe he was carrying onto the floor before taking a seat on his bed and looking over his French homework.

Arthur allowed his friend a few seconds to think that the casual shrug had fooled him. "Not much? *Really?*"

"Really," Merlin replied not looking up from his exercise book.

"Merlin," Arthur sighed in frustration. "I know that those French questions took you about three minutes to finish last night, so don't pretend you're actually checking your work. You've been gone all morning."

"The library."

"What?" Arthur huffed.

Merlin sighed with a grimace. "I was in the library. Mrs Beaulake sent me there. She decided it was probably best that I didn't disrupt my friends' education any further this morning."

Arthur could tell Merlin was directly quoting Mrs Beaulake.

"And?" Arthur pressed eventually.

"And what?" Merlin asked, still refusing to look at his roommate.

"*And*, what happened with Catterick?" Arthur asked. He refused to give into the urge to shout at Merlin for being purposefully difficult.

"He told me off for talking during the fire alarm." Merlin shrugged again.

Arthur narrowed his eyes and sat down on his own bed. "What aren't you telling me?"

Merlin opened his mouth to reply.

Arthur cut him off with a glare. "And don't lie."

For a few seconds Arthur thought Merlin was going to argue with him, but then his friend sagged slightly and finally looked up.

"When I was in Catterick's office I saw a letter on his desk. Well, part of a letter."

"A letter?" Arthur frowned.

"Yes, Arthur, a letter. Some people still write letters, you know, and Catterick's never really struck me as the most technologically minded. He probably doesn't know what an email is. He probably still writes with a quill."

Arthur rolled his eyes. "Alright, you're rambling now. What did it say?"

"I couldn't read it properly upside down because of the stupid, flouncy handwriting. The bit I could read said something about the legacy being tracked to Cambridge, but that the they'd lost the trail when they'd recovered Eliot."

"Who was it from?"

"I don't know." Merlin shrugged. "I couldn't see that bit. But that's what I'm worried about."

A chill settled over Arthur. "What *are* you worried about?"

"Your name was in the letter," Merlin said seriously, all traces of humour now evaporated. "A bit further on."

Arthur gulped. "And?"

"*Arthur Pendragon is not safe enough within Badon. They understand his importance, even if you do not.*" Merlin recited.

"Oh."

"There's more. Sorry." Merlin winced. "It said '*Our fears have been confirmed. They have it in their possession*.'"

"Have what? And who are '*they*'?"

Merlin flopped back onto his bed with a sigh. "I have no idea. The rest of it was covered with a book."

"Are you sure that's what it said?" Arthur asked. "I mean, really sure?"

"I was staring at it for fifteen minutes whilst Mrs Beaulake and the headmaster took turns telling me how disappointed in my behaviour they both were," Merlin replied archly. "The way they were talking you would have thought I'd actually set fire to the school."

Arthur started pacing, suddenly far too restless to stay still. "We need to get back into Catterick's study. We need to read the rest of that letter. It could help us work out what we need to do."

"What we need to do is step back from all of this, before one of us gets killed," Merlin sighed. "Arthur, there's so much more going on here than we understand. Elliot's back and he's okay. Maybe we should just let the Brotherhood handle it all."

Arthur took a step back at Merlin's words. "Are you serious? Come on, Merlin, just think what you can do! We can stop this sorcerer, I'm certain of it. The Brotherhood hasn't done a very good job so far, has it? Two people are *dead* because nobody's stopped the Beast yet. What if it comes back to college and kills a boy? What if it comes back to kill one of our friends? Or you? Or me?"

"Arthur, in case you've forgotten, let me just remind you that we're fourteen," Merlin replied fiercely. "We don't know what we're doing. We got lucky killing the giant, but-"

"That wasn't luck, Merlin!" Arthur shouted in frustration, before dropping his voice in case Hector overheard next door. "It wasn't luck. It was you. The power you have has been given to you for a reason, and I think that this is it. It's for stopping this sorcerer and making sure nobody else gets hurt."

Merlin was silent for a long moment. "You know, on my way up here I'd actually decided not to tell you about the letter. I *shouldn't* have told you about the letter. I can't help

261

you anymore Arthur."

"What? Why?" Arthur was stung by his friend's refusal.

"Well, Catterick thinks my behaviour means I'm not taking my scholarship seriously enough," Merlin tapped on his exercise book as he spoke.

"And?" Arthur threw up his hands. "When has what teachers thought of your behaviour ever stopped you from doing whatever you want?"

Merlin was silent for such a long time Arthur was convinced he was never going to speak again. Eventually, however, his friend looked up at him once more.

"I'm officially on probation," Merlin replied quietly, now looking horribly close to upset. "Catterick's put me on a final warning. If I end up in his office again before the end of the year I'm out of Badon for good."

Arthur gaped uselessly for a few seconds. "Are you serious?"

"If I get caught, that's it. Catterick will have me shipped back to Somerset immediately, and then Mum will probably lock me in my bedroom for the rest of my life as punishment," Merlin replied miserably. "I know I said I didn't like it here, but I really don't want to leave."

Arthur continued to stare in appalled silence at his friend.

"I think your cousin's got something to do with this," Merlin continued when it became clear Arthur was still processing the announcement. "Catterick didn't say anything specifically, but he kept making reference to the fact that me and you being friends was causing concern for some people. At first I thought he meant the Brotherhood, but as he thinks I have about as much magical talent as a doormat, it probably wasn't that. Then Mrs Beaulake suggested some of your family had contacted her with their concerns about you being friends with a 'bad influence'."

Arthur was now even more horrified. He thought of his cousin's sneering face after assembly "I knew Hugo looked far too happy about you being sent to Catterick this morning! I mean, even happier than he would usually be at seeing you in trouble."

"Doesn't he have anything better to do?" Merlin asked with a frown.

Arthur shook his head. "Hugo's always been vindictive. I wouldn't be surprised if he's complained to his father about you. My uncle's always been one for making a fuss as well."

Merlin looked alarmed. "I hope you don't think I'm ever going to visit you at home over school holidays. Your family sounds awful."

"Some of them are," Arthur agreed easily. "Look, we'll work something out. You're not leaving Badon, but we're not going to sit around and do nothing either. I know we can fix this."

Merlin didn't look particularly convinced.

Neither did Arthur.

*   *   *   *   *

"Sorry! Sorry, sorry, sorry," Gareth mumbled as he barged into Arthur and Merlin's room fifteen minutes after prep time had started. "I know I'm late. I bumped into Hugo."

Bertie's eyes widened. "Bumped into Hugo?"

"Yeah," Gareth replied as he sat down and took the biscuit tin form Merlin. "It was okay though. He just wanted to know if you were going on the Catterick College trip on Saturday, Arthur."

"Why would he want to know that?" Arthur asked,

frowning.

"And he didn't thump you?" Merlin grimaced. "Or threaten to chuck you off the bridge?"

"No," Gareth replied slowly as he picked out one of the remaining three custard creams.

"I think he saves those threats for you, Merlin," Bertie added.

Arthur scrunched his nose in confusion. "I don't understand. Hugo spoke to you, and all he asked was if I was going to Catterick College on Saturday?"

Gareth nodded. "Yes, that's all. Look, can we just forget about that for now though? I want to know what that envelope's about."

Arthur couldn't agree more, even as he remained suspicious about Hugo's motives. The mystery of what Elaine had handed him had been driving him mad all afternoon.

"Go on then, Arthur." Merlin nodded towards where the envelope sat by Arthur's textbooks.

Arthur carefully peeled back the sealed flap and tipped the envelope upside down. There was an immediate *clunk* as something heavy fell out and hit the desk. A small, folded piece of paper followed with a flutter.

"That's a key," Gareth said as he picked up the object with a frown. "What does the note say, Arthur?"

Arthur picked up the paper before clearing his throat and reading aloud. "*I don't think this will be missed for a few days. Thought it might help. Mum's being weird and I don't know what to do*"

"Is this the one for the Back Gate, Bertie?" Gareth asked, passing the key to his friend.

Bertie shook his head. "No. The Back Gate key is a plain black one. I don't know what this one's for."

"Would it have killed her to include a bit more information?" Merlin grumbled as he swiped the key from Bertie's grasp and inspected it. "Look, there are letters engraved on the end here."

Arthur leaned over to look at where Merlin was pointing. Sure enough, a swirling W and B were engraved into the head of the key.

"WB?" Arthur asked, wrinkling his nose. "What's that?"

"Not *what*," Gareth replied. "You should be asking *who's* that."

"You're being annoyingly cryptic, Gareth," Merlin grumbled.

"Elaine gave you the key, right? Which likely means it belongs to one of her parents. My guess is that it's her father's," Gareth replied, ignoring Merlin's surliness. "WB. I bet it stands for Walter Beaulake. That's Mr Beaulake's name."

"How do you even know that?" Arthur asked at the same time as Merlin's spluttered '*His name is* **Walter?**'

Gareth shrugged. "It's on the school website. Compared with some of the Winchester teacher's names, *Walter* is totally normal."

Bertie held up his hand. "Okay, before we get sidetracked, can we all just focus on the fact that Elaine's given us a mysterious key and we still have no idea what it's for."

"Let me see it again," Merlin said, grabbing the key once more and twirling it between his fingers. "It's not for a modern door, so assuming it's for something at Badon, that rules out most of the rooms within school buildings. It's not an old key, but I bet the lock it's for *is*. It's got initials on it, which means it's for a specific person. But why put initials on it, unless there's more than one copy?"

Arthur nodded as he understood Merlin's line of reasoning. "Maybe there's one copy for each person who might need access to a certain door?"

Merlin threw the key to Arthur. "I'd bet an entire stash of biscuits that it's a key for the Headmaster's Lodge."

"What does she want us to do with that?" Bertie asked.

Merlin rolled his eyes. "Hmm, let's see. What would Elaine, who's apparently just found out that her parents probably parade around in hooded robes, and who saw a giant, and who recently discovered that magic is real, want us to go rooting around in Catterick's study for?"

Bertie glared.

"Any guesses?" Merlin added with a smirk. "Anyone?"

"Well, we know one thing for certain," Arthur cut in quickly, knowing that Merlin probably wasn't anywhere near finished with his smart-alecky comments. He pointed at his best friend. "*You're* not going anywhere near the Lodge."

"Good!" Merlin shuddered. "I don't want to go back there ever again, if I can help it."

"I agree," Bertie added, agreeing completely having had Merlin explain what had happened that morning when they'd all met for lunch. "We can't have you getting thrown out of Badon." He grinned. "Not unless it's for something truly spectacular. Like vaporising Hugo."

Merlin snorted. "I suspect that'd do more than just get me thrown out of Badon."

"I'll go," Gareth said quietly.

So quietly, Arthur almost thought he'd imagined it. "What?"

"I'll go." The repetition was much more confident. Gareth squared his shoulders. "To Catterick's study. I

266

mean."

Bertie looked concerned again. "Gareth, I d-"

"I'm going," Gareth stated firmly, in a rare show of defiance.

"Alright," Arthur agreed after a long moment. "Now we just need to work out how to get over there without anyone noticing."

A slow smile spread across Merlin's face. "Thankfully, I already have a brilliant idea."

* * * * *

The following few days passed in a slow march of lessons and homework, but Saturday finally dawned with a perfectly blue sky and a heady sense of excitement.

Breakfast was noisier than usual as the entire school delightedly discussed that day's trip to Catterick College. After their 'imprisonment' in Badon, the prospect of freedom - even if that freedom was fully contained and supervised within the walls of Catterick College - was enough to have even the most sensible and reserved boys practically shrieking in excitement.

Even though Arthur was one of the very few students staying behind at Badon, and didn't share in his friends' excitement, he couldn't find it in himself to care much about missing the trip. He felt like Beaulake's key was burning a hole in his pocket, and he just want the others to leave as soon as possible so that he and Gareth could enact Merlin's plan. Thankfully his fellow Caerleonites mistook his apprehension for disappointment about missing the trip.

"Oh, cheer up, Arthur," Sib said, as he nudged his shoulder. "We'll try and get Mrs Beaulake to let us run into the shop for some sweets for you on the way back. You're one of her favourites, so she'll probably say yes."

"Thanks, Sib," Arthur replied, his stomach churning slightly at the thought of his housemistress.

"I don't think she'll let us get anything for Merlin though," Marc added with a snort.

"Ha ha ha." Merlin rolled his eyes. "You're hilarious."

Despite what the others thought, Arthur knew that Merlin wasn't all that disappointed that the headmaster had banned him from the Catterick College trip on the grounds of his poor behaviour. In fact, Merlin was positively delighted that he was getting to stay behind to cause some trouble without the headmaster being any the wiser.

Bertie appeared at the breakfast table right on cue.

"Where's Gareth?" Arthur asked, adopting as much curiosity as he could manage, considering he knew full well where Gareth was.

"He's not feeling well," Bertie replied. "He doesn't think he's going to be able to come to Catterick College today."

The first and second years sitting nearby shook their heads in sympathy.

"And I suppose," Bertie continued with a put-upon sigh, "I'll have to stay here with him to make sure he doesn't get too bored."

Charlie laughed. "If Ruari were ill I'd leave him rot if it meant I could get out of here for a day."

Ruari thumped his roommate on the arm. "Yeah, well Bertie's obviously a much better friend than you."

"I can stay with Gareth, Bertie," Arthur piped up. "I'm not allowed to leave school anyway."

"Nah, don't worry about it, Arthur," Bertie replied. "I've got some work to catch up on anyway. But if you and

Merlin are both around too we could see if Mrs Beaulake will let us all watch a film in the JCR, or something."

Merlin shrugged. "Sure. Have you told Mrs Beaulake about Gareth?"

"Not yet." Bertie shook his head. "I said I'd get him some toast first, just in case he might be able to eat it."

"I'm finished, so I'll go and find Mrs Beaulake," Arthur offered, standing up. "Merlin can get Gareth some toast while you have your breakfast."

"Why do I have to be the butler?" Merlin asked, pretending to be annoyed.

Arthur arched an eyebrow. "Would you prefer to go and speak to Mrs Beaulake?"

Merlin shook his head dramatically. "No thanks."

The Caerleon boys all laughed.

Phase one was complete. Bertie grinned up at his two friends, and then neatly turned the conversation towards what everyone else was planning to sign up to do once they got to Catterick College. Arthur and Merlin took the opportunity to quickly grab a plate of toast for Gareth, and slip out of the Dining Hall to begin phase two.

* * * * *

"Goodness, Gareth!" Mrs Beaulake exclaimed as she came into the JCR behind Arthur fifteen minutes later. "Are you alright?"

"I'm fine, Mrs Beaulake." Gareth added a whimper for good measure and Arthur had to bite his tongue to keep from laughing. "I just don't think I should go out today."

Mrs Beaulake sat on the sofa next to Gareth, pressing her hand to his forehead and making soothing sounds. Arthur hoped the hot-water bottle Gareth had been holding to his

269

forehead had left enough residual heat to fool their house-mistress. He also hoped it was stuffed far enough down behind the sofa cushions that it wouldn't be noticed.

"You're very warm," Mrs Beaulake announced. "Gareth, I think I need to send you up to Matron."

"No, please, Mrs Beaulake," Gareth replied quietly. "I'd just really like to go back to bed for a bit, if you wouldn't mind."

Arthur held his breath. If Mrs Beaulake didn't just let Gareth go back to his room their plan would fail before it even started.

"I really would prefer if you went up to Matron," Mrs Beaulake sighed as she checked his temperature with her hand again. "I can't stay with you, I'm afraid. I'm supervising the trip."

"I can look after him, Mrs Beaulake," Arthur said. "I promise if he looks any worse I'll go and get Matron. I promise."

"Well, that's very kind of you Arthur, but-"

"Mrs Beaulake," Gareth cut in quietly. "I really am okay. Arthur and Merlin are both staying behind, so they can keep me company."

Mrs Beaulake hummed slightly in disapproval.

"And Bertie too," Arthur added. When Mrs Beaulake looked surprised he added, "if that's alright with you, Mrs Beaulake. Bertie didn't think it was fair to leave his roommate on his own."

Mrs Beaulake hummed again. "Well, I suppose that would mean that you had two very sensible students with you, Gareth."

As it was clear what that suggested about his roommate, Arthur decided he would keep that comment from Merlin.

It was liable to set his friend off on a rant, and considering Merlin had agreed to practise some magic that afternoon while Badon was mostly empty, he thought it was probably best to keep him in a good mood. It really wouldn't do for the school to explode.

Mrs Beaulake still looked unconvinced when an idea struck Arthur. "And Hector's here too. You could talk to him about it before you leave."

"Alright," Mrs Beaulake agreed eventually. After all, she couldn't really argue that an armed member of the Protection Squad wasn't sensible. "I want you to go straight upstairs and go to sleep, Gareth. Arthur, I am expecting you to go to Matron as promised if there's anything you need. If Gareth feels any worse you are to tell Elaine immediately so that she can call me."

Arthur tried not to show any surprise that Elaine was in Caerleon; he'd assumed she and Thomas would be going to Catterick College with everyone else. With both Mr and Mrs Beaulake away from Badon it could be the perfect opportunity to speak to Elaine about her parents and the Brotherhood.

The corridor outside the JCR was suddenly filled with noisy chatter as the Caerleon boys all trooped downstairs and outside to assemble in Chapel Court.

Mrs Beaulake glanced down at her watch and Arthur knew they'd won her over.

"We'll be fine, Mrs Beaulake," he added, for good measure.

Mrs Beaulake gave Arthur another appraising look before nodding slowly. "I'm trusting you, Arthur. Don't let me down."

Arthur nodded, smiling as widely as possible. "Yes, Mrs

Beaulake."

When Mrs Beaulake narrowed her eyes ever so slightly Arthur let the grin fade a bit. Perhaps he was overdoing the enthusiasm.

"Upstairs, please, Gareth," Mrs Beaulake said. "We'll all be back in time for dinner."

With that, she swept out of the room and Arthur let out the breath he'd been holding. "I think we did it, Gareth. You should take up drama next term."

Gareth grinned. "I think I'd enjoy it a bit more than cross-country."

Arthur sat on the sofa next to Gareth and waited. They couldn't head for the Lodge until they had the all-clear from Merlin and Bertie.

It couldn't have been more than five minutes before they heard footsteps hurrying down the stairs.

"I think we're okay," Merlin announced, poking his head into the room. "I've told Hector we're taking it in turns to babysit Gareth."

"Oi!" Gareth hissed.

"Oh, you know what I mean," Merlin replied, rolling his eyes "There's a silencing spell on the entire left hand wall of the first year corridor. Nobody in Mission Control should hear anything."

"Mission Control?" Gareth asked with a confused frown.

"Merlin thinks he's being hilarious again," Arthur replied. "He's decided that the security team's room needed a better name."

"Well, it didn't have *any* name before," Merlin said as though this explained his reasoning perfectly.

Bertie's arrival thankfully halted the discussion.

"Are they gone?" Arthur asked him.

Bertie nodded. "Mrs Tilbury left on her bicycle a couple of minutes ago. Catterick was with Mrs Beaulake when everyone else left for the trip. Oh, Mrs Beaulake said one of us has to check in with Mr Wade in the Library once an hour so that they know everything's okay with us and Gareth."

"That's fine," Arthur replied. "Merlin should do it."

"Why me?" Merlin whined. "Mr Wade wants me to do inter house badminton after Easter. He'll just use today as another opportunity to guilt-trip me into signing up."

"Firstly," Arthur said with a smirk, "I doubt you could be guilt-tripped into doing anything. Secondly, if we get caught, who do you think Mrs Beaulake and Catterick are going to blame immediately?"

"You," Gareth said pointedly as he looked at Merlin.

"Yes, thank you, Gareth," Merlin huffed.

"If Mr Wade sees you a few times today he's less likely to think that you're involved if we *do* get caught," Arthur finished.

"Oh fine," Merlin agreed eventually. "I'll go and tell Mr Wade that I'm just sitting in my room *reflecting* on my behaviour like the headmaster wants me to."

Arthur laughed. "That's the spirit."

"Arthur, I think we should go," Gareth said, finally standing up.

"Here." Merlin held his school satchel out to Gareth. "There's paper and pens in there just in case you want to write anything down. You're our researcher after all."

Gareth looked delighted as he took the bag. "Thanks, Merlin."

Arthur nodded. "Right, Gareth, let's go."

Gareth looked momentarily terrified before squaring his

shoulders and leading the way out of Caerleon.

Arthur followed his friend towards the Headmaster's Lodge as quickly as possible, only just fighting the urge to cross his fingers for luck. The windows of various buildings looked down into Kings' Court and they both had to hope that they weren't being watched by any straggler students or teachers they hadn't know about.

Once they reached the ancient door Arthur pulled the key from his jeans pocket and quickly shoved it in the lock. He closed his eyes as he twisted the metal. "Please work."

Gareth let out a small sound of joy when the heavy lock unlatched and Arthur pushed the door open.

The two boys hurried in, closing the door behind them as quickly as possible. They'd done it.

Arthur carefully locked the door behind them. "Just in case."

"Good idea," Gareth whispered.

Arthur turned away from his friend and hurried up the staircase, keeping his footsteps as light as he possibly could. He trusted nothing about this school at the moment and even though they'd seen Mrs Tilbury leave, that didn't necessarily mean that the Lodge was empty.

Gareth copied his movements and soon the two of them were standing outside the heavy door of the Headmaster's study.

"You don't think it's locked do you?" Gareth frowned at the door.

"Only one way to find out," Arthur replied. He reached out for the doorknob, but his hand paused at the last second. "Gareth, look, if we get caught we're probably going to be expelled….at best. I know how much being at Badon means to you."

Gareth drew his shoulders back to make himself just a little taller. "Arthur, I'm not brave like you. Not really. And I'm not clever like Merlin; and, as we all know, my one attempt at magic didn't go very well. But this – finding things out – I *am* good at, so let me help."

Arthur nodded at his friend. He remembered all too clearly what had happened last time Gareth didn't think he quite fit in with his friends; he wanted Gareth working with them, not putting himself in danger trying to prove himself useful. "Okay."

"Also, let's just not get caught," Gareth added hurriedly.

Arthur snorted slightly as he finally twisted the doorknob and pushed open the door.

The study was mercifully empty. The only eyes on them now were the ones belonging to the painted lady above the fireplace. Arthur headed straight for the headmaster's desk, but it was completely clear of paper. "The letter's gone."

Gareth had stopped in front of the wall hanging of Cambridge that had captured Arthur's attention last time he'd been summoned. He was tracking the red lines that weaved through the buildings, stopping every now and then on an adjoining building and squinting.

"What?" Arthur asked after Gareth repeated this process a few times.

"There's something really weird about this map," Gareth replied, not taking his eyes from where his fingers were pressed into the material. "There are colleges on here that don't exist."

"So they've been knocked down over time?" Arthur asked. "That map must be hundreds of years old, Gareth."

"No." Gareth shook his head. "That's not what I mean. There are buildings on here that don't exist, and have *never* existed, Arthur."

Arthur frowned and went to stand next to his friend.

"This map should show fourteen Cambridge University colleges along with our school, making a total of fifteen buildings." Gareth waved his hands around in demonstration. "But this shows Badon, and *seventeen* colleges."

"Okay," Arthur replied slowly. "Why would there be three extra colleges?"

"Look." Gareth pointed at one of the golden outlines. "This one here – Cornwall College – is where King's College Chapel actually is." He pointed to another. "Tintagel College is apparently just across the road from Badon." He pointed to the final one. "Then over here there's *Alderley*."

Arthur's stomach lurched. "Alderley College?"

Gareth tapped the map again. "Yep, and it's right next door to Catterick College."

"Why are they on the map?" Arthur asked.

"I don't know, but I think the names are important." Gareth said. He thought for a moment before rooting through Merlin's satchel until he pulled out a small notebook and a pen. He hastily started scribbling a copy of the wall-hanging onto the paper. "Arthur, I know you don't like the idea of you being connected to the King Arthur in the legends, but both Cornwall and Tintagel are places that have strong connections to him. And to your family too. These names are linked to you."

Arthur looked back at the phantom colleges and sighed. "Alderley's not related to my family in any way."

"No, he's not, but he was a member of the Brotherhood, and the founder of our school. If James Catterick added a college to the University, it doesn't seem too far-fetched to think that Edward Alderley might have wanted to do the same after he finished building the school," Gareth replied as he continued with his drawing. "I don't think this is just a map, Arthur. I think this might have been a plan for the Brotherhood to become even more involved in the city for some reason. I suppose it would be a brilliant way to make sure members of the Brotherhood would always have reason to be here to protect any future kings going to school at Badon."

Arthur leaned forward to inspect the canvas more carefully. "But why keep this? If none of these colleges were ever built, then what use is this?"

Gareth shrugged. "No idea."

Arthur thought back to the tapestries that covered quite a few walls at home. As a child, he'd never had any interest in the giant, dusty weavings, until the day he'd found out about the secret entrances to old passages behind some of them. His eyes widened as an idea struck him.

"What?" asked Gareth, who'd looked up at his friend having finally finished his sketch.

"Sometimes hangings or tapestries are there because they look nice," Arthur said as he curled his fingers around the bottom left-hand corner of the canvas. "But sometimes it's because they're hiding something. Something that's supposed to be kept secret."

Arthur lifted the canvas carefully. At first, he could see nothing of interest; only the dark-wood panelling that covered the rest of the study's walls. Then, as he was about to give up, a slight glimmer caught his eye.

"Gareth, come here a second."

Gareth did as he was instructed. "What have you found?"

"I'm not sure," Arthur replied. "I need you to help me hold the canvas up so that we can see behind it. I think there's something stuck to the wall."

The two boys lifted the bottom edge of the canvas, drawing it carefully away from the wall until Arthur could duck underneath. Squinting into the semi-darkness he reached out a hand and his fingers brushed over something cool and metallic.

"This is where a phone, or even just a torch, would be handy," Arthur muttered as his fingers traced over grooves he assumed were letters engraved on the plaque. "I can't see what this is."

"Hang on one second," Gareth said. "I'll look for a light, but I'm going to need to let go of the canvas for a second."

"Alright," Arthur said and found himself plunged into further darkness as the canvas closed over him. "Gareth? I think there was a lamp of some kind on the desk last time I was here. I think it might be an oil lamp."

"I see it," Gareth replied. "I've got it."

"Give it here then," Arthur replied, pleased to have the weight of the canvas lifted from him once more.

Gareth's face appeared at the edge of the hanging, a slight golden glow to his face as he passed the lamp to Arthur, hesitating slightly.

"I don't think we'll be able to explain it away if you burn the Lodge down, Arthur."

"I'll be careful," Arthur replied. He used one hand to push the canvas up over his head and the other to hold the light closer to the plaque. "There's a metal panel here. There are some symbols and words on it."

"What does it say?" Gareth asked as he tried to get closer whilst keeping the fabric away from the lamp's flame.

"Oh brilliant." Arthur rolled his eyes in frustration. "It's in Latin."

"Can you read any of it?"

Arthur looked carefully at the words in front of him and shivered slightly:

Fraternitas ~ Firmitas ~ Magicas
ARTURUS REX
Rex quondam, Rexque futurus
VIVAT REX
Ad summa virtus

"Arturus Rex," he whispered eventually.

"What?" Gareth asked. "Arthur, what's wrong?"

"Arturus Rex," Arthur replied slowly. "It means 'King Arthur'. Vivat Rex is 'long live the King'."

The canvas swished slightly as Gareth obviously twitched in surprise, and Arthur's hand dropped down onto the panel as he ducked to avoid the hanging.

As Arthur's fingers pressed into the cool metal he felt the whole plaque give slightly beneath the force. He pressed a little harder and frowned as he heard a slight *click*. Ever so slowly he released the pressure of his fingertips, holding his breath as the panel popped away from the wall.

"What was that noise?" Gareth asked.

"It's not a plaque, it's a door," Arthur breathed. "Gareth, it's a secret door."

"Wow," Gareth whispered. "This is genuinely the coolest day ever."

Arthur was feeling more trepidation than excitement, but he hooked his fingers around the edge of the small door and pulled it towards him.

Behind the door was a cramped cubby hole, roughly hewn out of the stone wall surrounding it. The space was packed fairly tightly with books, documents and small wooden boxes. Gareth appeared at his shoulder and Arthur wordlessly handed him the oil lamp.

"What *is* all of this stuff?" Gareth whispered, moving the light closer to the stack of papers.

Arthur shrugged. Now that he had his hands free he carefully picked up the topmost book in the pile. It was large and leather-bound, with a thick gold band running around the spine and across the front cover. If there was a title Arthur couldn't see it in the low light.

He flipped open the cover and found that the yellowing first page was covered with writing that had been struck out with thick black lines of ink. It looked like names and dates, but the lighting was too dim to see properly. He turned the page and came across an intricately drawn family tree. The Pendragon family, Arthur realised with a flip of his stomach. He swallowed heavily as he saw his own name and birth date written on the final branch.

"Hang on," Gareth said. "Take the light for a second. I'll go and get a notebook and we can get some of this written down to research later."

"Mmm," Arthur replied, attention still focused mainly on the book he was holding as his friend ducked back out into the study.

"Arthur!" Gareth hissed, a slightly hysterical edge to his voice.

"What?"

"Mrs Tilbury's in the quad"

"She's supposed to be in the city!" Arthur's stomach lurched. "Is she coming this way?"

"I think so," Garreth whispered. "No, wait, she *definitely* is."

Arthur tucked the book under his arm and pushed the concealed door closed before ducking out from under the canvas.

"What are you doing with that?" Gareth asked, pointing at the book in faint horror. "Arthur, we're not stealing it, are we?"

"What else are we going to do with it?" Arthur asked as he ducked down slightly to peer out of the window. "It might be important, and we don't have time to copy it all out. She's nearly here, Gareth. We've got to hide."

"Where?" Gareth was clearly panicking as his eyes darted around the room searching for a hiding place.

"Not in here," Arthur replied quickly, crossing to the door that would lead them back out onto the landing. "There are other rooms off the landing. One of them has to be better."

"I don't like this, Arthur," Gareth replied, and Arthur could hear the slight quiver in his friend's voice. "Mrs Tilbury is one of *them*."

Before Arthur could reply, the sound of a key turning in the heavy lock of the Lodge's door caused both boys to freeze.

"Oh no, oh no, oh no," Gareth whispered. "Arthur, what do we *do*?"

"It'll be okay, Gareth," Arthur replied quietly. "I won't let you get into trouble for this. It was my idea, and this whole thing's my fault anyway."

The door creaked open below them and Arthur flinched. With Mrs Tilbury downstairs, there was no way the two boys would be able to move around without her hearing them.

Think, Arthur instructed himself, *think, think, think!* He closed his eyes, desperately hoping some divine wisdom would hit him if he concentrated hard enough. Mrs Tilbury catching them in the Headmaster's Lodge would be bad enough even if she wasn't a member of the Brotherhood, but getting caught in Catterick's study, clutching a stolen book no less, was unlikely to end well for either boy.

"Mrs Tilbury!"

Arthur's eyes flew open at the sound of the shout from outside.

"Is that Elaine?" Gareth squeaked.

Mrs Tilbury's typically grumpy tone floated up the stairs as Arthur shared a look of surprise with his friend. "Yes, Miss Beaulake?"

"One of the porters was looking for you," Elaine replied. "There's a phone call for you."

"Well, I'm very busy," Mrs Tilbury replied.

"He did say it was *urgent*," Elaine stressed. "Really, very, very urgent."

The silence that followed felt like it lasted hours, but eventually Mrs Tilbury sighed, a long-suffering sound of irritation. "Very well."

The door closed almost immediately and Arthur sagged in relief as he let out a breath he'd been holding for far too long. He only allowed himself a few seconds to recover, however, as Mrs Tilbury could return at any moment, particularly as Arthur was fairly sure that Elaine's story had been entirely fictional.

"Come on," Arthur hissed, motioning for Gareth to follow him down the stairs. "We need to get out of here without anyone seeing us." He wished, not for the first time in the past half hour, that he'd thought to get Merlin to cast that concealment spell they'd used the night they'd sneaked outside with Bertie.

When they reached the door, Gareth held out his hand when Arthur retrieved the Beaulake's key from his pocket. "Wait."

"What?" Arthur frowned in surprise. "Gareth, we need to leave *right now*."

"Hide the book in the bag first," Gareth said, undoing the clasp on the satchel. "At least then we won't be killed on the spot if we run into the headmaster or anyone from the Brotherhood on the way back."

"Good point," Arthur replied as he handed over the book and watched Gareth hurriedly wedge it between Merlin's French textbook and the notebook.

"Ready?" Gareth asked, once the book was safely stowed away.

Arthur nodded and unlocked the door, wincing again at just how loud the mechanism was. This was not a house that could be easily entered without anyone inside knowing they were not alone. Arthur was certain that this was exactly how Catterick liked it.

He twisted the doorknob and slowly pulled the door open. Peeking out, he was relieved to find that the quad was empty. He pushed Gareth out in front of him with a hissed *go* and pulled the door closed behind them with a sigh of relief.

Not wanting to be there a single second longer the two boys hurried past the Dining Hall as quickly as they could without drawing attention to themselves. Halfway across Kings' Court Arthur chanced a look up at his bedroom window and saw Merlin and Bertie staring back. They both looked as relieved as Arthur felt.

Merlin made a 'hurry up' gesture and Arthur rolled his

eyes as he and Gareth finally made it across the bridge, under the archway, and through the door into Caerleon.

Arthur had just reached the bottom step of the staircase when he heard Gareth squawk behind him. He turned just in time to see his friend yanked sideways into the JCR with another yelp.

"Gareth?" Arthur called as he hesitantly approached the door. He gulped. Had Mrs Tilbury seen them after all?

Arthur peered around the doorframe and immediately sighed in relief. "Elaine."

Elaine had manhandled Gareth into sitting on a sofa in the otherwise empty common room. She was sitting opposite him in an armchair, looking more than a little worried. Thomas was toddling around the room happily.

"Arthur," Elaine greeted quietly. "Now that we're even again, why don't you pop upstairs and get the others? I think we need to talk."

10

THE TRAITOR'S ESCAPE

By the time Arthur had finished explaining what he and Gareth had found in Catterick's study – with some added explanation to fill in the gaps about the Brotherhood for Elaine – his throat was dry.

"I don't understand," Elaine said eventually, shaking her head. "You're saying that this Brotherhood has got something to do with King Arthur, and my parents are involved somehow?"

"Yes," Arthur replied.

"That's the most ridiculous thing I've ever heard."

Bertie blinked rapidly. "*That's* the most ridiculous thing you've ever heard, even after what you saw before Christmas?"

Elaine crossed her arms. "Yes. My parents are good people. They wouldn't be involved in something weird like that."

"Elaine," Gareth said quietly, "if you didn't think your parents were part of something strange why did you sneak out onto the bridge? Why did you give Arthur the key?"

Elaine didn't reply. She just folded herself more tightly into the armchair.

"What are we going to do about that?" Bertie asked pointing at the book that was just sticking out of Merlin's satchel.

"I think we need to read it, read *everything* in it," Arthur replied. "If we're going to find out anything else about the Brotherhood, or about the sorcerer, I'm hoping that the book can help us. There's not much chance of us being able to get back into Catterick's study any time soon, so it's the best clue we've got."

"Why don't you copy out the family tree, Arthur?" Gareth suggested. "Maybe you could ask your parents about some of the names on there. See if anything weird ever happened to any of them?"

Arthur nodded. He looked around at his friends, frowning when his eyes landed on Merlin. His roommate hadn't said a single thing since Arthur started his explanation, and now he looked troubled.

"What's wrong?" Arthur asked.

"None of you think this is a bit..." Merlin trailed off. "Well, *simple?*"

"Simple?" Gareth tilted his head. "What do you mean?"

Merlin leaned forwards to rest his elbows on his knees. "I mean, Elaine decides to give you a key that just so happens to open Catterick's study-"

"Hey!" Elaine jumped to her feet. "I don't know what you're trying to imply, but-"

"I'm not implying anything," Merlin snarled. "My *point*, if you'd let me make it, is that this key is important. It's a way into the most important room in the whole of Badon. It's a key entrusted to a Brotherhood member, and we're just supposed to accept that it's been out of the Beaulakes' apartment for days and nobody's noticed?"

Elaine sat back down.

"And," Merlin continued, pointing at Arthur and Gareth, "when you two do, in fact, manage to get into Catterick's study you then find a secret door that isn't locked, and behind it is a book that seems to contain a helpful potted history of the Brotherhood."

"Come on, Merlin." Arthur grinned, trying to lighten the mood slightly, "maybe it really is just that simple. Mr Beaulake isn't here so he wouldn't have needed the key."

"Actually, Arthur," Bertie replied slowly, "I think Merlin has a point."

"That key was in my father's desk," Elaine said. "In his private study. My mother usually avoids that room, so there'd be no reason for anyone to notice the key was missing."

"And how did you know it was there?" Merlin asked, a hint of accusation in his tone.

"Because I pay attention," Elaine snapped. "Because I thought my parents had always told me the truth, and now it looks like they haven't. *Because,* I don't like what's going on around here any more than you do, and I wanted to do something useful. You don't just get to be some boys-only club running around trying to save the day. I want to help, so let me help."

Merlin remained silent, but shrugged.

"Okay," Arthur said, "you're helping. We're all trying to help, but let's just assume for now that this isn't some sort of Brotherhood plan to distract us. We need to get whatever we can from this book, because otherwise we just completely wasted our chance."

"I agree," Bertie replied with a nod. "I think we should split up the responsibility of different sections of the book and then meet back here when we've got something to share."

"Not here," Elaine said. "I'm not really supposed to be in the JCR during the week, and we really don't want my parents to find out that we have that book, do we?"

"Where then?" Arthur asked. "It's not like we can get out of Badon at the minute."

"Actually, we could. I've got a key for the Back Gate," Elaine replied. She frowned and looked at Merlin. "But can't you just open gates anyway?"

"I can, but I'm not going to," Merlin said vehemently. "We're not getting ourselves killed. Badon is the safest place we've got at the moment."

"I thought you were the rebel of the group," Elaine sighed dramatically. "Okay, fine. There's an old classroom at the top of Maris that doesn't get used for anything but storage these days. It should be free in the evenings, and on weekends too. I've used it for homework a few times when I wanted to get away from home but didn't want to head into the city."

"That's a good idea," Arthur agreed. "We'll need to make sure we get a message to you so that you know we need to meet."

"Secret meetings!" Gareth grinned. "Maybe we could send messages in code. I've got some books on ciphers. I've always wanted to be like a spy!"

"Maybe that would be a bit too far," Bertie said diplomatically. "Maybe we could just come up with a phrase or a word that means we need to meet."

"Can we at least have a name?" Gareth asked, looking somewhat dejected at the lack of secret codes.

Arthur shrugged. "I don't see why not."

"What about The Peril Men?" Gareth asked in delight.

"Er, excuse me!" Elaine huffed.

"Oh…" Gareth blushed. "Sorry. What about The Peril People then?"

Merlin wrinkled his nose. "That's rubbish."

"Hey!" Gareth began to protest, before frowning. "No, you're right. That *is* rubbish."

"I've got it!" Bertie announced. "Knights of th-"

"Don't finish that thought, Bertie," Arthur warned. "Maybe we don't need a name."

"What about Camelot?" Elaine asked after a long silence.

"Elaine, no." Arthur shook his head vehemently.

"Sorry, Arthur," Merlin grinned slightly. "That one's actually quite cool. The Camelot Society. I vote for that."

Traitor, Arthur thought with a grimace. Then again, Merlin actually agreeing with Elaine for once might actually be worth keeping the ridiculous name.

"The Camelot Society," Elaine repeated. "I like it."

"I agree," Bertie added.

"You would," Arthur muttered darkly, narrowing his eyes at his friend. He sighed. "Okay, fine. Gareth?"

"I like it too." Gareth nodded.

Thomas squawked what sounded like approval in toddler-speak.

"That's settled then," Elaine said primly as she stood up. "Let's get to work."

*　*　*　*　*

The first thing Arthur noticed when he and Merlin headed down for breakfast the next day was that Gareth's usual chair was empty. The second thing he noticed was that Bertie looked as if he were about to fall asleep in his cereal.

"Alright, Bert?" Merlin asked loudly, grinning when his hand to Bertie's shoulder caused the older boy to flinch in surprise.

"Keep it down, Montgomery," Bertie replied with a wince as he dropped his spoon into the milk with a dull splash. "I haven't slept. Gareth was shuffling papers and reading books all night. He was muttering so much about how complicated it all was that I eventually gave up trying to sleep and helped him translate instead. He's got some news for you both."

Merlin looked slightly guilty about his greeting now and pushed his plate of toast towards his friend. "Here, no spoons required."

Bertie nodded his thanks. "Did you two find anything out?"

"Well, we translated the motto," Arthur replied with a shrug. "And I spoke to my father about some of the names on the family tree."

"What did he say?" Bertie asked around a mouthful of toast.

"Not much. He was a bit surprised I was asking, to be honest. I told him it was for some history homework. The translation was a bit more successful."

"Well, you can tell me all about later," Bertie replied tiredly. "I don't think I can cope with Latin this early on a Sunday morning."

"Have you seen Elaine?" Arthur asked.

"No." Bertie shook his head. "I haven't seen her or Mrs Beaulake, and I've been sitting here for half an hour already."

Merlin looked towards the table where the Beaulakes usually sat. "You know Elaine better than we do, Bertie.

Do you really think we can trust her?"

"I do," Bertie said seriously. "I've actually known her for years."

"Really?' Arthur was surprised.

Bertie sighed. "My father had been a Badon boy, and he wanted me to come here just like him. The plan was that I would go to a school near home until I was old enough to start here. But, then when I was nine my father got very ill.

Arthur frowned as Bertie trailed off, but Bertie didn't elaborate.

"Anyway," Bertie continued eventually, "things were quite hectic, so my parents sent me away a few years early. They stayed at home, and I came to Cambridge. I ended up in the same school as Elaine. Even though she was a bit older, she was nice to me back when I had no friends and was just the new boy from Wales who kept bursting into tears at lunchtime. Not that either of you will ever repeat that to anyone." He looked between his two friends. "So, yeah, I really do think we can trust her."

Arthur didn't really know what to say to that so in the end settled for silently nodding his acceptance.

*　*　*　*　*

At five o'clock, the inaugural meeting of the Camelot Society began with Gareth hefting a stack of notes onto the table they were sitting around.

"Gareth, have you stopped writing at all today?" Merlin asked, looking at the handwritten notes towering in front of him. "Or slept?"

"No to both of those questions," Bertie replied as Gareth reached down to pick up yet more papers. "At the minute, he's basically powered by tea and biscuits."

Elaine gave Gareth a slightly concerned glance, but Arthur was glad that she decided not to comment on the younger boy's dishevelled appearance.

"Why don't we start?" Arthur said, nodding at Merlin. "We didn't find out that much, but hopefully some of it's useful."

"We translated the motto that was in the book," Merlin added. "Arthur *thinks* it's the same as the one that was on the door behind the map. By the way, if we ever have to do anything like this again, can we please send someone who's good at languages on the recon mission?"

"Oi!" Arthur protested. "There's a reason you didn't go!"

Merlin rolled his eyes. "Anyway, it says. 'Fraternity. Strength. Magic.' Then, 'King Arthur. King once, king to be. Long live the king. Courage to the end.'"

Bertie looked at the notebook Merlin was reading from. "So the Brotherhood's motto is all about King Arthur?"

"It looks like it," Merlin replied.

Arthur stayed quiet. He hadn't been very happy when Merlin had easily translated the text the night before.

"Which leads very nicely to this," Gareth said as he placed a large piece of paper on the table. It was a hand-drawn version of the map hanging in the headmaster's study.

Arthur studied it. Gareth had even managed to add in the red and gold lines from the original.

"I'm not sure if this is *quite* right," Gareth sighed unhappily as he placed a piece of paper on the floor between them. "I had to draw it so quickly, and then fill in the gaps from my memory."

"Gareth, this is amazing!" Merlin was clearly impressed as he picked up the hand-drawn map. "It looks just like the one in Catterick's study."

"The colleges that exist on this map, but not in real life, are these three," Gareth explained as he pointed to the buildings' outlines. "I haven't found out anything more about them, but there's about three quarters the book I haven't got through yet."

"Three quarters you haven't got through yet?" Merlin asked in horror pointing at Gareth's notes. "All of that is just for *a quarter* of the book?"

Gareth nodded with an apologetic wince. "Sorry."

Arthur frowned as he caught sight of another of Gareth's pages of notes. It looked like a small portrait of a young woman had been hastily sketched onto the page.

"She looks familiar," Arthur said pointing at the sketch.

"She should do. There's a portrait of her in the headmaster's study. Her portrait's in the book as well, so I thought it might be worth looking into." Gareth replied. "Turns out I was right."

"That's the portrait above the fireplace, isn't it?" Merlin asked as Gareth flicked through the book to the correct page. "What does it say beneath the portrait? I can't read it."

"It says A. Catrik. Her name was Anne Catterick," Gareth stated. "She was the daughter of James Catterick, the *first* headmaster. He had the portrait painted just before she got married. From what I've read in some of the earlier letters in the book, Anne had inherited her father's magical abilities, and was as much a part of the Brotherhood as he was."

"And they kept calling themselves the *Brother*hood?" Elaine grumbled. "Typical."

"I guess so," Gareth replied.

"Gareth, did you say she inherited her abilities?" Merlin asked with a frown. "She didn't learn them from books?"

"I think Anne Catterick was like you, Merlin," Gareth explained. "She didn't need books to learn magic from, not really. She was a sorceress. A really powerful one at that."

"So, if Anne had abilities, and she got then from her father, does that mean the magic has been passed down through every generation of Catterick since then?" Bertie asked, his gaze drifting across the court to the Headmaster's Lodge.

"Not quite," Gareth replied. "From what I can tell, being a Catterick doesn't automatically mean you inherit magic. Our headmaster has some ability but isn't anywhere near as impressive as Anne Catterick was."

"Hang on," Elaine said, holding up her hand. "Think about it. Your headmaster probably didn't descend from Anne Catterick.."

"What do you mean?" Arthur asked.

Elaine sighed. "This is the fifteenth century we're talking about right? Well, women didn't keep their surnames when they got married back then, did they? For the headmaster to still have kept the Catterick name, he would have had to descend from the male line. Right, Gareth?"

"Exactly," Gareth replied, clearly happy that someone was keeping up with him. "Anne Catterick became Anne Worcester when she got married. Our headmaster is actually a direct descendent of Anne's brother, William."

Arthur ran his hands over his face tiredly. "Gareth, this is all a bit complicated."

"I know," Gareth winced. "Sorry. I really have tried to keep all this to useful information only. There's just an awful lot of it."

Bertie, knowing particularly well how hard Gareth had worked on this, clapped his roommate on the back. "It's great, Gareth. *Really.*"

"Thanks." Gareth looked back at the notes on the table. "Anne Catterick was a sorceress, but it sounds like her brother had no magical ability whatsoever. Even so, once James Catterick died it was William who became headmaster of Badon."

"They didn't have headmistresses back then, did they?" Merlin asked. "So, Anne couldn't have taken over from her father?"

Gareth shrugged. "Generally, no. But, based on the way James Catterick, and an awful lot of Brotherhood members, wrote about Anne and her abilities, I think they would have wanted her in charge of Badon."

"So why wasn't she?" Elaine asked.

"Anne Catterick died when she was twenty-four. Her father wasn't even headmaster of Badon at that point," Gareth stated. He looked nervous suddenly. "And this is where the story gets a bit darker."

"What happened?" Arthur asked.

"Well, as you all know the first headmaster of Badon wasn't a Catterick at all," Gareth began to explain. "It was Edward Alderley. James Catterick only took on the role when his friend died and it became clear that Alderley's son, Richard, wasn't the sort of man you'd want in charge of a school."

"Lyonesse said he was a traitor to the crown," Arthur said.

"Who?" Elaine wrinkled her nose at the unfamiliar name. "Who's Lyonesse?"

"The man who nearly caught you when you decided to

go skulking around on the bridge the other night," Merlin responded shortly.

Arthur, sensing that an argument was about to erupt, continued speaking to Gareth instead, "Lyonesse said Richard Alderley was imprisoned in the Tower of London for treason and murder."

Gareth nodded again. "He was. Everything I've read in this book suggests that Richard Alderley had spent most of his life at odds with his father. Both Richard and his father were what the Brotherhood call Learners; people who have no natural magic, but are very good at learning spells. But, Richard wasn't interested in the Brotherhood, and instead spent his life devoting himself to the study of dark magic."

Bertie shivered. "I never believed that story about the dark magic. Everyone gets told the same one when they first arrive at Badon."

"Well, you should believe it," Gareth replied. "Richard Alderley was a first-class necromancer with ambitions to steal the crown, and he *was* a murderer. He killed Anne Catterick."

Arthur felt his eyes widen at the same time as Merlin's spluttered "*What?*"

"How did Richard Alderley manage to kill a sorceress as powerful as Anne Catterick?" Elaine asked.

"I have an idea about that," Gareth replied. "I might be wrong, but it's the only explanation I have for now."

"What explanation?" Arthur asked.

"What aren't you telling us, Gareth?" Merlin asked as Gareth hesitated.

"I will tell you," Gareth said eventually, "but you're not going to like it."

"Why am I not surprised?" Bertie sighed.

Gareth picked up the sketch of Anne Catterick and held it up so that the others could see it clearly. He pointed at the jewellery around her neck. "That locket. I think that's *why* Richard Alderley killed Anne Catterick, and I think it's also *how* he killed her."

Merlin raised a sceptical eyebrow. "A necklace?"

"That necklace was given to Anne Catterick on her thirteenth birthday," Gareth continued, ignoring Merlin entirely. "It was given to her by her father's closest friend."

"Edward Alderley?" Arthur asked slowly as the pieces began to slot together.

"Yes. It had been in the Alderley family for generations, passed down through the children along with an invitation to join the Brotherhood." Gareth grabbed one of his notes and looked carefully at what he'd written. "But, Edward Alderley wrote a letter to James Catterick just before Anne's birthday to tell him that he wanted her to have the locket instead of giving it to his own son."

"I bet Richard Alderley didn't like that," Bertie stated, now looking a little pale.

"He really didn't," Gareth replied. "Listen to what Edward Alderley said in this letter. *My dear friend, I believe that Richard is now lost to us permanently. He has once more refused the offer to join our Brothers, and I now firmly suspect that he is fully immersed in his pursuit of necromancy. He revels in the power it brings him, and I cannot in good conscience allow him to possess the locket. Instead I wish to pass it to your family line, beginning with darling Anne on the occasion of her birthday.*"

"I don't get why everyone's getting so worked up about a necklace," Merlin said, crossing his arms. "Richard Alderley was annoyed that Anne got his inheritance, and then just waited a decade to kill her for it. Is that what you're saying, Gareth?"

"By itself it's nothing really, it's just a necklace. But..." Gareth trailed off and looked squarely at Merlin. "But, give it to someone who can harness magic, and it acts like a conduit between the wearer and the Earth. A conductor for what the Brotherhood calls Old Magic. The locket amplifies the wearer's abilities. Imagine what it must have done to Richard Alderley's powers if he could go up against a sorceress like Anne."

Arthur shivered slightly. The thought of dark magic being magnified in any way was a horrifying one. He cleared his throat. "Where's the locket now? In Catterick's office?"

"I wish," Gareth replied. "That would probably make this all a bit more straightforward."

"Where is it?" Elaine asked. "Has this got something to do with where my father's gone?"

"I don't know about your father, Elaine," Gareth said apologetically. "But I do know that the Brotherhood caught Richard Alderley only moments after he killed Anne. It was nothing more than luck that they were in the right place at the right time, even if they were too late to help Anne. Maybe Alderley was too surprised by their appearance that they captured him before he had a chance to use the locket."

"And?" Merlin was clearly getting impatient now.

"*And*," Gareth continued, "they took the locket from him. It was returned to James Catterick. He became headmaster of Badon only a few days later. It was the same day that Richard Alderley was due to be sent to Newgate Prison to face his charges. He never went to Newgate though.

Instead, he just walked out of the Tower of London."

"How did he actually escape the Tower?" Arthur asked. It had been driving him mad since Lyonesse had told him the story, particularly after his father had confirmed that no traitor to the crown had ever escaped from there."

"I told you," Gareth replied. "*He walked out*. Apparently, he opened his cell door, walked straight past guards, and stepped back out into freedom. According to a witness he walked a few paces up the road and then just disappeared into thin air."

"Okay, that's creepy," Merlin said, wrapping his arms around himself.

Elaine gestured for Gareth to continue. "And the locket?"

Gareth shrugged. "No idea. According to the Brotherhood's writings the locket just disappeared from the Headmaster's Lodge at some point between Anne's death and when somebody thought to check on it after Alderley's escape."

"So, there's a chance that Alderley somehow got hold of the locket and then used it to get out of prison?" Bertie asked.

"There is," Gareth replied. "There's also the chance that the locket is out there right now. Remember when I said that only a true sorcerer could conjure creatures like the Questing Beast? Maybe I was wrong. What if our necromancer isn't a true sorcerer? What if they're a Learner, but-"

"-they have the locket?" Merlin interrupted, eyes wide. "That locket would be enough to enhance their power."

A horrible thought struck Arthur and he felt his skin growing clammy. "Merlin?"

"Yeah?"

"The letter in Catterick's office," Arthur replied. "What

did it say? The bit about the Brotherhood's fears."

Merlin looked confused for a couple of seconds before he paled. "Oh. *Our fears have been confirmed. They have it in their possession.*"

Arthur nodded. "How much do you want to bet that '*it*' is the locket?"

"That would be very, very bad," Gareth said quietly.

"I think that might be an understatement," Bertie added.

"None of this makes any sense," Elaine said, standing up and pacing slightly. "The locket disappeared over five-hundred years ago. Why hasn't anything with it happened before?"

"Well, there's actually more to the story," Gareth continued, and now he looked even more unsettled as he turned to Merlin and Arthur. "Apparently, the locket was forged in the same fire as Excalibur. And…um…some say it was enchanted by the Great Sorcerer Merlin himself. So, I guess it makes sense to be tied up with the Brotherhood, and what with you two being…you know, you two."

"Oh, not this again," Merlin sighed and dropped his head into his hands. "For the millionth time, Gareth, *he*" – he pointed at Arthur – "is not King Arthur. And I am not an ancient wizard!"

"Sorcerer!" Gareth corrected, looking appalled that Merlin, of all people, would make that mistake.

Merlin rolled his eyes. "Yes, fine, *sorcerer*. I'm still not an ancient one!"

"I'm not saying you are," Gareth countered, "but you *are* both a big part of what's going on here. No offence to either of you, but why would a necromancer be raising monsters in Cambridge, and in our school, if you weren't a sorcerer, Merlin, and if Arthur wasn't the future king?" He paused for effect when everyone remained silent. "Exactly. They wouldn't."

"And I suppose," Elaine said as she returned to her perch on the desk, "what with Catterick retiring in a few years, that would be the end of the Catterick line at Badon."

"Wait, what?" Gareth asked in confusion.

"The headmaster's going to retire in a few years," Elaine replied with a shrug. "Mum told me last year."

"No, that's not what I meant," Gareth replied, shaking his head and reaching forward for the Brotherhood's book and flicking back through its pages. "What did you mean about the end of the Catterick line?"

Elaine frowned. "Well, I would have thought that was fairly obvious, Gareth. The headmaster has no children. He has no family at all."

Gareth looked up, turned the book round and pointed at the final name on the Catterick family tree that came directly below *Cecil Catterick*. "If the headmaster has no family, who on earth is Irene Catterick?"

* * * * *

Merlin was moaning about being forced to participate in sport again as he and Arthur headed out of the changing rooms and towards the gym.

"Merlin," Arthur replied as patiently as he could manage, "it really isn't that bad. I know you claim to hate all sport with equal amounts of burning passion, but I really don't think an hour of exercise is going to kill you."

Merlin opened the door to the gym. He then stopped so suddenly that Arthur couldn't avoid the collision and bumped heavily into his friend's shoulder. He would have gone sprawling on his face if Merlin hadn't grabbed him roughly by the collar to keep him upright.

"What were you saying about this not killing me?" Merlin hissed.

Arthur followed his friend's gaze into the main gym where Miss Tristram and Hugo Pendragon were setting up for a fencing session.

"Ooh fencing!" Sib exclaimed as he and Marc came through the door. "I didn't think we were doing that until after the Easter holidays."

"You have got to be kidding me," Merlin sighed a he shot Arthur a look of horror. "Your cousin? Seriously?"

Marc laughed at him. "Oh, come on, it'll be fun. Anyway, Arthur, aren't you already really good at fencing? Surely you can teach Merlin?"

Sib laughed loudly and clapped Merlin on the back. "Marc, I'm not sure anyone could teach Merlin to be good at sports. Even *Hugo*, and he's a champion."

Merlin was obviously too horrified by the scene in front of him to be even remotely offended by Sib's comments.

"You did sign up for fencing as an extra-curricular for later in the year though, didn't you Merlin?" Marc asked, being slightly more diplomatic than Sib.

"Yes," Merlin whined, "but only because I was angry. I went back and scribbled my name out the next day."

Arthur looked at his friend in surprise. "You didn't tell me that."

"Yes, well," Merlin huffed, "I might have actually listened to what you said about Hugo taking the opportunity to skewer me with a blade even if the whole school was watching."

Sib let out a raucous laugh. "I know Hugo's a bit of a git, Merlin, but I don't think he's going to try and kill you during Games."

Marc nodded in agreement. "He's a third year anyway. Miss Tristram's probably not going to let him anywhere near us. He's probably just here to demonstrate."

"Hurry up boys, you're late," Miss Tristram said as she caught sight of the boys who'd just arrived.

"Sorry, Miss Tristram," Marc replied politely as the four of them jogged to where their fellow first years were already perched on benches against the wall. "We were helping Mr Mackenzie tidy up after an experiment."

"Hmm," was all Miss Tristram offered in reply before she started taking the register. "Gareth Allard?"

"Violin lesson, Miss," Charlie replied.

"Well, at least that's something," Merlin whispered as their teacher called out the next name. "One less target."

Arthur's eyes never left Hugo as his cousin began to fasten his fencing armour into place. There was no way this, whatever this was, could end in anything but absolute disaster, Arthur was sure of it.

"Now," Miss Tristram began as she put her clipboard down on the floor and turned to face the ten boys facing her, "those of you with a keen eye for the timetable may have noticed that we were due to begin our rowing training program in today's lesson. However, as access to the Boat House and the river is still restricted due to the wild animal attacks we have decided to swap your rowing and fencing blocks around."

Whispered exclamations of excitement rippled through the Caerleon boys.

Miss Tristram smiled slightly at their eagerness. "I'm sure you're all aware that Hugo York is a national fencing champion, and certainly the best fencer Badon has produced in many years."

Hugo smiled smugly as he looked at the first years. When he finally settled his eyes on Arthur, Hugo's expression grew colder and sharper.

Arthur felt like shrinking back, but was gratified to see that Merlin and a few of his other friends were glaring back at the older boy. It seemed that at least some of the Caerleon boys hadn't forgotten just how awful Hugo was.

"We'll start with basic moves today," Miss Tristram continued, either dutifully ignoring or having not noticed, the cold reception Hugo was receiving. "This lesson will be nothing more than an introduction. Hugo is going to help me give a demonstration in order to show you what you could aspire to achieve if you decide to select fencing as one of your extra-curricular activities. Once the demonstration is over you will be working in pairs and small groups on some footwork and balance exercises."

Miss Tristram reached down and picked up her fencing mask from where it lay on the ground. She gestured for Hugo to do the same and both moved to collect their blades.

"For the purpose of today's demonstration, gentlemen, we will be using what is called a foil," Miss Tristram explained as she held up the weapon. The foil was a thin, flexible blade with a bobble on the tip, and Miss Tristram held the handle securely beneath the circular guard that would protect her hand.

Both Hugo and Miss Tristram took their places in the centre of the gym, leaving a significant amount of space between them.

Hugo began pulling gloves on as Miss Tristram turned once more to the Caerleon boys. "Even though fencing is now a very modern sport, there are a number of traditions that form part of the regulations. At the beginning of each bout, whether it's in this gym or in a competition, you and your opponent will salute to each other. Once the bout is over you will shake hands, regardless of the outcome."

"Ready, Miss Tristram," Hugo said, his eyes sliding back towards his cousin for a split second.

Miss Tristram nodded. "Hugo and I will be working through a set routine so please watch carefully as you'll be trying out some of these moves in the coming weeks."

"Well," Merlin whispered to Arthur, "at least Hugo's all the way over there now that he's armed. Maybe this won't be so terrible."

Arthur looked at his best friend in horror. "You just *had* to say that didn't you. You've jinxed it now."

"We begin with the salute," Miss Tristram said as she and Hugo held the foils up in front of their faces before flicking the blades down towards the floor. The *swish* of the foils cut through the air and the Caerleon boys began whispering in anticipation.

Hugo and Miss Tristram then placed the masks over their faces and fastened them securely. Hugo nodded to the teacher once he was prepared.

"En garde!" Miss Tristram shouted, both her and Hugo adopting a new stance

"It was bad enough when it just involved swords," Merlin hissed, "but now I'll have to listen to Hugo kill me in French? He's probably as terrible at languages as you are."

Arthur ignored him.

"Prêts?" Miss Tristram called. *Ready?*

"Allez!" *Go!*

On her final shout, Miss Tristram and Hugo burst into action, moving quickly back and forth across the floor.

The reaction of their audience was instantaneous. Excited whispering grew to barely concealed hoots of glee as Hugo and Miss Tristram completed increasingly complicated attacks and counter-attacks.

Ruari punched Arthur on the shoulder from where he sat behind him. "Arthur, I really don't like your cousin, but this is so cool."

Arthur turned to where Merlin was watching the bout with a look of intense concentration.

"Oh no," Arthur said with a sigh, "don't tell me *you* of all people are impressed by Hugo now?"

Merlin snorted. "No chance. I'm just trying to work out how easy it would be to take Hugo down with a burst of well-timed magic."

Arthur's eyes went wide. "Keep your voice down! And definitely don't do…anything."

Merlin rolled his eyes. "Calm down, I'm not that stupid. I didn't mean right now."

As the Caerleon boys suddenly shrieked in delight, Arthur and Merlin looked over to where Miss Tristram was standing, the tip of Hugo's foil pressed against the teacher's shoulder. After a couple of seconds Hugo dropped the blade to his side. Miss Tristram completed the same movement, before both unmasking and shaking hands.

The Caerleon boys cheered. Apparently, the impressive display had been enough to win the temporary admiration of everyone but his cousin and Merlin. Arthur clapped politely, but Merlin just mulishly crossed his arms over his chest and glared at Hugo.

"Thank you, Mr Pendragon," Miss Tristram said to

Hugo with a smile. "Excellent work, as always."

"My pleasure," Hugo replied, inclining his head slightly.

"Right, boys," Miss Tristram continued as she turned to face the first years once more. "Hugo will be staying to help with this session."

"Of course he is," Merlin grumbled. "It's not like he should be in a different lesson right now, is it?"

"Get yourself into pairs and find a space," Miss Tristram called.

"Let's go over there," Arthur said to Merlin, nudging him towards the back wall of the gym. "Far, far away from Hugo."

"Arthur, Merlin," Miss Tristram called. "Wait there a moment, please."

Arthur paused, Merlin standing beside him.

"Arthur," Miss Tristram said as she approached, "I'm aware that you already have fencing experience, and therefore I'd prefer to partner you with someone who also has a few years of training behind them."

Arthur shook his head vehemently. "Miss Tristram, I'd really rather not work with Hugo. Please."

Miss Tristram frowned. "I wasn't going to suggest that, Arthur. Marc has similar experience to you and I thought that you'd work well together."

Arthur deflated in relief. "Okay. That's fine."

Merlin pointed towards Marc and his current partner. "Should I pair up with Kofi then?"

Miss Tristram shook her head. "Now, Merlin, I was surprised to see that you'd signed up for extra-curricular fencing. Surprised, but pleased. However, I was even more surprised when I received the final sign-up sheet to discover that you had removed your name."

Merlin cleared his throat but Miss Tristram held up her hand to halt his speech before it began.

"I would like to see you have a go, Merlin," Miss Tristram said. "I think you might actually enjoy it more than you think, and you were obviously interested enough to sign up in the first place."

Arthur thought it probably wouldn't be best to point out that Merlin had signed up in the middle of a temper tantrum after swearing vengeance on Hugo.

"I'd like you to work with someone who can really show you the best of the sport, and explain what it's like to be part of the school team. I'd like you to work with Hugo today." Miss Tristram smiled.

"What?" Arthur wasn't sure if the shout was from him, Merlin, or both of them in tandem.

Miss Tristram's smile dropped slightly at the horror on the boys' faces. "Hugo," she said slowly as though they hadn't understood which boy she'd been talking about. "Merlin, you're going to partner with Hugo today. I will work with Kofi until Mr Allard returns from his music lesson."

Before either boy could protest, Miss Tristram was calling Marc, Kofi and Hugo over to her to explain what was happening.

Arthur didn't hear the explanation; he was too busy watching Hugo grinning at him. This was bad, Arthur thought. This was very, very bad.

Merlin looked outraged as Miss Tristram sent him off with Hugo. Arthur just shook his head minutely towards his friend, hoping his message was clear. *Don't do anything stupid.*

If Merlin did anything that had him sent back to

Catterick's study, it would be the final straw. Arthur knew that Hugo had to be aware of Merlin's precarious position at Badon, just as he knew that his cousin would do everything he could to exploit it.

"Is Merlin going to be alright?" Marc asked Arthur, frowning slightly. "Do you think Miss Tristram knows that they don't get on?"

Arthur just shook his head silently.

"Maybe we should go and set up near them," Marc suggested. "Just in case."

Arthur didn't need to ask what Marc meant by 'just in case'. "Good idea."

"Alright, let's get started!" Miss Tristram announced.

Arthur kept a wary eye on where Merlin was standing as Miss Tristram began leading them through a series of warm-up drills. Merlin was standing as far away from Hugo as possible and half-heartedly completing the actions. Hugo was grinning maddeningly throughout.

"We're going to be focusing on balance and distance today," Miss Tristram explained after the boys were warmed up. "I want you to stand in front of your partner and place your right hand on their left shoulder."

The boys did as instructed, and it wasn't long before Marc was shooting worried looks towards Merlin and Hugo over Arthur's shoulder.

"What?" Arthur asked, dreading the answer.

"Nothing." Marc shook his head. "Just, if looks could kill…"

"Now I want you to take a step backwards, stretching yourself as far as possible whilst not letting go of your partner's shoulder," Miss Tristram guided them. "Stretch back until only the very tips of your fingers are resting on their shoulder. Okay, good, and stop."

Arthur chanced a glance behind him and wasn't surprised to see barely concealed loathing on Merlin's face.

"Now, we're going to play a quick game of tag," Miss Tristram said. "You will try and tap your partner on their left shoulder using your right hand. You are only allowed to move backwards and forwards in a straight line. The object of the game is to tap your partner's shoulder before they can do the same to you. You will receive one point for every successful tap you make. You will begin on my whistle."

The whistle blew and the boys sprang into action. The sound of laughing and good-natured threats filled the gym immediately.

Arthur's concentration wasn't on the game at all, so he wasn't surprised when Marc scored the first point.

"They've not killed each other yet," Marc said, his eyes drifting back to the pair closest to them. "I don't think they'd try to with Miss Tristram here."

"I'm really not so sure about that, Marc," Arthur replied. He shook his head. "Okay, let's try again."

The game continued for a couple of minutes, and Arthur found himself starting to relax into it. He told himself he was just worrying for no reason and everything would be absolutely fine.

The shrill screech of the whistle startled Arthur out of his thoughts.

Miss Tristram turned towards Arthur and thundered. "What do you think you are doing?"

Arthur jumped in surprise and opened his mouth to ask what he'd done wrong before Marc thumped him on the arm.

"Not you," Marc said, gesturing over Arthur's shoulder.

Arthur turned. His mouth opened in surprise when he took in the scene before him. Merlin was sprawled on his back, staring up at Hugo with an expression Arthur could only describe as terrified.

Hugo, for his part, was breathing heavily and glaring menacingly at the boy at the floor.

"What is going on here?" Miss Tristram barked. "Mr York, you will explain this instant!"

"Oi, York!" Ruari bellowed, taking a step forward. "What do you think you're doing?"

"Sit down, all of you!" Miss Tristram snapped as the Caerleon boys moved towards Hugo. "Now."

The boys didn't move for a long moment, and it took Arthur quietly saying 'come on' before anyone made a move towards the benches where they'd started the lesson.

"I tripped," Merlin said softly after a long moment of Hugo remaining stubbornly silent. "I just tripped."

Even from a distance Arthur could see how Miss Tristram's eyes narrowed dangerously. "Thank you for attempting to be chivalrous, Merlin, but may I remind you that I do have eyes, and I am therefore quite sure that you didn't 'just trip'."

Miss Tristram reached down to help Merlin to his feet. She turned and called, "Arthur, can you take Mr Montgomery back to Caerleon, please? I'll have Mrs Beaulake sent for. One of the other boys will bring your schoolbags to you later."

Arthur jumped to his feet and went to stand by his friend. He shot Hugo a filthy look that vowed a vengeance that Arthur felt brave enough to promise in that moment. "Come on, Merlin."

Merlin didn't need telling twice and he headed for the door of the gym, Arthur following closely.

They left the building and crossed Kings' Court in the direction of the bridge. When Merlin still hadn't said anything by the time they reached the Caerleon Arch, Arthur tried to get his friend's attention. "Merlin?"

"Not out here, Arthur," Merlin replied, his voice shaking slightly.

Arthur frowned but didn't say anything else as he followed Merlin into Caerleon and up the stairs to the first-year floor.

When Merlin opened the door to their room and disappeared inside Arthur stopped outside the next room instead. He knocked and waited patiently.

"Arthur?" Hector asked in surprise a few seconds later. "Shouldn't you be in Games right now?"

Arthur nodded. "I just thought you should know that something's happened."

"What?" Hector's surprise shifted into concern. "Are you alright?"

"I'm fine," Arthur replied, "but I'm worried about Merlin. There was a fencing lesson and Miss Tristram paired him with Hugo."

"*Hugo*?" Hector's eyes widened. Arthur knew Hector thought as little of Hugo as Arthur did himself. "Is Merlin alright? Is he hurt?"

"There weren't any actual weapons involved," Arthur replied. "Thankfully. I don't know exactly what happened but Hugo's in trouble with Miss Tristram, and we both know that he won't react well to that."

Hector pursed his lips. "And you think Hugo's going to try and cause trouble for your friend?"

Arthur sighed. "He's already had his father complain to the Beaulakes about Merlin. Like I said, I don't know what just happened - I didn't see - but it was definitely Hugo's fault."

"And you want me to make sure your parents know that if they call me to check on you?" Hector asked.

"Is that okay?" Arthur knew that Hector would understand.

"I'll need to speak to your teacher, Arthur," Hector replied. "I can't tell your parents anything unless I know exactly what happened."

"I suppose that's fair."

"Don't worry, Arthur,' Hector said, clasping Arthur's shoulder in a gesture that Arthur had always thought his own father probably should have tried once or twice. "When it comes to Hugo I'm generally inclined to believe the worst."

Arthur smiled grimly. "Thanks Hector." He blew out an exasperated breath and turned to head into his bedroom.

Merlin was lying on his bed staring up at the ceiling.

Arthur sat down at his desk. "Alright, what happened? What did you say to Hugo?"

"Nothing," Merlin replied quietly.

Arthur barked out a disbelieving laugh. "Are you actually not going to tell me what happened to make you look that scared?"

Merlin propped himself up on his elbows and narrowed his eyes at his friend. "No. I *am* going to tell you, but it has nothing to with anything I said to Hugo."

Arthur tilted his head. "I don't understand."

"Hugo wasn't exactly playing fair," Merlin said eventually. "He just kept going on, and on, *and on* about how

I don't belong at Badon. How this school isn't meant for people like me. How I didn't have any reason to be here."

"That sounds like Hugo," Arthur replied.

"I was ignoring him, Arthur," Merlin continued, "I really was. But then he grabbed my arm and just said *I know*."

Arthur's eyes widened. "What? What did he mean?"

"He shoved me backwards and by then I'd had enough," Merlin said, his voice getting quieter again. "I know I said I wouldn't do anything stupid, but I just thought if I could cast one spell, just something small, it might teach him a lesson."

Arthur was outraged. "*Merlin!*"

"I know, alright?" Merlin balled his fists as he sat up properly. "I know. But I couldn't help it. I just thought I'd distract him by tying his shoelaces together."

"You can do that?" Arthur was slightly impressed.

"Usually, yes," Merlin replied, "but that's really not the point, Arthur."

"The spell didn't work?" Arthur asked, frowning. Hugo was perfectly upright when they'd left the gym.

Merlin shook his head. "It should have done. And then…"

"And then what?" Arthur's stomach dropped as he watched his friend grow even paler.

"And then…" Merlin took a deep breath. "And then just before he gave me a final shove, he looked right at me and smiled. He just said one more word…"

When Merlin trailed off again Arthur leaned forward slightly in concern. "What?" his voice came out barely above a whisper. "What did he say?

Merlin took another deep breath and looked directly at his friend. "*Sorcerer.*"

11

SHADES OF THE PAST

News of the disastrous first-year fencing lesson had spread through the house like wildfire, which was why Eliot Troyes' return to Badon attracted far less attention than his disappearance had. Even if the Head Boy had flown over the wall and landed in the middle of Kings' Court the Caerleon boys, at least, were unlikely to have noticed. By dinnertime everyone was far too distracted plotting Hugo's imminent demise to notice much else.

Well, almost everyone.

Merlin, still white as a sheet but with a steadily growing cloud of anger now surrounding him, had shut himself away in his bedroom, whereas Arthur was too busy worrying about Hugo's apparent knowledge of magic to join in his housemates' lively discussions on how 'the royal swine' could be taught a lesson.

It was Marc who eventually broke the news of Eliot's return. He'd been called to Mrs Beaulake's office to give his version of the events that had led to Merlin in a heap at Hugo's feet, and had bumped into the Troyes family on his way back to Caerleon.

"Was Eliot missing any limbs?" Sib asked when Marc

recounted the tale at dinner.

He was immediately elbowed by Will. "Don't be ridiculous. The headmaster already told us that Eliot's fine."

"Bit weird though, isn't it?" Charlie asked. "Him coming back after only a few days. I'd stay away from school for as long as I could get away with."

"Of course you would," Ruari replied as he rolled his eyes. "But Troyes is Head Boy. He's not going to want to miss a single second of school is he?"

"I'm sure we can ask Eric later," Gareth supplied.

"Well that's boring." Sib shook his head, ignoring the incredulous looks from the others. "Fine, back to Hugo then. Has anyone had any more thoughts about my idea for a giant catapult?"

Arthur's eyes widened as Charlie produced a piece of paper from his pocket. "I have. I've done a quick sketch of the mechanics."

"Are you alright there, Arthur?" Kofi asked. "You haven't said a single thing since we sat down."

"Yeah, fine. Sorry." Arthur shrugged as his friends erupted into animated argument about whether or not it would be possible to borrow equipment from the University's Engineering department.

"We know you're not the same as your cousin, right?" Kofi continued, ignoring the rising noise. "It's not your fault he's…well…"

"A complete git?" Bertie supplied, as he took the empty seat next to Arthur.

Kofi grinned in agreement and turned back to where Charlie was now suggesting possible locations for storing the proposed catapult, which, if Arthur caught the snippet of conversation correctly, seemed to have just been officially named the 'Hugo Hurler'.

Bertie looked around the table, frowning at Arthur. "Where's Merlin?"

"In our room," Arthur replied. "He's refusing to come down."

"Even for lasagne?" Bertie asked.

"Even for lasagne. Don't worry, I'm going to check with Mrs Beaulake about taking up a plate when I'm finished."

Bertie's frown deepened. He lowered his voice so there was no chance he'd be heard over the lively discussion of amendments to Charlie's design. "What happened, Arthur?"

"Hugo said something to him," Arthur replied quietly. "We think he *knows*."

"About-" Bertie cut himself off with a shake of his head as his eyes widened. "Are you serious?"

Arthur nodded grimly.

Bertie put his knife and fork down. "I'm not surprised he's not hungry. Is he alright?"

"Well, he'd stopped being silent and had moved on to throwing stuff around the room and cursing Hugo when I came down for dinner."

"*Actual* magical cursing?" Bertie asked, paling slightly.

"I don't think so." Arthur winced slightly. "Although, I don't think everything he said was entirely in English so I'm not actually sure."

"Arthur?"

Arthur looked up in surprise to see Mrs Beaulake standing at the end of the table. He'd been expecting their housemistress to come looking for him and Merlin as soon as word had reached her from Miss Tristram, but in the hours between the fencing lesson and dinner she hadn't made an appearance.

"I've just been up to see Merlin," Mrs Beaulake continued.

Arthur tensed slightly. Surely she wasn't going to tell him that Hugo had caused enough trouble to have his roommate expelled? She wouldn't just do that over dinner, would she?

Something must have shown on Arthur's face as suddenly his housemistress was holding up her hand with a small smile. "Don't panic, Arthur, Merlin's not in trouble."

Arthur could practically hear the '*this time*' Mrs Beaulake didn't say. "Oh?"

Mrs Beaulake shook her head. "No." Her face darkened again. "Miss Tristram explained what happened, as did Mr Dubois." She pointed towards Marc. "I'm fully convinced that Merlin is an innocent party in today's events. Hugo will be dealt with by the headmaster upon his return."

"The headmaster's not here?" Arthur asked before he could stop himself, already wondering if the headmaster was wherever Mr Beaulake had disappeared to.

Mrs Beaulake tilted her head in surprise at the question. "No," she replied slowly. "Ha has some business to attend to away from Cambridge."

Arthur realised he probably shouldn't have sounded so interested in Catterick's whereabouts. "Oh, right. Yes, sorry, I just thought..." He mentally searched for anything to finish that sentence with. "I just assumed he would be here, what with Eliot coming back today. Not that it matters. Obviously. I mean..."

Mrs Beaulake looked ready to respond when Bertie cut into the conversation. "If Merlin doesn't want to come down, would it be alright to take some food up to him,

Mrs Beaulake?"

The housemistress blinked in surprise for a moment as she shifted her focus to the other boy. "Of course, Bertie. That's very kind of you."

"Why don't you go and see if you can convince Merlin to come down for dinner, Arthur?" Bertie asked. "If you don't come back with him, I'll bring a plate up once I'm finished."

"Thanks, Bertie," Arthur said, taking the escape opportunity Bertie had created for him. "Excuse me, Mrs Beaulake."

Arthur hurried across the Dining Hall to clear his tray before Mrs Beaulake could say anything else. He might want to get away from his housemistress's look of suspicion, but he wouldn't dare risk the wrath of Agnes and her kitchen staff by leaving his plate on the table, even in an emergency.

He tucked his hands into his jacket pockets as he headed out of the Dining Hall. There were hints of spring reaching Cambridge in the small flowers that were beginning to sprout on the edges of the lawn in Kings' Court, but the dark early evenings still felt bitterly cold.

The light in Arthur's room was on, and the glow was bleeding between the edges of the curtains and the stone wall. At least that meant Merlin hadn't decided to just go to bed early and refuse to talk.

He crossed the bridge, wondering if maybe they should never have tried to get involved with whatever the Brotherhood was up to. For just a second, he also wondered if maybe it wouldn't be such a terrible idea to tell Hector everything, and hope that a full complement of highly-trained employees of the Royal Protection Squad would somehow have a plan to make everything alright again.

"Alright, Arthur?"

Arthur twitched in surprise. He looked up to see Eric Troyes leaning against the wall near the door into Caerleon, hands in his pockets.

"Eric," Arthur replied. "Welcome back."

"Thanks. What are you doing out here? Isn't it still dinner time?"

"Merlin's sulking," Arthur replied, feeling only slightly guilty at reducing the truth to such a simple phrase, "and I can't listen to any more half-formed plans that end with chucking Hugo in the river."

Eric snorted slightly. "Yeah, I heard about what happened. What did Merlin say to Hugo this time?"

"Nothing," Arthur replied. At Eric's raised eyebrow he added, "*Really*. For the first time ever it wasn't actually anything Merlin said."

"Mrs Beaulake seems to think it was entirely Hugo's fault," Eric added.

"That makes a change," Arthur replied.

"I've never liked Hugo."

Now it was Arthur's turn to snort. "Join the club."

"I think even my brother would have a hard time not punching him," Eric said, shaking his head.

Arthur grinned slightly at the thought of the perpetually well-behaved Head Boy ever doing such a thing. "How is he? Eliot, I mean."

"He's fine," Eric replied quickly. Then he looked down at his shoes and seemed to consider his response. "Actually, I'm not sure he *is* fine."

Arthur's stomach dropped slightly. "I thought that the headmaster said his injuries weren't too bad."

"They're not," Eric replied, shaking his head. "Physically he *is* fine. Well, apart from the sprained ankle. But, he's being weird."

Arthur's frown deepened. "What do you mean?"

Eric shrugged. "I can't even really explain it. He's barely spoken to me at all this week. I know we don't talk to each other much at school, but it's never like that when we're at home. He won't even tell me what he was doing in Grantchester before the accident. He just says he can't remember and then stops talking."

"He can't remember?"

Eric shrugged again. "Apparently not. I don't believe him though. Eliot's always had a brilliant memory, and the doctors repeatedly told my parents that he had no head injuries. So, all I can think is that he's lying to me."

"Why would he lie to you?"

Eric grimaced. "I have absolutely no idea."

* * * * *

Merlin had turned all the lights off before Arthur had arrived back at their room. He'd then refused to come down for dinner, and the heaped plate of lasagne Bertie had arrived with was still sitting untouched on the desk hours later. All attempts Arthur had made to engage his friend in conversation had failed and he'd ended up finishing his homework in the room next door with Hector and the rest of the Protection Squad.

Hours later Arthur thought he should probably try again. "Merlin?"

A rustle in the darkness. "What, Arthur?"

Arthur was so surprised that Merlin had actually replied this time that it took him a few seconds to remember what he was going to ask. "Oh. What did you mean earlier? When you said that the spell *should* have worked on Hugo."

"I meant exactly what I said," Merlin huffed in the dark. "Now, will you please just shut up so I can go to sleep?"

Arthur ignored the request. "Well, if it *should* have worked, why didn't it?"

"I don't know," Merlin replied through gritted teeth. "I've used it plenty of times before. It was one of the first things I taught myself that actually worked. It came in pretty handy at primary school. It's never let me down before."

Arthur looked over to where Merlin was still lying on his bed facing the wall. "Do you really think Hugo knows about you? About magic?"

This time there was a lengthy pause before Merlin answered. "I don't know. Probably not. He was probably just mocking my name again or something. Can we leave it alone now, please?"

The conversation was clearly not going to go anywhere useful, so Arthur changed tack as he sat up. "I bumped into Eric earlier. He came back with Eliot this evening."

Merlin remained silent.

"He said that Eliot's being weird," Arthur continued. "Apparently he's claiming that he can't remember why he was going to Grantchester before he disappeared."

"So?" Merlin grumbled. "He was probably going to meet a girl or something, and doesn't want anyone to find out."

Arthur scrunched up his face. "That's really what you think he was doing?"

"Well, what do *you* think he was doing, Arthur?" Merlin huffed as he too sat up in bed. "You've obviously got a brilliant idea that you want to share with me, so why don't you get it out so that I can go back to trying to sleep?"

For a second Arthur toyed with the idea of letting Merlin's harsh tone get to him, but he thought better of it. Eliot Troyes obviously wasn't the only person trying to avoid certain topics of conversation. "Well," he continued levelly, "what if Gareth was right? What if Eliot ending up in Grantchester was because of the necromancer?"

"And what?" Merlin frowned. "He's now in league with them?"

"Maybe." Arthur shrugged. "Maybe not."

"Eliot 'I-do-everything-by-the-rules- Troyes?" Merlin replied as he lay back down. "No way, Arthur. Now, I'm going to sleep."

Arthur was silent for a long time, listening to the sounds of the school settling around him. If he concentrated he could just about hear Hector and the rest of the Protection Squad talking quietly next door. Only the distant sound of traffic driving along the Backs filtered through the window, and there was nothing that seemed out of place. Still, Arthur could feel a sense of wrongness in the air.

"What?" Merlin asked grumpily. "I can hear you thinking from all the way over here, and it's annoying."

"Something's not right," Arthur replied, shaking his head even though he knew his friend couldn't see him. "It's been too quiet. There's been no sign of the necromancer, or the Beast in weeks. Eliot's back, but hiding something, and Hugo knows…" he trailed off in frustration. "Well, I don't know *what* Hugo knows really. But it can't be good, can it?"

Merlin didn't reply.

"You even said it yourself," Arthur continued, "about the key to Cattterick's office, and the book we found. I think we're being led, but I don't know why. If the Brotherhood doesn't think I'm important, or you for that matter, then why is one of them going to the trouble of making sure we know a bit about what's going on? Why not just keep us all as far away from it as possible?"

"How can you be sure it's the Brotherhood?" Merlin asked.

Arthur twisted his hands together, a nervous gesture he hadn't turned to in years. "I *can't* be sure. Merlin, what do we do if Eliot's involved somehow?"

"We can't do anything, Arthur," Merlin replied and he sounded more resigned than Arthur had ever heard him. "I think we just need to hope that whatever was going on has been dealt with. I can't imagine Eliot being involved in dark magic, can you? As far as I know he hasn't done a thing wrong his entire life. He practically worships the headmaster."

"I still think he's lying about not remembering why he went to Grantchester," Arthur replied. "And none of that explains how or why Hugo might know about your magic, does it?"

"Look," Merlin said returning to his previously grumpy tone, "if Hugo knows what I am, then it means someone's told him. I know you didn't, and I trust that Gareth and Bertie have kept my secret." He sighed, before grudgingly adding, "Elaine too, I suppose. I doubt anyone in the Brotherhood likes your cousin all that much, so that rules them out. After them, there's nobody else left who really *could* tell him, is there?"

Arthur hummed noncommittally.

"And we both know my grasp of magic is a bit temperamental sometimes," Merlin added. "So maybe I did something wrong because I wasn't concentrating properly."

"But, Merlin, you actually stopped time when that giant tried to club me over the head." Arthur blew out an exasperated breath. "Then, you *destroyed* it. That's not a little party trick, is it? That's real, proper, *actual* magic! Just remember what the headmaster said about your magic that night out in the Court. You're far more powerful than anyone seems to realise, but now you're saying that you can accept that your easy-peasy little spell didn't work against Hugo? Not likely."

"So you think Hugo somehow managed to, I don't know, *block* that spell?" Merlin asked incredulously. "Arthur, don't you think that sounds a bit mad?"

"Madder than anything else that's happened to us this year?" Arthur arched an eyebrow.

Merlin sighed. "Okay, fine, you may have a point there. But why would anyone tell Hugo about magic? About me? It's not like anyone would believe him if he announced to the world that I'm a sorcerer. It sounds ridiculous when *I* say it, and I know it's the truth!"

"I'm sure he'd find a way to use it against you," Arthur replied bitterly. "Hugo's very good at that sort of thing." A horrible thought occurred to him and his blood ran cold at the idea. "You don't think Hugo has magic himself do you?"

Merlin looked sceptical. "Hugo? Magic? Sorry, Arthur, but I don't think it runs in the Pendragon line. You're about as magical as a tea towel, and I suspect Hugo's probably the same."

"I still don't like it," Arthur replied.

"That's because you don't like Hugo." Merlin scowled slightly. "Not that I blame you, obviously. He's an awful little-"

"Merlin!" Arthur warned before his friend could finish that thought.

"Well, he is," Merlin sniffed.

Arthur grinned slightly despite his concern. "He is, isn't he?"

* * * * *

Arthur, Merlin and Bertie were already waiting in the abandoned classroom when Elaine arrived after school the next day, with Gareth only a few seconds behind her.

"What's wrong?" Arthur asked, frowning at Elaine as she closed the door behind her.

"My Dad came back," she whispered, fidgeting with the strap of her school bag. "I heard him and Mum talking in the middle of the night, but this morning he was gone. Mum told me that I dreamed it, but I know I didn't."

"Did you hear what they were talking about?" Arthur asked.

Elaine knitted her brows. "Some of it. He was saying something about being in France."

"France?" Merlin's eyebrows shot up beneath his fringe.

Elaine nodded. "France. Then he said something about only just getting away and apologised for not calling Mum. That he'd only just escaped being injured like Lyonesse had been."

Arthur remembered the limping figure on the bridge the week before. "We were right, Merlin. That must have been Lyonesse."

"Anything else?" Merlin asked Elaine.

"I heard him say that they'd tracked the legacy to Catterick," Elaine added.

"The headmaster?" Arthur asked.

"Maybe he meant Catterick College," Merlin supplied. "That would make more sense."

Elaine shrugged. "I don't really know, but the last thing I heard him say was that Cecil was still searching."

"Cecil?" Arthur repeated, frowning. "That's the headmaster. When Mrs Beaulake said he was away from Badon last night, it wasn't about school business at all. The Brotherhood must still be searching for the necromancer."

"Looks like you're not the only one who thinks this isn't over yet," Merlin said to his roommate. "If the headmaster's left Badon to join this search he must be worried."

"*And,*" Elaine said with a heavy sigh as she took her usual perch on the desk, "I've solved the mystery of Irene Catterick."

"You have?" Gareth asked, eyes wide with interest.

Elaine nodded. "I just asked Mum if the headmaster had any family."

"And you didn't think that would sound suspicious in any way?" Merlin asked.

"No, I didn't," Elaine shot back. "We were already talking about family, and it didn't seem weird to bring it up. She's been so distracted about Dad being away I figured she probably wouldn't notice anyway."

Merlin grumbled as he shook his head.

"What did she say, Elaine?' Arthur asked.

"Irene Catterick is the headmaster's daughter, like we thought," Elaine replied. "She was born after Catterick became headmaster here, and she grew up at Badon with her father. Mum didn't say what happened to Irene's mother."

"And where's Irene now?" Bertie asked.

Elaine grimaced. "She's dead."

The boys all blinked in surprise.

"Mum said it happened years ago, the year I was born actually, back when Mum and Dad had only worked here for a little while," Elaine continued. "Irene was going to stay in Cambridge for university, and had a place at Catterick College. But, when all the teachers came back here after the summer holidays, the headmaster told them that Irene had died."

"What happened to her?" Gareth asked quietly.

Elaine shrugged again. "Mum said she didn't know, but…"

Arthur's eyes narrowed in suspicion. "But what?"

"But I think Mum was lying to me," Elaine replied hurriedly. "There was just something about the way she said it. I think she knows what happened to Irene, but won't tell me."

Merlin practically jumped out of his chair. "What if it was *them*? The Brotherhood, I mean. What if she found out about them and then they just decided to get rid of her?"

"Why would they do that?" Bertie asked. "As a Catterick she was surely destined to be part of the Brotherhood anyway. Maybe she was even a sorceress herself."

When Arthur looked over to Gareth he caught his friend frowning. "What?"

"I think, maybe…" Gareth trailed off as he stood up and retrieved a notebook from his bag. His eyes scanned the pages quickly as he flipped through them.

"What are you looking for?" Elaine asked.

Gareth held the book out in front of him, and Arthur found that they were once more looking at a copy of the Catterick family tree.

"Do you notice anything about these names?" Gareth handed the book to Arthur.

Arthur scanned down the names. "Not really. There are some names that repeat – family names, I guess. Is that what you mean?"

Gareth shook his head.

Elaine peered over Arthur's shoulder. "They're nearly all men. Every name on here except for Anne and Irene are male descendants of the Catterick family."

"Exactly," Gareth replied, nodding vigorously. "Don't you think it's a bit weird that Anne was killed by Richard Alderley, and then there are no more female descendants listed until you get to Irene Catterick over four-hundred years later, who dies in unusual circumstances too?"

"We don't really know that Irene died in unusual circumstances," Bertie said. "There was nothing about her when we tried searching the internet. If there had been something odd, surely we would have found a news article about it."

"I wouldn't bet on that." Merlin shrugged. "Think about it. If the Brotherhood's managed to conceal the fact that magic exists for such a long time, surely they could hide a news story if they wanted to."

"I agree with Merlin," Gareth added. "If something weird happened to Irene Catterick the Brotherhood would have made sure nobody found out about it. Just think about how everyone in Cambridge thinks that an escaped animal is to blame for what happened to the two men killed by the Questing Beast."

Bertie looked at his watch. "Sorry guys, I need to go."

"Where?" Merlin frowned. "I thought we were going to look through more of that book."

Bertie winced apologetically. "With the inter house rugby on Saturday, Mr Wade's called an extra practice for the Caerleon lower team tonight. If you want to give me some pages to read I can do it later."

"Rugby practice is more important than this?" Merlin asked, wrinkling his nose in distaste.

"If we want to beat Kings' and wipe that smirk of Hugo's face then yes, it is more important right now," Bertie replied with a hint of disgust at the utterance of Arthur's cousin's name. "I could probably come up with an excuse though. I could tell Mr Wade I've got too much homework."

"No. Go, Bertie," Arthur said, shaking his head. "You lot better beat Kings' on Saturday. Otherwise we'll never hear the end of it."

"Oh, we will," Bertie grinned. "We will."

* * * * *

Inter house was all the school seemed to be able to talk about as the weekend approached. Rugby was up first this year and with a Caerleon winning streak stretching back over a decade for both the lower and upper teams, Arthur's housemates had been particularly vocal in their excitement.

When Sunday morning dawned slightly damp and overcast it suited Arthur's mood perfectly. His father's ban on leaving the school remained in place, and Arthur had been snappish over breakfast with his friends.

By mid-afternoon even Hector had given up trying to cajole his young charge into doing something that would take his mind off being trapped at Badon. Merlin, who was also banned from leaving the main school grounds, but decidedly happier about it, had simply retreated into his books and ignored his friend's increasingly cross muttering.

Arthur had been glaring at Merlin for the best part of half an hour. With the bedroom window opened a crack the shouts and cheers from the Badon rugby pitches were floating over the school's walls and fuelling Arthur's annoyance. He hadn't been pleased when the rest of the school had trooped off to the pitches after lunch, but his irritation had ratcheted up dramatically now that he could hear the evidence of everyone else having fun.

"No, Arthur," Merlin replied steadily, not looking up from his Chemistry homework. "For the fiftieth time, *no*, I'm not helping you sneak over to the pitches."

"Oh, come on, Merlin," Arthur huffed. "Can't you just do that concealment charm again? You don't even have to watch the rugby. You can bring your work with you. Everyone else is there."

"Yes, well everyone else isn't being targeted by one of Richard Alderley's followers, are they?" Merlin continued staring at his textbook.

"The sorcerer hasn't done anything in ages," Arthur grumbled. "For all we know the Brotherhood's already stopped them. Would Mr Beaulake be back if they hadn't?"

Merlin finally looked up. "If you're going to keep whining about this rugby match I'm going to go and work in Mission Control with Hector and co. They've got to be more fun than you."

"Whining?" Arthur was horrified. "I'm not *whining*. I've just had enough of being stuck in this stupid building all the time. I might as well be back in London with my parents."

Merlin just rolled his eyes and gathered up his books. "Look, I get it. You wanted to be on the rugby team. You know, you actually *are* on the team, Arthur. When this is all over you'll get to play again, but I'm not helping you leave

331

Badon today. Sorry."

A knock at the door startled them both.

"I hope that's not Hector trying to cheer me up again," Arthur grumbled as he headed for the door.

"He actually looked really sad when you said you didn't want to play Scrabble," Merlin replied with a grin.

"I don't really *do* board games, Hector," Arthur said as he opened the door. "Oh."

Eliot Troyes was standing in the corridor blinking in surprise.

"Sorry, Eliot," Arthur said, bobbing his head slightly. "I thought you were someone else."

Eliot smiled tightly. "That's quite alright, Your Royal Highness."

"Eliot, please, just call me Arthur." He shuffled his feet slightly. After hearing his official title on an almost daily basis for most of his life, it was funny how, after only a couple of terms at Badon, he now felt awkward when addressed as anything but 'Arthur'.

Eliot's features twisted slightly into something approaching a sneer. "But that wouldn't be appropriate for such a special occasion."

Arthur quirked his lips in confusion. "I'm sorry, what?"

The smile he received in return was cold, with a peculiar sharpness at the edges. It wasn't an expression Arthur had ever seen on the Head Boy and he took a small step backwards

"Seriously, Eliot," Arthur tried again, "I have no idea what special occasion you're talking about."

"The occasion of your death," Eliot replied with a disturbingly casual shrug. "obviously."

Merlin laughed uproariously from behind him and

Arthur turned around in surprise. He watched as the smile dropped off his friend's face. Merlin's features morphed into alarm at whatever expression he must have seen on Arthur.

"Wait, you think he's *serious*?" Merlin asked Arthur as his eyebrows disappeared into his hair in disbelief.

"I *am* serious," Eliot stated, as though his solemnity couldn't possibly be in doubt. "As Head Boy, I'm serious in all of my duties, particularly when carrying out any task given to me by a figure of authority."

"Figure of authority?" Merlin repeated as he stood next to Arthur and folded his arms. He looked Eliot up and down and wrinkled his nose. "Are you quoting from a handbook?"

"This is a really weird joke, Eliot," Arthur added, huffing out a strained laugh. Even though he was mostly certain that the Head Boy was pulling his leg, Arthur's eyes drifted to the door of the RPS's room nonetheless.

"Oh," Eliot said, following Arthur's gaze, "you won't be needing your guards. Think of it as giving them an afternoon off. I'm sure they need it."

Arthur side-stepped Eliot and ventured into the corridor. "I think I'll just have a quick chat with Hector anyway."

"Shouldn't you be at the rugby, Troyes?" Merlin asked. "Rather than hovering around here being weird."

Arthur knocked on the door to the next room. "Hector?" He waited patiently for a couple of seconds before knocking again. "Hector, can I have a word, please?"

"Sorry," Eliot said, his lips stretching into another parody of a grin, "I mjst have forgotten to mention that."

"Mention what?" Merlin asked, his eyes narrowing as Arthur tried knocking a little louder.

"They can't hear you." Eliot tilted his head to the side

and turned his calculating stare to Arthur, who now had his back to the security room door. "Even if they could hear you, they wouldn't be able to help you."

The words sent a flush of sickly warmth crawling up Arthur's skin, before the hairs on his arms prickled as if chilled. "What have you done?"

"Me?" Eliot frowned. "I haven't done anything." His eyes widened before his face settled back into the unnerving smirk of earlier. "Oh, you still don't understand, do you?"

"Understand *what*?" Merlin demanded. "Why are you prattling on like a cartoon villain?"

"The Silver Lady wants to see you," Eliot said, keeping his eyes fixed on Arthur. "She's been trying to get your attention since September. Surely you've noticed."

"The Silver Lady?" Arthur asked, shaking his head.

"He means the sorcerer," Merlin said when Eliot didn't add anything further. "The necromancer. Don't you, Troyes?"

"Oh, she won't like being called that," Eliot said pityingly. "The Silver Lady is not wicked. She will bring enlightenment."

Arthur pounded on the door again. "Hector! Hector, open the door!"

Eliot sighed dramatically. "I've already told you that they can't hear you. They will remain unharmed as long as you do as requested."

"What?" Arthur asked hurriedly. "What do I have to do?" The thought of Hector or any of the other Protection Squad members being harmed in any way made Arthur feel sick. They would risk their lives for him, he knew that, but he couldn't just let something terrible happen to them if there was some way he could prevent it.

"You need to come with me," Eliot said, staring coldly at Arthur.

"Not bloody likely!" Merlin huffed. "Arthur, you can't possibly wander off alone with this lunatic."

"Not alone," Eliot said, shaking his head and turning to Merlin. "The Silver Lady is particularly looking forward to making your acquaintance, Mr Montgomery."

Merlin looked alarmed. "Well, I'd rather not make hers, if you don't mind."

Eliot's eyes narrowed. "She won't like to be kept waiting."

Arthur looked at Merlin. He gulped. "Well?"

Merlin waved a hand in front of him. "After you, Your Royal Highness."

On any other day, Arthur would have rolled his eyes at Merlin's use of his official title, but in that moment he chose to ignore it. He nodded towards Eliot instead. "Lead the way."

Eliot looked pleased as he turned away and began heading down the corridor.

Arthur could see no evidence of an injured ankle as Eliot quickly descended the staircase with the two younger boys close behind.

"Let's just try not to die, Arthur," Merlin whispered as they followed the Head Boy outside and towards Badon's main gate into the city. "It's not really what I had in mind for my first year in Cambridge."

The short walk to Catterick College seemed longer than it should have. As they passed a row of shops around the corner from Badon, Arthur briefly looked up at the window of one of the flats above. He knew another team from the Protection Squad should be up there, but with Eliot's vague threats towards Hector and the others at Badon Arthur didn't dare make a scene.

"Why are you doing this, Eliot?" Merlin asked as they reached the entrance to Catterick College minutes later.

"I am a seeker of knowledge and truth," Eliot replied, once again sounding as though he were quoting from a book. "The Silver Lady has promised me both in return for my help in bringing you both to her."

They walked straight past the Porter's Lodge without being stopped by anyone, and Arthur frowned at the lack of people. It was the middle of the day, and the quad should have been busy with students and tourists alike.

"There's definitely something up with him," Merlin said to Arthur quietly as they followed Eliot down a long, wood-panelled corridor. "More so than usual, I mean. There's something off about the way he's talking. It's like the words aren't really his."

Arthur nodded. He opened his mouth to reply, but snapped it shut as Eliot finally stopped in front of some large wooden doors.

"I've been here before," Arthur said as he and Merlin were ushered in the large room beyond. "That dinner I went to earlier in the year." He looked at Merlin pointedly. "When you turned Hugo green."

"Arthur," Merlin hissed, pointing towards the far wall. "Look."

Arthur followed the line of Merlin's arm and flinched backwards as his eyes fell on a figure swathed in a silver, hooded robe.

"My Lady," Eliot said reverently as he bowed his head respectfully.

Merlin looked ready to say something that would no doubt make the situation worse, so Arthur elbowed him in the ribs before his friend could utter a sound.

The Silver Lady walked towards the teenagers, her robe making it seem as though she were gliding above the stone floor. As she came closer Arthur could see that Anne Catterick's locket was hanging from a chain around her neck.

"Thank you for your assistance, Master Troyes," the woman said, face still shrouded by folds of dark material.

Arthur reared back at the voice, snapping his head to the right to Merlin. He found his friend staring back at him, eyes wide in surprise.

"Oh good," said the woman as she removed her hood, gracefully settling it over her shoulders. "I see that you recognise me."

For a long moment, Arthur couldn't do anything more than gape as he took in the sight of the woman who had stood before him and his schoolmates only a couple of weeks earlier and extended an invitation for the boys of Badon to visit Catterick College.

Lady Burton was wearing a wide smile, and a look of triumph as she watched understanding begin to settle on Arthur's face.

"You're the necromancer?" Merlin choked out.

"Necromancer is such a dirty word. I much prefer 'enchantress'," she replied silkily. "I also do rather prefer to use my own name, rather than that of my terrible bore of a husband."

"And what's that?" Arthur asked as steadily as he could manage in the face of a woman who'd raised not-so-mythical creatures from the dead.

"Emma Alderley."

12

The Silver Lady

They'd tracked the legacy to Catterick.

That's what Elaine had heard her father say, wasn't it? Emma Alderley must be the legacy they'd been searching for. How long had she been at Catterick College, and right under their noses?

Arthur could have kicked himself. Even after all the time he'd spent looking at the Catterick and Pendragon family trees in the book he'd taken from the headmaster's study he'd never stopped to consider that the Alderley family line could have continued through the centuries too.

Emma waved her hands towards Eliot, whispering something too quietly for Arthur to hear.

Eliot lurched forwards suddenly, moving jerkily like one of the marionettes that had terrified Arthur as a child. The Head Boy walked up behind Merlin before clamping his hands around the younger boy's upper arms and began to bodily push him towards the door.

Merlin cried out in surprise, trying to twist out of Eliot's grip. "Hey! Let go of me!"

Arthur surged towards his friend but he was stopped by Emma raising her hand in his direction.

"Don't even think about it," Alderley hissed. Her eyes drifted up to the grand clock above the fireplace. "It's not quite time for you yet."

"Merlin, *do* something," Arthur called to his friend, not daring to take another step as Emma still hadn't lowered her arm. "Magic!"

"You don't think I've tried that yet, Arthur?" Merlin yelled in exasperation, wrenching one shoulder forward but still not managing to dislodge Eliot's iron grip as they came to a sudden halt. "I've been trying since Troyes turned up at our door."

Emma shook her head pityingly. "You've been such a disappointment, Merlin. I had expected so much more from you."

Merlin's panic morphed into an expression of downright mutiny as he glared at Emma. "What's that supposed to mean?"

Emma continued, ignoring the glare, "I think the Brotherhood is wrong. They've decided that you don't possess Old Magic." She narrowed her eyes. "I think you *do* possess Old Magic, but your control and understanding of it is pitiful at best."

Merlin looked ready to argue. Arthur thought it best to step in to divert Emma Alderley's attention again.

"But I've seen you with the headmaster," Arthur accused, daring to point a finger. "He can recognise magic. He surely would have noticed that you had magic when you were at Badon."

"Cecil Catterick doesn't deserve to be the headmaster of Badon," Emma sneered. "He might have been give the gift of magic, but his power is weak, and his ambition even weaker. Do you really think that I couldn't conceal my true nature from a pathetic conjurer like him? Besides, I had a little help."

Arthur watched in concern as Emma approached Merlin. She reached into her robe and extracted what looked like a small, golden brooch. She held the trinket up to the light and smiled at it.

"Did you know that Richard Alderley was a genius?" Emma asked, turning her head slightly to look back over at Arthur. "Not only was he a skilled alchemist, he was also an inventor. This little treasure is one of his designs."

"What is it?" Arthur asked, wincing at the reedy quality his voice had developed.

"Well, it's a clever little thing," Emma replied lightly. "Richard called it a Ventura. It's lucky for the wearer, you see. It can block magic. It can dull the senses of those who would otherwise be able to detect magic, and it can repel magic cast at its wearer."

"But my favourite thing," Emma added, taking a few steps towards Merlin, holding the brooch in front of her, "is how, if a sorcerer is close enough to the Ventura, it will stop them accessing their magic entirely. Just as it's stopping you right now, Merlin."

Arthur watched as Merlin fought against Eliot's hold once more, but the Head Boy's grip remained unfalteringly secure.

"As Eliot here had accepted an offer to study at Catterick college," Emma continued, stopping just in front of Merlin, "I thought he would be happy to accept a Catterick pin to wear until his studies at Badon concluded. He was. He's been so delightfully helpful."

It was only now that Emma pointed it out that Arthur noticed the small, golden badge attached to Eliot's blazer, nestled between his Head Boy shield, and the Winchester House pin.

"But you're using magic," Arthur said to Emma as his mouth finally caught up with his brain. "If that *thing* can stop magic, how come you can still cast spells?"

"Oh, you are a clever little thing, aren't you?" Emma smiled brightly, before lightly grasping the locket around her neck. "It's because I have this. With it I'm strong enough to resist the Ventura. I'm strong enough to change the world."

"Then why haven't you just killed me before?" Arthur asked, even though he'd prefer not to hear the answer. "That's why you brought me here, isn't it?"

"Really?" Merlin hissed in horror. "That's the sort of question you think you should be asking a murderous lunatic?"

Emma glared at Merlin, and then sighed. "It's not just about killing you, Arthur. It's about timing. Killing you means nothing in itself. But, killing the boy destined to become the great man of the ancient prophecies, and on the night of the equinox, well…" Emma trailed off with a grin, "that's something a bit more special."

Arthur didn't have time to reply before a surprised shriek from Eliot cut through the hall.

Arthur turned to see the Head Boy clutching his forehead, and Merlin running towards Emma Alderley with a determined look on his face.

Emma's mouth opened into a perfect 'o' of surprise, and for a second Arthur really thought Merlin was going to take down the sorceress with what looked like a surprisingly decent rugby tackle.

But when he was only a step from Emma, Merlin was

suddenly thrown sideways as an ornate chair that had been positioned against the wall shot across the floor and ploughed into him.

"Merlin!" Arthur called as he watched his friend sprawl to the floor with a pained grunt.

"Take him upstairs!" Emma barked at Eliot. "Put him in my office, lock the door, and don't move from outside until I tell you to."

Eliot, the skin around his left cheekbone already slightly mottled from the jab of the elbow Merlin had managed to unexpectedly connect with the Head Boy's face, nodded slightly before hauling a groaning Merlin to his feet, and dragged him, stumbling, from the room.

Arthur rounded on Emma angrily. "What are you doing? If this is all to do with me then just leave Merlin out of it."

"I'm afraid that's just not possible, Arthur," Emma replied, shaking her head. "Just as your birth was prophecised, Merlin is fated to be your most trusted ally. More importantly, he's fated to be a supremely powerful sorcerer. The Brotherhood cannot comprehend the power he could wield, and they have all written him off as useless, as an incorrect interpretation of an age-old prophecy. I'm going to give Merlin the chance to harness his true nature and find a *better* path than the one Fate has dealt him. A path where he'll be able to see the wonder in what I plan to do, following Richard Alderley's vision for a brighter future."

Arthur pursed his lips. "You want Merlin to *help* you?"

Emma laughed. "I want to help *him*, Arthur. Magic like that shouldn't just be allowed to wither and die. Richard Alderley had such grand plans for what could be achieved once the Great Sorcerer appeared again. With my help, Merlin would experience greatness."

"He doesn't need you," Arthur replied angrily. "He's already more powerful than you think."

"Oh, please." Emma rolled her eyes. "Without proper instruction he's not capable of anything more than party tricks. His silencing spell on the Caerleon corridor was child's play. I was able to replace it with a far more powerful version from outside the college walls."

"Merlin stopped that giant," Arthur replied stubbornly. "*Your* giant. He could stop you too."

"A child didn't vanquish the giant. *He* did it. The first Merlin, the *real* Merlin. He scattered the words into the earth centuries ago, and that young *pup* found them by chance," she spat. "I was there. I saw it happen. The magic came from deep within the fabric of the earth. He plucked them out of the air with nothing more than good fortune."

"Then why have you locked him up?" Arthur asked. "Are you afraid of him?"

"Afraid?" Emma repeated incredulously. "*Afraid?*"

Arthur was reminded of wicked witches from stories he'd heard as a child when Emma tipped her head back and cackled. Her eyes narrowed as her gaze fell on Arthur again, a malicious smile plucking the corners of her lips upwards a little.

"I have no need to fear a child," Emma continued in a voice devoid of warmth. "If he doesn't immediately cooperate it will be nothing more than a temporary inconvenience. But first, I need to deal with you."

Arthur refused to be cowed as the woman took a step towards him. He glanced around him quickly, searching for anything that would give him hope of getting out of this situation alive. "If you want to kill me, why haven't you done it before?"

The sorceress tilted her head and appraised the boy before her. Eventually she shook her head pityingly. "They really haven't told you anything, have they?"

This time Arthur did take a step backwards as Emma moved towards him, her robe fluttering behind her as she walked.

"Richard Alderley was a great man," Emma said reverently. "He could see beyond the prophecy his father, and his forefathers, had clung to for centuries. He had been blessed with the ability to harness magic, so why should he waste it waiting for the ghost of a man who had failed in his duty to protect his people?"

"Failed?"

Emma pursed her lips. "Yes, failed. The Brotherhood talks of their King Arthur as if he were a hero, but he was nothing more than a warmonger who roamed up and down the land taking what was never rightfully his. The stories, the legends, all of it was created by the Brotherhood to poison minds against the truth."

"Which is what?" Arthur asked.

"King Arthur was a beast," Emma replied. "He was an brainless brute with a sword, undeservingly protected by the magic of the greatest sorcerer on earth. He was surrounded by men who were no better than he. Bullies and thugs the lot of them. They thought Merlin's magic belonged to *them*."

"And you think *this* Merlin's magic belongs to you!"

"King Arthur wasn't a hero, and he certainly didn't die a hero's death," Emma replied, ignoring Arthur's outburst. "He died at the hands of a noble soldier of the truth. Mordred Malbranche sacrificed himself for the good of the kingdom by removing that parasite from the throne." She sneered once more. "But the Pendragon line didn't end, did it? Over eight-hundred years later and here you are, just waiting to take the place of that criminal."

"But it's just a story," Arthur snapped. "It's all just a story. King Arthur from the legends didn't exist."

"Do you really believe that?" Emma asked, raising her eyebrows. "If you do, then you're even more naïve than they believe you to be."

Arthur stayed silent.

"I thought not," Emma spat as she began pacing the hall. "Some of it is fiction, of course. Things get twisted and changed as time moves on, but King Arthur was as real as you or I, as were his faithful *knight*s. As was the Great Sorcerer, Merlin himself"

Arthur shivered as Emma turned back to him but seemed to stare straight though him to the wall beyond.

"The prophecy the Brotherhood so devoutly believes in says that King Arthur will, alongside his most trusted allies, lead his people to greatness," Emma continued, scorn dripping from every syllable. "It is said that he will tear down barricades and create unity when the world is most fractured."

A bell chimed somewhere in the college and Arthur jumped in surprise.

Emma snorted derisively. "Look at the world, Arthur. If King Arthur will save us all, where was he through the wars, through the pestilence, through the death and destruction that has stained our history for centuries?"

Arthur had to concede that Emma Alderley might have a point. "So the Brotherhood is waiting for him to rise from the dead somehow?"

Emma frowned. "King Arthur isn't destined to rise from

the dead."

"He isn't?" Arthur shook his head. "So I'm not…"

For a moment Emma looked confused, but then she looked absolutely delighted as she laughed loudly. "You thought you were *him*? Of course you're not. People don't just come back from the dead. Even ones who've lived their lives protected by the most powerful magic."

A strange sense of relief rippled through Arthur. At least now he knew that Gareth's vague theory of Arthur and Merlin returning from the dead was incorrect. "Then what is it that the Brotherhood is protecting? What exactly are they all waiting for?"

"They cling to the hope that one day a worthy successor of King Arthur will return and lead his people to ta time of ultimate peace," Emma explained coldly. "They see themselves as protectors of a divinely selected king, but they are nothing more than hypocrites and opponents of progress. Can you imagine what the world would be like if someone like Richard Alderley was on the throne?"

Arthur didn't want to imagine what it would be like to have a magic-wielding murderer in a position of power.

"I can," Emma continued, ignoring Arthur's silence. "It would be a world of advancement. A world where people like my family weren't threatened by the Brotherhood for believing in a different path."

"Richard Alderley was a traitor and a murderer," Arthur said, injecting as much courage into his voice as he could muster.

"Richard Alderley was betrayed by his own father," Emma snapped. She clutched the locket in her fist. "This was supposed to be his, but instead his coward of a father passed it to that Catterick girl. What need did she have for it? Richard had learned to harness the powers of the Earth in a way she never could. With the locket, he would have been unstoppable."

The bell chimed again and this time Arthur felt the cold weight of dread settle in his bones.

Emma looked up at the clock once more. "It's time."

Arthur tilted his chin up in a show of bravery that he didn't really feel. "Time for what?"

Emma didn't respond. Instead she closed her eyes as she held her hands out in front of her, palms facing the ground. She held herself completely still for a long moment before curling the fingers of her right hand back into her palm to make a fist.

"What are you doing?" Arthur asked, backing away slightly now that Emma wasn't staring at him.

Emma smiled and her eyes snapped open. "Even though he desperately wants to believe that you are the one he's dedicated his life to, Cecil Catterick thinks you're just too weak to be the king they've been waiting centuries for. I thought you might like one final attempt at proving him wrong."

Arthur's eyes widened in surprise as he felt the floor begin to shake slightly. He stumbled slightly as he tried to move further away from Emma.

"You won't, of course," Emma added snidely.

Arthur flinched as the first, quiet barks began. "No, no, no," he whispered to himself as the barking grew louder. There was no way he could defeat the Questing Beast on his own, and certainly not without a handy dash of Merlin's magic.

"Why?" Arthur asked, desperation leaking into his voice. "Why the Beast? You still haven't really explained why you can't just do it yourself!"

"I suppose I like the poetic justice of you facing the same trials as the legendary King Arthur himself," Emma replied thoughtfully. "Although I have studied his writings for years, and I am the first Learner in the Alderley family tree in over a century, I unfortunately do not possess the same talents as Richard Alderley. I can't sustain such powerful magic for more than a short period." Her face then morphed from dissatisfaction to pride almost instantly. "Oh, don't worry, Arthur, with the power of the Equinox amplifying the spell it will be more than enough time for the Beast to deal with you. Magic is at its most powerful when the earth is in flux, and without the magic that's sewn into the walls of Caerleon to protect you, you are defenceless."

"You're completely mad," Arthur replied. He clenched his fists at his sides and tried not to flinch when the barking grew in volume, and wisps of a shadow began forming on the wall behind Emma.

"Each time I've called the Beast into existence it has drawn out the Brotherhood." Emma's smile spoke of pure cruelty. "And each time it has taken one of their number. They've had plenty of opportunities to vanquish it, Arthur. Really, it is the Brotherhood that you should blame for this. Both you, and that excuse for a wizard."

"He's a *sorcerer*," Arthur spat out, refusing to be cowed as Emma's face hardened once more, "and he's my friend."

Emma stretched her arm out in front of her, and Arthur squirmed as he felt his arms and legs lock into place where they were. He sucked in a breath of panic as he realised that he could no longer move.

"This isn't fair!" Arthur cried in protest.

Emma shrugged. "Well, I had thought about letting you

have a sword to see how far you got before the Beast tore you to shreds, but I think just letting it happen would be more humane. Don't you?"

Terror wasn't a feeling Arthur had ever really encountered before, but as the shadow on the wall began to morph into a tangible entity of skin and bone, scales and claws, he knew undeniably that it was pure terror he was experiencing in that moment.

Arthur was so focused on the hammering of his heart that he barely noticed the creeping shape of what might have been a person, pressed against the far wall of the hall, just next to the fireplace. The shape shifted slightly, and Arthur briefly thought he might recognise it, before it began creeping slowly and silently towards Emma's back, losing any resemblance to a human as it moved.

The serpent-like head of the Questing Beast burst into existence with a sharp cry that had Arthur's blood running cold at the sound. This was followed by a spotted, furred body flickering in and out of existence as though it didn't quite have the strength to remain properly in the world.

Arthur's attention was pulled away from the grotesque creature when Emma shrieked suddenly as a hand reached around her neck and pulled hard on the necklace. The locket was yanked from her neck and she tumbled to her knees in surprise.

The pressure Arthur had felt pinning him in place lifted immediately and he blinked in surprise as he suddenly saw Merlin leaning against the wall with the locket's chain dangling from his clenched fist.

"Give that back!" Emma shrieked as she scrambled to her feet. Her legs tangled in her robes, causing her to lurch forward unsteadily. Hissed words Arthur couldn't understand fell from her lips as she advanced on Merlin.

Merlin had a look of deep concentration on his face as he held out one hand. Just like the first time he'd tried to stop the giant.

And, just like the first time, nothing seemed to happen.

Arthur, finally able to move again, darted forward and grabbed the trailing fabric of Emma's robe.

Merlin scrunched his eyes closed and held the locket to his chest as Emma raised her hands above her head menacingly, barely even noticing that Arthur was trying to slow her down.

The chain Merlin held seemed to glow brighter for just a second, and Arthur watched with rapt attention as silver threads, as delicate and ethereal as spider silk, bloomed from within the locket twisting outwards to swirl around his friend.

"No!" Emma wailed as she stopped suddenly, twisting her head quickly from side to side as though shrinking back from a noise nobody else could hear. She blindly reached into her pocket as she fell to her knees again, and produced the Ventura she had taunted Merlin with earlier.

Arthur watched in morbid fascination as the bronze pin resting in Emma's palm burst into flames for a moment before exploding outwards in a blast of silver sparks and black ash.

"No!" Emma howled again, clutching her burn-reddened palm to her chest. "How did you do that?" She screamed at Merlin. "How are you doing this?"

"Merlin, what's happening?" Arthur yelled as the Questing Beast's screeching grew impossibly louder even though he could have sworn that the monster looked slightly fainter than it had a moment ago.

"Arthur, I think now might be a good time for you to run," Merlin shouted with his eyes still clamped shut.

Arthur, agreeing entirely with his friend's plan, ran forwards and grabbed Merlin by the arm. "Come on then!"

Merlin's eyes shot open in surprise and he dropped the locket to the floor.

The entire room shook as the Questing Beast brought a giant clawed foot down on the stone floor.

"Uh oh," Merlin whispered, gulping.

Arthur didn't have time to reply before a hand closed over his ankle and he looked down to see Emma Alderley clutching his shoe and laughing hysterically.

"See?" Emma cackled, and Arthur's skin crawled at the sound. "I told you he was useless. Just think what he could do if he had me to show him the way. The connection may have been broken, but the locket was enough for me to bring the Beast through properly this time. You can't stop it. Neither of you can."

The barking and screeching reached fever pitch and Arthur pressed his hands to his ears as high-pitched screaming joined the melee of sound. A wind had picked up and small debris was beginning to spin through the air at an alarming rate.

"Arthur, look!" Merlin bellowed loudly enough for his friend to hear.

Arthur followed Merlin's gaze and found himself looking straight at Lyonesse and a young woman he'd never seen before.

"Arthur! Merlin!" The unknown woman cried desperately, running towards the boys. "Get out of here now!"

"Who are you?" Arthur asked in confusion as the woman grabbed his arm and yanked him from Emma Alderley's surprise-slackened grip.

"Irene Catterick," she answered quickly, dark hair whipping around her face as the wind continued to pick up. She held her hand out in front of her and the boys watched in fascination as the locket rose from the floor and flew into her waiting palm.

"Irene Catterick?" Arthur's eyes widened. "But you're dead!"

"Obviously not," she replied with a grimace, gripping the locket tightly and placing the chain around her neck.

Arthur could see her knuckles turning white. Irene turned her head and shouted over the noise of the whirlwind, "Lyonesse! Get them out!"

Arthur barely had time to react before a pair of strong arms clamped around his middle and he felt himself being tugged backwards out of the room, and into the shadows of the path that skirted the outside of the quad. He was dropped unceremoniously on the ground, with Merlin landing in a heap next to him a couple of seconds later.

"Get back to Badon," Lyonesse snapped.

"What about Eliot?" Merlin asked, scrabbling backwards towards the hall as a particularly loud roar burst through the open door. "The Head Boy. He's still upstairs."

"I'll find him." Lyonesse barked. "Now go."

Arthur looked around wildly, staring up at the college buildings. "But there are students here. We have to warn them."

Lyonesse snarled, crouching down and pointing his finger threateningly between both boys. "Run for your very lives, and don't stop until you're both safe inside of Caerleon. Stop for no-one, and tell nobody that you were here today. *Nobody*."

Arthur gulped. "But-"

"NOW!"

Merlin grabbed Arthur's wrist in an iron grip and hauled him to his feet. The two boys stumbled towards the college gate, almost tripping over their own feet in their haste to obey Lyonesse.

They didn't pass a single soul as they ran, and Arthur couldn't help but wonder how Emma Alderley had managed to keep an entire college of students from noticing what had happened in the hall. The shrieks and wails that had been almost-deafening in the old hall could barely be heard by the time they had slammed the heavy wooden gate behind them and raced towards the river.

"What just happened?" Merlin asked breathlessly as he tried valiantly to keep up with Arthur's lightning pace.

Arthur didn't answer beyond shaking his head slightly. The cold evening wasn't helping as Arthur's lungs burned with the exertion of running faster than he ever had in his life. His heart hadn't really stopped pounding since he'd first laid eyes on Emma Alderley clutching the locket in her hand.

They raced up the road and Arthur ducked his head as they passed the row of shops again. He didn't know if whatever spell Emma had cast would still be working and he had no desire to be spotted and stopped by the Protection Squad.

"Back Gate. We're less likely to be seen," Merlin panted.

Arthur nodded silently, hastily changing course to take them away from Badon's main entrance. They ran along the pavement next to the school's perimeter wall, dodging clumps of tourists taking photographs of Badon, and finally over the road bridge that crossed the Cam.

Merlin grabbed Arthur's arm just as they reached the Back Gate. He held up a hand to show Arthur that he wanted him to wait while he got his breath back. Arthur looked at Merlin's bright red face critically; if they were going to make a habit of running away from crazed, magic individuals then he was going to force his best friend to join a sport's team come second year just to make sure he got some regular running practice.

"What happened to Eliot?" Arthur asked eventually, when it looked like Merlin might be able to answer.

"I managed to use the shoelace spell that didn't work on Hugo as we got to the top of the staircase. Then I ran." Merlin paled. "I know what Lyonesse said, but do you think we should go back for him?"

A roar rose over the walls of Badon and Arthur flinched in surprise. Belatedly he realised that it wasn't the noise of the Beast, but the shouts of the crowd on the rugby pitch. Whatever had happened at Catterick College clearly hadn't been noticed by his schoolmates.

Arthur looked over his shoulder to where the spires of Catterick College were rising into the early evening sky. "I think-"

Arthur's thought was cut-off as the gate they were standing next to opened suddenly.

Merlin, with a speed Arthur couldn't quite believe, uttered the words of the concealment charm and shoved Arthur back against the wall.

Mrs Tilbury stepped through the gate, flanked by the librarian, Mr Franklin, and Miss Tristram. They barely paused as they pulled the gate closed behind them, and began running towards the city.

Arthur sighed in relief as the teachers disappeared around

the corner.

"They're all Brotherhood," Merlin whispered. "They must be."

"We need to get back to Caerleon before anyone sees us," Arthur replied hurriedly. "I know you don't like using magic that much at school, but can you please open the gate? Quickly?"

Merlin huffed as he waved his hand slightly, the lock's mechanism sliding open with a clunk. "I highly doubt anyone's going to notice me unlocking a gate with everything going on at Catterick."

"Catterick," Arthur repeated as the two boys stepped through the gate and hurried across the court towards the bridge. "Do you really think that was Irene Catterick?"

Merlin shrugged. "I don't know. She knew who we were, whoever she was."

Arthur nodded as they reached the door into Caerleon. "We need to be quiet going upstairs. Emma Alderley said that she'd replaced your silencing spell with her own, so I don't know if it's still there." He frowned as his stomach dropped again. "Hector and everyone will be alright, won't they?"

Merlin nodded, looking mostly convinced. "Of course they will."

"I might just check," Arthur said as they reached the Caerleon landing. "Go and see if there's any of those biscuits Hector bought for you left in the tin. I could really do with a chocolate digestive."

As Merlin headed into their room, Arthur paused outside Mission Control and knocked.

For a long moment nothing happened, but then the door clicked and opened to reveal a slightly confused, but completely intact Hector. "Arthur?"

Arthur opened his mouth to say something, but closed it again when he couldn't find any words. Instead he reached forwards and clamped his arms around his bodyguard in an awkward hug.

"What?" Hector asked as he stumbled back slightly. "Arthur, are you alright?"

"Fine," Arthur said quickly as he stepped back with a slightly embarrassed cough. "Absolutely fine. I, um, just wanted to apologise for being awful this morning. I'll definitely play Scrabble with you next time I'm stuck in school."

Hector looked like he didn't know what to say, and eventually settled on nodding.

"I'm just going to, er…" Arthur trailed off, backing towards his room. "Go in there. Okay, bye Hector."

"Are they okay?" Merlin asked as Arthur closed the bedroom door behind him.

Arthur nodded, hoping he looked less embarrassed than he felt. "Fine. I don't think they know anything weird has happened."

"Good," Merlin replied, prising the lid off the biscuit tin.

The door burst open without warning. Arthur would later deny the high-pitched shriek the surprise elicited. Mr Beaulake was leaning heavily against the door frame, panting as though he'd run a marathon.

"Mr Beaulake!" Arthur blinked in surprise. "You're back!"

"Is everything alright in here, boys?" Beaulake asked after a long moment of looking between Arthur and Merlin as he got his breath back.

"Yes, Mr Beaulake," Arthur asked, trying to keep his voice steady. "Fine."

"Are *you* alright, sir?" Merlin asked as he casually nudged a small pile of scrabble tiles laid out on his desk.

Beaulake's eyes drifted to the game as had obviously been Merlin's intention. "Yes, thank you, Merlin," the housemaster replied eventually. "Quiet afternoon?"

Arthur nodded with what he was sure was far too much enthusiasm. "Yes, sir. Board games. Quite boring really."

"We didn't know you were back at Badon, sir," Merlin said, eyes narrowed.

Mr Beaulake stared back as though searching for something in Merlin's expression.

A wave of laughter drifted in through the open window, and the sounds of returning boys filled the courts below.

"Who won?" Arthur asked, trying to divert Mr Beaulake's calculating stare away from him and Merlin.

"Won what?" Mr Beaulake looked momentarily confused, before his face cleared as joyous chants of 'Caerleon, Caerleon' filtered in from outside. "Oh, yes, of course, the rugby. We did. Caerleon, I mean."

Judging from the slight look of panic that remained on Mr Beaulake's face, Arthur was fairly certain than Beaulake hadn't been anywhere near the rugby, and it was probably though sheer dumb luck alone that he and Merlin hadn't encountered him on the way back from Catterick College.

"And you've been here all afternoon?" Beaulake asked eventually, frowning as though he couldn't quite believe that the two boys were sitting calmly in front of him. "Both of you?"

"All afternoon," Arthur repeated. "You can ask Hector."

* * * * *

Arthur found that he really couldn't enjoy the celebrations in the Caerleon JCR that night. He still didn't know what had happened at Catterick College when Lyonesse had sent him away. Was Emma Alderley still out there? What had Irene Catterick done when she'd found herself holding the locket that was rightfully hers?

"Are you alright, Arthur?" Marc asked passing over a plastic cup of orange squash.

"Fine," Arthur replied, taking the drink. "Sorry, it's been a bit of a weird day."

"I'm sorry you couldn't be out there today," Kofi added, patting Arthur's back roughly, "but would it make you feel any better if I told you that your cousin got sent off ten minutes after he came onto the pitch, *and* that he looked like he'd swallowed something awful when Caerleon won."

"He was *almost* green again!" Marc guffawed.

Arthur felt sick at the mention of his cousin and put the cup down. "Erm, that's great. Look, I'll be right back, okay?"

Marc and Kofi frowned but let him go with no more than a 'see you later, Arthur'.

"What's up with you?" Merlin asked as he followed Arthur out of the JCR and into Chapel Court.

"Hugo."

"Hugo?" Merlin arched an eyebrow. And here I thought it might be something to do with a murderous necromancer trying to kill you today. You do remember that, don't you?"

Arthur shook his head. "Don't be stupid, Merlin. Look, we still don't know how Hugo knows about you? *Or* the reason that spell of yours didn't work against him."

A dark shape loomed up before them and two hands reached out to grab the shirtfronts of both boys.

Arthur could do nothing more than hiss in alarm before

he realised the arms belonged to Lyonesse.

"What were you doing at Catterick College today?" Lyonesse growled. "Are you both mad?"

"It's not like we wanted to go," Merlin replied mulishly as he wriggled free of Lyonesse's grasp. "*She* made Eliot take us there."

Lyonesse grunted, but let go of Arthur too. The man wasn't wearing his Brotherhood robes and if it not for the distinctive scarring on his face, Arthur wouldn't have recognised the man wearing jeans and a shirt standing in front of him.

"What did she do to Eliot?" Arthur asked, putting more distance between himself and Lyonesse.

"Her power was great enough that she could influence his mind," Lyonesse replied with a disgusted twist of his lips. "Although she was nowhere near as powerful as Richard Alderley, she seemed to have inherited his ability to exert control over others. The boy will be fine now that the connection has been severed. He won't remember a thing, and thinks he spent the day in his room. The unfortunate black eye he received has been dealt with." He glared at Merlin.

"Oh, I'm sorry I wasn't more careful when trying to avoid death!" Merlin sniped.

Arthur elbowed his friend, then frowned at Lyonesse. "Why didn't she try to control me? Or Merlin? Wouldn't that have been easier?"

Lyonesse smiled at Arthur then, but it was sharp and humourless. "I don't doubt that she *did* try, but some people are easier to control than others. You are much stronger than most, Arthur." He looked at Merlin, now with something akin to wonderment. "And then there's you."

"What about me?" Merlin asked. Arthur could tell his

friend was trying to sound mulish, but his voice wavered ever so slightly.

"You possess the power to change the world," Lyonesse replied after a few moments of silent regard. "It is only a lack of faith in your abilities that is stopping you from doing so. The day you realise your true purpose will be the day Nature bows before you."

Arthur shot Merlin an incredulous look, only to find his friend staring at Lyonesse in a mix of surprise and horror.

"That's what the Brotherhood believes?" Arthur asked, when he realised Merlin had been stunned into silence.

Lyonesse moved his focus to Arthur. "The Brotherhood may change its position now that the Alderley threat has surfaced once more, but as they do not know exactly what occurred at Catterick College this evening, they will still believe that Merlin is not the Great Sorcerer. Someone of far greater power and importance than any number of our order believes in you Merlin. Believes in you both."

"Who?" Arthur asked.

Lyonesse bowed his head reverently. "My lady, Irene."

"Irene Catterick?" Arthur asked quickly. "So that really was her? She's not dead?"

"It was," Lyonesse replied. "And no, she is very much alive."

"What happened to her?" Merlin asked. "Why does everyone think she's dead?"

Lyonesse looked away and Arthur could only wonder that meant. Eventually he looked back at the boys. "That is not for you to trouble yourselves with. As far as the wold is concerned, and will continue to be concerned, Irene Catterick has been dead for fifteen years. I'm sure I don't need to explain the dire consequences that will befall you both if anything you saw or heard today is repeated outside of this conversation."

"Are you threatening us?" Arthur asked as steadily as he could manage.

Lyonesse stepped towards the boys once more, narrowing his eyes. "I think you already know the answer to that, Arthur Pendragon."

"Does her father know?" Merlin asked, ignoring the threat in Lyonesse's tone.

Lyonesse sighed in annoyance. "No, he doesn't know, nor will he find out."

"What did she do to Emma Alderley?" Arthur asked. "She is gone now, isn't she?"

"You'll have no further trouble from Emma Alderley." Lyonesse spat on the ground after speaking her name.

"That wasn't what Arthur asked," Merlin said pointedly.

"It's the only answer you're getting," Lyonesse snarled.

Arthur's eyes widened slightly as Merlin took a step towards Lyonesse and tilted his chin defiantly.

"And what about Hugo?" Merlin asked angrily. "Did you know that he called me 'sorcerer'? Did you tell him what I am?"

Lyonesse looked alarmed. "When did this happen?"

"A few days ago," Arthur said. "During a lesson."

"We have always been concerned about Hugo York, and indeed his presence at Badon." Lyonesse sighed tiredly before he looked at Merlin, almost apologetically. "If Hugo has accused you of sorcery, Merlin, then I'm afraid I'd be inclined to believe that he knows something."

Arthur traded a worried glance with his friend, before looking to Lyonesse. "What should we do? Does the headmaster know what's happened? The Beaulakes?"

"The truth of what occurred today at Catterick College exists only between us, and it will stay that way," Lyonesse replied sharply.

"But what do we do about Hugo?" Arthur asked. "We can't just let him know about Merlin!"

"*I* will deal with Hugo York." Lyonesse pointed at Merlin and then Arthur. "You two will stay as far away from him as possible."

"Oh, well that's going to be easy, isn't it Arthur?" Merlin grumbled. "It's not like he goes to school here with us or anything."

"Merlin, maybe just shut up for a second," Arthur hissed as Lyonesse narrowed his eyes at Merlin.

The sound of footsteps crunching on the gravel behind them had Arthur turning quickly, and Lyonesse glancing wildly towards the sound.

"Are you alright Arthur? Merlin?" Bertie asked as he appeared, Gareth at his side.

"Fine," Arthur replied, but he had returned to warily watching Lyonesse.

Lyonesse cast his eyes over the four boys standing before him as the shadows around the court began to lengthen rapidly as the sun. "And so it begins."

"And so what begins?" Arthur asked as Lyonesse began to turn away without explanation.

Lyonesse paused and turned back. He remained silent as he regarded Arthur seriously for a long moment. Eventually he inclined his head slightly in what was a clear bow of respect. When he righted himself he smiled slightly "A new age."

~

Epilogue

Arthur didn't see Lyonesse again as the school year picked up pace and hurtled the first years through a blistering round of ever-increasing homework and revision. Even Hugo seemed to have been sucked into the whirlwind of schoolwork, and the Pendragon cousins barely crossed paths, for which Arthur was very grateful. He was less grateful, however, that the extra work meant he spent less time with his friends.

The Camelot Society hadn't met again after the events at Catterick, and even though Arthur knew Elaine still had plenty of questions about the Brotherhood, and her parents' involvement, she seemed to be purposefully avoiding talking to the boys about anything.

The Brotherhood's book was wedged carefully under Arthur's bed with Merlin's concealment charm protecting it from anyone who might stumble across it. Each time Arthur suggested that they read a bit more of it, Merlin just shook his head with a wary glance towards the book and a *'not yet, Arthur.'*

Finally, the end of year exams they'd heard the second years speak of with a mix of reverence and terror dawned, and Arthur *almost* forgot about everything to do with legacies, magic and legends. Instead his days were filled with Latin verbs, algebra, and listening to Gareth desperately practice for his violin exam through the wall.

"What did you put for question eleven, Arthur?" Gareth asked Arthur only seconds after they'd been released from Mrs Beaulake's Chemistry exam. "I put zinc."

"I don't know," Arthur replied. "I can't remember."

Gareth looked worried. "Actually, I think zinc might have been the wrong answer."

"It *was* the wrong answer," Merlin added from Arthur's other side. "It was cadmium."

"Cadmium!" Gareth announced in horror, covering his eyes dramatically. "Of course it was."

"I wouldn't worry about it, Gareth," Arthur added with a grin. "In fact, don't even think about it. That was the last exam, so we're finally free!"

Merlin wrinkled his nose. "Only until lessons start again on Monday. Why we have to bother with two more weeks of school now that exams are finished I'll never know."

"At least we're not the fifth years," Arthur pointed out as a group of Winchester fifth years, including a completely-back-to-normal Eliot Troyes, darted across Kings' Court clutching revision folders and looking panicked.

"Oh," said Gareth as he watched Eliot and his friends head towards the library, "did you hear that Eliot's changed his mind about going to Catterick College in September?"

"Really?" Arthur asked in surprise. "But hasn't his entire family gone there for generations? I remember him telling me all about it back on my first day here."

"I guess what happened with Emma Alderley must have affected him, even if he doesn't remember it," Gareth said quietly. "Apparently he's decided to go to Edinburgh instead."

"Far away from here," Merlin commented. "Far away from anything to do with the Brotherhood."

"Do you think the Brotherhood would have wanted him to join them?" Gareth asked, lowering his voice further as they crossed the Caerleon bridge.

Merlin nodded. "Don't you? Remember what Lyonesse said about certain families being linked to the Brotherhood. If the Troyes family has been sending boys to Badon and Catterick for centuries then it seems likely that Eliot might be a member one day."

"I suppose," Gareth agreed. "I'm glad I don't have a legacy like that." He glanced at Arthur. "No offence, Arthur. I don't think I'd be as good at living up to that sort of thing as you."

Arthur didn't reply.

"Oh cheer up," Merlin said, nudging his roommate hard in the ribs with a grin. "Exams are over, freedom is coming, everything's back to normal, *and* Mrs Beaulake said there's going to be cake in the JCR after dinner."

"You think cake solves everything, don't you?" Arthur asked, rolling his eyes.

"Usually, yes," Merlin replied, pushing open the door and heading up the staircase.

"It's weird to think we have to move upstairs when we come back in September," Gareth said as they reached the first-year floor.

"Maybe we'll get bigger rooms," Arthur replied as he headed down the corridor.

"I don't care how big the room is," Merlin replied, "as long as it doesn't look out over the bridge. I've had enough of looking out that window for a lifetime."

* * * * *

They had marched onto the battlefield in their thousands as the sun had cast its first weak fingertips of light across the wintery planes. Scarlet dragons emblazoned on the standards billowing above their heads in stark warning to the enemy; a shock of colour against the dull sky.

Each man had taken up his sword knowing that this day could well be his last; for Fortune's Wheel had already turned, and no man possessed the power to escape his own destiny.

The battle had begun with a roar from the King as his men had charged towards their fates, and the bone-shaking clang of steel on steel had split the air until dusk heralded an abrupt silence.

Two figures remained standing in the centre of the carnage, and from afar it looked as though they were locked together, each man with a tight grip on the forearm of the other as if supporting him. The fallen soldiers of both sides littered the fields in a macabre canvas of red and blue, bearing the insignia of the King or his adversary to their graves.

A good distance away, Sir Bedivere scrambled to his feet as he saw the taller figure stumble slightly. He squinted into the growing twilight and hissed as he realised that the remaining two men were not the King and his Court Sorcerer as he'd first assumed, but instead the King and his greatest enemy, Mordred Malbranche.

"My Lord!" Bedivere called as he sprinted towards the final two combatants as quickly as his battle-weary body would allow. "My Lord Arthur!"

The King did not reply, instead he remained almost motionless as he faced the man who had sought to destroy the prosperous kingdom Arthur had been building for over twenty years.

Bedivere looked around wildly for help, sick to his stomach as he recognised the death-slackened faces of many loyal knights - loyal friends - he had fought alongside since he was no more than a boy.

He was barely ten strides from the King when he came across the fallen body of Sir Gawain, Arthur's most loyal and trusted knight. Gawain's sword was still grasped in his hand, a clear statement that he'd defended the King until his final breath.

But where was Merlin? The Court Sorcerer had barely been a hair's breadth from the centre of every battle since he'd been appointed as chief advisor on the day of the King's coronation. Yet, here was the King facing his most dangerous foe and Merlin was nowhere to be seen.

All thoughts of the missing sorcerer were banished when Arthur suddenly retracted his arm, his sword sliding free from where it had been buried deep in Mordred's side.

Mordred staggered backwards, his right hand releasing his own weapon to clutch at his surely mortal wound. His eyes remained open, staring at the King even as he fell to his knees with a painful thud.

Bedivere moved forward quickly to stand with his King, drawing his own sword as he noted that Arthur was now leaning heavily on the pommel of his faithful Excalibur. "My Lord?"

"The Traitor is defeated." Arthur spoke quietly as he watched the final spark of life fade from Mordred's eyes, the younger man slumping to the ground at the King's feet. "He will threaten these lands no more."

Bedivere swallowed heavily when he saw that Arthur's mail was stained with blood in a mirror image of Mordred's wound. "My Lord, you are injured."

Arthur nodded his head with a grimace. "Sir Mordred found his mark. I fear the blow will prove fatal."

The King's voice was eerily calm as he spoke of his impending death and Bedivere shivered in horror at the acceptance he heard there. Arthur's knights had all but fallen entirely; surely the kingdom could not lose their leader too?

"My Lord, I must take you to a surgeon," Bedivere stepped forward, fear for the King making him bold. "The nearest village is but two miles away."

This time Arthur shook his head. "It is too late, Sir Bedivere. I ask instead that you take me to the water's edge."

Bedivere, who had sworn loyalty to Arthur, agreed even though he wished to argue. He took Arthur's weight as the two staggered away from the blood-soaked grass, the King refusing to let go of his sword as his eyes roamed the faces of every man who had fallen in the name of the kingdom.

They did not speak again until they reached the water. Bedivere was surprised to see a barge nudging lightly against the grassy bank as it bobbed in the calm water of the Granta.

"Sir Bedivere." Arthur's voice was little more than a whisper, but his tone was still commanding as he shrugged himself out of Bedivere's grasp and held Excalibur out before him. "I must take leave of this world. This night I have already been allowed to remain far longer than any man should be granted upon the occasion of his death. You must take Excalibur and return her to the water."

"My Lord!" Bedivere shook his head and stepped away from the sword. "Excalibur is the greatest sword ever to have been created. Without it there will surely be nothing but darkness."

Arthur almost smiled. "You have been a loyal knight, Bedivere, and I am certain that you will do as your King asks. Excalibur must return to the water, for if it does not, Fortune *will not be satisfied and the world will be lost to eternal night."*

The King grasped Bedivere's hand, pushing until the knight's fingers clamped over the hilt of Excalibur. Then he turned, stepping into the awaiting barge; a small hiss of pain the only sound of distress he had made since meeting Mordred's sword.

Excalibur had always seemed to gleam when the King had entered battle and there were those who swore that they had heard the blade sing as it had protected the King's lands and people. But as Bedivere looked at the sword in his hand the usually smooth metal looked dull and brittle.

With a final glance at Arthur, Bedivere hefted the sword back over his head before swinging his arm forward with a ferocious cry. The blade flew from his fingers, arcing gracefully through the air towards the still water as though it weighed no more than a pebble.

Bedivere yelled in surprised when the blade stopped dead above the water, the tip only a hair's breadth from the surface. Moments later the sword slowly descended into the water yet no ripple blemished the pool. The one gemstone upon the hilt catching light from somewhere to glow impossibly in the inky darkness of a moonless night.

When Bedivere looked back to where his King had been he was met with only swirling fog and the hint of a shadow moving away from the bank. It was almost impossible to see in front of him, but Bedivere was sure that he'd glimpsed the silhouette of his King surrounded by a group of figures in dark robes.

A mournful cry rose from the lake and it sounded as though the earth itself was weeping for the loss of the King. Bedivere shivered as a frost crept across the grass far quicker than could be considered natural and he wrapped his arms around himself to try and warm his bones through the chilled mail he was *wearing.*

"*Sir Knight? Sir Knight!*"

Bedivere whirled at the sound of the voice echoing somewhere behind him. "*My lord, Merlin?*"

"*Bedivere, is that you?*" Merlin's voice cut once more through the night, but the sorcerer remained out of sight.

"*It is!*" Bedivere called back, darting his eyes around to try and locate the other man.

Merlin suddenly appeared only a few strides away from where Bedivere still stood at the bank. It was difficult to see in the darkness, but Merlin looked to be limping and leaning heavily on the tall, razor-thin wooden staff he always carried when away from Camelot.

"*The Traitor is dead,*" Bedivere announced as Merlin reached him.

"*And the King?*" Merlin asked anxiously. "*I could not find him on the battlefield.*"

Bedivere cast his eyes to the ground, unwilling to voice the truth that only he knew.

"*The King is dead?*" Merlin asked eventually, his voice as hollow as Arthur's had been before death.

Bedivere nodded. "*He asked to be taken to the water's edge. A boat bore him away into the mist.*"

Merlin dropped his head to his chest. "*Then Fortune has at last fulfilled her prophecy.*" He cast his staff to the ground and dropped to one knee before the lake, inclining his head in respect. Bedivere, as if compelled by some unseen force, copied the action and stared into the water.

They remained in silence for a long time and the air around them seemed to freeze in gossamer strands that clung to their hair and clothes. Bedivere was so cold that he began to wonder if this would be the night he also left the grind of the mortal

370

world behind him.

"What happens now, my lord?" The knight asked eventually, his teeth chattering over the syllables.

Again silence stretched between the two men until Merlin turned to fix his companion with an indecipherable expression on his face. "We wait."

Merlin reached his arm forward until his fingers just skirted the surface of the water. Bedivere was once more surprised as the ethereal glow that had appeared to envelop Excalibur steadily began to grow under the water until the pool was radiating light from below.

"Here lies Arthur," Merlin whispered reverently as he bowed his head further, "the Once and Future King."

Arthur's eyes snapped open and he lurched out of bed without any coordination

"What?" Merlin asked sleepily, sitting up slowly. "Arthur, what's wrong?"

Arthur gulped as the memory of the dream refused to fade even with the sunlight now piercing the bedroom. He shook his head, but offered no explanation.

"Arthur?" Merlin asked again, more worried now that he was awake. "Do you need me to get Hector? Mrs Beaulake?"

Arthur wearily sat down on the edge of his bed and took a few deep breaths to calm the hammering of his heart. Eventually he looked up and turned to his friend, thankfully seeing no similarity between the 'Merlin' from his dream and the Merlin before him. "Remember what you said about being glad that everything was back to normal? That it was all over?"

"Yeah?" Merlin replied slowly.

Arthur shook his head again. "I don't think this is the

end."

Merlin frowned. "What do you mean?"

The early morning sun bathed the room in an intense golden glow and Arthur shivered slightly as he remembered the final words from his dream.

Here lies Arthur, the Once and Future King.

"Arthur?" Merlin asked, looking concerned as he threw back his duvet and got to his feet.

"I think this might only be the beginning."